MUR
MALLOW
COTTAGE

An addictive crime thriller with a twist you won't see coming

GRETTA MULROONEY

Detective Inspector Siv Drummond Book 3

JOFFE BOOKS

Joffe Books, London
www.joffebooks.com

First published in Great Britain in 2021

Cover art by Dee Dee Book Covers

ISBN: 978-1-78931-918-7

For the two Ds who graced my life
Much missed

PROLOGUE

Then

They'd been having a terrific evening. One of the best ever, in fact. School had finished for the Easter holidays and they felt heady, uninhibited. It was a balmy, clear night and the prospect of a fortnight's freedom lay ahead. They'd consumed beer, wine and gin, all liberated from their parents' drinks cabinets, and when the excitement and alcohol overwhelmed them, they'd got up and danced to everything from Rihanna to Manic Street Preachers, spinning around and taking turns to neck from a bottle. They laughed, without knowing what they were laughing at, helping themselves to the pretty triangular pink, blue and yellow tablets like they were sweets.

It was dark. She was dancing, arms waving above her head in the air. Her skirt had silver glitter around the hem and it sparkled in the lamplight. She looked at the boy who was whooping and urging her on. His bony chest was bare, and he shone a torch under his spade-shaped face as he rolled his eyes up and grimaced, trying to alarm her. He wasn't kind to her, taking her for granted and teasing her. He could be cutting and sarcastic, but he was intriguing, unpredictable, and his anarchic anger called to her own deep-seated rage. He was the opposite of safe, but that must be what she wanted, as she was here with him. She thought briefly of another, gentler boy. A safe boy. She'd hurt his feelings, but it was all way beyond her control now.

Her head throbbed and she was hot, giddy. So hot. She reached up to the floating moon. It looked cool, remote. One minute she was twirling, the next she was twitching, shaking violently. She slumped to the ground, burning up, covered in sweat. The others talked to her, but she couldn't understand them. One of them poured water onto his shirt, using it to dab her forehead. When she went quiet, her eyes closed, body still, they shook her, called her name. No response.

'Christ, she's so hot! What's happening?'

'Dunno. Must be a bad reaction. I feel OK. You?'

'Yeah. How many'd she take?'

'Not sure.'

'What are we going to do? She's unconscious.'

'Don't ask me. You bought the stuff and brought her here.'

They squabbled, panicked. What if she didn't wake up? They'd be in deep shit.

There was that film they'd seen recently, with a situation similar to the one they were in. Why not copy it?

They lifted her, carried her between them to the car. She was petite, light, her head dangling from her limp body. They drove fast towards the hospital, leaving her in a doorway just along the street, before stopping at a phone box to make an anonymous 999 call.

Afterwards, they reassured each other that they'd done the right thing, that they'd done everything possible in the circumstances. It wasn't their fault. It was just a terrible accident.

Over time, they drifted apart, losing touch, relieved at the absence of contact. But through the years, they dreamed about her, waking in the small hours, their skin burning, on fire. Just like hers had been.

CHAPTER 1

Now

A chill woke Toby Foxwell just before his six o'clock alarm on that Tuesday morning. His wife had stolen most of the duvet and cocooned herself in it, her face rosy with warmth. His feet and nose were cold. They'd discussed having separate duvets on their queen-sized bed, but he was reluctant. Their marriage was sound, but Toby was superstitious, worrying that such a change could be the first step on a slippery slope to trouble. Cold limbs and a partner beside you were better than solitary warmth, and every successful marriage demanded sacrifices.

He slid out of bed, so as not to disturb Annie, and peered through the window into the dark. The bare trees looked fragile and forbidding. The *whump* of the boiler kicking in was reassuring. There would be plenty of hot water when he returned home from his run.

He put on the new tracksuit that Annie had bought him for Christmas, and did some stretches before leaving. Closing the front door gently behind him, he began his usual thirty-minute route along Greenlea Way, down Bere Hill, into Clifton Crescent, skirting the back of Berminster General and then up Pembroke Road back towards home. The air was glacial, invigorating, and it gave him a glow of health — something he couldn't be more grateful for after last year's cancer scare. Ten months ago, he'd been worried that he would end up in a coffin, ready for the furnace at Berminster Crematorium, rather than returning to his job as the manager there. After surgery for mouth cancer — he'd been a devoted smoker in his twenties — he'd made a good recovery and had adopted a fitness regime and plant-based diet. No dairy. His superstitious streak again. He'd told himself: *If I heed the warning, exercise and take care of myself, the universe will repay me with good health.*

Back home, he showered and prepared a bowl of muesli with almond milk. While he ate, he checked the day's schedule on his laptop. January was always a busy month at the crematorium. The grim reaper upped his work rate in the dark hours of winter. Many older people hung onto their final breath until after Christmas — some sort of last hurrah — and then turned up their toes. (Although Toby often thought in these terms and used them with Annie, at work he spoke respectfully and came down hard on employees who joked about death.)

There were two chapels at the crematorium, unimaginatively named East (consecrated, stained-glass windows) and West (unconsecrated, plain windows). Three funerals were booked in East today, and two in West. All the deceased were over seventy, except for the one o'clock in East, for a Lisa Flore, just twenty-six. That was a double slot, an hour. A young person's funeral was hard on everyone, the usual comforting platitudes just not cutting it. The celebrant couldn't refer to a full life. A life well lived.

Toby took great pride in the service his team provided. He'd been appointed to his role two years before, with a brief to update and streamline the crematorium, and it was a success story. He was all too aware that some of the older, more entrenched staff resented his 'new broom' style, referring to him as 'Slick Foxy'. A couple of them had been hanging around for far too long in Toby's opinion, but Berminster Council was a conservative organisation. They didn't want job losses or employment tribunals, leaving Toby with no choice but to alter the course and speed of the boat without rocking it. So, he cajoled when needed, ignored snarky comments and mutters about 'change for the sake of it' and 'style over substance', while pushing through his changes. And there had been many, all efficiently actioned. The chapel anterooms had been refurbished, the gardens rejuvenated. He'd worked on culturally sensitive ceremonies and had created a new vision statement which featured in the information pamphlet.

We provide a peaceful space where you can pay respect to and commemorate your loved one. We offer personal choice, excellent care and dedication.

Toby made sure these weren't just pretty words, that this ethos was put into practice, today being one such example of this. He'd arranged to be available for Ms Flore's funeral and had double-checked the readings and the music with the celebrant.

Just after seven, he took Annie a cup of tea. She wasn't a morning person and was slowly coming to.

She muttered, 'Weather?'

'Bracing.'

'Yuck. Been for your run?'

'Yep.'

She yawned. 'Well done. Gold star.'

Her skin was rosy and inviting, her golden hair tousled. For a moment, he wanted to slide back in beside her, but the dead were calling him.

* * *

Toby drove through the crematorium's wide iron entrance gates topped with fleur-de-lis finials, and along the handsome larch and yew-lined avenue. The original cemetery was Grade II listed and dated from the Victorian era, the hundreds of years' worth of graves discreetly screened from visitors by beech hedging. Completed in the 1860s, the site sat on a ridge above the River Bere. It was a rather grand affair for a small town, but Berminster had always been a prosperous place, based on big money from fishing in the mid-nineteenth century. The architecturally in-keeping crematorium had been added in 1949.

Toby loved the buildings and impressive cemetery and gardens. Every day, he relished the drive down the avenue to the Gothic Revival chapels and Bere Lodge, the flint-built house that accommodated the staff offices and the council's bereavement service. It couldn't have been in greater contrast to where he'd started his career, further along the coast, in a modern, boxy, concrete monstrosity of a crematorium that offended the eyes. It had always reminded him of something Hitler or Stalin would have built.

At the entrance to Bere Lodge, he keyed in the security code, then dropped off his bag and started the coffee machine brewing. He was always the first one in. 'First in, last out' was his mantra as a manager. Then, as was his habit, he went to open and check the chapels. He liked to see that the evening cleaners had left everything just so. The smallest of oversights could upset mourners: a rosary or order of service left behind, a discarded tissue on a parquet floor, a piece of chewing gum stuck to a chair, one dead blossom in a vase.

Outside, the sun was just starting to rise, turning the sky a deep lavender. A solitary magpie hopped on the grass. 'One for sorrow', appropriately enough. The forecast was for a sunny, cold, dry day. Ideal for funerals. Families and friends wouldn't linger in the chill, and the timetable should tick over nicely. It could get awkward when a service ran over and mourners were kept waiting outside. The staff offered refreshments if the delay started to drag on, and that affected Toby's budgets.

The large sandstone chapels had separate side entrances but were connected by an impressive central foyer with its own front-facing oak door. This was accessed by three broad steps and topped by a tower with a belfry. Some families liked the bell to ring at the beginning or the end of a funeral. Others disliked the sombre peals. Whenever he heard them, Toby recalled the Edgar Allan Poe poem he'd learned at school.

Oh the bells, bells, bells!
What a tale their terror tells
Of Despair!

The entrance foyer had been partitioned into two anterooms, one for each chapel. There were toilets in each, seating, a drinks machine and packs of biscuits. Toby had arranged the flow so that mourners entered via the foyer and exited through the chapel doors. The north-facing, steeply pitched roof of the building was dotted with moss. Clumps sometimes detached themselves, falling onto the steps below. Andy Smeaton, the caretaker, was scheduled to clean them off at the end of the month.

As he approached the main entrance, Toby was startled to see a line of large yellow, red and green wreaths resting along the bottom step below the foyer door. His expert eye spotted calla lilies, orchids and cornus stems entwined with asparagus fern. The red centres of the lilies were the colour of fresh blood when it bubbled up from a cut. What on earth was going on? Perhaps a funeral director or a relative had placed them there, although he couldn't imagine why — certainly, they shouldn't have been left there overnight. He'd have to have words with the cleaners.

Drawing nearer, he halted, stared, then clasped his gloved hands together, his brain not able to compute what he was seeing.

The wreaths weren't on the step, as he'd originally thought. They were balanced on top of a prone figure, almost covering it. Toby glimpsed a pale hand drooping downwards and a foot in a black ankle boot. He stepped closer. He could just see the crown of a head. The hair was fair, thinning into a bald patch. Confusion filled him. For a wild moment, he wondered if someone was playing an appalling practical joke.

Toby took a breath and foolishly croaked, 'Hello?', half-expecting the figure to jump up at him. Nothing. He stared, mesmerised, before finally bending down to place a fingertip on the exposed skin. He yanked his hand back at the feel of the cold and rigid flesh.

Toby had seen plenty of corpses in his time, but always in the lined, dignified confines of a coffin, suitably prepared, undergoing due process. He swallowed hard, this morning's muesli at the back of his throat. He backed away from the steps, closing his eyes to the terrible sight before him, taking deep gulps of the invigorating air. It wouldn't do for the manager to vomit up his breakfast outside the chapels.

* * *

Saffie took a couple of painkillers, swallowing them down with strong coffee. She could hear Damian snoring long and loudly just along the hallway. How on earth did Viv not wake up? She rubbed her temples. Last night had been a bit mad and her head felt like a brick. She didn't usually drink, but she hadn't wanted to be a party pooper, and Henry had kept ordering more red wine with the meal. This week by the sea with his friends meant a lot to him, so she'd joined in, knowing she'd pay for it today.

And would Henry thank her for it? At the end of the night, he'd abandoned her — gone crawling back to his mum's up the road, leaving Saffie with his mates at the chalet. She supposed he was still sprawled in his childhood bed, dead to the world. His mother kept his bedroom exactly as it had been before he left home. It encapsulated the world of a sporty, indulged, middle-class teenager: pictures of footballers and cricketers, trophies for fencing, a wide-screen TV fixed to the wall opposite his double bed, a maple study desk and chair and a huge poster of Natalie Portman, his

Hollywood crush, in a low-cut jade dress. Saffie had been jealous when she'd seen the comfortable room — her parents had rented out her tiny bedroom on Airbnb as soon as she'd left home. Now, she pictured Henry clutching the pillow while Natalie smiled down on him. He had to wear a mouth guard when he was sleeping because he ground his teeth, but he wouldn't have put it in last night. It was lying on the chest of drawers in their chalet bedroom. He might not emerge from his mother's house until lunchtime. She could never sleep in. Her mother was a childminder and, over the years, Saffie had become used to the racket of marauding kids from seven in the morning.

The tablets were starting to kick in and her headache was a little better. She swept up her long, blue-black hair in one hand, smoothed it down her back and put a slice of bread in the toaster. There was no clean cutlery in the drawer, so she opened the dishwasher in search of a knife. The chalet wasn't well equipped — there were just four sets of cutlery and four cups, plates and bowls. But as Henry's mother owned it and they weren't paying anything for it, she could hardly comment. Otherwise, she'd have said something. No, that was fooling herself — she never complained. She prepared objections in her head, practised whole speeches, built up to delivering them, but never actually articulated them.

A smear of ketchup from the dishwasher door clung to her finger. She wiped it off. The others didn't bother to clear up. Viv and Damian were incredibly messy, dropping clutter everywhere they moved. They had a cleaner twice a week at home and seemed to expect that their chaos would mysteriously vanish here. It was one of the reasons she couldn't wait to get back to London. Damian didn't even flush the toilet sometimes, which was disgusting, and he always left the seat up. How did Viv tolerate it? Saffie resented picking up their soggy towels in the bathroom, removing their hairs from plugholes, wiping away toothpaste spatters and cleaning the work surfaces, but she did it to make her own life bearable. She couldn't tolerate disorder of any kind — the very thought of it was enough to make her pulse flutter and her breathing quicken.

And there were still four days to go.

I shouldn't have come. I knew I wouldn't like it. It would be different if it was summer and I could go out more. But Henry was looking forward to it so much, and he'd have been upset if I'd refused.

She shoved dirty mugs and a couple of empty beer bottles out of the way, spread marmalade on her toast, poured a second cup of coffee and sat at the table, gazing at the choppy sea.

She had to admit that if you liked this kind of thing, the chalet, cosily called Driftwood, was in a terrific location, set just above Minster Beach, with steps leading down to the shore. And there was an assumption that everyone *did* like this kind of thing. Who wouldn't want a break by the coast, and a free one at that? One of her work colleagues had even called her 'jammy'. She couldn't tell anyone the truth, that she disliked being by the sea, found the fathomless cold waters vast and worrying, dreaded the teasing winds. She liked woodland and parks, places with signposted paths, sheltered from the elements. If the weather had been milder, she could have sat on the decked, covered porch that ran along the front of the chalet. There were a couple of hanging heaters out there, and she'd lingered under them with Henry for a while on Sunday evening. She'd enjoyed being wrapped up in her coat and scarf, a mug of steaming hot chocolate in hand, as they watched the moonlight ripple on the quiet waves below. In the dark, the sea was almost invisible, tamed.

Viv and Damian had gone out, and it had been good to have Henry to herself in that romantic setting. He'd just drawn her close when his phone had pinged. Something to do with work, he'd said, frowning. He'd better go and make some calls. He'd vanished for a while, and then he'd told her that he had to wait for callbacks, so he was going to nip out for a drink.

'You don't mind, do you? You don't really like pubs. Won't be too late, promise.'

She'd been disappointed, but she'd agreed, of course. Henry liked to socialise and he'd find people to chat to. He was popular, always had been, had a dizzying collection of acquaintances. She'd tagged along on a few occasions when they'd first met and felt rather like a spare part because the experiences these people shared were so foreign to her. The conversations were about rugger, sailing and various other sports, stories of holidays they'd been on that involved lots of strenuous activity. All this amid a sea of alcohol.

She opened one of the sliding doors to the porch and stuck her head into the salty, bracing air. It smelled good after the hot fug of the house. She looked longingly at the white bench outside, but she didn't want to switch the heaters on at nine in the morning. Imelda, Henry's bossy mum, had a habit of popping in, and Saffie was nervous around her. She seemed to have lots of rules and ways of doing things, and Saffie felt that the instructions laid out in the prim welcome booklet were aimed particularly at her, as if she was the others' chaperone or housekeeper.

I've set the timers for the hot water and heating. You shouldn't need to change them and they're a bit complicated, so it's best if you leave them alone. Don't alter the toaster setting — if it gets too hot, the smoke alarm will go off. You have to give the loo two quick flushes. The bin lid has a habit of springing open, so make sure you press it down.

It would be easy to transgress unwittingly, so Saffie moved around the place with caution, as if Imelda were peering over her shoulder and finding her wanting. With her brisk, cheery energy, Imelda reminded her of one of those women who'd kept the home fires burning in 1940s black-and-white films.

She should have a shower before Damian or Viv got up and used all the hot water. Or they might shower together and have noisy sex, like yesterday morning. Henry had laughed as they'd lain in bed listening, but Saffie was embarrassed. She liked quiet, private lovemaking and found Damian and Viv's constant and uninhibited kissing, fondling and groping hard to take. The way they carried on, you'd think they'd met only yesterday. Saffie had been even more nonplussed at the sex toy they'd left lying on the shower tray. She should really get into the bathroom before them, but she didn't move from her chair, absent-mindedly moving toast crumbs around her plate with a finger. She wished Henry would come. She glanced through the side window, at the path up to the road where his mother lived. No sign.

They'd been together for just over a year, but Saffie still caught her breath when she glimpsed him. He overwhelmed her, but she liked the sensation. He was so sure about everything, whereas she lived her life in a state of uncertainty. She wasn't sure if this was her nature or due to being the child of immigrants. Her parents had come to London from Tehran when Saffie was five. Her first language had been Farsi, and although her English was perfect, she always had a sneaking suspicion that she wasn't entitled to it.

Henry exuded confidence, he belonged. That was why she'd fallen in love with him. He masked Saffie's insecurities. At times, she wondered if he loved the idea of her, rather than the real, self-doubting Saffie. The only thing she was certain of was her own beauty, her striking, dark-eyed looks. Henry liked watching people's reactions when he walked in with her on his arm. They'd met in an antiques market and he referred to her as the 'Persian princess he'd found in the bazaar'. It was said fondly, but it made her feel categorised, as if she were a collector's item. Like an Elgin Marble or a fragment of Egyptian statuary.

She emptied the dishwasher and rinsed her breakfast things, then tidied away half a dozen empty gin and tonic cans, crisp and biscuit packets and sandwich crusts. She pressed the bin lid down firmly, recalling Imelda's instructions, wiped the surfaces and darted to the bathroom as she heard sounds of waking from Damian and Viv's room.

CHAPTER 2

DI Siv Drummond checked her phone first thing that morning to see DC Patrick Hill had already tweeted.

> *@DCBerminsterPolice*
> *Today is DC Lisa Flore's funeral. Please remember the devastating effects of drink & drug driving. Thanks for your messages, which we've passed to Lisa's family. Thanks also to the majority of people who do the right thing & only drive when sober.*
> *#KeepingBerminsterSafe*

Patrick was friendly with Lisa's family and had been hit hard by her death. He'd liked Lisa and had once asked her out, but it hadn't worked, mainly because he'd been too preoccupied worrying about and caring for his brother. Lisa's mother was a widow, on her own at home now that her only child was gone. Her brother, Lisa's uncle, lived with his family in Chicago. Patrick had stepped in to help her with the bureaucracy that a funeral entailed, and Siv had told him to take the day off. He'd sent an email to everyone at the station the previous evening.

I've spoken to Lisa's mum. She said there's no need to wear black. In fact, she'd prefer it if people wear cheerful, bright colours. Ms Flore said it's what Lisa would have wanted.

Although Lisa, being dead, had no say in the matter.

Siv hadn't worked with Lisa long — the young constable had transferred to a domestic violence unit shortly after joining the force — but she'd liked her. A drunken New Year reveller had killed her. He'd lost control of his car, mounted the pavement by the harbour, running her over and killing himself too in a tangle of metal.

Siv descended the steps from her compact home at half past seven, sipping at a mug of tea. The steam from her drink warmed her nose. When she'd moved back to Berminster, she'd rented the renovated circus wagon at the bottom of a meadow by the river. It was tiny, snug, isolated, almost maintenance free and had provided a secure sanctuary after Ed, her husband, had been killed. She wandered along the riverbank. The biting air jolted her, rousing her dull head somewhat. She pulled up the cowl neck of the chunky purple sweater she'd bought from Corran. He and his partner Paul were her landlords. Corran was also a weaver, and he'd acquired a knitting machine on eBay and was expanding his repertoire into producing attractive clothing. The sweater was like a warm embrace on this raw morning, and Siv made the most of it. It was the only kind of hug she'd had for a while: she couldn't imagine wanting one that wasn't from Ed.

It was handy, having the River Bere as a boundary to her little home. She found its background song soothing, and she sauntered by it in all weathers. She watched the dark swift-running waters and touched a frosted, twiggy bush of rosehips. They were ice cold and firm. Clumps of gleaming snowdrops were opening on the riverbank, their green stems pushing up through the wet earth. Finches searched for mast in the beech trees. Despite everything, nature carried on, business as usual. Before her death, Lisa had been planning her birthday celebrations for later this month. They'd involved an afternoon's go-karting, followed by a champagne supper. So much for joyful anticipation.

Time for a shower. Siv retraced her steps, pausing to bend and stroke a delicate snowdrop head. It made her smile. She decided to steer a middle course for the funeral and pair black trousers with a crimson shirt that reflected the colour of the bright rosehips.

She showered, dressed, ate a slice of toast and peanut butter, then drank another mug of tea. When she was ready to leave, she took a belted navy wool coat that she hadn't worn for ages from the wardrobe. It was a London coat, calf-length and city smart. Ed had helped her choose it. They'd rarely shopped together and had bickered amiably as she tried on several styles. Because he'd been hanging around, she'd found herself unusually indecisive. When she'd donned this one, Ed had declared that she looked chic, then pleaded with her to just buy it before he jumped out of the nearest window.

She checked herself in the mirror. She'd do. She was still pale and skinny, but her dark hair had grown back again. No more bald patches to conceal artfully. She paid a small fortune every month at the hairdresser, her one vanity. A good haircut distracted the eye from her pallid skin and the cold sores that grieving had gifted her.

She massaged her scalp, easing the fuzzy head that the chill air hadn't quite cleared. She woke up with one quite a few mornings, after she'd overdone the akvavit the night before. Her recycling bin was always full of bottles with a blue fish label, and last night she'd emptied one to help her numb the thoughts of this funeral. It had the desired effect, but she was aware that the aftermath wasn't so good.

By the door, she unhooked her green leather bag from the back of a chair. Her friend Bartel had given it to her for Christmas and she loved it. It was soft leather, with two buckles and was expensive — she'd spotted it for sale in town afterwards, then had worried that she'd been a cheapskate, only giving him, in return, a few bottles of his favourite cherry vodka.

Lisa's funeral was at one o'clock, so Siv headed to the station first. She drove slowly down the track to the road, waving to Corran as she passed him, carrying a bucket full of kitchen scraps, on his way to feed his goats. They were named after famous divas, and two of them, Judy and Nina, were crazy for banana and orange peel.

She gripped the wheel firmly with her gloved hands. This would be the first funeral she'd attended since Ed's. Life had become a series of firsts after her husband was knocked from his bike: the first Christmas — she'd spent it alone in their London flat, eating beans on toast — the first Easter, the birthday when he should have turned thirty-four. And so it went on.

Was it getting any easier, without Ed? Not really. She was just better at muffling the pain. He didn't talk to her quite so much these days, although he still dropped the odd comment. *I can't remember much about your funeral,* she told him. *I was too numb. Sorry. Hope you didn't mind.* His parents had arrived and taken over. She'd let them. They'd meant well, and she could barely speak, let alone make the necessary arrangements.

She was dreading the crematorium today, but it wasn't about her. She had to show up and take part as Lisa's colleague.

Chin up and sing loud, Sivster, Ed said in her ear. Lisa's gone. The service is to comfort others.

She smiled and was about to reply when her phone rang. Sergeant Ali Carlin's Derry accent always cheered her up, although this time, she noted, he sounded strained.

'Hi, guv, where are you?'

'On my way to the station. Are you there?'

'No, I'm with Noah. Patrick had to go and help Ms Flore. She's in a bit of a state. Her brother's flight was delayed and he won't arrive until mid- morning. Talk about leaving it till last minute! Noah's carer didn't turn up, so I've come round to give him a hand.'

Noah was Patrick's brother. A stroke had left him disabled and using a wheelchair.

'Is Noah OK?'

'He is, aye, very natty in a seasonal shirt patterned with robins. But there's a man who is very much *not* OK on the steps of the crem. We have a body to deal with. Sounds a grim scene, guv. Corpses are the crem's bread and butter, but they're usually in coffins.'

She listened with amazement as he described where the dead man had been found, beneath a line of wreaths, on the steps of Berminster Crematorium.

'Who found the body?'

'Toby Foxwell, the crem manager. Guv, what do you wanna do? Will Lisa's funeral go ahead? It'll be terrible if we can't hold it, especially for her mum.'

Siv was appalled at the prospect of Lisa's funeral being cancelled. She glanced at the time. Eight thirty. Could they have the scene processed and cleared in time?

'I just don't know, Ali. I'll see what I can do.'

'Just . . . we need to let Patrick and Ms Flore know if there's a delay or a cancellation—'

'I'll drive to the crematorium now and see what needs to be done. I'll get back to you as soon as I can.'

'OK. I'll be there when Noah's sorted.'

Siv had been to the cemetery once before, for her father's burial, and Ed had been there to hold her hand. It occurred to her now, as it had then, that it was like driving into the grounds of a country mansion. She'd read that the Victorians never did things simply when they could put on a show, and they'd been fascinated by death and dying and elaborate funeral rituals. If she'd been married to Ed in the nineteenth century, she'd have had to wear a black mourning dress for at least a year and shun society for two. Queen Victoria had set the bar high by wearing a full mourning outfit for Prince Albert for the rest of her life. Siv had done the shunning bit — that had been easy. Her colleagues often found her unsociable, and she'd overheard someone at the station refer to her as 'that weirdo'.

It was so hard, not having Ed beside her. Her support and confidant, the man she'd gone home to and leaned on.

* * *

Steve Wooton, the crime scene manager, was with his team by the steps when Siv arrived at the crematorium, parking some distance away from them. The body was like an offering, laid out, ready and waiting for those who dealt with the dead. She gazed at the line of opulent wreaths. The colours jarred. She hated the things. They were gaudy and brash — give her low-key, graceful wildflowers any time.

As she approached, Steve followed her with his narrow, darting eyes. They didn't like each other. She found him self-important. She also suspected that he didn't like the fact that she was several inches taller than him. Ali said Steve had WMS — Wee Man Syndrome.

'Looks like strangulation,' Steve said. 'Marking around the throat and petechiae.'

'Killed here?'

'Hard to say. Bad joke, leaving a corpse on the crem steps.'

'Any ID?'

'Nothing. He's not one of the crem staff. I got the manager to take a peek. He was up for it, and I reckoned it would save time.'

She wasn't sure that she approved of that, but she let it go. 'I'll just see his face.'

Steve lifted a wreath for her, exposing the man's head and shoulders. His red-dotted eyes stared upwards. In his twenties, he had unremarkable features, silky fair hair and a wispy moustache. He was wearing a black fleece.

Siv stepped back, assessing the situation. She'd need to determine if the crematorium could keep on working today.

'When can you move the body, do you think? Is the pathologist arriving soon?'

He shrugged, puffing himself up. 'Rey Anand's on his way. I don't see why it can't be shifted pronto if he agrees.'

'Where do I find the manager?'

'Toby Foxwell's in his office,' Steve said chirpily. 'He's anxious about today's funerals, including Lisa's. He has a nightmare vision of hearses queueing around the block and relatives tearing their hair out. I told him it'd be your call.'

He could make it less obvious that he was relishing the difficult situation she was in. But it was indeed tricky and she'd not faced anything quite like this before. 'Any evidence that the chapels are crime scenes?'

'No. Foxwell usually unlocks them and this central foyer, and he found the corpse before he got round to that. I've checked. All doors for public access are still locked and no sign of tampering. There are double doors at the rear, leading only to the crem offices and chamber. The crem technician opened those and confirmed that they were secure when she arrived.'

Siv searched for a plan of the crematorium on her phone. There was a map on the council website detailing the numbering of the graves. Studying it, she was able to get a vague idea of the grounds. The visitors' car park was situated at a short distance and there were separate paths from it to the chapel side entrances. Maybe with a bit of organisation, a restricted area could be preserved for mourners. If she spoke to Rey, they might be able to shift the corpse once he'd done his examination, and Lisa could have her service.

Siv left Steve and walked around the building to check the area for herself, and then headed along the path to the crematorium offices in Bere Lodge. It was a double-fronted building with a half-timbered upper floor and canted bay windows. She supposed that, when it first opened, the cemetery keeper and his family would have lived there. Inside, she found modern office furniture in pale wood, magnolia walls, blue carpet tiles and notices in the dark green-and-grey motif used throughout the crematorium. Siv thought this a little tasteless. *Even death has to be branded now.*

She introduced herself to the woman at the reception desk — Phoebe Palmer, according to her name badge — and showed her ID.

'Mr Foxwell's waiting for you in his office. First door on the left,' Phoebe said politely.

Toby Foxwell was seated at his desk, clutching a mug of coffee. He got up as Siv entered and held out his hand. She took it.

'I'm DI Siv Drummond. Difficult start to the day for you, Mr Foxwell.'

'Indeed. Unexpected. It's a challenge. The kind of thing that tests our mettle and keeps us on our toes.'

That was an interesting response to a dead man on your doorstep. Siv accepted the offer of coffee, reading the laminated mission statement on Toby Foxwell's desk while he prepared it.

We provide a peaceful space where you can pay respect to and commemorate your loved one.

He wasn't going to be managing a peaceful space in the coming days, that was for sure.

Foxwell didn't seem thrown by his grim discovery. He crackled with energy. He might have been putting on an act, needing to appear the professional manager, or perhaps he'd been on one of those management courses about turning threats into opportunities. His name suited him. He was lean and smartly dressed. He had burnished, tawny hair, parted just so, and a narrow, sharp nose. His desk was neat, pens in a straight row. Siv guessed that he ran a streamlined, efficient outfit, despatching the dead sympathetically, albeit promptly.

'Do you have an identity for that poor man yet?' His accent was modulated cockney and his voice made her think of melting treacle. It was emollient. Handy for working with the bereaved.

'We haven't established that,' Siv replied. 'What time is your first funeral?'

He glanced at his watch and bounced a little in his chair. 'Ten thirty. Inspector, I need to know if we can cremate our dead today. I've checked with my manager and she said I have to be guided by you. If you say we can proceed, that's fine. If we can't go ahead, I have to issue instructions immediately and get my team on the phones. You can imagine the disruption and the anguish for families that would cause. I need to consider our public profile and reputation—'

‘I understand. I’m supposed to be attending a service myself — Lisa Flore’s. I need to check a few things with you.’

He blinked his sandy lashes. ‘Oh, of course. Ms Flore was one of your colleagues. I’m so sorry, Inspector.’

‘Thank you.’

‘Yes, dreadful event indeed. Well, I suppose you want to clarify exactly what happened when I found the body. I drove through the gates just after half seven—’

Siv waved a hand, cutting him off. ‘That can wait for now — we’ll get to those details later. Do you unlock the central foyer door and the side doors to the chapels each morning?’

He seemed annoyed at her interruption. ‘Oh, um . . . yes. That’s always my task. I like to inspect the chapels and anterooms personally.’

‘But you didn’t today.’

‘No. I saw the body at around a quarter to eight before I managed to do my rounds. I rang the police immediately.’

‘And what about other parts of the crematorium — are different staff responsible for them?’

‘The caretaker opens the main gates around seven, as well as the pedestrian access gate off Barker’s Way, at the top of Bluebell Copse. It’s called Emmeline’s Gate, after the wife of the cemetery’s designer. The cremation technician unlocks the back gate and the door to the retort at eight.’

‘The retort?’

‘The cremation chamber, at the back of the chapels. Diane Lacey, the technician, checks the equipment and the day’s schedule on arrival.’ He put his shoulders back and leaned forward, spreading his hands flat on the desk. A clear I’m-in-charge pose. ‘I’ve checked with the caretaker and Diane. They say that they didn’t see anything suspicious, and they confirmed that the front and back gates and the pedestrian access were locked when they arrived at their usual times. Diane is my excellent deputy manager, by the way, as well as senior technician. She’s highly qualified in her field. She covered for me last year when I was unwell.’

'Do you have any burials scheduled for today or in the next couple of days?'

'We have none this week. Just cremations.'

'Give me a moment, please. I need to consult with my colleagues about the crematorium's functioning.'

She stepped outside into the corridor and rang Rey Anand, who'd since arrived at the scene. As always, she appreciated the pathologist's precise, no-nonsense approach. His view was that the body could now be taken to the mortuary. Other arrangements were her responsibility. With less enthusiasm, she phoned her boss, DCI Will Mortimer. He'd need to make the final call on this one. It was a longer conversation, as she described the grounds and the layout and the potential complications they could create. He ummed and ahhed before he made a decision. Siv leaned on a window ledge and jotted quick notes, making sure they'd covered all the bases. She returned to Foxwell's office. He looked up anxiously.

'I'm afraid you have to cancel this morning's funerals, Mr Foxwell, so that we have time to secure the scene, but you're OK to go ahead with this afternoon's from one o'clock,' she told him. 'But there are conditions. There will be a police cordon and presence around the grounds, at the front and back gates and all the other areas with public access. The public can't visit graves or memorial areas until further notice. Mourners must enter and exit via the paths leading directly from the car park to the chapels' side doors. The central door and anterooms have to remain locked, and the steps and roadway outside will be cordoned off. You need to make sure that visitors go straight to the chapels from their cars and leave immediately after the services. No loitering. Have you got the staff to marshal them in and out?'

He blew his cheeks out, slowly releasing the air while he thought. 'This will be difficult, with no access to refreshments or toilets . . .'

Like it or lump it, Siv thought. If it wasn't for Lisa, she'd have been tempted to advocate closing the place down completely. 'I expect mourners can go without a cuppa and hold onto their bladders for the sake of saying goodbye to their loved ones.'

He gave her a shrewd glance. 'Very well. I'll inform the staff.'

'A few more things, Mr Foxwell. Have there been any problems here recently? Difficulties between staff or any of the people who use your services?'

'No, I'm pleased to say. The whole operation has been running smoothly.'

'You can't think of anyone who'd want to bring the crematorium into disrepute?'

He tweaked his tie. 'Absolutely not.'

'I'd appreciate a map of the site and a staff list as soon as possible.'

He handed her an envelope. 'All ready for you.'

Before Siv left his office, he was already on the phone, issuing instructions. It was clear he was enjoying tackling the adversity the day had brought, despite the disruptions involved.

* * *

The gates accessing the rear of the crematorium were similar to the main ones, but on a smaller scale, and the door into the retort area was robust and had a mortice lock. In contrast to the industrial bank of steel, the technician's office was warm and homely. A huge vase of roses, lilies and freesias stood on the desk, scenting the room. Reds, yellows, purples, pinks and creams. Unseasonal colours for January. Diane Lacey picked out a couple of blossoms that were drooping as Siv watched.

'Families insist on giving us bouquets by way of thanks. We're not really supposed to accept gifts, but Toby says flowers are OK. We get so many I never need to buy flowers for home now,' Diane commented.

Siv listened to the low background hum of the cremation chambers. It was soothing. Lisa would be in there soon, crumbling to ash in the furnace. Then she recalled reading that it was bone fragments that remained after cremation, and they were then ground to a fine powder like ash. She'd sprinkled Ed's ashes in the Thames at Greenwich, below the Old Royal Naval College, and watched them merge with the ebbing tide.

Diane shuffled the flowers and moved the vase to one side. She was in her mid-forties, had an earnest manner, spiky brown hair and soft down on her top lip. With her long fingers and slightly hunched shoulders, Siv would have guessed she was a musician — a violinist.

'We're all stunned and disgusted by what's happened,' Diane continued. 'We deal with death every day, but for someone to place a body on the steps and abandon it in the open like that . . . It's a bit like desecrating a church.'

She looked as if she'd been crying and gave the impression that she was of a shy, nervous disposition, so Siv started with easy questions.

'How long have you worked here?'

'Fifteen years, almost.'

'Talk me through what you do.'

Diane was a slight woman, very pale and serious. Her blouse and skirt were in a dowdy fawn, baggy and shapeless, and as she sat back, her high office chair swallowed her up. 'I meet families and guide them through the process. I check coffins when they arrive and the ID of the deceased, make sure that regulations are followed to the letter when bodies enter the retort and keep records. Every morning I check that the equipment is working correctly. If families want to watch the actual cremation, I assist them with that. Then, post cremation, I have to make sure that remains are identified and disposed of correctly.'

Siv's attention had been snagged by one sentence. 'Families can *watch* a body being cremated in the furnace?'

'Of course. We have a small viewing room. Some people want, need, to complete the journey as part of the ceremony. Keeping their loved one company to the end. It's not that much different to standing by a graveside to pay your last respects.'

Keeping company. Last respects. The room dimmed.

'Can I have a glass of water?'

Siv watched Diane unscrew the bottle on her desk. Had she failed Ed at the last, not staying by him as he burned away? She'd been clueless about his funeral arrangements, had wandered through the weeks after his death as if she were having an out-of-body experience. She'd agreed to whatever Ed's parents had suggested, wanting them to go away and leave her alone.

'Are you OK?' Diane was holding out the glass to her. 'A crematorium can often be upsetting. I could get you a hot drink, if you want.'

Siv shook her head and drank half the glass. After a moment, her vision cleared. 'Just thirsty. Have there been any problems at the crematorium, between staff or with the bereaved?'

'None that I'm aware of.'

'What's Mr Foxwell like as a boss?' Siv imagined he'd be a tad snappy, a keen bureaucrat. Some staff might resent that.

Diane measured her words. 'He likes things run well. So do I. This is such a responsible job. We deal with people who are in a vulnerable state and we have to get it right.'

Siv took the staff list from her bag. 'Saul Robbins is a general support worker and a retort assistant. Is he working with you this morning?'

'It's his day off today. Most of the time, he meets and greets families, accompanies visitors to the chapels and memorials and helps the caretaker with maintenance of the grounds. Saul helps out in the retort at busy times. I've given him on-the-job training to provide him with some more stimulating, responsible tasks and get him a little bit more pay. He doesn't actually want to stay in this kind of work, and he certainly has academic potential. I've encouraged him to study for an MBA.'

Then Diane took Siv through her arrival that morning. Straightforward, nothing unusual.

'Where were you late last night?'

'At home. I live with my grandfather. We watched TV until around eleven, then I made him some cocoa and we went to bed.'

Siv finished the water and shook her head when Diane offered a refill.

'Do you want to see around the facility?' she asked. 'It can help, especially those who find the idea of cremation daunting or upsetting. We have open days a couple of times a year for that reason. Many people find it fascinating.'

That must make for a jolly day out.

Siv flinched at the compassion in Diane's eyes. She resented having her discomfort noted. 'I'll pass on that, thanks.'

'I understand. Something a bit less full-on that might interest you, if you've never done it, is this.' She took a flyer from her drawer and handed it over. 'This has details of some regular talks I give here. You'll see the days and times and a bit of background information. I have a particular interest in thanatology. It formed part of my MA. I conduct tours of the nineteenth-century sector of the cemetery once a month, year round. There are some fascinating graves and monuments, as well as strange stories of the families who lived in Berminster then. '

'Thanatology?'

'It's the scientific study of death and loss. The tours are very popular. I never tire of doing them.' Diane beamed.

Siv glanced at the flyer and tucked it into the side pocket of her bag, smiling weakly.

On the way out, she stopped at a retail area to the side of Diane's office, where you could sit on an example of an engraved memorial bench. There were a couple of cabinets holding urns and keepsakes. The bereaved could choose from classical-style metal urns in gold, black or cream, blue ceramic with brass details, rose china shaped like a teardrop or grey smoked glass. If you wanted to have your loved one by you always, there were porcelain keepsake urns with the inscription, *I'll carry you with me until we meet again*, marble boxes and a collection of teal and silver-painted egg-shaped stones with hollowed centres.

It didn't occur to me, but I wouldn't have wanted to cart your ashes around with me. Seems a bit naff, Siv said to Ed. No reply. Did that mean it was a touchy subject and he'd have liked to be kept by her side, maybe zipped in her bag or sitting on her bedside table? *Too late now.*

Outside, the air was brisker, nipping at her face and neck. A hearse arrived, its windows filled with lilies spelling *LISA*. Tears sprang to her eyes and she blinked hard as she watched the coffin being unloaded and carried in through the rear of the building.

CHAPTER 3

An hour is too long for a funeral service. Ali would tell Polly to keep it short and sweet when he popped off.

Lisa's mum had spared no expense. The coffin was top of the range, elegantly crafted in cherry wood with braided trim and gold handles. Ali had seen the details on Patrick's kitchen table. It had cost over three thousand pounds, and that was before all the flowers and wreaths that were surrounding it — enough to fill a florist's shop. The funeral business must make a mint out of people's grief and vulnerability.

He stood sturdily between the guv and Patrick, feet planted apart, aware of the tension radiating from Siv. He was a touchy-feely man and would have liked to have put an arm around her, hold her steady. Back in Derry, folk were more demonstrative at funerals, sharing publicly in their grief. Here, everything was restrained and muted. Polite. There'd been no wake before the funeral and there'd be no singing at Nutmeg afterwards. At least the grub would be good. Ali's wife, Polly, was the chef there. She'd spent last night prepping the buffet and as soon as the service finished, she'd be leaving the chapel to make final tweaks. Every so often, he could hear her clear, high voice behind him, joining in the singing.

He pictured the sausage rolls, pasties, cheese twists and savoury tarts that Pol had slaved over the night before. His stomach grumbled, and he reprimanded himself for letting his mind wander to food when he should be paying attention. But Lisa would have laughed. She'd had a hearty appetite, and she'd egged him on to eat the naughty carbs a diabetic should avoid. Sometimes, when they'd worked late, she'd ordered in double-crust pizzas and he'd tucked in, picturing his blood sugar heading out of control and Nurse Keene's frown at the diabetic clinic.

Ali glanced at the guv. She was as pale as paper, one hand gripping the back of the chair in front of her, the other clutching the order of service. Another funeral would be a tough call after you'd been to your husband's. It wouldn't help that Crista, the guv's mother, was at the service on the arm of DCI Mortimer. Heads had turned when she walked in. She resembled a fashion model in her elegant black coat, lacy mantilla and huge dark glasses. Ali had first seen her at the Halloween party last year. He gathered that she was Finnish, had arrived in town recently and there was no love lost between mother and daughter. He was dying for the full story, but you didn't ask the guv that kind of stuff unless you wanted your head bitten off.

He was fond of Siv. She was a cracking detective, but he wished she'd let people in a bit more. Polly said she just needed time, that she must still be in shock over her husband, and Pol was usually right. Patrick sighed as Noah spoke about Lisa's love of marathon running and dim sum. Ali gave his arm a light squeeze.

The chapel was packed with police colleagues, Lisa's friends and her small family, just her mother and uncle. Now the celebrant was praising the lively woman they'd been friends with, who'd had so much to give before she was cut down in the bloom of youth. Ali liked that phrase, 'the bloom of youth'. It reminded him of the song 'Tir na nÓg'. Like the lover in the song, Lisa's hair had been the colour of barley and she'd had pale, almost silvery eyes. He hummed it silently to himself and pictured the other young corpse who'd been removed from the steps outside. Steve had estimated that he was in his twenties. This really was turning out to be a strange, sad day.

When the service ended, Ali, Siv and Patrick hurried to Ali's car, shivering after the warmth of the chapel. The sun was pale and lemony in a faded blue sky. The guv sat in the back for a minute. They were all silent, watching the cars pull away. The chapel bells were clanging. Ali's stomach made a noise like a drain emptying and he pressed a hand against it. He reached into the glove compartment for his stash of sugar-free jelly bears and offered them round. The guv passed and Patrick took a green one.

'Good turnout,' Ali said.

Patrick nibbled his sweet. 'She was popular. Everyone liked Lisa.'

'What's happening with her ashes?' the guv asked. She sounded a bit wobbly.

'Her mum's thinking of scattering them along one of Lisa's marathon routes,' Patrick said. 'She checked with me that it wasn't illegal. Said she liked to think of Lisa always running into the distance.'

The guv cleared her throat and put a hand on Patrick's shoulder. 'I'm sorry, Patrick, but I can't come to Nutmeg. Please give my apologies to Ms Flore. It's terrible that this murder is hanging over our goodbyes to Lisa. I need to get on with this investigation and start interviews. We've no idea why this man was left here. We'll focus on the crem and its staff for now, in case there's a link between this location and the deceased. It's as good a place to start as any, until we know his name. You stay with Ms Flore as long as you need.'

'Thanks. These things aren't easy. I can't stomach the thought of food myself. This sweet's sticking in my throat.'

Ali wasn't sure that Patrick understood. He'd been in a kind of trance all morning. 'We'll raise a glass for you, guv,' Ali said. 'I'll not stay long, just half an hour or so, if that's OK with you, and then I'll be back.'

Siv opened the car door. 'That's fine. I'll meet you at Bere Lodge.'

Ali glanced at her in the rear-view mirror as he drove away. She looked solitary, pinched. Life was such a bastard sometimes.

* * *

The light bulb was stiff in the socket. Imelda Kilgore pushed and twisted. At last, it freed and she was able to replace it. She folded the stepladder and left it by the door. She went through the rooms and checked each one again, making sure the inventory was up to date. The guests weren't arriving until Friday, but once the keys were in the key safe, she needn't worry about Hazel Cottage again for a week. In the kitchen, she checked that the information pack was on the table, with the small box of welcome shortbread that she bought wholesale. Imelda realised that some rental owners left loo rolls, a basic store cupboard, milk in the fridge and scones and local wines for guests, but she kept things simple and low-key. She'd never seen the need to over-egg the pudding, and she wasn't running a charity.

On the way to the car, she pulled a few weeds from the side of the path and deadheaded some roses that had struggled on through the winter. A property owner's job was never done, but she didn't mind. The tiny front garden was pretty, even in this bleak month. Hazel Cottage didn't have a sea view, tucked as it was down a quiet lane, just two miles from town, and the beach was a twenty-minute walk. It was her smallest property, only one bedroom, and was usually booked by couples wanting a secluded place. *Ideal for a snug honeymoon getaway*, as the brochure said.

Imelda owned six holiday homes in the area and maintained them all herself under the name Berminster Breaks. She'd gone for a portfolio with variety: two traditional cottages, two chalets, a bungalow and a flat by the harbour. She did all the routine maintenance, cleaning and laundry.

Life was easier since bookings had gone online, but in high season, her feet hardly touched the ground and that was the way she liked it.

And thank goodness she had gone into holiday properties in her fifties. Wilf, her husband, had been made redundant from his lecturing job and she'd insisted that they use the pay-off to buy two cottages, Hazel and Mallow. He'd died at fifty-five and she'd invested the life insurance in more holiday lets. The rentals gave her purpose, satisfaction and a comfortable income. She'd been able to give Henry a hefty deposit towards his flat in London — if only he wasn't sharing it now with that twitchy girlfriend. Imelda could see the attraction of a beautiful, exotic woman but failed to understand why he'd had to move her in with him. Soppy Saffie, who seemed to have no opinions and jumped when someone coughed. If only he'd stayed with Viv, who was a bit of a lazy madam but fun and gutsy. Imelda would keep her mouth shut though, hoping that the affair with Saffie would run its course.

She spent an hour at the bungalow, touching up some paintwork, cleaning the fridge and the dishwasher filter and plugging in a new kettle. She drove home, invigorated. It was such a beautiful crisp day, the kind that you hope for but can never rely on in late January. She was anticipating elevenses and catching-up with Henry and the gang. She'd pop down to Driftwood after twenty minutes' respite with coffee and the crossword.

Tonight was the big night — Damian and Viv's engagement celebration. From what Imelda gathered, there would be more, but this was the Berminster bash. They were all going to Amalfi, the best restaurant in town. The chef had won a TV competition last year, and you had to book weeks ahead. Word was that the lobster with ginger was amazing.

Imelda saw Saffie as she drove along the road. There was no mistaking that drooping stance. You'd expect that a young woman with such stunning looks would be confident, holding herself erect. She was hanging around by the front door, hands stuffed in her pockets, her hair blowing over her face. Imelda smiled stiffly as she locked the car.

'Hello, dear. Do you need something?'

'I'm just here for Henry. We did say that we'd have lunch in town and he hasn't surfaced yet. I rang the bell, but he must still be asleep—'

What was she talking about? 'Henry's not here, dear.'

'But—are you sure? He's not at the chalet.'

'I expect he's out for a run, blowing away the cobwebs.'

'No. Sorry, I mean he said he was staying here last night.'

Is she a bit dim, as well as nervy?

Imelda opened the door impatiently and strode straight upstairs to Henry's room, standing aside to show Saffie the empty, perfectly made-up bed. 'You must have got confused, dear.'

Saffie shook her head. 'I woke up at three this morning and wondered where he was. I checked my phone and realised I'd forgotten to switch it on. He'd left me a message around eleven last night, said he'd had one too many and was about to have several more. He said he'd crash at your place so that he didn't wake me and he'd see me this morning.'

Imelda felt the first tingle of anxiety. 'Have you asked Damian and Viv where he is?'

'They're not up yet.' Too busy having max-volume sex.

Imelda sat on the edge of the empty bed beneath sultry Natalie Portman. She took her phone from her bag and rang her son's number. Voicemail.

'Henry, I suppose you're messing around somewhere. Give me a call when you get this.'

She got up and straightened the duvet. 'We'd better go down to Driftwood. I'm sure there's an explanation. These young men can be daft when they're let loose on their own.' But even to her own ears, her words sounded hollow.

She led the way on foot from the house, down the path to the chalet, Saffie following.

* * *

Siv was leaving the car park and heading back towards the crematorium buildings when a silver Lexus saloon purred up beside her.

'DI Drummond, how's it going?' DI Tommy Castles had rolled down his window and was peering at her over the top of his aviator sunglasses.

Just what she needed. One of her least favourite people. 'OK, thanks. How are you?'

'Fine. Here for Lisa's funeral. You want a lift to Nutmeg?'

'I can't come. I have a murder investigation.'

'Ah. I'd ask more, but I don't want to be late. I was fond of Lisa. We dated once. She was good fun.'

That's not what she said about you, Tommy. I believe 'conceited prick' was the term. Whenever Tommy's name had been mentioned, Lisa had started humming the Carly Simon song, 'You're So Vain'.

'There are worse epitaphs, I'm sure,' said Siv.

Tommy eyed her suspiciously and then smiled. 'You never did get back to me about that drink.'

'That's right, I didn't. It slipped my mind.'

He pretended to be wounded, putting a hand over his heart. 'And I thought I'd made an impression on the woman from the Met!'

'Well, I mustn't keep you.'

'OK, Ms Frosty. Have it your way.'

You've disappointed that poor man, and he's only trying to be nice, Ed sniggered.

She watched the Lexus accelerate away. DI Castles used to work in town, and DCI Mortimer had wanted him for the job Siv got. Following a promotion, Castles had gone off to Kent, but he was still good mates with Mortimer and there were rumours that he'd like to come back, given a chance. Siv suspected that her boss used him to snoop on her and the team. Castles had turned up for Mortimer's Halloween party last year and emailed her afterwards, suggesting a drink. She'd deleted it.

She stepped into the foyer of Bere Lodge and was greeted again by Phoebe Palmer. She was a fidgety but pleasant middle-aged woman, with a grey birthmark the size of a pound coin on her forehead, above her right eye. She led Siv to a tiny, quiet room at the back of the building where she could conduct interviews. It had a window facing flowerbeds filled with pansies, and pergolas draped with winter jasmine and wisteria.

'This is where the bereavement service invites distressed relatives to sit,' Phoebe told her in a diffident, fluting voice. 'We're all terribly upset about what's happened.'

'It must be dreadful. Are you a tightly knit group?' Siv asked, trying to get some idea of the setup at the crematorium. The murder might be connected to the place.

'Well . . . I'm not sure I'd say that.' Phoebe's voice held regret. 'Maybe not as close as we used to be before we were restructured.' She held her hands clasped in front of her. 'It's been very different since Mr Foxwell took over. He's full of ideas, made big changes. New broom and all that.'

Siv took note of the subtext. 'Did you prefer things the way they were before?'

'Oh, well . . . I expect we needed shaking up. That's what Mr Foxwell told us when he was appointed.'

'How about Diane, the deputy manager — she's been here longer than Mr Foxwell, hasn't she?'

'Diane's very approachable and helpful. She loves her job and she gets on fine with Mr Foxwell. He realises that she's the expert in what she does, so he respects her. She's a quiet, reliable person and she's terribly knowledgeable about the history of the cemetery. The retort is very much her domain. As she's told me more than once when I've been a bit fed up with Mr Foxwell's changes, you can't stay in a rut.'

Phoebe sounded like she longed to stay in a rut. 'How long have you been here?' Siv asked.

'Thirty years,' she said proudly. 'It's good to do a job where I can help people in their time of need. I may not have any qualifications, but I do have life experience and compassion. I realise I sometimes get a bit over-involved though.'

'In what way?'

'Oh, talking to people for too long, helping them with things that aren't in my remit.'

That sounded like management speak. 'Is that what Mr Foxwell told you?'

Phoebe nodded. 'I have to give the same quality service to everyone. We have to be careful not to discriminate.' She spoke like a child repeating a lesson and gave a little laugh. 'I'd best get back to the desk now.' She hurried out to reception, leaving Siv alone in the room.

There were two small sofas and a cheap coffee table on which stood a large box of tissues. One framed glossy poster of a sunrise over the sea hung near the window. The photographed sky was suffused with tangerine and ochre tints. Maybe it was to indicate hope, or maybe the cycle of life. Siv tilted her head and stared at it. She wondered how many saw it as a sunset, the dying of the day.

In that moment, Siv saw that. Her mood was definitely flat. She'd suspected that her mother would be at Lisa's service. Crista, Siv's *mutsi*, hadn't met Lisa, but now that she'd attached herself to her daughter's boss, she popped up everywhere with him. Mortimer was smitten. The only place free of her was Mortimer's office, and Siv half expected to find Mutsi propped on the desk in there one of these days. It was a horrible thought, but this corpse on the steps had let her off the painful hook of having to socialise with Mutsi and her boss at Nutmeg. She shouldn't be grateful that a murder had happened, but it was fortuitous, certainly.

She pulled out the staff list that Foxwell had given her. She was starting interviews with the caretaker, as he would have been the first staff member at the cemetery this morning. Once Ali arrived, she'd ask him to take over.

Andy Smeaton was in his sixties with a smoker's cough and a straightforward, rough manner. When he arrived, he got down to business immediately.

'I'm not just caretaker for the crematorium, you see. I open the main gates here every morning at seven, then I drive to Emmeline's Gate at Barker's Way and unlock that. After that I go straight to the swimming pool and open up there, then the museum. It's called "working across the piece" in council jargon.' He smiled, as if it were a private joke. 'I'm also responsible for checking general maintenance and security at all three sites. I look after the grounds here and the scrap of a garden at the museum.'

'Did you see anyone around this morning? Any cars or pedestrians?'

He shook his head. 'I just got out of the car, opened up and headed off.'

'And do you lock the gates at night?'

'That's right, the main one and Emmeline's, at eight sharp. The cleaners are in between six and eight. I check around the site to make sure everyone's gone.'

'And that was the case at eight last night?'

'That's correct.'

Siv was running on empty after the funeral. She struggled to come up with another question. Smeaton grinned, as if he sensed she was adrift.

'I'm not responsible for the back gate,' he offered. 'The senior technician opens and locks that. Diane Lacey, that is.'

'Yes, thanks. Have there been any problems here recently? Any upset customers or staff?'

'Not that I know of. Mr Foxwell runs everything like clockwork. Very on the ball. This place has been ship-shape since he took over. Pity he can't be prime minister — the country wouldn't be in such a mess.'

'Quite a recommendation. I didn't notice any CCTV at the main gate.'

Smeaton shook his head. 'We don't have it, or at the back either. I suppose nobody's ever seen a need for it. We've never had any break-ins or vandalism here. Unless you're after someone's remains, there's nothing much to nick.'

A crematorium was an unlikely place for crime. Until this morning.

'Who do you work with most closely here?' Siv continued.

'Saul, I suppose. Saul Robbins. This is just a stopgap job for him, though.' He added sarcastically, 'If what he says is true, he has his mind on higher things.'

'In what way?'

'He's studying for some kind of degree. Rates himself. You can see he reckons he's slumming it with us. Personally, I can't wait for him to leave so I can have someone who gets stuck in.'

'Where were you last night?'

'I had a pint at the Silver Band club. I got home about half ten and went to bed.'

'Do you live alone?'

'Yep. On my tod since my missus died.'

She let him go, relieved when Ali arrived not long after. He'd made an effort with his appearance today and was wearing a dark grey suit. His tie was askew, and as usual his shirt was fighting with his tubby middle, escaping from his waistband. He was like an overgrown schoolboy in need of a pair of braces. He tugged his trousers up and handed her a paper bag.

'Here, a bit of scran for you from the restaurant — a couple of Polly's pasties. Funerals always make people hungry.'

The bag was warm, a savoury aroma escaping from it. Ali loved his food and could always be relied on for supplies. She was lucky to have a sergeant with a warm, generous nature, not least because he softened her own sharp edges. Ed would have got on with Ali.

'Thanks. I'll eat them in the car. Is Ms Flore OK?'

Ali shrugged. 'Difficult to tell. Putting on a good show. Patrick's a bit wan. It's all gone off well, that's the main thing.' He stood, hands in pockets, rolling back and forth on his feet, examining the picture. 'Too much orange in this for me. I can't be doing with orange. Reminds me of Lambeg drums and "The Sash My Father Wore".'

They didn't share many confidences, but he'd told her once during a car journey that he'd been beaten up after a Loyalist parade when he was a teenager in Derry. Some marchers had spotted him watching from a street corner and had taken exception to his mixed heritage and his black Catholic mother. Siv watched the cold sunlight gleaming on Ali's cornrows. He'd had them braided for today in a zigzag pattern, the style Lisa had liked best. All these young people dying. It was so stupid and wasteful, but all she could do was find out what happened to the poor man on the steps who'd had his life snatched away.

'Sit down, for goodness' sake, you're blocking the light,' she said, annoyed that she sounded so curt. This day was wearing, but she needed to stay resolute and keep the team steady.

Ali said nothing but sat on the narrow sofa beside her. She had to shuffle along to make room for his plump thighs as she showed him the list of staff.

'The asterisked ones work part-time and some aren't here today, so we'll have to check the rota and play catch-up with them. Phoebe Palmer, the receptionist, has been here ages, so she should be useful for background. But she's not overfond of her boss.

'There's no evidence of a break-in at any of the buildings and the gates haven't been tampered with. Unless Toby Foxwell, Diane Lacey or Andy Smeaton dumped our body, then whoever did may have driven through the main gates after Smeaton unlocked them. If that's the case, our man was left on the steps between seven and seven thirty this morning, cutting it fine between the caretaker opening up and Foxwell arriving.'

'Seems whoever did it has an understanding of how the place operates.'

'This crime might be linked to the crematorium or might be a bizarre statement by the killer, or both. Foxwell claims he's had no problems here recently. According to him, everything's running smoothly, and Diane Lacey and Andy Smeaton echoed him, but check that out with everyone you interview. I want to touch base with Steve and Rey—' She looked up to see Ali's eyes were watery. 'You OK, Ali?'

'Aye. Just a wee bit sad. You?'

'Hmm. Difficult day,' she said quietly. 'It's a lot to cope with for all of us. We just have to get on with the job.'

'Sure. Best keep busy, catch the bad guys, eh?'

She gathered up her things and smiled at him. Hopefully getting back to work would help keep his mind occupied.

In her car, she ate a spiced spinach and potato pasty ravenously, brushing crumbs from her lap, phoning Steve Wooton through a mouthful.

'Still no ID for our dead man?'

'Hello to you too, DI Drummond. And, no, his pockets were empty and there's no phone. He's been taken to the mortuary now. Rey Anand's scheduled the post-mortem for tomorrow morning. We're starting to search the general area, but the light will go soon, so we'll resume tomorrow. Did Lisa get a good send off?'

'Yes, it went well.'

She wiped her hands on a tissue. The pasty had energised her. She could see why Ali was always so cheery. She wouldn't mind being married to Polly and having delicious meals served up every day. She wondered if Polly ever found it frustrating that she had to tailor her home cooking to a man who struggled to manage his diabetes. If she did, she never showed it.

The low sun was striking through the windscreen, warming her face. Siv pushed back her coat collar, planning the rest of the dwindling afternoon.

She started the engine. She'd had enough of this place for one day.

CHAPTER 4

Viv and Damian were tucking into a fry-up when Saffie followed Imelda into Driftwood. The kitchen was full of smoke and the smell of carbonated bacon, a meat that Saffie hated. She winced when she saw the dirty pan in the sink, its sides trailing egg yolk. Imelda threw open a window and ran hot water into the pan, followed by a squirt of washing-up liquid. She swished it round with her plump fingers. The green liquid merged with the yellow yolk into a blend of colours resembling diarrhoea. Saffie's stomach turned.

She looked at Viv and Damian. 'Have either of you heard from Henry?'

Damian was gnawing at a crisp rasher, holding it between his fingers. He had elegant hands and a haughty expression, but his table manners were atrocious. His thin sleeveless vest exposed his hefty shoulders. 'Should we have?'

Saffie started to explain that Henry hadn't been at his mum's, as expected, but Imelda butted in, drying her hands on a tea towel. 'We're not sure where Henry is. Has he contacted either of you since last night?'

Viv checked her phone. 'No. Haven't talked to him since we had a drink at the Three Swans after dinner. He made a phone call and said he was off to meet some old school friend.'

'Bertie, that's his name,' Damian said. 'They fenced together.' He sniggered. 'Swords, not stolen jewels.'

Viv rolled her eyes and laughed. Saffie's mother often asserted that men never grew up, but Damian seemed stuck at around eight, when boys developed a fascination for silly jokes.

Imelda frowned. 'Bertie Greene? I can't imagine why Henry would have wanted to meet him. I didn't think they were in touch these days.'

Saffie's contact lenses were stinging from the smoke. She sat down, defeated by these people and the rules they played by.

'You OK, Saf?' Viv asked. She moved her plate away. 'Sorry, you don't like bacon. We should have put a warning on the door.'

It was hard not to like Viv. She was irritatingly jolly, but she had a goofy, kindly smile.

'Sensitive Saffie. You're too good for the likes of us. You make me feel like a Neanderthal.' Damian beat his chest and winked at her, picking up another chunk of burnt bacon. He gave a groan of pleasure as he bit into it.

Imelda was now on the phone, talking to Bertie, presumably. She ran a sponge around the frying pan while she listened. She finished the call and tapped the phone against her square chin. Saffie comforted herself with the mean thought that, in some lights, with her strong, heavy features, Imelda was rather like a man in drag.

'Bertie says that Henry didn't turn up last night, and he assumed he'd changed his mind,' Imelda told them.

'He probably got distracted. He was well-oiled when he left us.' Viv mopped her plate with bread.

'I expect you're right.' But Imelda sounded unsure. Then she said stoutly, 'I'm just going to call a few of his other friends. I'm sure he's on a sofa somewhere.'

She stepped through into the living room. She started every call in the same way: 'Hello, this is Imelda Kilgore speaking.' Damian held a pretend phone, mimicking her softly. Viv giggled on cue. Saffie put the kettle on for something to do and pressed her nose to the window. A few scrappy white clouds hung low in the sky and there was a light mist on the horizon. A solitary paddleboarder was navigating the waves below. She tried Henry again on her phone but only got his voicemail.

Behind her Damian and Viv discussed ice skating later in the afternoon, in the double-act vaudeville style they frequently adopted. Damian instigated the wordplay and Viv acted as his foil. Henry often joined in with them, leaving Saffie out of the game. Imelda found them hilarious when they carried on like this and would smile at them indulgently.

'I say, I say, I say, Ms Carpenter, would you care for a trip to the ice rink later on?'

'I don't mind if I do, Mr Kyalo. I once visited one in the West Indies with my sister.'

'Jamaica?'

'No, she went willingly!'

Imelda returned, shaking her head, her face decidedly paler than when she left. 'No one's seen him and he's not responding.'

'I just tried him again,' Saffie said. 'I'm really worried. Why did he call me to say he was staying at home with you?' She noticed Viv and Damian exchange glances. 'Do you know something I don't?'

'No, it's not that,' Viv said quickly. 'It's just that Berminster is Henry's old stamping ground. He's probably reliving his glory days and didn't want to worry you.'

Saffie held the edge of the worktop. They suspect he might have been with an old flame. He's never mentioned anyone here. Henry wouldn't do that, would he? Surely not after Sunday?

'You should have come to the pub with us after dinner,' Damian said, 'then he'd have told you where he was going.'

'I had a terrible headache after the red wine.'

Damian glanced at Viv. 'So you said.'

Saffie winced. His tone indicated that she was a killjoy. But that didn't matter right now. 'What if he's had an accident?'

Imelda stared through her. 'I'll check Berminster General. Perhaps you can tidy up here, Saffie, dear. It's such a small kitchen, it gets cluttered quickly. Viv, give Saffie your crockery.'

Viv brought their dirty plates to the worktop while Damian played a game on his phone.

'Aren't you worried about Henry?' Saffie rolled a dishwasher tablet in her hand, inhaling the lemony scent.

'He's a big boy,' Damian said, concentrating on his screen. 'He'll have been sleeping off a hangover somewhere, on a sofa or a floor. He's probably groaning and feeling sorry for himself right now.'

'Yeah. He'll be laughing at you and his mum being worrywarts.' Viv smiled. She handed Saffie her plate. 'There you go, Saf. I'll leave these in your capable hands and check the ice rink's open in Hastings. Want to come with us? Play hard to get. Let Henry stagger back with a terrible hangover and find you out enjoying yourself, that's my advice. You have to lick him into shape. I did with Damo, and now I've got him eating from the palm of my hand.'

Damian blew a loud raspberry on his forearm and Viv giggled. *Everything's a joke with them.* Saffie turned her back and opened the dishwasher.

* * *

Imelda cleaned out the already spotless kitchen cupboards at Driftwood while they were waiting for the police. She had to do something to control her anxiety. Berminster General had said there were no admissions under Henry's name or matching his description, and there was still no news from her son. She kept checking her phone.

The police had asked them to stay put. Saffie had vanished to her bedroom while Viv and Damian went outside to sit on the bench, both wearing sunglasses, wrapped up against the cold, with the heaters on. Damian was stretched out with his head in Viv's lap while she played with his hair.

Imelda stared at them enviously for a few moments. It was a long time since she'd been part of a cosy twosome. Wilf had gone off sex before he died — gone off sex with her, anyway. She'd assumed it was because her body had thickened in middle age, as if each year had laid down a layer of immovable flesh. She rubbed the cupboard handle vigorously. No time for self-pity.

The light exposed yet another smudge on the window by the door. A child had stayed here over Christmas and seemed to have spent most of his time with his nose glued to the glass. Probably bored, because it had rained constantly. Not that a bit of boredom did a child any harm. Although she didn't mind taking their money, Imelda never understood why people spent the festive season away from home. Henry and Saffie had gone to Madrid this last Christmas, and he'd sent her photos of boiled shrimp, cured ham and a ring-shaped cake, decorated with glazed fruits. What was wrong with a beautifully roasted turkey or goose, and traditional Christmas pud? She'd helped out at the Salvation Army lunch on Christmas Day, wearing a silly paper hat and feigning enthusiasm when, really, she'd have preferred her darling Henry's company. Boiled shrimp, indeed!

She was rubbing the greasy mark away when she saw a tall, slim woman approaching from the road above. The woman stopped halfway down, glanced up at the sky and then out to sea, a hand shielding her eyes. She tightened the belt on her coat and carried on towards the chalet. Imelda had been as slender as this woman back in the day. She could have pulled her belt in like that, cinching her waist. She waited to see if the woman was going to head down to the beach, but she stepped aside onto the narrow stone path to Driftwood.

Imelda opened the door. 'Can I help you?'

'Yes, and hopefully I can help you. Imelda Kilgore? I'm DI Drummond, Berminster Police.'

Imelda was relieved and taken aback. This willowy woman, with her classy coat and expensive haircut, seemed too elegant to be a detective. 'Oh, thank goodness. You'd better come in. I've been keeping busy while I was waiting. I'm terribly worried. I keep hoping my phone will ring.'

The detective stepped into the kitchen and took off her gloves. 'You've reported that your son, Henry, is missing.'

'That's right. I'm baffled, to be honest. I checked the hospital, but they haven't seen him. I'll round up the others, if you like, so you get the full picture. Then you can make sure you've all the details you need.'

'No, that's not necessary,' the inspector said. She spoke quietly, but assertively. 'I'd like to talk to you alone for now. Does your son live here?' She pulled a chair out, took a notepad and pen from her leather bag and sat, waiting.

Imelda sat opposite her. She explained that she owned a number of holiday properties around town and that this chalet was one of them, that Henry lived in London with his partner, Saffie Armand. 'He and Saffie arrived from London on Saturday. His friends, Damian and Viv, drove down. They're staying for a week.'

'January's a bit cold for a break by the sea,' the inspector said. She was watching Damian and Viv on the bench with eyes the same navy as her coat. They hadn't noted her arrival, wrapped up in each other.

'Damian and Viv have just got engaged and this is a little jaunt to celebrate . . . Young people don't feel the cold, and this chalet is lovely and snug.' Imelda realised that she sounded defensive. She clasped her hands on the table. 'I'm very worried about my son. No one has heard from him since last night and he didn't meet the friend, Bertie Greene, who was expecting him. I've left messages on Henry's phone, but he hasn't called.'

'I can understand your anxiety, Ms Kilgore. Do you have a photo of your son?'

Imelda snatched her phone up. 'Here's one I took yesterday afternoon.'

The detective took the phone, using thumb and forefinger to enlarge the photo and scrutinise it. She gave a tiny sigh and frowned. 'If it's OK with you, I'll just send this to myself.' She picked up her pen and went through Henry's personal details, checking that they were accurate. 'Your son is your only child and he's twenty-eight. He works in London?'

'Yes, he's in events management.'

'Who was the last person from the group to speak to him?'

'Damian and Viv saw him last, in the Three Swans. Saffie had a call from him to say that he was staying at home, with me.' She gestured. 'I live above on Strand Way. Henry has a key, but he didn't sleep in his room. I started to get concerned when Saffie came up asking for him.'

'Are he and Saffie happy together?'

'They appear to be. Henry's very . . . smitten, certainly.'

'Is there anyone else he might be with?'

'I've tried all his friends, people he was at school with.' Imelda's throat had gone dry. This woman was so composed. Shouldn't she be talking about a search? Didn't every minute count? That's what they said in those crime dramas on TV that Wilf had liked. She tapped on the table, almost shouting. 'Inspector, time's getting on. Henry's been gone for hours. What happens now? What are you going to do?'

DI Drummond was unruffled. 'I appreciate your worries, but I have to get an overall impression of your son. Had there been any arguments here? Between your son and his partner, or the other friends? Did he have any personal or work problems?'

Imelda shook her head. 'No one has mentioned any disagreements and Henry's been in good spirits. They've been having a wonderful time, enjoying their holiday, relaxing.'

The inspector gestured at the window, the view outside. 'It's a lovely spot. Did Henry grow up in Berminster?'

'That's right. He went to university in Reading. That's where he met Viv and Damian.'

The inspector tucked her pen into her notepad. 'How many holiday properties do you own and are they all rented out at present?'

'Six. There's just one other than this one occupied this week, a flat near the harbour. Why do you ask?'

'I'll need to get officers to check that Henry isn't at any of them. I'll arrange for someone to collect the addresses and sets of keys from you.'

The inspector was wasting time. 'Henry won't be at any of the other properties, surely? Why would he do that without telling me? Plus, he doesn't have the keys. It doesn't make any sense.'

'Vanishing doesn't make any sense. We have to check all possibilities. Do you live alone?'

'Yes. I'm a widow.'

'Where were you last night?'

Imelda bridled at the question. 'Me? I was at home. I watched a film and was in bed by half ten. Why?'

'We always ask these things, for the record. Ms Kilgore, if you could go home now, I'm going to contact my colleagues at the station to start a missing person alert and a search of your properties. Officers will visit you shortly. I'll speak to Henry's friends here.'

Imelda was put out. 'Well, surely I should stay with you?'

'That's kind of you, but it's better that you're at home, just in case Henry turns up there. He might be distressed for some reason and head back to his mum. Could you write out a list of friends Henry still has in town and their contact details? That would be invaluable.'

'Yes . . . I see . . . but I've been in touch with them all. Some of them are away at present.'

'Even so.'

Viv had spotted them and she and Damian uncurled from the bench and came in, holding hands. A gust of icy air accompanied them, carrying the salt tang of the sea. Imelda opened her mouth to explain what was happening, but the inspector had taken over, and before she could protest, she'd been ushered out of her own property and was heading up the steps towards home.

CHAPTER 5

Siv watched Ms Kilgore walk away, pulling her padded jacket around her ample frame. The kitchen seemed much airier without her imposing presence and emphatic, ringing voice. Viv Carpenter and Damian Kyalo stood close together, their faces glowing from the sun and chilly wind, like two children who'd been out playing. Siv told them to stay indoors, explaining that she needed to speak to Saffie first and then she'd talk to them.

'We were supposed to be going ice skating,' Damian whined. He was tall with full, pouty lips and tiny square, rimless glasses.

'Aren't you concerned about your friend?'

'A bit, but he's probably been a naughty boy, got a blinding hangover and wants to get rid of it before he comes back. He'll be downing pints of water and mugs of black coffee. Saffie gets tight-lipped when he's had a skinful and his mum nags him.'

'Most people have recovered from a hangover by the end of the next morning,' Siv said. *I should know.* 'Does Henry have any addictions?'

'He drinks a fair bit,' Viv answered, wide-eyed. 'He's into Alabama Slammers when he gets going and sort of loses track.'

'Isn't it odd that he hasn't phoned?'

Viv said, 'Fair point. It is getting on in the day. Although he might have only just woken up if he was drinking into the early hours.'

Damian pulled a petulant face. 'Henry will hate all this fuss. So do I. We're supposed to be having fun.'

Oh, grow up. 'It must be very hard for you,' Siv said.

Viv, noting Siv's sarcasm, took Damian's arm. 'Better do as the inspector asks. Let's go in the living room.'

Siv shut the door after them and pondered. It was a bit early to start a missing persons search, but Henry Kilgore's absence seemed odd. She called the station to order it and then examined the young man's photo again. A compact frame, just the right side of chunky, with dark cropped hair and a confident smile. *Henry, have you gone missing because you've done something naughty? Could you be connected to my mysterious body at the crematorium?*

Patrick called as Siv was switching on the kettle.

'I've left Ms Flore with her brother now, guv. She's OK. He's staying with her for a couple of days. Where do you want me?'

Patrick was holding himself together, but he sounded mournful. She was used to him being distracted by concern for his brother, but he'd been even more preoccupied since Lisa's death and, at times, irritable — or, as Ali put it, 'carnaptious'. She needed him back on form. But maybe she should be more sympathetic. She did have a duty of care. 'You sure you don't just want to go home?'

'Certain sure.'

She was relieved, as a heavy workload had landed and she could do with all hands on deck. 'I've been speaking to a woman whose son is missing in case he was our murder victim, but there's no resemblance. I'll talk to Ali and get him to contact you. Can you check if anyone else has been reported missing? And we need to publicise the murder.'

She found tea bags in a cupboard and made a pot. The fittings in the kitchen were cheap and basic. Thin, unlined curtains hung at the windows. Imelda Kilgore certainly didn't splash out on interiors for her guests. She lined up two mugs and spoke to Ali while the tea was brewing.

'How are you doing?'

'Just finished here at the crem. Nothing unusual. They're all shaken up, and some were a bit tearful. No one spoke of any problems or disagreements. I'd say some of them like their boss less than others, but show me any workplace that doesn't have issues. I'm heading back to the station now.'

'This Henry Kilgore who's gone AWOL isn't our dead body. That would have been too neat. But there's a chance he might be our killer. I've started a misper alert, so can you liaise on that? As I'm here, I'm going to talk to Kilgore's friends. Can you get a photo of the dead man sent to me? Patrick's back at work, so update him on the murder and this misper and sort out a schedule between you.'

Siv took her coat off, hung it over the back of a chair and then opened the door to the hallway. She could hear a TV from the room opposite, so walked down the narrow passage, past a bathroom. The door was open to a dimly lit bedroom on her left that seemed to bear evidence of a tornado. Curtains still closed, a crumpled bed with a wet towel hanging from the headboard, clothes and shoes strewn on the floor, an open suitcase with a coat slung on it. The door along from it was closed. Siv knocked, then walked in. A striking woman with a cloud of fine black hair was lying, head back against a pillow, staring at her phone screen. This room, in contrast, was neat and tidy, the bed made.

'Hello, I'm Detective Inspector Siv Drummond and I'm with the police. Are you Saffie Armand?'

The woman bolted up from the bed, pulling down her sweater as she rose. 'Yes. Have you found Henry?'

'Not yet. Come through to the kitchen with me. I've made tea.'

The young woman followed her and sat down meekly while Siv poured out two mugs. Her wide, heavy-lashed eyes were tear-stained, but rather than marring her appearance, they only enhanced her loveliness. She had a gentle voice, a perfect, symmetrical face and wore her dark jeans and blue cashmere sweater with an easy elegance. Her feet were bare and as beautiful as the rest of her, neat and even-toed. Siv recalled Imelda's snarky comment that Henry was 'smitten'. There was clearly no love lost on the lumpy, heavy-handed mother's side.

'I gather you haven't heard from Henry?'

Saffie shook her head. 'Nothing. I've called him half a dozen times. This waiting is awful. What if he's had an accident?'

'I understand how worried you must be. How long have you been together?'

'A year or so. I moved in with Henry last summer.'

'Has he ever gone missing like this before?'

Saffie held her mug tightly but didn't drink. She had gold rings on the three middle fingers of each hand and perfect oval nails. 'Of course not! What makes you ask that?'

'People do, sometimes. Flight can be a bit of a habit if life gets stressful.'

'Well, Henry never has. He's not the stressed-out type. He's really laid- back.'

'Does he have a drink problem?'

That made her pause. 'He drinks more than I'd like him to. But then, I don't like alcohol much, so I probably overreact. There's a lot of corporate hospitality with his job, so I suppose it's easy for him to indulge. I can understand that it gets to be a habit.'

Listening to her, Siv reckoned that she made excuses regularly for her partner's inebriation and love of Alabama Slammers — whatever they were. 'Talk me through last night.'

Saffie cradled her tea. Her eyes welled up. 'The four of us had a meal at the Barnacle. It's not far from here, so we walked. We finished about ten. The others wanted to go onto a pub for a drink, but I'd had quite a bit of wine with the meal already and the restaurant was full and noisy. I had a headache and I didn't fancy staying out. Henry, Viv and Damian met at uni and they'd been reminiscing.'

'And you were left out?'

'A bit. And a bit bored, to be honest. They were talking about people I'd never met, a play they'd been in where Damian forgot his lines, someone setting fire to the kitchen in a hall of residence, that sort of stuff. My head was pounding and I just wanted to get back here. That sounds horrible, doesn't it? Like I'm a spoilsport.'

'I wouldn't beat yourself up about it,' Siv said.

Saffie gave her a ghost of a smile. 'I walked back here and they went onto a pub called the Three Swans. I got in around half ten, had a hot bath and fell asleep. I woke in the early hours and realised that Henry wasn't home and my phone wasn't switched on. He'd called at eleven twenty and left a message saying he'd stay at his mum's.'

'Can I listen to the call?'

She handed her phone to Siv, who checked the time the message had been left and listened to the deep, hearty voice.

'Hi, Saf, expect you're fast asleep. Listen, I've had a few and expect I'll be having a few more. Don't want to disturb your beauty sleep, so I'll crash at Mum's. See you in the morning. Kiss kiss.'

The man's voice was slurred but he didn't sound troubled. Siv listened to the message again. He was panting slightly, as if he was walking. She wondered why he'd bring his girlfriend on holiday and sleep at his mum's. Plenty of drunken people crept home during the early hours and crawled in beside their sleeping partners.

'Were you surprised that Henry was opting to sleep at his mother's?'

Saffie shook her head, her hair rippling. 'He was just being considerate. I'm a light sleeper and he knows I hate waking up to the smell of alcohol. Sometimes he sleeps on the sofa at home when he gets back late. When he hadn't come back here this morning, I walked up to his mum's.'

'Do you know this Bertie Greene whom he was supposed to meet?'

'No, and I don't remember Henry mentioning him. But then, Henry's got so many friends I sort of lose track. He's a popular guy.' She bit her lip and sniffed, slipping a tissue from her sleeve. 'What's happened to him? This just isn't like him at all.'

Siv finished her tea. Damson-coloured clouds were rolling across the sky and the kitchen was shrouded in shadows. She rose and switched the lights on. 'Has Henry argued with you or anyone else recently?'

'We haven't argued. If he has rowed with someone, he hasn't told me, and I'm sure he would.' But Siv heard a trace of doubt in her voice.

Her phone buzzed. Ali had sent her a photo of the victim with his eyes now closed. She held it out to Saffie. 'Any idea who this might be?'

Saffie recoiled. 'I've never seen him before. Wait, is he . . . is he *dead*?'

'Yes, sadly.'

'You don't think that Henry's dead, do you?'

'Don't be alarmed, Ms Armand. The person in the photo is part of another inquiry, but I just had to make sure you didn't know him. I see that you live in London, in Farringdon.'

'Um, yes, that's right, we have a flat.'

'Does anyone have a key to your flat?'

'The neighbour at number five does and we hold one for her. Why?'

'We'll need to ask our London colleagues to check your property, make sure Henry isn't there.'

'But he wouldn't have gone back to London without telling me.'

'I agree that it's unlikely, but we have to be certain. Your neighbour's phone number would be useful.' The woman recited it. Siv noted it down, then said, 'What about other friends in London? Are there people who Henry sees regularly?'

'Viv and Damian are his main London friends, the ones we see together. The three of them moved there and shared a flat for a while after they left uni. He plays squash with people from work now and again, and I've met some of his colleagues, but just occasionally. He travels around a lot with his job, and it's long hours.'

'Does Henry have a tablet or laptop with him? If so, I'll need to take them for now.'

'He has a laptop.' Saffie disappeared to the bedroom and returned with it.

'Thanks. Let's leave it there. We've started a search for Henry and we'll keep you updated, but you'll need to stay in town for the time being.'

Siv wasn't sure that Saffie had heard her. She'd picked up her phone again and was concentrating on it as if she expected Henry to pop out of the screen. Siv shouldered her bag and slipped away to the living room.

* * *

Viv and Damian were lying entwined on the sofa, watching TV. The room was warm and snug, lit softly by a lamp. They sat up and turned the programme down when she said she had some questions, but Damian continued to loll against the cushions, his legs spread wide, with Viv pressed up against his side. Siv had them take her through the events of the previous night, which matched both Imelda's and Saffie's accounts.

'How did Henry set up the visit to Bertie Greene?'

Damian answered. 'Henry rang him. He's like that, suddenly takes it into his head to go off and see someone.' He snapped two fingers. 'We're used to it.'

'When Henry left you at the Three Swans, what time was it and how was he getting to the meeting with Bertie Greene?'

'Walking,' Viv said. 'He said Bertie's place was only ten minutes away. He took off along Adam and Eve Street. It was about a quarter to eleven.'

She had huge, doll-like, china-blue eyes. Candid. She'd make a good liar with that honest gaze.

'Have you met Bertie Greene?'

'Neither of us has,' Viv said. 'Henry knew him from school.'

'Was Henry very drunk by the time he left you?'

Damian rolled his head. 'Fairly. Like, happy-go-lucky drunk.'

'What did you two do when you left the pub?'

'Came back here. We got in around half twelve,' Viv said.

Siv calculated the distance. 'The Three Swans is only a mile from here, surely?'

Damian puckered his lips at Viv. 'We idled along the beach and stopped for a snog at the bandstand on the way back. We've just got engaged and as the song says, "It's delightful, it's delicious, it's de-lovely."'

Viv smiled and ruffled his hair. She glanced at her watch. 'Do you really reckon something bad's happened to Henry?'

'I can't say. Has he had any concerns, worries lately, that you're aware of?'

Viv picked at a thread on her shirt cuff. 'He said that work had been a bit slow recently and there might be redundancies. But he didn't seem that worried.'

'He was updating his CV on LinkedIn the other day,' Damian offered. 'Henry has the golden touch — always has, always will. He'll slot into something else dead easily if need be.'

'Any problems between him and Saffie? She didn't mention that he had any work worries.'

'Nah,' Damian said. 'They're solid. She worships him, which is how Henry likes it.' He grinned. 'His mum's always adored him, and now he's got two women who think the sun shines from his arse. He's in pole position!'

Damian spoke affably, but Siv suspected that Henry Kilgore might not be her type of person if she ever got to meet him. She showed them the dead man's photo, but, like Saffie, they said they didn't recognise him. They expressed no interest in who he was, leaning into each other, loved-up and self-absorbed. She wasn't sure either of them would have noticed if their friend had problems.

Viv saw her watching them and sat forward. 'We were talking about driving around to search for Henry, asking Saffie if she'd like to come. What do you think, Inspector?'

'Of course, it might help Saffie. Just don't get in the way of the police teams.' Siv stood up to leave. 'You all need to stay here in the chalet until you're permitted to go home. Make sure you contact me immediately if any of you hear from Henry.'

'Yeah, thinking about it, it is a bit odd that he's not back by now,' Damian said with a grimace. 'I suppose we'd better cancel our dinner booking this evening. I'll give Henry a bloody headache when he turns up, even if he's already got one!'

Viv stroked his hair, consoling him that they'd celebrate another evening, when Henry was back and they could all be together.

Outside the chalet, walking back to her car, Siv paused to gaze at the darkening horizon. A misty full moon was rising in the sky. Her breath clouded in front of her and then vanished like a wraith. What was going on here? It might just be a coincidence that a young man was murdered and another vanished in the same twenty-four hours, but the timing seemed odd. She debated whether to visit Imelda Kilgore at home, but decided to send Patrick instead. She found the overbearing woman hard going, whereas he was good with mothers. They seemed to sense that he'd lost his own mum and responded to his startled appearance and waifish charm. With his skinny frame and spiky hair, he resembled a Quentin Blake illustration.

She turned up the heater in the car. Better check in with the boss. She rang Will Mortimer, hoping that he'd be unavailable. They'd had a tense relationship since she'd started the job, displacing his mate Tommy, and she spent a lot of her time trying to avoid him. Then, when her mother had started seeing Mortimer last autumn, things had become truly weird. He was friendlier now, but in a strained, nervy way. She'd preferred it when there'd been straightforward mutual dislike. He answered — unfortunately — and Siv updated him.

'Sounds complicated,' he said. 'Make sure DC Hill's back at work tomorrow, you'll need him on board. I realise that he's been cut up about Lisa, but he does like to indulge in a bit of drama, given half a chance.'

He had a point — still, Siv's hackles rose. 'He's already working, sir. Came back without being asked.'

'Pleased to hear it. We did Lisa proud. Good turnout.'

'Yes, sir.'

'Good, good. Well, speak tomorrow.'

She put down the phone. An image of Mortimer sitting at his desk with her mother nibbling his ear came to mind. She shuddered.

* * *

The two police constables had gone. The kids had been excited about their uniforms and stayed high as kites after they'd left. Now they'd slumped and were parked in front of cartoons with apple juice. Bertie could probably count on about ten more minutes of peace before one of them started on the other. Carrie yelled that she was cold, so he inched the central heating to eighteen. Hang the bills, and he could turn it off once the kids were in bed. When they were back with their mum, he had the heating on for just an hour in the evening and sat wrapped in a duvet.

He headed to the kitchen, flipped open a can of cider and took long gulps to soothe his agitation. The police had checked his contact with Henry the night before, asking what time he'd called. Then they'd asked politely — but with an edge, Bertie noticed — if they could have a look around. He'd wanted to refuse, but, of course, he'd agreed. He didn't want to provoke them and he could see in their eyes that they were aware of his record. Typical of bloody Henry to bring trouble to his door. One of the constables had told him that detectives would want to talk to him. That would mean time off work and complications. He had to try and stay calm and work out what to tell them.

Fuck Henry. Bertie hadn't even wanted to see him, but he'd been plastered and insistent last night when he'd rung. Wanting to chat, which meant picking at scabs that were best left alone. Chatting with Henry was the last thing Bertie needed. He'd explained that the kids were staying and he had work this morning, but what Henry wanted, Henry got, and Bertie had always been a doormat where he was concerned. He'd been relieved when the guy didn't turn up and thought no more about it. Now it seemed Henry was missing. What was that all about? Maybe his smug, entitled manner had finally riled someone enough to make them snap.

Bertie stared at the tub of iced biscuits that the girls had made with the childminder. She'd kept him chatting for a good twenty minutes when he'd picked them up. She was a single mum and lonely and she fancied him. It wasn't mutual. He didn't go in for plump blondes. But he had to keep her sweet because she was reliable, and good childminders were hard to find, as his ex constantly reminded him.

The damp patch on the wall by the window caught his eye. It was shaped like Spain and he was sure that it had got bigger. He went across and touched it. It was clammy and the paint was crumbly, the salts rising from the plaster. The ground-floor flat was in a terraced house near the river, and Bertie reckoned that it drew water up through its foundations, especially when it rained. The walls seemed to sweat, and even the bedding was damp at times. Still, beggars couldn't be choosers, and he'd been lucky to find it to rent when he was trying to rebuild his life. It wasn't far from the kids' school, and there was a tiny patch of gloomy garden out the back.

He loaded the washing machine — how come a six- and an eight-year-old produced so much dirty clothing? — stuck a couple of potatoes in the microwave, grated a hunk of cheese and opened a can of baked beans. He leaned back against the counter, downed the cider and watched the spuds spinning. The hand holding the can trembled. What a day . . . If it's not one thing, it's another. He'd seen Jock Keyes when he was delivering a parcel late afternoon. The man had been walking along the street, head down, a crumpled carrier bag hooked on one finger. Jock had gone completely grey now. Hardly surprising with his son banged up for a long stretch. Bertie's heart had started thumping. He'd got back in the van and closed his eyes for a bit, then drank a bottle of water straight down, as if he'd reached an oasis in the desert. Just as he'd got a grip and started the engine, he'd had a call from the police about Henry.

Bertie paused the microwave and turned the potatoes. If only he could have moved away to a place where no one knew him. Consigning bad memories to the past. A real fresh start. But he was well and truly trapped here, and the kids needed him. They stayed with him now for two nights a week. He was lucky that his ex had forgiven him. Some exes would have been tricky about access after a jail sentence, but she had a new man and it suited her to have the kids gone regularly.

He knocked back the last of the cider. God, he'd gone from hero to zero in the blink of an eye — from prison officer at HMP Berminster to being detained himself for almost two years at Her Majesty's pleasure.

His job at the prison had suited him down to the ground. He'd liked wearing a uniform and being part of a team, the tight structure. He had a weak nature though, and he'd always been something of an outsider, one of those people others took for granted. In the prison, he'd been able to blend in and play his part, head down. You didn't need to be talented or witty or a bit of a character. You just turned up, stuck to the rules and did the hours. And all of that had been fine until the day when, supervising the library visits, he'd been taken to one side and reminded of his past associates. He could no longer play by the rules, at least not the official ones.

Since then, he'd been like a fly caught in a web, and he'd learned that if he tried to struggle, he'd become even deeper enmeshed. Ever since he'd finished his sentence last autumn, while he might have been released from his cell, he was still a captive, long term with no parole in sight. He did as he was told, kept appointments and passed messages, still working for the prison, but this time for the inmates. He'd never be free of it, but he'd told himself that if he kept his head down, he'd be OK. Look how well that was going. Now the police were back in his life, thanks to Henry. He'd just have to tread carefully. He flicked open another cider.

He split the cooked potatoes, loaded them with cheese and stuck them in the oven to brown. There was a loud thump from the living room, followed by a pitiful cry of '*Daaaaad!*' He went through, calmed the fuss and sat between his daughters on the ropy old sofa. He was sure he could smell mud in here.

'Dad, your telly is so *small*,' Carrie said.

'Haven't you heard that small is beautiful, like you two?' He kissed the top of her head. She was a pernickety child. Last week, she'd complained that his flat was smelly and yucky. Well, she was right. He winked at Alice, who was staring at him anxiously.

He leaned his head back on the worn fabric and gazed at the uneven ceiling. At least he had the warmth and weight of his children within his grasp.

CHAPTER 6

Bartel was making rye bread — his Polish grandmother's recipe. He'd treated himself to a bread maker, but after a few failed attempts that had been discarded quite quickly in favour of the tried and trusted method of kneading the dough with his huge hands for a few minutes.

'My *babcia* would be disgusted with me for even thinking about using a machine, but she's not mending roofs all day in the freezing wind. And, of course, she's right.'

Siv was eating a thick slice of the bread he'd baked the previous day, topped with *Oscypek*, a smoked cheese made of sheep's milk. Polska, the Polish centre in town, had a little shop where emigrants needing a taste of home clustered. She'd layered the cheese with the dill pickles that Bartel's mother had sent him and washed the feast down with tea. Bartel had offered her a malty golden lager from Krakow, and she'd eyed it but refused — reluctantly — in case she was needed later. She'd intended to call in briefly for a pit stop and a quick cuppa because she hadn't seen Bartel for a couple of weeks, but it was never that simple with him. You always had to eat and drink, and if you could be merry too, that was encouraged. His glass was always half-full, and no matter how low Siv's mood, her heart lightened when she saw his tank-like frame. They'd met when she'd been investigating murders by the river. Bartel fished there and he'd provided useful information. Now, it felt as if she'd always known him.

He'd bought and moved into this small Victorian house in the Poets' Piece area of the town in mid-December and spent Christmas dismantling and renovating the kitchen. He'd replaced the damaged cabinets and worktops and was repairing the original floor tiles. He was a huge man, tall and powerfully built. Siv had wondered how he'd manage in these narrow spaces designed for smaller people, but he got by, and he was planning to knock through the two downstairs rooms.

'There!' He put a cloth over the dough and left it to rise, then made himself an open sandwich and brought it to the table with his lager. The cat, who'd turned up one day in late December and adopted him, stalked in and jumped onto his lap. Bartel had named him Pumpkin because he was a rich mix of gingery fur. Siv noted his colouring was rather similar to Toby Foxwell's.

'You got through the funeral, *madame*?'

'It was OK, but Mutsi turned up with Mortimer.'

Bartel caught a slice of pickle and dropped it in his mouth. His pointed reddish beard glowed in the light. 'She's like a pimple. Pops up when you don't want her.'

Siv smiled. 'Exactly.'

Bartel put his head to one side and rubbed the bald dome of his head. 'She's not going away.'

'No. At least, not for a while. Her pace has slowed with age.'

'So, you have to deal with the problem.'

'You think I've been ignoring it?'

Bartel pursed his lips. 'Hiding from it, maybe. You might make your peace with her sometime. It's not healthy to be on bad terms with your mother.'

Siv chewed on a crust. There was so much history. If this were a book, Bartel had only got through half a page; she doubted it would have a happy ending.

'Reconciliation has to work both ways, and I can't see Mutsi wanting to be friends — or, at least, not for long. If there was peace, I'd always be expecting her to tear up the treaty and conduct a surprise attack. There's a constant hidden agenda with my mother. You'll find that hard to understand.'

'That's true. But I can see it's a problem now that she's cosying up to your boss. Do you reckon that will last?'

Siv considered all the men Mutsi had romanced down the years. All the 'uncles' she and her older sister, Rik, had been introduced to. They'd usually lasted at least six months. The longest relationship had been with Bjork von Essen, a baronet who lived in Helsinki. He didn't care for children, so Mutsi had dumped Siv and Rik with their father in Berminster before she married him. Siv had never met the baronet, but she'd always been grateful to him because he'd inadvertently secured her a stable adolescence, after a chaotic, hither-and-thither childhood.

She ticked her boss's advantages off on her fingers. 'Mortimer's got a boat, which Mutsi can grandly refer to as a yacht. He has a handsome house with sea views near Cliffdean Point. A good salary and attractive pension prospects. And he's besotted with her, for some reason — can't believe his luck. Mutsi's not getting any younger and she must worry that her sell-by-date is approaching. So, it might work out, as long as she doesn't decide he's boring, mean or selfish — her usual criteria for moving on when it suits her.'

Bartel scratched his beard, then took a bite out of a slice of yesterday's loaf. 'This bread needed a couple of minutes longer in the oven.'

'Tastes fine to me.'

'Says the woman who never cooks.'

'Lies. I make scrambled eggs and I heat things in the microwave.'

Bartel tutted. 'Appalling. No wonder your bones show through your skin. Have more cheese.'

'No more cheese, but I'll eat another pickle. They're amazing.'

'My mother puts in extra mustard seeds. Fire in your belly for January.'

'If Mutsi gave me home-made pickles — which is about as likely as the Pope converting to Judaism — they'd probably make me ill. She often neglected me as a child. She was more like a wicked stepmother in one of your tales than a mother.'

Bartel reached over and patted the back of Siv's hand. 'Mutsi's the glamorous witch, the one who seems trustworthy, but has gone to the dark side. Have I ever told you the story of 'The Hare's Heart'? I don't believe so.' He coughed, patted his chest.

He was ready to tell her one of his long folk tales. Really, she should ring Patrick and Ali, catch up with them. But the funeral had knocked her back and it was warm and cosy in the kitchen, the yeasty bread mix smelling like home. Pumpkin had shifted to Siv's lap and was weighing her down as he dozed. It would be cruel to wake him. So, she sat back, eased her feet up on a chair, so as not to disturb the cat, and listened to Bartel's sonorous voice.

'Many years ago, a large castle stood on an island in the middle of the River Vistula. A rich, proud knight lived in the castle. A trumpet sounded over the entrance gate whenever he returned victorious from battle.

'His prisoners were kept in the castle's dark dungeons. They were forced to work hard. Among them were an old woman and her husband. The old woman was a witch, and she was determined to take revenge on the knight. She waited for an opportunity to find him alone.

'One day the knight returned to the castle and fell asleep on the grass outside. The witch crept from her hiding place and sprinkled poppy seeds over his eyes to make him dream deeply. Then she struck him on his chest with a twig of an aspen tree. The knight's chest opened, and the wicked witch could see his brave heart beating. The malicious woman took out the heart so quickly with her bony fingers that the poor knight never woke. Then she put in its place the heart of a hare, closed the opening, hid herself among the thick bushes, and waited.

'When the knight woke, he realised his heart had grown timid. He, who had never been afraid, now trembled. As soon as he got up, he heard, with terror, the barking of the dogs. He ran away like a frightened hare. As he fled to his room, the clatter of his armour alarmed him so much that he threw it away. From then on, he was terrified of everything.

'After a time, the knight's enemies besieged his castle. He heard the roar of fighting and he fled to the ramparts and trembled at the sight. He shook from head to toe, and he ran and hid in the deepest vault. His army, however, was victorious. His soldiers searched for their cowardly leader and they found him in a cellar, half-dead from despair.

'The unhappy knight did not live long. One day, he opened his window that he might breathe fresh air. A martin, which had built its nest near the roof, caught him on the head with its wing. The poor knight fell down, as if struck by lightning, and died.

'A year afterwards, when some witches were being punished for spoiling crops, one of them confessed that she had removed the knight's heart and put a hare's heart in its place. Then the people understood how a once courageous knight had become a coward. They wept bitter tears over his cruel fate, and, as a punishment, burned the wicked witch over his grave.'

Bartel smiled as he finished his story and fingered one of his gold earrings. 'I can guess what you're going to say. The witch was misunderstood.'

'Too right. The knight was a show-off and cruel to his prisoners. She was a clever old woman who beat him at his own game. Also, she made the punishment fit the crime. I like that.'

Bartel threw his hands up in the air. 'The magic of my tales is lost on you.'

'I love them. I wonder why she caved in and confessed.'

'Perhaps she was questioned by someone like you, *madame*. She had nowhere to hide.'

Siv's phone rang. Patrick. She put Pumpkin on the floor, much to his disgust, and stepped into the hallway to take the call.

'Guv, hi, I'm at Ms Kilgore's. She knows our dead guy. He's called Eugene Warren. He and Henry were at school together, so are about the same age. She hasn't seen him for ages, says he'd moved away from the area. As far as she can tell, Henry lost touch with him once they left school and he never mentioned him. Warren's parents are dead, but he has a sister, Tara, in Berminster. Shall I find her?'

'Leave that to me. Is Ms Kilgore OK?'

'Bit shaky. Last time I checked, there was no news of her son, but IDing Warren has thrown her a bit.'

Siv saw the time and was guilty because she'd been chatting cosily with Bartel. 'Make sure Ms Kilgore is all right, then go home. You've had a long day.'

She rang off, feeling clear-headed now that there was a link between these two men. She leaned against the grubby woodchip wallpaper, searching for Tara Warren in the phone directory and saw that she lived just four streets away from Bartel. When she called Ali, Siv could tell immediately from the background music that he was in Nutmeg. He didn't like his own company and often hung out there when Polly was on an evening shift.

'Uniforms visited Bertie Greene,' he reported. 'No sign of Henry Kilgore and Greene confirmed that he never showed up last night.'

'Wasn't he worried?'

'Apparently not. He had his kids staying and was glad that he could get to bed. He said Kilgore sounded drunk, so he assumed he'd gone home to sleep it off. Uniforms walked the likely route that Kilgore would have taken to Greene's. It's a little network of side streets with no CCTV. There's a tiny pocket park at one point, Larch Dell, with a kids' playground. They didn't find anything. Greene's got form, by the way. Used to be a prison officer, but he did time for smuggling mobile phones to inmates. He's been out a couple of months.'

She told him Patrick's news.

'Maybe Kilgore killed this Warren and now he's done a runner,' Ali said with relish.

Despite having had the same idea herself, she warned him, 'No jumping to conclusions. I'll meet you at Ms Warren's. She lives in Milton Road.'

She gave Ali the address and went to say goodbye to Bartel, who was feeding Pumpkin tiny bits of cheese and singing softly to him in Polish.

* * *

Tara Warren lived in a compact first-floor flat. She was quiet, in shock after hearing the news of her brother's death, walking in circles around her sofa. Siv felt a little dizzy watching her. Ali had made three mugs of tea and Siv was relieved when he brought them in from the kitchen and Tara finally sat down.

Tara stared into her mug. She kept stirring it, as if mesmerised by the swirling liquid. 'I don't get it. Why would Eugene have been here? He hasn't been in town for years. He didn't even come back for our parents' funerals.'

Where was he living?' Siv asked.

'No idea.' Tara had a low, whispery voice. 'I've never had an address or phone number. Just an email.'

Siv could see that Ali was mystified by this. In his world, families clung to each other like burrs. His were farmers in Derry, but he was in frequent contact with them, as if they lived up the road. He spoke to them most nights, conversations that often lasted for more than an hour. He knew the price of livestock in their local market. Siv occasionally had brief email conversations with Rik, her sister, but knew almost nothing about her personal life, only that she lived in Auckland and had mentioned an interest in aromatherapy. Rik hadn't returned for Ed's or their father's funerals. She had her reasons for living on the other side of the world and Siv understood them. There were usually deep-seated causes for fractured families, and it was possible that Eugene Warren's death was rooted in old feuds.

She asked, 'How was your brother's relationship with the family? You said he didn't go to your parents' funerals. Had they argued?'

Tara lifted some tea in the spoon and dribbled it back into the mug. 'Argued? No, not really. He sort of detached himself. It was just the four of us — him, me and our parents. He was such a sweet, happy-go-lucky little boy. We got on well, but then he seemed to change overnight . . . turned into a stroppy teenager. There were the usual disagreements about loud music and staying out too late. But it was as if his personality altered. He became unhappy, dissatisfied. He started to moan that Berminster was a backward dump, and said when he left home he was never coming back. It just seemed like the kind of thing bolshie adolescents say, but he stuck to his word. He's never been back, not since he left suddenly, the May before he was due to finish school. He just bailed out on his A levels.'

'Were your parents in touch with him?'

'They couldn't get hold of him other than trying his email, and he never answered those. His phone number was disconnected. They were terribly upset, but what could they do? Mum died a year after he left, Dad five years ago. There was some inheritance for Eugene, and I emailed him about it, but he didn't respond. When I moved in here last summer, I sent him my new address, just in case, but there was no reply.' She shrugged. 'I never imagined I'd end up in my twenties with my parents dead and my brother murdered.'

She was dry-eyed, her tone flat. Siv watched her pick at a thumbnail. Maybe she was through the worst of the pain and had already mourned for a brother who'd cut family ties a long time ago.

Ali was adding sweeteners to his tea. 'Do you know Henry Kilgore?'

'Vaguely. Eugene used to knock around with him back in the day.' Her voice grew stronger. 'Why?'

'He's missing. When did you last see him?'

'Henry? I'm not sure.' She drank tea, trying to recall. 'It would have been in town, a couple of years ago. I saw him across the street, not to speak to though. He was with his mum, carrying shopping. What has this got to do with Eugene?'

'Did your brother and Henry ever fall out, or did Eugene row with anyone else when he lived in town?' Ali pushed forward, ignoring Tara's comment.

Tara scratched at the back of her hand. 'Eugene was a mystery to me before he left home. It wasn't really home to him by then, just a place where he slept, did his laundry. When he was in, he shut himself away in his room. I rarely saw him. Why do you ask about Henry? Do you think he had something to do with Eugene's death?'

'We're just making enquiries at this stage,' Siv replied. 'What can you tell us about Bertie Greene?'

'He was another mate of Eugene's. A bit drippy. He went to prison a while ago. Can't remember what for. I just don't get it. This is really odd, hearing these names again . . .'

'Would you have a photo of your brother as a teenager?' Siv asked. 'It would be useful for publicity.'

Tara went to a cupboard, took out an album and detached a photo. She handed it wordlessly to Siv. A teenage Eugene Warren was lounging against a hedge, dressed in ripped black jeans and long-sleeved T-shirt, with an embroidered skullcap on his head. His pierced tongue lolled out, exhibiting a steel barbell. Siv recognised that disdainful adolescent expression, the one that kept the world at bay while turmoil raged inside.

Tara had drifted away. She was standing by the wall, her hands over her face. Time to wrap this up. Siv checked that Tara was willing to ID her brother's body and asked whether she wanted them to call anyone for her.

'As you've gathered,' Tara said dully, 'I don't have anyone you can contact.'

'A friend then?'

'No. I'd rather be on my own. I'm used to it.'

At the door, Siv paused. 'Did your family have any connection to the crematorium?'

'No. My mum and dad were Catholic. They're buried in the cemetery at St Peter's.'

A fine, icy rain was falling when the police officers stepped outside, silver needles glancing in the streetlights.

'That's Baltic now,' Ali said. 'Talk about a long day!' He took a bottle of water from his pocket and drank thirstily. Then he slid out a packet of Gitanes, lit one and sucked on it. 'Your woman didn't look that upset.'

'Seemed as if she and her brother were so estranged his death barely registered. I wonder if Eugene got into drugs. That might account for a personality change.'

'Aye, but that's a long time ago now. How would that cause ructions ten years or more later?' He took another deep drag on the cigarette, its end glowing red in the dark. 'I can't believe that those parents didn't do more to find their son.'

That's because you believe in happy families. 'Any idea what an Alabama Slammer is?'

He flicked ash away. 'A dance from the Deep South? Like a hoe down type of thing.'

'It's a drink of some kind. Thought you might have heard of it. Henry Kilgore was on them last night.'

Siv stifled a yawn. The rain was stinging her face. Liquid acupuncture. It was both pleasurable and uncomfortable. 'Let's call it a night.' She lingered for a few moments while Ali went to his car. When she glanced up, she saw Tara Warren standing in her bay window, forehead pressed to the glass, hands clutching the frame. Her face was a picture of despondency.

* * *

Jimmy Curtis was weaving his way home from a darts match at the Stag's Head, using the torch on his phone to light his way. He pulled his cap lower over his ears. It was brass-monkey weather and raining now, but a couple of whisky chasers were keeping him warm, as well as his team's victory in the match. It seemed a long time since he'd eaten an early dinner. When he got in, he'd make himself cheese on toast with loads of Worcester sauce. That would do the trick.

He wobbled unsteadily but told himself no harm done. This stretch of road never got much traffic. He wheeled around on the tarmac, arms spread wide, and laughed up at the moon. Oh, he felt a bit dizzy. So he stood still for a moment before carrying on.

Somewhere in the night, a dog started barking. It must be someone out for a late-night walk with their pooch. The barking got louder and then changed to desperate whining. Jimmy stopped and played his torch around. There was an opening to a field just up ahead, and he could make out the shape of a car. It was definitely where the whining was coming from. He hiccupped and walked towards the verge. The car was parked with its bonnet almost against the field gate.

As he hurried towards it, he slipped over, banging his knee. Cursing, he got to his feet, wiping his muddy hands on his jeans, ignoring the pain in his leg from where he'd hit something sharp. His torch illuminated the dog's face against the car's rear window. When it saw Jimmy, it started to yelp and thrash around, throwing itself against the glass.

Jimmy called, 'Is anyone there?'

Maybe the driver had slipped out for a pee. He tried again, 'Hello there!'

No answer except for the panicking dog.

He put a hand on the car's bonnet. It was stone cold. He tried the doors, walking around the car, slipping on the damp grass, but they were locked. The dog grew even more frenzied when it saw him checking the doors, switching to high-pitched howls. Jimmy shone his torch into the field and called out again. He went back to the road and stood, mulling this over. He'd heard of dogs being rescued from cars in hot weather, but never on a January night. He returned to the car and stared at the writhing dog. It would die of a heart attack if it carried on. Jimmy rang the emergency services, his visions of cheese on toast fading.

CHAPTER 7

Siv had had better starts to the day. She'd overslept and turned her ankle in her rush to get out of the house. It was raining heavily on the way into the station and she'd got drenched. Her phone buzzed with an incoming email from Mutsi as she hung up her coat in her office. She left it unopened, closed the blinds to the team room and rested her chilled hands on the old cast iron radiator. It was lukewarm. The police station had once formed part of the corn market and was a listed building. Now and again, there were rumours that it would get an upgrade, but the ancient heating system continued to grumble and groan, the single-glazed windows let in nipping draughts and some of the loos still had chain flushes. Still, Siv had a handsome view across to the museum and the theatre. The trees were bare now, but in summer they cast leafy shade, and when there was a breeze, she opened the window so that she could hear them rustle.

She took a deep breath. Might as well get it over with. She opened the email. Her heart sank.

Darling Sivvi,

I hope you're well. I missed you at Nutmeg after poor Lisa's funeral, but Will explained that you were dealing with an urgent situation. Always so busy, Siv, and no time to contact your mother!

Now, I have some lovely news. I'm giving up my flat and moving in with Will this week. We're so happy and excited. I hope you'll be pleased for me. We'd love you to come round for lunch to celebrate with us. I'll make lihapullat, as Will's never had them and you've probably not eaten them in ages. (I do wonder if you eat anything! You looked so thin at the funeral. It ages you. Slim is good, thin is unappealing.)

Is this Saturday OK for you? About 1 p.m.?

Love from Mutsi xx

Mortimer had capitulated sooner than Siv had expected — but then he'd met a seasoned campaigner. She laughed — lunch made by Mutsi! She'd rarely seen her mother cook. Meals with her had been random items from delicatessens — expensive slivers of cured meats that teased the palate like amuse-bouches with tiny pots of salad that left you wanting a main course. When Mutsi had run short of cash, dinner came from cheap takeaways, the kind that sold food by the bucket. Siv wondered how her mother was going to execute spicy meatballs. She'd probably find an IKEA with the nearest Swedish equivalent and stock up.

Siv pushed her phone to one side — she'd deal with that later — and picked up the reports on both Warren and Kilgore from the previous day, made a few notes and checked Bertie Greene's record. He'd been a valued prison officer until he'd been caught with mobile phones and SIM cards. One of the prisoners he'd supplied, an Ian Keyes, had used his phone to order an attack on someone who owed him money. Greene had pleaded guilty. His defence had stated that he'd become compromised after failing to report finding a mobile phone in a cell. He'd been threatened with exposure by Ian Keyes and started taking phones into the prison.

She rang Greene and said she needed to speak to him. It sounded as if he was by a busy road.

'I've a full day at work, not sure when I can make it.'

'I need to see you as soon as possible. Henry Kilgore is missing and you're one of our last contacts with him.'

'I told the constables who came round about Henry,' he blustered. 'He didn't turn up. I haven't got any other info for you.'

'I'll decide that. When can you come to the station?'

'I've got to deliver my quota of parcels. How about tomorrow?'

'Today, Mr Greene. Do you get a lunch break?'

'Yeah, suppose,' he grumbled. 'Around midday. I can't take long. I've got over a hundred parcels left in the van.'

'I'll see you at twelve to twelve thirty, then.'

Patrick tapped on her door, indicating that he'd brought in a tray of coffees from, the Italian café they patronised. She joined him and Ali in the team room. Ali had organised the incident board and brought in a bag of Danish pastries. Forbidden goodies for him. He pretended it wasn't such a sin if he was sharing.

As she sat down, Siv glanced at the empty desk in the far corner of the room where Lisa used to sit. Someone had placed a single yellow rose in a glass in the centre of it.

'Is Steve not joining us?' Ali asked.

Siv shook her head. 'His team's still searching the site. The rain's been hampering them, so he's keen to crack on. He emailed me a brief update. I'll fill you in as we go along.' She crossed her legs and kicked off the discussion. She always experienced a buzz at this point in an investigation, when all roads were open and promising.

'We have a dead man, Eugene Warren, aged twenty-seven, and a missing man, Henry Kilgore, aged twenty-eight. Turns out they grew up in town and used to be friends. Both went to Fulbrook Upper School. It's possible the two incidents are connected.

'Warren's body was left on the steps of the crem yesterday morning, beneath a row of wreaths, possibly between seven and seven thirty. Strangulation, judging by the marks on his neck — we'll see if the PM this morning gives us anything else. We don't know how the body was brought there, but Steve reports there were no tyre tracks near the steps, which isn't surprising as the tarmac was cold and dry. No footprints either. Warren's sister said that he left town years ago after a mutinous adolescence and lost contact with his family. She believed he'd never been back and had no idea where he was living.

'Henry Kilgore went missing late Monday night. No trace of him since. He was staying in one of his mother's rental properties with his partner, Saffie Armand, and another couple, Viv Carpenter and Damian Kyalo, who've just got engaged. They're here for a break and to celebrate the engagement. According to them, Kilgore had been boozing — sounds to me as if he has an alcohol problem.' She sipped coffee. *I worry that I have too.* 'Kilgore was on his way to meet Bertie Greene, an old friend who has a prison record, but Greene said he didn't turn up. Kilgore called his partner and left a message at eleven twenty, saying he was out having a good time, and planning to stay the night at his mother's house, but his mother confirms his bed wasn't slept in.

'Ms Kilgore said that she was at home on her own on Monday night. Saffie told me that she got back to Driftwood about ten thirty, bathed and fell asleep. Viv and Damian said they were together. The Met have visited Kilgore's flat in Farringdon, but it's empty. I'm seeing Bertie Greene later this morning. He was friendly with Eugene Warren too, back in the day. Patrick, did you get anything else from Imelda Kilgore?'

Patrick had a hoarse voice at the best of times, but that morning he sounded as if he'd swallowed sandpaper. 'She's an imposing woman. The house is full of photos of Henry, from baby to adult. A huge one of him in fencing gear with his sword drawn by the front door. Maybe it's supposed to ward off intruders.' He chuckled. 'She's a widow and runs a holiday rental business, Berminster Breaks. Does very well, according to her, and I'd say she does all right if her house is anything to go by. She handed over a list of her son's closest mates in town. There are five, including Greene. We've searched all her other properties and no sign of Kilgore. She was proud of the fact that he's always been a popular, gregarious guy and that he's done well for himself. Though she doesn't rate Saffie Armand. Her mouth turned down when she mentioned her.' Patrick gave a good imitation of Ms Kilgore's expression. 'I checked in with the three at Driftwood. None of them had heard of Eugene Warren or recalled Kilgore mentioning him.'

Ali was swinging around on his chair and munching sneakily on a pastry. He kept it shielded with one hand. Guilty pleasure. 'I talked to four of the crem staff. None of them came up with any problems there or any dissatisfied customers. Doesn't seem like anyone had the kind of grudge against the place that would make them dump a corpse. I wondered if there might have been any mix-ups with bodies or ashes — you do hear about families getting angry because they've scattered someone else's relative, and I remember reading that a crem somewhere burned the wrong person, poor sods. But there's been nothing of that nature reported.'

'From what I saw of Diane Lacey, I wouldn't imagine she'd let any mistakes through,' Siv said. 'She's serious and dedicated. Her colleagues hold her in high regard.'

Ali caught a sliver of icing on a fingertip. 'By the way, I googled Alabama Slammer, Kilgore's preferred drink. It's a cocktail made with amaretto, Southern Comfort, sloe gin or vodka and orange juice.'

'I could have told you that,' Patrick said. He was shaking chocolate powder onto his coffee. 'I went out with a woman who liked them at Police College. I was amazed she could afford them at six quid or more a pop. I tasted one once. It was revoltingly sweet. You'd like it, Sarge.'

'I'm glad we've got that sorted, although I wouldn't have listed it as a priority,' Siv said.

'OK, OK. I haven't been squandering my time,' Ali protested. 'I also searched for Eugene Warren online, to see if we could track down what he's been up to all these years. I got a couple of hits but no one who resembled the dead man. He's not on social media. I'll try the electoral register.'

'We need to establish how he got to Berminster and when he arrived,' Siv said. 'Kilgore's mates at the chalet indicated he had some worries about redundancies at work and noticed him updating his CV. Neither his partner nor his mother mentioned that. He's an external relations manager at a company called Footprint, near King's Cross.'

'Maybe he's gone AWOL because he lost his job or is about to lose it, and can't face telling anyone. He might be sitting with a bottle, trying to find his *bottle*.' Ali licked his fingers, looking pleased with himself at the joke.

Siv finished her coffee. 'Right, let's see. Ali, can you call Kilgore's employer to clarify his status and attend Warren's PM this morning? Patrick, follow up on that list of Kilgore's friends here. I'm going to request urgent and extensive searches of beach areas and any abandoned properties around town. Kilgore has to be somewhere, either dead or immobilised in some way. Then I'll check if Eugene Warren had any links with the crematorium and I'll see what Mr Greene has to say.'

* * *

Viv had persuaded Saffie to come for a walk along the beach. She'd said with her usual exuberance that it wasn't good to stay in all day and they needn't go far. Saffie had been sluggish and reluctant. She'd barely slept, jolting awake to look at her phone, wondering if she'd heard the front door open. Several times, she went out to the hall to check. When she got back into bed, she hugged Henry's pillow, sniffing his lime shampoo. Damian was sulking, as if Henry was deliberately spoiling his holiday. He was watching TV, lying full length on the sofa. Then Imelda arrived and started bustling around the house, so Saffie had taken up Viv's offer to go out.

Early heavy rain had cleared and it was another bright, sunny day, but with a stinging breeze. They had the shingle beach to themselves as they crunched along. Saffie was lonely and miserable. Without Henry around, she felt like a spare part more than ever. She had no connection with this place. The town was pretty, but it had a complacent, established atmosphere. She stuck out like a sore thumb. London was her comfort zone, a city where she could blend in effortlessly. She glanced at Viv, who was setting the pace, arms swinging. She wasn't close to these people, and she couldn't believe that Damian was acting as if he didn't care that his friend was missing.

Viv seemed to read her mind. 'Damo is terribly cut up about Henry. He just goes into himself and blanks people when he's upset. It's because his dad left when he was young, and he experiences abandonment all over again.'

Saffie nodded, but she couldn't care less about Damian's sensitivities. Actually, it sounded like pop psychology. He was just self-absorbed and Viv played along with it. She wandered down to the water's edge, watching the imprints her boots made as the pebbles gave way to soft sand. She shivered and turned sideways to the wind. Viv wandered over to her, blowing on a long, spiral-shaped shell she'd picked up.

'What lovely markings. I'll take it home to my collection.'

Henry had once told Saffie that he'd gone out with Viv at uni for a couple of months before she met Damian. Just a brief thing, he'd said, nothing serious. She wished he hadn't said anything because she found herself watching them when they met up. It was ridiculous, because Viv and Damian were clearly devoted and getting married in the summer. Henry was going to be best man, Saffie a bridesmaid — although she still wasn't sure why she'd been chosen. Viv was so different to her — so blonde, muscular and sporty. She kayaked and played squash. It confused Saffie. How could a man be attracted to such entirely different women? She realised that Viv was speaking.

'Um, Saffie . . . did Henry tell you that he was a bit worried about his job?'

The sun was in her eyes. She squinted at Viv. 'No. What do you mean?'

'It's just that we mentioned it to that DI Drummond yesterday, because she asked if anything was troubling him. Henry'd told us not to say anything to you. He didn't want to worry you, or his mum.'

'He talked to you about it?'

'To Damo and me, yes. I wanted to tell you now, because the police will probably mention it to you.'

She took a breath. 'When was this?'

Viv sounded earnest. 'A couple of weeks before Christmas. He dropped by one evening. Things had been a bit slow at Footprint, and he'd heard that senior management were planning to reduce staff. He wasn't *that* worried, just aware that there might be redundancies and he could be in the firing line.'

Saffie's mind had gone blank. She tried to make sense of this. Viv was rolling the shell between her gloved hands. She cleared her throat.

'So, what are you saying? Henry might have gone off somewhere because he was worried about his job?'

'No, I'm sure that's not why he's missing—'

'What is the reason then? No word from him. Nothing,' she snapped, turning away. *I can't believe he talked to you about something important, not me. Why?*

'Saffie, I'm sorry. Damo said not to tell you, but that didn't seem right.'

'I'd like to be on my own, Viv, if you don't mind. I'll be back later.'

She walked away quickly, leaving Viv standing on the beach, and kept going until her limbs were warm and her face glowing. She stopped at the café that she'd visited with Henry on Sunday afternoon and ordered a tea. There was only one other person there, a woman with a toddler half-asleep in her lap. Saffie sat at a table by the window, the one that she'd shared with Henry, and remembered the many evenings she'd spent alone in the beautiful Farringdon flat.

Henry's job entailed frequent travelling and meeting clients in the evenings. It was a competitive industry, where you sweated to clinch a deal. He earned an enormous salary and huge bonuses and spent it accordingly. By contrast, Saffie was a telephone counsellor for a private health provider, employed to provide a first-line response to the ill and the worried well. She earned a modest wage and enjoyed Henry's largesse and lifestyle. She trusted him. She *had* trusted him. Now, from what Viv had said, while he hadn't exactly lied to her, he'd certainly concealed the truth. The other evening, outside Driftwood, he'd said that he had to deal with calls about work. Perhaps he'd been lying then too, or he'd been unwilling to share the true nature of those calls.

In her job, Saffie spent her days listening to people pour out their troubles. Stories of depression, family stresses and schisms, marital woes, debt caused by illness, fears about surgery, cancer treatments, diagnoses, anxieties about mental health. Occasionally, she could make a practical suggestion or offer a route to ongoing therapy. Mostly, she allowed the callers to talk aloud to themselves. But she'd never heard about the pain of someone going missing. What would she have said if she had? Henry treated her job with sceptical amusement, saying that the people who phoned her paid for the privilege of unburdening themselves. That was harsh, and she'd respond that everyone was deserving of a willing ear. But, beneath it all, she nurtured a niggling suspicion that he had a point, and that she could be doing something more worthwhile with her life.

He'd sat beside her here, laughing at seagulls being buffeted by air currents, and then linked his fingers through hers.

'Maybe we should get married, Saffie. What do you say? How about later this year? We can have the wedding wherever you like. Mum would love it if we married here, but you can choose. It's the bride's day.'

She'd said simply, 'Yes, please.'

'We'll get a ring when we're back in London. Something beautiful but unshowy, like you.'

They'd agreed to keep the news to themselves for this week, so as not to encroach on Viv and Damian's celebration, but she'd bubbled with joy. She longed now to see Henry walking across the beach towards her, giving the mock salute that was his trademark. *I'd just popped out*, he'd say. *Look at you all, so worried.* But she had so many questions. Where to start? Maybe the first, who were Eugene Warren and Bertie Greene, and why had Henry never mentioned them?

She listened yet again to his last call to her. If only she hadn't forgotten her phone was off! If he'd got through to her, he might have said where he was going, who he was with and why he'd changed his mind about visiting Bertie Greene. Saffie's shoulders sagged with the guilt of that thought. If only she'd picked up that call, Henry might not be missing.

The toddler woke up and started howling. Saffie wished that she could utter similar desperate cries.

* * *

Bertie Greene wore scruffy cream-and-brown cowboy boots, the buckles jangling as he walked in. He lacked a cowboy's weathered complexion, his more the colour of the wallpaper paste that Bartel was using in his house. Prison pallor took a while to disappear. He was a stringy man with a twitching muscle in his right jaw. He kept his head down and his shoulders up, as if expecting trouble.

He asked, 'Will this take long? I only get forty minutes.'

'You're a delivery driver, by the sound of it.'

'Yeah. I have to empty my van by five.'

'I'll try not to keep you, but this is a serious investigation.'

She could see that he didn't like the answer. He'd been a prison officer, and then a prisoner. He'd be familiar with dodges and weaves, so she surprised him with her first question.

'Tell me about Henry Kilgore when you were at school.'

'At school?' he echoed. 'What sort of thing do you want?'

'Anything you like.'

'Well . . .' He relaxed a little. 'He was fun. Outgoing, a laugh and used to getting his own way. Good at sports.

We were in the school fencing team. We won some cups at tournaments. He always had spare cash to splash. His mum doted on him, pretty much gave him whatever he wanted. Girls liked him and vice versa.'

'Any particular girl?'

He tapped his chin. 'He went out with Etta Parton for a while.'

'Does she still live here?'

'No, she moved away. I've no idea where she is now.'

Siv adopted a conversational tone. 'So, when you were having a laugh, did Henry drink a lot?'

Greene scratched the crown of his head. Flakes of dandruff drifted onto his shoulders. 'He liked a drink, yeah. Most teenagers do.'

'Tell me about Eugene Warren. You were at school with him as well.'

He worked his jaw muscle and said warily, 'I haven't come across his name for a long time. I didn't get on with him that well, just hung out occasionally because Henry liked him.'

She'd been hoping he wouldn't be aware of the murder and was glad of the confirmation. 'Haven't you heard about him? It was on the news this morning.'

He shook his head. 'What news?'

'His body was found at the crematorium yesterday. He'd been murdered.'

'My God.' He took a drink of water, spilling some. 'Here? The crematorium in town?'

'Yes. So, one person you know is dead and another is missing. Two of your old school friends.'

He gazed into his water. 'That's pretty weird.'

'Isn't it?' She let the silence sit for a little while before continuing. 'Is there anything you can tell me about them?'

'Me? No. Why was Eugene here in town? Word was, he said he'd never come back.'

'No idea. People say things and don't necessarily mean them. Mr Greene, is there anything that connects your friends, other than growing up together? Have you heard of any difficulties they had, anything that might anger someone?'

'Sorry, I can't help you. I mean, they both left here years ago now. Henry comes back now and again, but only for visits.'

'Do you usually see him when he visits?'

'Not usually, no. We hook up once in a blue moon.'

The way he said it, Greene sounded as if he wasn't overjoyed by the prospect. 'It seems odd, then, that he'd suddenly ring you late at night and want to visit you.'

He laughed, the sound high, staccato. 'You're right there.'

He was good at short answers and his manner was impassive. Siv was frustrated.

'Eugene's sister said that he was troubled as a teenager. Unhappy, maybe. Does that stir any memories?'

'Show me a teenager who isn't troubled, but I don't remember Eugene being particularly miserable.'

That didn't ring true from what Tara had said. Although, of course, teenage boys wouldn't necessarily show vulnerability to each other.

'It doesn't sound as if Henry was troubled back then.'

'Hmm. He was the exception that proves the rule.' Greene was crafty, his answers controlled, although clearly not sharp enough not to get banged up.

'What about drugs — did the three of you ever indulge?'

He glanced to the left and coughed. 'Now and again.'

Siv didn't miss the tell and knew instinctively that this was an understatement. 'What type?'

'Bit of dope.'

'Ever fall out with a dealer?'

'Not sure. I didn't buy it. Eugene used to get hold of it and insisted I smoked, so I joined in to keep him happy.'

Convenient strategy — blame the dead man. Siv could see why Tara Warren had described Greene as drippy. Despite his guarded replies, he seemed spineless. 'Talk me through exactly what happened on Monday night, starting from when Henry called, wanting to meet up with you.'

He relaxed slightly, obviously more comfortable with this narrative. 'Henry rang me just after ten o'clock, saying he was in town for the week. He said he wanted to have a chat. I could tell he was drunk, and I tried to put him off because my kids were staying over and I was worried we'd wake them up. But he was insistent, just as he always is, so I gave in.' He drank more water, draining the cup.

'Did he say what he wanted to talk about?'

'Just a chat.'

'Did he sound worried?'

'Nope. Just drunk.'

'Then he didn't turn up.'

'I waited until just before midnight and then went to bed. I had to be up at seven. I thought he'd changed his mind or forgotten, given that he was pissed.'

'You didn't try to call him?'

'No. That might have encouraged him to come.'

Greene was making an effort to stay alert, bouncing his leg under the table, although he averted his gaze, his eyes darting about nervously. Siv was sure of one thing — he knew more than he was saying.

'Mr Greene, is there anything else you can tell me about your friends that might help this investigation?'

'Sorry, no. Can I go now? I'm going to be late back as it is, and I need this job. I was lucky to get it.'

Siv let him go but had a feeling that there was more below the surface with Greene. She'd rarely seen anyone look so shifty.

Checking her phone, she saw that she'd had an email from Toby Foxwell, informing her that his database had records for the previous eight years. There was no trace of Eugene Warren or anyone of that surname having a connection with the crematorium. Another blow. He'd added:

We've decided to have a little service for the staff group near the chapel steps on Thursday morning at 9 a.m. Just a quarter of an hour, with some secular readings. It seemed fitting to do something out of respect for Mr Warren and it might help staff with their shock and grief. If you or any of your colleagues would like to attend, you're very welcome.

A nice gesture, Siv thought, and one of the team should put in an appearance. She might well go herself.

Steve phoned when she was back at her desk, sounding cheery. 'Bloody rain has been bugging us, but we've made progress. Andy Smeaton has a shed in the grounds here, at the back of Bluebell Copse. We found that the padlock had been snapped. We asked him to come and see, and he told us that his wheelbarrow had been moved. He said he hadn't used it for a while, and he's sure no one else has either. The wheelbarrow had been left in the middle of the floor, not upended and stacked where he puts it. We're examining it now, and we've found fresh wheelbarrow tracks in Bluebell Copse and the garden of remembrance. Smeaton says he hasn't needed to take the barrow there since October. We're going over that whole area now with a fine-tooth comb.'

Did the killer use the wheelbarrow to move Warren's body? It had to be a possibility. It was a start, anyway. Siv was relieved that there was some evidence to follow. 'I'll come and see,' she said before signing off.

Siv jumped up and strode out of the interview room. Finally, a lead. Perhaps the killer had slipped up and left their DNA all over the barrow. If only. Then, they'd have this case shut down in no time.

As she ran down the stairs, she nearly collided with Mortimer coming the other way. From her elevated angle, she saw that his grey roots needed touching up. Mutsi had introduced him to hair dye and a more casual cut. Siv wasn't sure it was working. She paused, updating him briefly.

'That sounds like progress, DI Drummond.'

'Also, sir, I'd like to ask the media team to publicise Warren's murder nationally. Although he grew up here, he hasn't been in Berminster for years. We've no information about where he was living or working since then.'

'Go ahead.'

'And I'd like blanket press coverage about Henry Kilgore all around town. I was thinking posters as well as TV and all the usual news outlets. It's worrying that there's been no sign of him, despite the searches. Someone out there might recall seeing him.'

'Very well.' Mortimer glanced around. 'I believe . . . I believe that your mother has told you our domestic news. I'm delighted, of course.'

Siv tried to remain expressionless while the lines of a poem popped into her head.

'Will you walk into my parlour?' said the Spider to the Fly,
''Tis the prettiest little parlour that ever you did spy . . .'

She cleared her throat. 'Yes. Congratulations, sir.'

'Thank you. Well . . . yes, better get on then.'

'Absolutely.'

She sped away. What would she be expected to call him outside work? It was too much to contemplate without a glass of akvavit to hand.

No. Make that two.

CHAPTER 8

Patrick was at his desk, sipping coffee. Despite the blow of Lisa Flore's death, he couldn't help but feel optimistic. Things were going well with Kitty, his new girlfriend, and Noah was happier than he'd been in a long time. That was partly down to the guv. She seemed a bit remote to most, but she'd been a sound and discreet ally when he'd needed one. She'd steered his lonely brother away from the clutches of an exploitative woman who'd offered him sex and ended up stealing from them. Instead, the guv had given Noah information about some sex workers in town. Noah was actually close friends with one of them now, Eden Jarvis. They went to the cinema and had meals together. Eden even stayed over sometimes. She cooked a mean breakfast. That morning, Patrick had demolished a plate of her waffles with maple syrup. It was like starting the day on pudding. Ali would die for it, but Polly would never allow such a calorific feast. They also employed Eden to clean the house. Patrick didn't enquire if Noah paid for her companionship. It wasn't his business. He was just glad that his brother was smiling these days.

He posted on his popular Twitter account.

@DCBerminsterPolice
We're investigating the murder of Eugene Warren and the disappearance of Henry Kilgore. The two men grew up in Berminster and were friends. They attended Fulbrook Upper School. If you have any information that might help, please contact us immediately.
#KeepingBerminsterSafe

Patrick phoned Tara Warren and read out the list that Ms Kilgore had provided of her son's friends. Tara confirmed that she knew Teagan Grenville, the one woman on it. Eugene had been keen on her for a while, and they'd hung around with Henry and a girl called Etta Parton. Teagan used to work at an upmarket fashion emporium — Ormonde, she thought it was called — but Tara wasn't sure if she was still there. When Patrick phoned the shop, the manager confirmed that Ms Grenville was still on the staff. He arranged to see her and called two of the men on the list. They told him that they hadn't spoken to or seen Henry for a while, that he hadn't contacted them recently and they weren't aware of any problems. Another friend was in the Royal Navy and had been deployed to West Africa for the last six months. Bertie Greene, the final name, was accounted for.

It was only ten minutes' walk to the harbour, where Ormonde was situated in a stylish three-storey Georgian building. Kitty said it was the kind of shop that catered for women who had nothing better to do with their money. But then Kitty eschewed make-up and fashion. She worked as a warden at Halse Woods, a local country park, and dressed in jeans and T-shirts. Patrick liked a smart suit and appreciated a well-cut jacket when he saw one — not that his police salary extended to such items very often. He'd never bought anything in Ormonde, although he'd admired the menswear window. Too pricey for him. As he entered, he lingered by a Harris Tweed sports jacket, fingering the cloth. It was fern green with a ruby check pattern. The label said *£285*. He winced and moved on. The shop interior smelled opulent, a heady brew of scents, hair preparations and expensive cosmetics.

The top-floor staff room, where he met Teagan Grenville, was less glamorous. It looked tired, although an effort had been made to brighten it with candy-pink paintwork and pastel cushions. The air reeked of stale food. Teagan was waiting. She was tall and rather stately, with heavy make-up and a little fixed smile. Judging by the appearance of all the staff, the Ormonde dress code was grey and black, and Teagan wore pale grey trousers and a black polo neck, with chunky jet beads. She was about the same age as Patrick, but her elegant outfit and lofty expression made her seem older.

'You must have come about Eugene. I saw it on the news. How *awful*. Was somebody trying to have a laugh, leaving him at the crematorium?'

'Someone with a strange sense of humour.'

She examined him. 'I know you, don't I? Is your brother Noah Hill?'

'That's right.'

'I went out with him a couple of times. Before his awful accident.'

Before he went running on the cliff path and had a massive stroke. 'I'll tell him you said hi.' He gave an awkward smile.

'He was such a nice guy. So sad, isn't it?'

'Mm. He still *is* a nice guy.' Patrick was annoyed at Teagan's use of the past tense. 'Where were you on Monday night, until late?'

The question didn't faze her. 'I was at the pub, with my hubby. We got home about eleven and went to bed.'

'You used to go out with Eugene, is that right?'

'Yeah, when we were at school. We were an item for a while.'

'How old were you?'

'Seventeen. He was sort of intense. Interesting.' She touched her lips with a lacquered fingertip. 'Good kisser.'

'Why did you split up?'

'He was a love rat. My brother saw him snogging someone else and told me. I don't like two-timers.'

'Who was this other person Eugene was with?'

'No idea. My brother saw them down on the beach one evening. He didn't say who it was, and I didn't want to know, frankly. I just told Eugene to get lost. He didn't even try to win me back. My mum said that told me everything I needed to know about him. I'm married now.' She held up a finger with a wedding ring displaying an impressive chunk of diamond.

Patrick smiled. 'Lovely ring. Have you heard from Eugene or anything about him since?'

'I heard he'd left town, but I haven't seen him since we were at school.' She ran a finger through one of her long, loose curls. 'Is it hard, your job? It must be, dealing with criminals, sweeping up society's rubbish. I bet you come in for a lot of stick. Interesting as well though.'

'I enjoy it. Lots of challenges, never a dull moment.'

Her eyes glinted. 'You're quite nervous though. The way your eyes flick around and you keep tapping your pen on your thigh. Maybe you're always expecting danger, staying alert.'

Patrick stifled a laugh. She must watch too many TV shows. 'Hardly, in Berminster.'

'We have the odd shoplifter in here. They're just pathetic. We've got good security and CCTV, so they're never going to get away with it, yet there are some people who try more than once. I saw this woman shoving lipsticks into her pockets as if no one was going to notice. She was so obvious. I mean, how dumb can you get? And she worked herself into a real strop when I challenged her. I thought she was going to hit me! My hubby was ever so upset when I told him. He said, "Tea, you've got to leave that kind of thing to your security guy. That's what he's paid for." I know he's right. It just annoyed me when I saw that woman helping herself. I mean, the cheek!'

'Are you a friend of Henry Kilgore?' Patrick asked, trying to get the conversation back on track.

'Course, yeah. He was a mate of Eugene's as well. His mum rang me yesterday, asking if I'd seen him. I told her not since late November, when he came in here to get his mum's Christmas present. Fab Estée Lauder gift box I recommended myself. She said she'd loved it. Is he OK?'

'He's missing, so we're searching for him.'

Her mouth turned down. 'Oh gosh, I'd no idea. His mum must be frantic.'

'How was Henry last time you saw him?'

'He was fine. We had a coffee. He was making a quick guilt visit to his mum because he wasn't coming back for Christmas.'

'What's Henry like? I believe he was a popular guy at school.'

She smoothed the neck of her jumper and picked a wisp of fluff from the arm. 'That's the trouble with wearing black, you're always dusting yourself off. Henry? Yes, he's good fun. A bit full of himself, I suppose. Never seems to take anything that seriously. He got a car when he was seventeen, so he was in demand with his wheels back in the day. His mum shops here sometimes. We do a special cosmetics range for the older woman. I saw her a couple of weeks back, buying concealer.'

'When you and Eugene were together, I believe you mixed with Henry and his girlfriend, Etta Parton.'

'Yeah, the four of us used to do stuff sometimes. Etta was a brainbox. Bit dull, to be honest. She'd cancel coming out at the last minute if she had an essay to finish.' Teagan gave a mock yawn, patting her mouth. '*Boring!* It used to annoy Henry.'

'Is Etta around now?'

'She got a place at Oxford and I think she works there now, at the university. So, I suppose all her studying paid off.' She didn't sound impressed.

'And Bertie Greene, is he a friend of yours?'

Teagan pulled a face. 'Not likely. I saw it on the news when he was sent to jail and I don't mix with offenders. He knocked around with Eugene and Henry at school. I didn't have much time for him. He was a bit of a hanger-on. I must ring Henry's mum, see how she is. I hope he's okay, not had an accident or anything awful.'

Patrick didn't think there was anything else he could get from Teagan, so he thanked her and went on his way.

As he was leaving the store, he saw Crista, the guv's mum, perched on a stool, her long, shapely legs crossed and her eyes closed. She was a bit of a stunner, beautifully dressed, classy. She wore a cherry red coat and her honey-streaked hair was held back in a matching scarf. A woman was dabbing a cosmetic brush in a little tray and sweeping Crista's face with it. She'd sidled up to him in Nutmeg after Lisa's funeral and put a hand on his arm. He'd been mesmerised by her long nails, decorated with triangles of red, gold and silver lacquer. She'd started asking questions about the guv — did she have many friends, did she socialise much, did she mention her family? He'd been uncomfortable and muttered that they didn't talk about things like that.

Must be odd, having such a fashion plate for a mum. He'd picked up that Crista and the guv had issues, but he steered clear of asking any questions. He had enough going on in his own life.

* * *

Siv studied the map of the crematorium that Toby Foxwell had given her the previous day. The extensive cemetery lay to the left of the main entrance gates. To the side of the east chapel was the columbarium, a resting place for funeral urns which sat in niches behind marble plaques. Each niche was deep enough for several urns. Beyond the west chapel lay the garden of remembrance, which ran along the perimeter. Ashes could be interred there beneath brass plaques or scattered on the lawn. A path from there led to Bluebell Copse, where ashes could again be strewn around memorial benches. A narrow road, Barker's Way, snaked down one side of Bluebell Copse, where Emmeline's Gate was situated. At one end, Barker's Way joined a road that connected with a main route into town, and at the other, it branched into the coast road.

The sun was hazy now, the light thinning. She donned protective gear and found Steve in the garden of remembrance, which was bisected by a broad path. He walked her along it to Bluebell Copse, a circular grassy area of birch trees with benches beneath. It was underplanted with bulbs: narcissi, wood anemones, crocuses and the bluebells that would form a carpet of colour in the spring. A wide, sturdy timber shed flanked by two large green compost bins stood on a paved area at the far end. It was screened by a laurel hedge with a narrow access gate between two cypress trees just beyond.

'This is where all the basic gardening equipment is kept,' Steve said. 'The door was closed and the padlock left hanging, so it wasn't immediately obvious that it had been snapped.'

He opened the shed door. Siv glanced in at orderly rows of spades, shovels, hoes, rakes, bags of fertiliser, a leaf blower and a hedge trimmer. 'Where is the wheelbarrow usually stored?'

'Over in that corner, upended against the wall, but it had been left just there.' Steve pointed to the floor inside the door. 'We've examined in here and taken the wheelbarrow to the lab. It's a one-wheeler. Now, I'll show you the tyre grooves. To start with, there's a faint impression by the gate over here, in the soil below one of the trees.'

They crossed to Emmeline's Gate. It was about five feet high. Beyond it, Siv saw members of Steve's team on the road, searching the area.

Steve bent and pointed to an area beneath a cypress. 'You can just about see that the barrow was set down here. There are depressed patches in the soil where the feet would have rested. So, it was wheeled across the paving from the shed. After this, tyre tracks run down the side of the grass in both directions. They stop at the garden of remembrance. Whoever used it could have taken the path from there to the chapel steps.'

She followed Steve and focused on the two sets of tyre grooves meandering across the grass, more indented in places and interweaving at some points.

'So, say the wheelbarrow was taken from the shed, trundled over to Emmeline's Gate and something was put in it.' She was thinking aloud. 'It's reasonable to wonder if our body and the wreaths were in it.'

'Exactly, exactly, and that would explain why some of the tyre grooves travelling away from the gate are deeper.' Steve seemed invigorated by the idea. 'Now, the paint on the metal gate is worn and uneven, which is good from a forensic viewpoint. We found some black fibres snagged on the side facing the road, about halfway up. We'll need to analyse and compare, but our dead man was wearing a black fleece jacket, so that suggests they're from him.'

Siv felt a flutter of anticipation. Could this be a break? 'The gate isn't high, and Barker's Way would be quiet late at night. You could park on the road without much chance of being seen, and if you were strong enough, you could hoist a body over the gate and then climb over yourself,' she added.

'It wouldn't be difficult,' Steve confirmed. 'There are no tyre tracks on the road, but then it was dry on Monday night. Just our luck that the rain keeps arriving on and off now.'

'You've not found any footprints?'

'No. The grass is a bit flattened. I'd say that our barrow pusher wore shoe covers. I'll keep you posted.'

She walked back to Bere Lodge. If the killer had transported Warren's body in the barrow and had worn shoe covers, that indicated a significant degree of preparation and planning. This wasn't a heat-of-the-moment crime. Someone had built up to the murder and probably derived pleasure from the process. They'd gone to the bother of getting wreaths, setting a scene. All these details added to the picture.

She met Toby Foxwell by the door of the lodge. He seemed rather down compared to the previous day.

'I heard about Andy's shed. I see you've now cordoned off a lot of the grounds,' he grumbled.

'I understand you're unhappy about that, but it's how we work.'

'Yes, yes, of course. But . . . Oh, dear. Such a terrible thing. The staff can't decide if they're coming or going.'

'I'd like to speak to Saul Robbins, if you could find him for me.'

While she waited in the room with the sunrise/sunset picture, she phoned Andy Smeaton, who was extremely cross that someone had tampered with his shed.

'That shed's been safe and secure for years and the wheelbarrow's an expensive model. We only bought it last July. What's society coming to when a place for the deceased is disrespected?'

'Indeed,' she soothed. 'When were you last in the shed?'

'Last week, Friday. It's a quiet time of year in the grounds, but I wanted to tidy up a few leaves. Everything was tickety-boo and the wheelbarrow was where it ought to be.'

'And when did you last use the barrow?'

'Must have been November.'

'Saul Robbins helps you with maintenance. Have you asked him to do any jobs recently?'

'Like I said, it's a quiet time of year with little growth, so I can cover most of it myself. He used the leaf blower last week. We'd had high winds and he cleared piles of dead leaves. Moaned about it too, I might add. I got him to remove wilted flowers before Christmas. Lots of people bring wreaths and such at that time of year, and you don't want them finding decaying stuff on their loved one's grave. Will I be able to get back into my shed soon?'

'That depends on whether we need anything in there as evidence.'

'Evidence of what?' He sounded confused.

There was a tap on the door and a slight man with a mop of mousy curls appeared. 'We'll have to leave it there, Mr Smeaton. Thank you.' Siv put her phone down and turned to the new arrival. 'Saul Robbins?'

'That's right.'

'Take a seat.' She got up and opened the window a notch.

'Was that old Andy on the phone? He's in a state about his shed and his top-of-the-range wheelbarrow. The way he goes on about it, you'd think it was gold-plated. It's not as if it's his personal property.'

'He's worked here a long time, it's his territory. People take these things personally.'

'Suppose.' He had a tiny chip on one of his front teeth and a cold. A scarlet rash bloomed around his nose. He sniffed and swallowed.

'How long have you worked here?'

'Three years.'

'Happy?'

'Enough.'

'You don't sound too enthusiastic.'

'The pay's pretty crap, and most of the time, it's dogsbody work. It's a means to an end for me, pays the bills. I'm doing an MBA online, and as soon as I get it, I'll be moving on.'

'Any problems or disagreements here?'

'I haven't heard of any. What's this, a careers interview?'

She wasn't keen on his familiar attitude. 'I'm investigating a murder, Mr Robbins.'

He wrinkled his pinkish nose at her. 'Course. Just that I'm up to speed on my career, you see. Once I have my master's, I plan to work in the financial sector, maybe move to London.'

'Yes, yes, but for now, you do various tasks here, including assisting Diane Lacey.'

He snuffled loudly. 'Correct. Diane's been great and encouraged me. She helped me with my study application, checked it all over. I don't have a first degree, so I doubt I'd have got accepted without her help. She's from a dead ordinary background like me, never much dosh, but she was determined and she's got two degrees. She's really too highly qualified for the job she does here, but she loves it. Diane's so clued-up about this place — anything you need, she's your woman.'

It sounded like Saul had a little bit of a crush on Diane Lacey. He seemed one of those boastful, brittle people who can be needy beneath the surface bravado. Perhaps Diane saw that vulnerability, although Siv was finding it very hard to glimpse. 'Yes, I've met Diane. I'm pleased to hear that you have ambitions. Have you ever met Henry Kilgore or Eugene Warren?'

'Never heard of them until Diane rang me to say a body had been found on the steps, and then it was on the news about the murder and the Kilgore guy being missing.'

'Does the name Bertie Greene mean anything to you?'

He wasn't so keen on that question. He adjusted his collar, looking uneasy. 'He was married to my cousin. One of those something-removed ones. They're divorced now.'

'Mr Greene was friendly with both of the men I'm investigating.'

'Oh, OK. Doesn't mean anything to me. I haven't seen Bertie for a while. He's a bit of a blot on the family character, and you know how it is when couples divorce — the demarcation lines are drawn. I expect you're up to speed about him being in prison. What an idiot. Gamekeeper turned poacher. I don't get why anyone would want to be a prison officer, mixing all day with losers, having to watch your back. Too much like a paid jail sentence.'

Siv privately agreed with the last comment. 'When did you last use the shed at the back of Bluebell Copse?'

Robbins blew his nose. To her disgust, he inspected the mucus collected in the tissue before crumpling it in his palm. 'Last Wednesday. I fetched the leaf blower. Andy asked me to clear leaves and bits of debris. Very challenging intellectual work.'

'And the wheelbarrow, when did you last use that?'

'Just before Christmas. I cleared old flowers and stuff from graves in the cemetery, so I used some garden waste bags and the barrow. Riveting stuff.'

Siv sighed inwardly. He was wearing company. 'I'm sure you'll be happier when you move to high finance,' she said coolly. 'These details are riveting to me. Did you use the barrow in Bluebell Copse or the garden of remembrance at all?'

'No, I just took the path from the top of the copse to the cemetery and back, and I put the degradable stuff in the compost bin. Actually—' he held up a finger — 'I've just remembered something. When I was clearing the cemetery, a woman stopped and admired the wheelbarrow. She startled me, because I was kneeling, with my back turned, and suddenly she was right there, behind me. It was a misty afternoon and it *is* a graveyard. She said the barrow was just the sturdy kind she needed. She asked if she could push it a few paces to see how heavy it was. I thought it was weird, but I let her.'

'Can you describe this woman?'

'Not sure. I didn't take that much notice. The light was starting to go, and I wanted to finish the area I was tidying.' He closed his eyes for a moment. 'Thirties, quite tall. Dark hair. It was a freezing day, so she had a long, padded coat with a hood up. Slim.'

'Was she a local person?'

'Hard to say. We didn't get chatting.'

'Can you remember anything else? The colour of her coat?'

'Black or grey, maybe. Not a bright colour. It was just a minute or so, then she walked on. You get visitors in and out of the cemetery all the time.'

'Where were you on Monday night?'

'I had a burger with a friend and then I went home about half nine, watched telly and went to bed.'

Siv reckoned there was something slippery about Robbins. Maybe it was just his jarring manner getting under her skin. 'Can anyone corroborate that you were at home?' she said curtly.

'I've got a flatmate, but he was on a night shift, so no. Is that a problem?'

'I can't say as yet.' But she shut the interview down shortly after that.

When Robbins had gone, Siv collected her things, closed the window and left the building. It was raining heavily again now, chilly slanting needles, and as she walked to her car, a call came through from the duty desk at the station.

'Guv, uniform have been dealing with a distressed dog left in a car.'

'A distressed dog? Isn't that RSPCA territory? Why do I need to know?'

'The RSPCA couldn't respond quickly enough, so the constables who attended had to break in to rescue the dog, which isn't chipped. But a brochure for Berminster Breaks was retrieved from the glove compartment. Along the top someone's written, *Remember fun at Mallow Cottage*. And, guv, the car was left beside Mallow Cottage, one of Ms Kilgore's holiday properties listed in the brochure.'

Siv's grip tightened on the phone. 'Where's the car now?'

'Still where it was found, on a turning off Derwin Lane, by a gate to a field. When uniform followed up, they couldn't trace an owner, so they checked out the brochure and made the connection with your investigations. The car hasn't been searched thoroughly yet, though.'

'Tell those constables well done.'

She took the details, rang Steve and asked him to get a team to the location. Then she phoned Ali and told him to meet her there.

'That's cracking news. Are we going to find Kilgore's body in the car boot, d'you reckon?'

'Possibly. Let's get there and see.'

Siv dashed to her car, shaking rain from her face, fumbling with the keys. More importantly, if Kilgore was there, would he be dead or alive?

CHAPTER 9

Jock Keyes visited his son, Ian, in prison once a month. They had little to say to each other, but it was the right thing to do and Ian's mother would have expected it. The meetings were always a little awkward as Jock sat and made small talk. Trivial stuff about his work at the sorting office, what he'd grown in the allotment and the scenery he'd painted for the local am-dram company. Ian barely replied, and when he did speak it was to complain about the food, the noise and boredom. He listed all these things as if they were his father's fault and responsibility. There were times when Jock worried that he might snap and say, *You're in here because you made the wrong choices and you committed crimes*. But he stayed silent. There was no point in rubbing it in and, in the end, he was sorry for his son, in spite of what he'd done.

Jock's dad had been a petty crook, always in and out of trouble and prison, and leading his family in a merry old dance. This had turned Jock into a law-abiding citizen, determined to give his son a better, more secure life. He'd moved from Dumfries to Sussex to leave behind the taint of his father's criminality. Yet here was Ian, repeating the pattern, now serving a minimum of twenty-five years for murder. Jock had no idea how it had all gone so wrong. Maybe there was a risk-taking gene that had passed him by, but he'd handed it on.

So, he sat month in, month out in the visiting room with its odours of sweat, disinfectant and bad plumbing. He scratched around for things to talk about and listened to Ian's woes, watching the clock behind his son's head inching towards the hour, willing it onwards. Today, the minutes dragged unbearably, and Jock could tell that his son was as relieved as he was when time was called and that was it for four weeks.

After every visit, Jock drove towards Cliffdean Point and walked a couple of miles along the headland, whatever the weather. He craved the fresh air and the open skies after the claustrophobia of the prison visitation room. Then he'd drop down the path to the Horizon Café for fish and chips. He treated it as his reward. But for what? He should do his duty by his son, after all. His food always tasted of relief mixed with guilt.

He was tired today, having done a couple of night shifts at work. They always left him out of sorts and a bit irritable. But if he went home, he'd brood about the visit. He parked the car on the headland and strode out, letting the sharp wind buffet him and leave him breathless. The sea glittered blue–grey, rolling in on a high tide.

In the café, he relished the crunchy chips. While he ate, he caught up with the local news on his phone. He read about a missing man and another who'd been murdered. The name Eugene Warren and the face in the photo were familiar, but he couldn't recall why. He'd always worked for the post office, for many years delivering the mail and for the last two sorting it. He was familiar with many people around town from the names on envelopes and parcels. His memory teased away at it as he cut into his battered cod, but eventually he gave up.

By the time he'd finished eating and had a cup of tea, he was ready to fall asleep in the chair.

* * *

Siv held her breath when they opened the boot of the car. There were some personal items and dog food in the grubby space, but no body. Good news, she thought grimly, but where did that leave them in the search for Kilgore?

Siv and Ali donned gloves. She searched the rucksack and wash bag in the boot, while he looked in the body of the vehicle. The rucksack contained clean men's clothes, jeans, jumper, socks and underpants. They smelled of fabric softener. No ID in any pockets. The washbag held a well-worn toothbrush, a creased tube of minty toothpaste, soap and a disposable razor.

'No ID in here?' she asked Ali.

'Nothing in the glove compartment except a pack of tissues. Other than that, just a bit of rubbish and a disgusting smell of dog muck.' He wrinkled his nose.

'We'll get on then, see what prints we can find,' Steve said.

Siv and Ali gladly left Forensics to it — the rain was cascading down on them. By early evening, they were all back at the station and were met by the incident board. Siv updated the others on Steve's findings at the cemetery and asked Ali for the post-mortem results.

Ali finished a glass of water as he itemised the initial points. 'Warren was strangled from behind with a thin leather strap or belt. Estimated time of death between 11 p.m. on Monday night and 3 a.m. of Tuesday morning. His own finger marks were around his neck, indicating that he'd struggled and tried to free himself. He hadn't been drinking and had no traces of drugs in his system. He'd eaten a chicken dinner around seven hours before he died. He was a healthy young man, although a bit underweight. The lab's working on his clothes.'

Siv summarised details of the car, rubbing her hands together. She'd left her gloves in Bere Lodge and her fingers were numb.

'Late on Tuesday night, a Mr Curtis was walking home from the pub along Derwin Lane. He heard a dog barking and found that it was locked in an old Vauxhall Corsa. The constables who rescued the unchipped dog couldn't find anything in the car to ID the owner. It's untaxed and unregistered. There was a brochure for Berminster Breaks in the glove compartment.' She showed them a photo of the brochure in its evidence bag. 'Someone had handwritten on the top in black biro, *Remember fun at Mallow Cottage.* The car was parked near to that cottage, one of Ms Kilgore's holiday rentals. She's owned it since 2006, and the last guests in there left a week after Christmas. One of our uniformed colleagues was on the ball and linked it to our cases. The body of the car was empty, just a couple of sandwich packets and a blanket covered in dog mess on the back seat. There was a sleeping bag, a cushion and a wash bag with basic bathroom stuff in the boot, plus a rucksack with some men's clothes and a pack of dog biscuits. Nothing to indicate who the owner is.'

'Could it be Warren's car? He might have been sleeping in it,' Ali said. 'That would account for why I haven't been able to trace him.'

'That thought crossed my mind,' Siv agreed. 'Or perhaps, if it is his, he couldn't afford to stay anywhere in town while he was here, so he planned to camp out in the car. Uniform report that the dog was dehydrated and ravenous. The vet who saw it said it hadn't had water for approximately twenty-four hours — so it was left around the time that Warren was killed and Kilgore went missing. The car's proximity to Mallow Cottage, and the brochure inside it, indicate that there may be a more recent link between these men than their school days. Forensics are going over the car and arranging for it to be taken to the pound. They'll also check the brochure for prints and examine Mallow Cottage. I've asked Uniform to trace the car's ownership history and take a look at ANPR cameras approaching town.'

Ali said, 'I'd wager that Eugene Warren came to Berminster in the Vauxhall and expected to return to his dog.'

'That's my thinking too,' Siv agreed. 'You've been going over the locations we're working with. What have we got so far?'

'Hang on, I just need to nip to the loo,' Ali said, exiting the room sharpish.

Siv and Patrick stared at the incident board while they waited for him.

'Nice comfort break?' Patrick asked when he came back.

'Nice enough, since you ask,' Ali said loftily. He pulled his chair closer, his iPad to hand. 'Aye, it's interesting regarding locations. Mallow Cottage is on Derwin Lane. If you drive on down Derwin and take a left, you join Barker's Way. It'd be ten minutes' drive max from Derwin to the pedestrian access gate at the crem, where Steve and co. were examining the wheelbarrow tracks.'

They all studied the map. Patrick pointed to Barker's Way with the tip of his pen. 'If the fibres found on the cemetery gate are from Warren's jacket, either he climbed over — presumably to meet his killer, who then strangled him — or his body was pushed over. It's a complicated way of dealing with a body: hoisting it over a gate, breaking into the shed for the wheelbarrow, loading the corpse in the barrow with wreaths and arranging it on the steps and then returning the barrow to the shed. If that's what the killer did, they went to a lot of effort and trouble. This was planned, not opportunistic.'

'Agreed. The killer knew about the shed and the wheelbarrow,' Siv said. 'Wherever Warren was actually murdered, the disposal of the body on the crem steps was done in that way because it was meaningful to the killer and worth the display. The night manoeuvre would have been intricate, but a calculated way to access the crem without being seen, and it gave the killer time to arrange Warren on the steps. Back in December, a woman asked Saul Robbins about the wheelbarrow when he was using it in the cemetery. He gave me a vague description. Worth bearing in mind. What else have we got?'

Ali swivelled in his chair. 'I've been chasing Henry Kilgore's boss at Footprint. He rang me just now. He met with Kilgore last week and told him he'd be made redundant at the end of this month. Kilgore was pretty brash about it. Said he'd been expecting it.'

'It must have been a knock-back, all the same,' Siv said. 'We might be looking at suicide. He was a popular man, seen as successful. Losing his job, losing face — it wouldn't fit his script, and he hadn't told his partner or his mother about it, so maybe he was stressed.'

'If he's drowned himself in the sea, we might never know,' Patrick said glumly.

Ali nudged him. He'd been unusually prone to melancholy of late. Now Lisa's funeral had passed, the team hoped Patrick would return to his old self. But they could give him a helping hand if need be. 'True enough, Patrick, but let's stay hopeful.'

'Bertie Greene didn't volunteer much,' Siv continued, 'although he admitted that he, Kilgore and Warren used to smoke dope. He confirmed that Kilgore rang him unexpectedly on Monday night, but then didn't turn up. He mentioned that Kilgore had gone out with an Etta Parton at school, so that link needs checking. Greene seemed genuinely surprised when I told him about Eugene Warren's death, but there was something iffy about him. I'm not sure what, but he was shifty. Saul Robbins, who works at the crem, is a distant cousin of Greene's ex-wife, but he told me he hasn't seen Greene recently.'

Patrick filled them in on his meeting with Teagan Grenville. 'She said that she finished with Warren because he two-timed her. She last saw Kilgore in November and he seemed fine. She described Greene as a hanger-on when they were at school. Guv, Etta Parton might live in Oxford now — she went there for uni and stayed on for work.'

Ali said, 'Right, so it looks like something happened after Kilgore set off to see Bertie Greene. Either he's been murdered, killed himself because he was losing his job or he's murdered Warren and done a runner.'

'But why would he arrange to see Greene if he was planning either of the last two?' Siv asked. 'If Warren's death was messy, a crime of opportunity, sure, but it was organised and carefully executed. It seems odd that none of Kilgore's friends noticed anything was wrong with him, and surely someone who was planning suicide or murder might give off some signals.'

She rubbed her face wearily. 'I had a report from Uniform. They've been searching all over town and found no trace of Kilgore. Volunteers are looking along the beach. Imelda Kilgore's joined them. I sincerely hope she doesn't stumble across her son's body. The three at the chalet have been out looking for him too.'

That group at Driftwood niggled her. The unease had been lurking at the back of her mind. She wasn't sure why, but she didn't quite buy the cosy set-up. She had an odd feeling about them. They'd have to be questioned again.

'Saffie says that she was asleep in bed when Henry left his message, but we've no corroboration that she was at home. We only have Viv and Damian's word for it that they didn't see Henry again after he left them to head to Bertie Greene's. They're each other's alibi and they didn't get home until half past midnight. But it was a cold night for idling and snogging at the bandstand.'

'Love keeps you warm,' Ali offered. 'Or in my case, love and a spare tyre.'

'And in my case, a Kitty-cat,' Patrick said.

Siv pulled a face. She felt left out of this smug lovefest. The empty space in the bed that Ed had left was always cold now. She had to stop herself thinking about what it used to be like waking up to warmth and love every morning. She stared at the incident board with concentration as she pushed away the memory and said tightly, 'Patrick, I wish you'd stop clicking your pen, it drives me nuts.' Patrick stopped, instantly chastened.

Siv continued. 'We need a timeline for everything the four at Driftwood did from when they arrived in town, and we want background checks on all the crem staff. The writing on the brochure might be Warren's or Kilgore's. Patrick, can you show Tara Warren, the three at Driftwood and Imelda Kilgore a photo of the brochure and ask if they recognise the writing. Get samples of handwriting from everyone we've interviewed to date. And those wreaths — try and find where they came from. There can't be that many florists in this town.'

'I've been mulling over the wreaths,' Patrick said. 'What do they indicate? Why go to that bother? I know from Lisa's funeral that fresh floral wreaths aren't cheap.'

'An unpleasant or sarcastic gesture, or maybe a genuine one, take your pick,' Siv said.

'Genuine?' Patrick looked puzzled.

'It depends on the killer's motive. If this murder was done with some regret, the wreaths might be saying that.' Siv turned to Ali. 'I sent Kilgore's laptop for scrutiny. Can you chase the results? And I want you to talk to Damian Kyalo, shake him up a bit. The guy's attitude is just plain weird. Get him away from his comfort zone with his fiancée.' Siv knew Ali would be good at that. He could switch from easy-going camaraderie to brisk intensity in an instant. It even unsettled Siv at times.

This was usually when she'd tell them her actions. Instead she stood up and shoved her chair in, still irritated by their cosy references to their partners. Ali raised his eyebrows, but Siv ignored him. She noticed her team exchange glances as they sloped off back to their desks.

She left the office and called at Gusto, waiting to be served in the warm fug of the café. She inhaled the aromas of garlic, onion and rosemary, gazing at the tempting shelves of food: cannoli with Parma ham mousse, rigatoni and peppers, panzerotti, cheese arancini, crostini with tuna, courgette fritters. The atmosphere calmed her, eased her aching heart.

This was the kind of place Mutsi had always liked, especially in the early evening — a café where she could swoop in and buy assorted snacks. Siv glanced over her shoulder into the darkness outside the lighted windows, but the street was empty. A dislike of cooking was the one trait Siv shared with her mother. She ordered a couple of arancini to take home for supper and a latte, reflecting on the day's events, that phrase on the front of the brochure. *Remember fun at Mallow Cottage.* Had it been written as a fond memory or a warning?

* * *

Imelda Kilgore had browned leeks and celery in a large casserole dish. Now she added chunks of floured chicken dusted with paprika, moving like an automaton. She didn't have any appetite, but she had to do something with her desperation. It was Henry's favourite meal. She'd lost count of how many times she'd made it over the years. Maybe it would summon her son, call him home, as if he could smell the spices on the breeze. She'd told Saffie, Viv and Damian to come for supper. They needed to eat and they needed to stay together, stay strong. Plus, she needed the distraction.

She'd just put the dish in the oven when the young detective, DC Hill, rang the bell. He must have seen the anxious expression on her face — he told her immediately that he didn't have any news. She took him into the kitchen and offered him coffee.

'I won't this time, thanks,' he said, taking out his phone. 'Is this Henry's handwriting?'

She put on her glasses. 'No, nothing like. Where has this come from?'

'A Berminster Breaks brochure was found in an abandoned car. Is the writing familiar at all?'

'I don't recognise it. Of course, you don't see many handwritten things nowadays.'

'Does the phrase ring a bell at all? Perhaps it refers to something in particular?'

She mouthed it to herself. 'Sorry, no. Lots of people have had fun at Mallow Cottage.' She cringed slightly at the cheesiness of her comment.

DC Hill shifted in his chair and rubbed his chin. He was a smart, well-mannered man. Fresh cheeked and bright-eyed. A bit on the lean side. Probably about the same age as Henry.

'Do you see much of your mum?' she asked him. She hoped he was going home to his mother tonight, to a hearty meal.

He took a breath. 'My mum died a while ago.'

'Oh, I'm sorry. That was clumsy of me.'

'It's OK. She was great and I miss her. Ms Kilgore, there's something else I need to tell you. We spoke to Henry's boss earlier today and established that your son's employment was coming to an end. He'd just been told that he'd be made redundant at the end of January. Had he said anything to you about that?'

The oven whirred, the red light clicking on. Imelda had a sharp twist of fear. Henry's job meant everything to him. 'I don't understand. He's been with that company for six years, achieved promotion. They were very successful. Why would they be letting him go? He didn't mention it.'

'I don't have the details. I understand that business had dropped off. It's just that it might have affected Henry's state of mind, especially as he doesn't appear to have told anyone. He'd mentioned to Viv and Damian that he was worried about his job security, but nothing more.'

She got up and poured herself a glass of water. The rice was ready to go on soon. Basmati, because Henry preferred it. She checked the lid was tight on the saucepan, then sat down.

'Are you saying that Henry might have been depressed?'

'It's possible.'

She saw his kindly expression, gathered what it meant. 'You believe that he might have harmed himself?'

'We have to consider that possibility, yes. I'm sorry.'

'No. I don't believe that. It's a ridiculous idea. You're completely on the wrong track there.'

'I expect you're right.'

'I am. Henry wouldn't do that.' *Would he?*

'Has anything else come back to you about Eugene Warren?'

Eugene had been flitting in and out of her mind, especially after the news coverage. He'd always had a mocking expression, as if everything was a private joke. His hair had been lank and greasy, in need of a good wash, and he'd smelled of sweat only half-masked by cheap body spray. She'd always opened windows when he'd been in the house. She'd once caught him helping himself to a bottle of gin from her larder, trying to hide it in his jacket. He'd laughed and put it back, cool as a cucumber, with no apology. But the police wouldn't be interested in those memories.

'Nothing important,' she said. 'He was one of those youths who don't say a lot, darting in and out of the house like a shadow.'

DC Hill seemed satisfied. 'Will you be OK now, Ms Kilgore?' he asked. 'You've had a shock. Do you want me to call anyone?'

'No, no! The others are coming for supper. They'll be here soon. Thank you.'

She longed for him to go. She showed him out, closing the door on his heels, and then stood for a long time, staring at the photo of Henry in his fencing gear. He held his visor in the crook of his left arm, his foil over his right shoulder. She recalled all the evenings she'd driven him to classes and the chats they'd had. He'd always confided in her. They'd been so close. So why hadn't he told her about his job? She could have reassured him that with his talents and experience, he'd get another very quickly.

Viv rang the bell, and Imelda realised she hadn't even put the rice on.

CHAPTER 10

Siv slept fitfully and gave up around 6 a.m. She slipped on pyjama bottoms and Ed's old sweatshirt and made coffee. When she raised the blind on the narrow kitchen window, the night was still lingering outside, shroud black and silent. She recalled a book of Finnish proverbs that Mutsi used to have, a yellow hardback with the Maiden of Finland on the cover. A woman with streaming blonde hair, dressed in a peasant skirt and blouson, she'd stood on a sun-dappled mountaintop, brandishing the Finnish flag. There'd been a saying in the chapter on the seasons that had always struck Siv as ominous: *The winter does not leave without a backward glance.* She must have liked the ripple of fear it gave her, because she returned often to that page. Her sister, Rik, provocative and fearless, would use the proverbs to taunt their mother. When Mutsi presented them with scratch suppers, Rik would say with a sigh: *A tiny morsel is a feast to a starving man.* She'd greet news of Mutsi's latest love interest with: *There are many means, said Granny, when she was wiping the table with the cat.* Whenever they had to move home yet again, Rik would shake her head, proclaiming the unfathomable and portentous sounding words: *The cheese betrays the milk.*

Siv wondered if she'd have survived childhood without Rik, who stole to buy extra food, mysteriously acquired school equipment that Mutsi had neglected to buy and looked out for her sister in her combative, sharp-tongued way. She'd got them into trouble too, when they were left on their own. She'd turned into a teenage delinquent — necessity evolving into fun when Rik became fond of shoplifting — but she'd also been skilled at talking her way out of the consequences of her actions. Siv had once tried to thank Rik in an email but had received a dismissive reply: *Don't get misty-eyed on me. I've always been a sinner, not a saint.*

It had been a while since she'd heard from Rik. Siv took her iPad and emailed her sister.

Hope you're OK. Breaking news. Mutsi's moving in with Will Mortimer, my boss. That will make work interesting. I've been invited to lunch at their love nest. Maybe I'll have to join you in Auckland. x

She pulled down her kitchen table and switched a lamp on. The wood- burning stove was warm from the night before and she threw a couple of logs in to keep it ticking over. Her landlords, Paul and Corran, kept her supplied with wood, as well as bringing her the occasional meal. They were generous and kind, but not intrusive, the perfect combination.

Her little home was cheery, despite the dank, dark world outside. She took out the paper she was currently working with, checked the diagram and made creases. She was a skilled origamist and had been accepting commissions for a while. Her latest was from Berminster Museum. They were creating an exhibition about the sailing and fishing history of the town and had asked her to make a set of boats and ships. Berminster had once been an important trading seaport — the natural harbour having lain five miles inland since medieval times — before nature, with a helping hand from humanity, had changed the course of the River Bere. She'd completed a square-rigged ship with tall masts and billowing sails and was now working on a trio of fishing boats. Her next project would be a nineteenth-century steam yacht and, after that, with a nod to Roman Britain, a coracle and a seafaring cargo boat, based on one found at Blackfriars in London. She worked steadily, pausing only to pour another coffee. Only once was she brought out of her reverie when she started at a sharp, passing shower rattling on the roof.

At half past seven, she put her work away reluctantly, showered, had breakfast and cleared up, which took just minutes. Her doll's house on wheels was pristine. She might stay here forever if her landlords agreed.

* * *

Siv stood near the chapel steps, to one side of the service organised by Toby Foxwell. A light drizzle was falling from low, murky clouds. It was useful to observe the cemetery staff as a whole, ranged as they were in a semi-circle. Phoebe Palmer stood with another woman, their heads bowed. They were both dressed in black and stood out from their colleagues, who wore their usual work clothes. Andy Smeaton had put on a wide black tie. He'd nicked himself shaving just below his chin. He held an umbrella over Diane Lacey and stared straight ahead, blank-faced. Toby Foxwell wore a dark grey coat and a sombre expression as he stood before them. The rain darkened his hair to a muddy copper.

'I wasn't sure what to read, but I felt this poem by Ernest Dowson would suit.'

They are not long, the weeping and the laughter,
Love and desire and hate:
I think they have no portion in us after
We pass the gate.
They are not long, the days of wine and roses:
Out of a misty dream
Our path emerges for a while, then closes
Within a dream.

Siv studied the staff as she listened. Saul Robbins was standing to the left of Phoebe Palmer, tapping his foot. He slid his phone from his pocket and checked the screen. Phoebe noticed and gave him a look of disgust, not that it registered with him. Diane Lacey stepped up beside Foxwell, raised a pair of reading glasses to her nose and spoke quietly, eyes down on the sheet of paper she held. She read 'Roads Go Ever On' by Tolkien. There were a few shuffles and coughs and the faint, steady hiss of the rain. Siv couldn't imagine that this miserable little gathering in the damp morning was going to help anyone. Well, except maybe Foxwell. It would satisfy him and he could report to his manager that he'd cared for his team during a difficult time. Job well done.

Foxwell thanked Diane and said, 'Eugene Warren was a stranger to us, but we are saddened by his death. He was a young man with his life before him. He is in our thoughts as we go about our work, and we can find solace in the professional service we provide here. Just to remind everyone that I'm available if any of you need space and time to talk about this awful event. Thank you all for coming. You should get back into the dry now.'

As the group turned to leave, Siv heard Phoebe comment to her friend, 'A hymn or a simple prayer wouldn't have gone amiss, but I suppose that would have been too traditional in these times. It might have offended someone.'

Saul Robbins moved across to Diane and murmured to her. She touched his shoulder reassuringly. Andy Smeaton stared at him, twirling his umbrella. 'Saul, don't forget to check all the waste bins this morning,' he barked.

Robbins clicked his heels and smirked.

'Thank you for coming,' Foxwell said to Siv as he approached. 'I'm glad that all the staff could attend and show respect. How is your investigation progressing?'

'It's coming along. Has any member of staff seemed particularly distressed?'

He wiped his forehead with the back of his glove. 'No, Inspector, I wouldn't say so. We've all tried to support each other. I've been checking in with everyone daily and Diane has been a calm and reliable tower of strength, as always. I know that several staff members have been to talk to her, and she keeps an eye on Saul, who can be rather immature.' He raised an eyebrow ever so slightly before the professional facade slid back into place. 'Phoebe has been upset, but then she takes things to heart. I find her difficult to talk to. Maybe it's a generational thing or perhaps just that she's passive aggressive. Do you have that problem with some colleagues?'

Siv pictured Mortimer. 'Oh, yes.'

She stood, gazing at the watery landscape and shivered as rain trickled down her neck. January was such a drab, tired month. She craved a rich, dark hot chocolate and a warm, sugary doughnut.

* * *

When Ali arrived at Driftwood, Saffie opened the door, dressed, with damp hair. Her eyes were raw and inflamed. She tensed when he introduced himself.

'Have you any news?'

'No, sorry. I've come to see Damian Kyalo.'

'Oh. They're not up yet.'

'Can you give him a knock for me?'

They waited in the kitchen, which was a mess. He could see that he'd interrupted Saffie tidying up. He tried to keep out of her way as she moved around, which wasn't easy, given his girth.

'How are you bearing up?' he asked.

'OK.'

The guv had phoned him to say that she would talk to Saffie again this morning, so he didn't want to press too hard. 'Do you know if Henry had any of the Berminster Breaks brochures at your home in London?'

'No. Why would he? There's a pile of them here though, on the living room table.' Saffie stopped what she was doing, twisting a tea towel between her hands. 'Something bad must have happened to him, mustn't it?'

Ali, who never saw the point of holding out false hope, said, 'At this stage, that seems likely.'

Damian appeared in the doorway, wearing only boxer shorts. He was scratching his thick black weave of chest hair. Saffie frowned, turning away to the sink.

'I'm DS Ali Carlin. I need to talk to you about Henry Kilgore and Eugene Warren.'

'Bit early, mate,' Damian said. 'I need to grab a shower and some brekkie. Can you come back in an hour?'

Ali already had a nagging headache and Damian wasn't improving it. 'No, I can't,' he snapped. 'Get dressed now and we'll take a walk. You can shower later.'

Damian opened his mouth to protest, then reconsidered. He went away, muttering to himself. Ali wondered if he'd delay deliberately, but the man was back within minutes, huddled into a thick jacket. Ali led the way out of the chalet, down the steps to the beach. The rain had stopped, but the sky was still grey, with a pearly sheen. The sea lay beneath it, flat and sullen, matching Damian's apparent mood. Ali had been going to suggest they stop at a café, but now he couldn't be bothered being good cop.

He lit a Gitane and offered one to Damian, who flinched away. 'Are you sure you've never heard Henry mention Eugene Warren? They were good friends at school.'

'Sure. Why do the police keep asking us about him?'

'The death and Henry's disappearance might well be linked. Did Henry ever say anything about any problems he'd had when he lived here?'

'Nope. Sounded like he'd had a good time when he was growing up. Lots of socialising and the money to fund it.'

'How long have you known him, then?'

Damian flicked up the hood on his jacket, although the air was mild. 'Ten years or so. We met at uni — Reading — in our first term, playing snooker. Henry's great company. Always the life and soul of the party.'

‘You’re close friends?’

‘We are, yes. Best friends, I’d say. Viv and I shared a flat with him in London after we graduated. We see him at least once a fortnight. Sometimes I have a drink with him, just us two, other times we meet up as a foursome, or he drops into ours after work. He’s going to be our best man.’

‘Have you been here to stay with him before?’

‘No, this is our first time in Berminster. Henry suggested it as a way to celebrate our engagement, and we liked the idea of a few days on the coast.’

It crossed Ali’s mind that Kilgore might have had another motive for inviting them, but what might that be? He watched Damian’s plump, feminine lips. Some people looked sulky when they were upset, and from the way this man was pouting, he must have been utterly miserable. Then again, his best friend had gone missing and might be dead. He softened his tone a little. ‘Talk me through what you all did, from when you arrived on Saturday until Monday night.’

Damian’s demeanour indicated he found the question tiresome. ‘How many times do we have to tell you guys this stuff?’

Ali said nothing.

‘OK, OK. Fine.’ He shoved his hands in his pockets and hunched forward. ‘We drove down Saturday, arrived about two, just after Henry and Saffie. We unpacked and hung around for a bit, and then the four of us had a walk on the beach. We had a couple of drinks in the Three Swans, then decided to get fish and chips to have back at Driftwood. Viv and I walked back here, while Henry and Saffie got his car to fetch them. When we’d eaten, we watched a couple of films — *The Favourite* and *Joker*.

‘Sunday, we got up late, went to Imelda’s for lunch.’ He pulled a face. ‘We didn’t really want to do the whole roast dinner thing, but Imelda was keen, so . . . Then Viv and me drove along the coast and walked at Bere Marsh Nature Reserve. We stopped at the café there afterwards and decided to catch a film at the Talisman cinema in town. They're doing a Hitchcock season and we went to the six o'clock showing of *Vertigo*. After that, we had a snack and a drink in the bar there. Must have got home about ten.' He stamped his feet, kicked a few shells.

'What did Henry and Saffie do the rest of Sunday?'

'No idea. They were in watching telly when we got back.'

'And Monday?'

'Me, Viv and Henry went kayaking. He keeps a couple of kayaks in his mum's garage and we hired a third one from a place at the harbour. Saffie doesn't like sporty stuff. I'm not sure what she did. We got back late afternoon, just before dark, and she was in. We've told you where we went Monday evening.'

'So, Henry didn't go off anywhere on his own?'

'Nope.'

They'd walked a fair way. Ali would be able to report to Nurse Keene at the diabetic clinic that he'd been taking exercise. She might be less stern and disapproving.

'You're close to Henry, but he didn't tell you he's lost his job?'

They'd walked near the water's edge. Damian's red-and-yellow trainers were a flash of colour in the bleak day. He jumped back as a wave surged in.

'Who told you that?'

'Henry's employer. They're making him and some other people redundant at the end of this month.'

Damian shook his head. 'Oh, poor bloke, that's rough. He didn't say. Viv and me knew he was worried and was scanning other jobs. When did they tell him?'

Ali ducked as a gull screamed over his head. He'd been nervous of the things since one whipped an ice cream from his hand. 'Last week.'

'I don't get why he didn't say something. Maybe he didn't want to spoil our engagement with bad news. Henry's kind like that. Or maybe he just needed to process it before he told us.' He sighed and stared out to sea. 'This has turned out to be such a shitty week, and it was supposed to be fun. Saffie spends all her time in tears, Viv's really cut up and Henry's mum keeps making us meals we don't want.'

'And you? How are you coping?'

'I'm gutted, mate, all adrift. We've been driving all over the place, hoping we'll spot Henry.' He gripped the edges of his hood as a sudden breeze snapped at it. 'What a fucking mess. Can we go back to London soon? I can't see that there's anything we can do here, and I'd rather be at work than hang around.'

'We'll inform you when you're free to return home. Is Henry happy with Saffie?'

'Very. Ready to settle down, I'd say.'

'Did you see her when you came back in the early hours of Tuesday morning?'

'She was in bed, so no. Saffie's a clean-living, moderate kind of person. She'd bore me stiff with her quiet, virtuous ways, but they suit Henry. She likes early nights, compared to us. That's why she's good for Henry. She keeps him in line and, of course, she's gorgeous.'

They were approaching a café, a low timber building with blue window frames and two sets of solar panels. The scent of coffee wafted their way on the breeze.

Damian pointed at it with his thumb. 'I'm going to that café for breakfast, if that's all?'

Ali had another fag after Damian had gone. The man's account of the days after the group arrived at Driftwood sounded straightforward enough, but he needed to compare notes with the guv. He eased a finger into the nipping waistband of his trousers and tried sucking in his stomach. He let it out again with a sigh. No matter what he did, the weight crept on. He'd be one on those middle-aged men with protruding bellies that made them look pregnant. Then Polly would leave him for some slim, fit guy, brimming with energy, who didn't smell of fag smoke. He saw him in his mind's eye, one of those carefree, hale-and-hearty types who could eat what they like without gaining an ounce. He was sickened by the thought that the picture fitted Tommy Castles. He took a last, panicky gasp of his Gitane before stubbing it out on the edge of a nearby bin.

It started to rain again and by the time he made it back to his car, the downpour had drenched him. The SOCO colleagues working at the crem would be fed up, plodding around in this.

* * *

Siv sat on the end of the bed. Saffie was dressed but lying against the pillows. Her face was gaunt, and she was sipping through a straw from a carton of fruit juice. Siv took in the Bulldog face scrub, copy of *Canoe and Kayak* magazine, mouth guard and Ian Rankin paperback on what was clearly Henry's bedside cabinet. It was hard, when someone had gone, to see their everyday bits and pieces waiting for them. She knew from experience.

'This is difficult for you, but I need to ask you for more information.'

'I understand.'

'Thank you. First of all, did you hear Damian and Viv come back in the early hours on Tuesday?'

'No. I was asleep.'

'We've been informed that Henry was being made redundant at the end of the month. It's odd that he didn't tell you.'

Saffie froze, the straw in her mouth. Her hand trembled as she put the juice down carefully. 'He was really losing his job?'

'Yes. I can see that you're shocked. Viv said he had worries about his employment.'

'She told me that yesterday. Henry hadn't said anything to me.' She pulled herself up a little. Her voice was quiet. 'He asked me to marry him on Sunday afternoon. We said we'd keep the engagement to ourselves for now and not take the spotlight off Viv and Damian. Why wouldn't he tell me something so important?'

'I've no idea.'

'Did he tell his mother?'

'No.'

'That surprises me.' Saffie shook her head, closed her eyes.

Siv gave her a few moments. She wondered how much Saffie was Henry's trophy, in his life to be paraded about but not really part of it. Perhaps he'd proposed marriage because he was seeking security in another area of his life while his job disappeared.

When Saffie opened her eyes again, Siv continued. 'Can you talk me through your movements from when you got here on Saturday?'

Saffie spoke dully. 'We arrived about half one, and Viv and Damian turned up just gone two. We all went to the beach, had a drink in the Three Swans and we had fish and chips here in the evening and watched films. We all just hung out or sat out on the porch on Sunday morning. I was reading, Henry was on his laptop. Damian and Viv never get up much before eleven. I expect they watched TV in bed. They spend a lot of time doing that. We went to Henry's mum's for lunch. Then Viv and Damian went off in their car. They didn't come back until much later, not long before I headed to bed. They'd been to the cinema.'

'And what did you and Henry do after Sunday lunch?'

'Henry checked out the kayaks he keeps in his mum's garage. Then we walked on the beach and went to a café — that was when he proposed.' She trailed off and took a sip of juice before continuing.

'After that, we came back here. We had a snack and we sat out on the porch for a bit. Henry got a phone call. He said it was about work and went off to deal with something. Then he popped out to have a drink while he was waiting for another call.' She gazed at Siv, her eyes wide, demanding honesty. '*Was* that call about work? Why would he need to deal with work issues if he wasn't going to be there much longer?'

'Good question,' Siv said bluntly. 'Maybe Henry was tidying up things. Did his mood seem different?'

'No.'

'How about Monday?'

'Henry, Viv and Damian went kayaking. That's not my thing, so I walked into town mid-morning, did a bit of window shopping. I bought gloves in Zara. I wandered around the harbour and had a coffee. I came back here and read. The others got back around four-ish. Then, Monday evening, we had a meal at the Three Swans. They carried on, but I kissed Henry and came home because I had a headache.' She started to cry very quietly.

Siv stood, turned away, observing the white spray on the choppy sea.

'Did Henry ever mention a woman called Etta Parton? He went out with her in his teens.'

Saffie wrinkled her brow. 'I don't remember that name.' She fiddled with a tissue. 'He had a thing with Viv at Reading, before she got together with Damian.'

'Were they together long?'

'Not sure.'

Siv showed her a photo of the brochure with the handwriting on her phone.

'I told your DC Hill, that's not Henry's writing. I wish you'd stop asking me the same things, again and again.' She said in a little voice, 'I hate it here. Imelda doesn't like me and the only thing I have in common with Viv and Damian is Henry. I've been out searching and I'll carry on for now, but I want to go home soon. I rang my mum and she wants me to stay with her.'

'Where's that?'

'Acton, West London.'

Siv felt Saffie's pain, but she couldn't agree to anyone leaving the area yet. It bothered her that they'd found no trace of Henry Kilgore. She'd been hoping that the publicity in town would produce results, but to date it had brought no reliable information, just the usual timewasters, cranks and lonely people who wanted a chat. She needed time to compare the details that Damian, Viv and Saffie had given them. 'We'll let you know when you can go back to London,' she said finally.

Siv left the young woman in her room. As she shut the door, she couldn't help but hear Saffie's sobs.

Imelda Kilgore came through the kitchen door as she was putting her coat on.

'I don't suppose there's any news?'

'I'm afraid not.'

Henry's mother looked weary, but her mood was pugnacious. 'How can someone just disappear? There are cameras everywhere these days. Are you checking them all?'

'Where we can. There are none in the residential back streets that Henry took to Mr Greene's.'

Imelda clawed her hair back. 'I hope you're questioning him closely. He's been in prison. He's clearly untrustworthy.'

'I can confirm that we're following up with everyone we need to. We're doing everything we can, I promise you. We've publicised Henry's disappearance widely.'

'The police always sound so reassuring, so why aren't I comforted? Have your people finished with Mallow Cottage yet?'

'No. These things take time. Ms Kilgore, what do you recall about Henry's school friend Etta Parton? She went out with him for a while.'

'Ah, Etta!' Imelda said wistfully. 'She's lovely. So pretty, well-mannered and sensible. Intelligent too. She'd bother to hold a conversation when she came to the house. Her parents were both barristers. I had hoped that she and Henry would stay together, but it didn't last. Henry moped for a while after they finished.'

'Why did they? Was it Etta who ended things?'

'I wasn't told. But what does Etta have to do with anything?'

'Probably of no relevance, Ms Kilgore.' Siv's thoughts went to the abandoned car and the brochure found within. 'Are the brochures for Berminster Breaks widely available?'

'They're in all the holiday lets, and in the library, museum and various shops around town. Anyone can print one from the website as well.'

'Thanks. That's helpful. We'll be in touch.'

The woman didn't reply, just shrugged her jacket off and donned some rubber gloves. She was spraying the cooker hob when Siv left, rubbing it with a cloth as if her life depended on it.

CHAPTER 11

Viv Carpenter needed to go to a chemist, so Siv had arranged to meet her in the harbour café. She was late. Siv sat with her hot chocolate, stirring the froth. She used to come here sometimes, after school and on Saturdays. Then it had a cosy seafaring theme, with fishing nets draped from the ceiling, shells decorating the walls, wooden floorboards and pictures of sailing boats. Rik had pursued her pastime of petty crime in the café. Siv had given it a wide berth after her sister took off without paying a couple of times. Now, there were new owners, who'd gone for a pared-back look of pale pastels, black vinyl flooring, silver spotlights and metal tables and chairs. It felt hygienic but not that comfortable.

'Siv! Siv Drummond! How amazing!'

She looked up, pleased, startled, to see a woman with a mischievous smile and riot of hair the colour of mulled wine standing near her.

'Hope! Hello!'

'Hello yourself.' Hope Merrick balanced her coffee and a bulging leather bag. 'My goodness, where to start! Are you visiting?'

'No, I live here now. Moved back from London.'

'When?'

'Last year.'

'Are you still in the police?'

'That's right. How about you?'

'Social worker. God, it's been how long?'

'Must be fourteen years.' Hope had been a school friend, and the sight of a familiar face was more comforting than she'd expected.

'Well . . . we're a bit older. Are we any wiser?' Hope laughed, a throaty chuckle that Siv remembered well.

Siv grinned in response. 'Probably not.'

'You should have got in touch when you came back to town.'

'You're right. I'm sorry. I've been a bit preoccupied. New job and everything. Lame excuse.'

'Never mind, fate has intervened. And Rik, what's she doing now?'

'Rik's in Auckland. I'm not sure what she does.'

'She was always a riddle hidden in a mystery. Listen, I'm late for a meeting, but I'd love to catch-up.'

'That would be great.'

Hope put her coffee down and fished a card from her pocket. 'That's my work email, contact me there and we can do phone numbers.' She gazed at Siv for a few moments, picked up her coffee, then hurried away.

Siv read the card.

Hope Merrick
Berminster Social Services
Adult Community Care Team

Hope Merrick. They'd been such good friends at school. Correction: Hope was her only real female friend ever. For so long Siv had looked up to and trusted no one but Rik, her big sister and protector. They'd been a tight unit for many years, and Siv had loved, admired and possibly been a little frightened of wayward, difficult Rik. So, when Siv had landed as a newbie at yet another school in mid-term, Hope, with her open and engaging nature, had been hard to resist. They'd had a few adventures together, dating twin brothers at one point, and sneaking out to parties their parents didn't know about. In the summer, they'd swum in the river. It really was good to see her — Siv felt cheered by the encounter. She tucked the card away for safekeeping — she would follow up on that drink with Hope, she'd make sure of it — as she saw Viv arriving.

Viv opted for coffee and a huge cheese scone. She slathered it with creamy, golden butter that was the same colour as her hair. Siv regarded her robust frame and fresh complexion. She was the hearty type who'd have been chosen as team captain in PE lessons.

Siv took her through her itinerary since Saturday. Viv responded easily, without hesitation.

'We had a terrific time kayaking. I really needed the exercise. I wasn't sure that we should leave Saffie on her own for the day, but she doesn't like outdoor stuff so . . .' She crumbled a piece of scone. 'There are times when I struggle to understand why Henry got together with her. I mean, she's not that sociable, whereas he's a party animal, and they don't share many interests.'

Siv decided to keep back the information about Henry's and Saffie's marriage plans. 'Henry might like coming home to peace and quiet, a calm island in the storm of modern life.'

'I suppose.'

'You and Henry were an item at university.'

'Did Saffie tell you that?'

'Yes.'

'No surprises there. She's the type who broods and makes mountains out of molehills. I went out with Henry during the first term. It was lust at first sight, but it didn't last. Soon as I met Damian, I knew he was the one.'

'The prior relationship never causes any discomfort?'

'No. Why should it? These things happen.'

Siv found that a tad blasé but let it pass. 'You met Henry when he was fresh from school. Did he talk to you about his friends here in town? We've asked you about Eugene Warren before, but are you sure you'd not heard of him?'

'We did a bit of that background stuff when we got together. I've been trying to remember. To be fair, we mostly had a lot of sex and didn't do that much talking. Hope that doesn't shock you.'

'I could tell you a few stories about police college. Anything about Henry and his life is helpful.'

'He *may* have mentioned Eugene when we first met. He said someone had gone a bit weird and fallen off the radar. I honestly can't be certain it was this Eugene guy, though. Henry definitely did drugs as a teenager, because he said he'd had to wean himself off them. He realised that he had an addictive personality, and he was determined to try and limit his dependency on alcohol. He was clean when I met him — as far as I could tell.'

'What types of drugs did he take?'

'No idea. I've always been terrified of them, so I didn't ask.'

'Henry was informed last week that he'd be made redundant at the end of the month.'

'Yeah, Damo said your sergeant had told him. That's hard.' Viv bit her lip. 'It probably didn't come as a surprise, though. D'you think he's gone off somewhere to lick his wounds?'

'Would that be like him?'

'Hard to say. Thing is, Henry's always been successful, so I've never seen him deal with something like this. He's a buoyant, glass-half-full type, though. Usually, anyway. Maybe coming back here affected him.'

'In what way?'

Viv chased melting butter around her plate with the last wedge of scone. 'It's a lovely town and it must have been a great place to grow up, but after living in London, it's sort of slow and provincial. It can be difficult, returning to the place where you were young. I grew up in Leicester and when I visit, it reminds me mainly of my teenage dissatisfaction and heartbreak. After a day or two, I'm ready to leave. Did you grow up here?'

'I moved here when I was a teenager. It was something of a haven for me.'

'Sorry, I didn't mean to be rude about your hometown.' Viv smiled the cheerful smile of a person who doesn't really believe they've given offence. 'I reckon Henry has the best of both worlds, with London as his base and free accommodation by the sea a couple of hours' drive away.'

This conversation was frustrating. It wasn't leading anywhere. They knew all this, and it wasn't getting them any closer to finding Henry, Siv thought. She finished her coffee. 'Picture Henry as he walked away from you on Monday night. Did he seem his usual self?'

Viv narrowed her eyes. 'Absolutely,' she said firmly. 'Just merry with booze, that's all.'

This is pointless. Siv gave up. She left Viv buying postcards in the newsagent's next to the café.

* * *

When she entered the station later, the constable on the duty desk beckoned her over with an embarrassed grin.

'Guv, there's a girl asking to see you. Came in about ten minutes ago, insisting that she wants to speak to the lead detective about the missing man. Very cocky. Ali and Patrick are both out. She says she saw a poster about Henry Kilgore and she might have vital information. Her name's Fern Quinn.'

At last, something from the publicity drive. Siv glanced over at a girl, aged about eleven, sitting in the waiting area. She wore a black skirt, white shirt, ankle socks, cheap slip-on shoes and a school blazer that was too big. A hand-me-down from an older sibling, Siv guessed. The girl was eating a massive sausage roll, spraying flakes of puff pastry, while reading a magazine.

Siv walked over, sat down beside the girl. She smelled of cheap soap. The slivers of pastry on the surrounding floor resembled a scattering of dry skin. Her magazine, *Kookie*, was open at an article on supernovae. Siv was impressed.

'Hi, Fern. I'm DI Siv Drummond. How can I help you?'

Fern put the half-eaten roll in a paper bag. 'You the boss on the Kilgore case?'

'That's right.'

Fern had the blurry features and pimply skin of adolescence, but her narrow eyes were shrewd, and she had a calculating manner. 'I want to go somewhere private, not out here. Haven't you got interview rooms where you're supposed to take witnesses? Like, procedures you're supposed to follow.'

Siv kept a straight face. 'Shouldn't you be at school?'

'Lunch break,' Fern said. 'I'm entitled.'

'I see. Well, come through and I'll see if there's an interview room.'

Siv led Fern into an empty one. She grimaced at the grubby chairs and cup rings on the table.

'It pongs in here. You don't make much of an effort for the public,' she said.

'You're right. Tight budgets, Fern.'

'Don't I get a cup of tea or a Coke?'

'Let's see how we go. Have a seat. I hear you have vital information.'

Fern hugged her rucksack against her chest. It was blue with stick-on rainbows and silver unicorns. Some of the unicorns were jumping over the rainbows. 'I won't bother saying if you're going to be sarky.'

Siv regrouped, softening her voice slightly. 'Fern, have you got something to tell me?'

'I saw a picture of that man who went missing. Kilgore.'

'Right. Is it about him?'

'Yeah. I saw cops poking around Larch Dell. Thing is, I saw a man there.' She took a tube of Smarties from a side pocket of her rucksack, tipped one out and popped it in her mouth. She offered the tube to Siv.

'Thanks.' Siv took a red one. 'I used to use these as pretend lipstick.' The girl seemed unimpressed. 'When did you see this man?'

Fern gave her a stony stare. 'Shouldn't you be taking notes, or recording me? I'm serious *and* I've given up my lunch break.'

'I appreciate that. I've got pretty good recall, so this will be OK for now. Tell me about the man.'

Fern nestled back in the seat and crossed her ankles. 'I live opposite Larch Dell, though Mum says it should be renamed "Condom Dell".' She sniggered. 'Anyway, Monday night, I woke up. There're cats around our way who scrap and yowl. Bloody awful racket. They're territorial, so they're defending their ground. I looked out of my window and I saw a man just by the park railings, on the pavement. He was on his phone.' She popped another Smartie.

'What time was that?'

'Ten fifty-five. I checked my clock when I got up.'

'Can you describe him?'

Fern gave a sly grin. 'I can do better than that. I took a photo of him. I take loads of photos of people when they're unaware. It's my thing. I'm an observer. I catch the unguarded moment.'

I'm sure you do. Siv was beginning to like this girl. 'Can I see this photo?'

'Sure. But can I have a Coke first? I bet you've got a machine here. I *have* given you a Smartie.'

Siv got up. 'I'll see what I can do. Don't move.'

When she returned with the frosty can from the machine, Fern was scrolling through her phone. She flicked the can open, took a deep gulp and then showed Siv the screen. It was Henry Kilgore, leaning with his back to the railings, his phone pressed to his ear. Siv sent the photo to herself.

'Thanks, Fern. That's very helpful. Did you see where the man went when he finished the call?'

'Yep. I waited and watched. I'm patient like that. I reckoned he might be suspicious, hanging around late at night. He went towards town.'

'I'm glad that you're so observant.'

Fern burped loudly. 'It's him, isn't it? Kilgore. Does my photo give you a lead?'

'It helps place him on that night and adds to our information.'

'Will you find him?'

'I hope so, but these things can be complicated. You'd better get back to school now.'

Fern glanced at her watch. 'Helping you with your enquiries has made me late. Can I have a lift?'

Siv laughed. This girl reminded her of Rik — sassy. 'You don't take any prisoners, do you?'

Fern smiled with satisfaction. 'Not if I can help it.'

'Come with me and I'll see what we can do. By the way, be careful of taking random photos. Some people might not appreciate it.'

Fern hoisted her rucksack. 'I'm covert ops. They never know.'

Siv was relieved to see Patrick coming through the door as she led Fern back.

'DC Hill, just the man! Can you take Fern back to school? She's given us some very useful information. In fact, you could mention it on your Twitter feed.'

'Sure.'

'Will you flash a blue light?' Fern asked with glee.

'He might, if you give him a Smartie,' Siv said.

* * *

After a little research, Siv was able to pin down Etta Parton, who was now a lecturer in computer science at Oxford University. Siv got through to her college with surprising ease and explained the reason for her call.

'I understand that you went out with Henry Kilgore for a while.'

'That's right. It seems like another lifetime. I'm terribly sorry to hear about him, and about Eugene's death. How can I help?'

'Was there any trouble between Henry and Eugene back then?'

Etta had a robust voice and spoke deliberately. 'I can't recall anything like that. They hung around together a lot, sparked off each other. Egged each other on, the way boys do. I wasn't keen on Eugene, he was reckless. He'd urge Henry to drive too fast. He went out with Teagan Grenville. I didn't have much in common with her. We did stuff occasionally as a foursome, but I wasn't keen on the company.'

'How do you mean?'

A pause. 'I suppose I found them a bit silly. Teagan wasn't that bright. Henry was fun and witty, but I lost interest in larking around. Eugene was keen on hanging out in the cemetery late at night, with Henry and lots of alcohol. He used to say, "Let's have a grave party." Thought it was exciting and illicit. He and Teagan used to climb over the gate, and I imagine they had sex. Henry drove us there one night, but I refused to join them and I made him take me home after the other two had climbed in. It was just distasteful.'

Siv was glad that Etta couldn't see her down the phone because she had the biggest grin on her face. Finally, they were getting somewhere — a connection between Eugene Warren and the cemetery, and one that suggested behaviour that might have angered or disgusted someone. This was music to her ears. 'Which gate do you mean?'

'It wasn't high, and a narrow road ran alongside. Sorry, I can't remember its name, but I know it joined the coast road further on because I lived that way.'

Barker's Way. Siv liked it when a piece of the jigsaw fit. 'Is that why you stopped seeing Henry, because of the cemetery stuff?'

'One of the reasons. I wasn't that into drinking and, as I said, it all seemed a bit infantile to me. They never offered me drugs, but I suspected they took them, and I didn't want to get involved in illegal stuff. Let's say Henry's gloss wore off rather quickly. We ran out of things to talk about. That sounds like something middle-aged people experience, but it's just how it was.'

'Have you had contact with any of these old friends since?'

'No. I got a place at Oxford and I stayed here. My parents moved away so I've had no reason to return to Berminster.'

'Henry had a friend called Bertie Greene. Was he involved in messing around in the cemetery?'

'I can only remember him vaguely. I couldn't say.'

Siv didn't think Etta was a likely suspect, but she asked anyway. 'Where were you on Monday night and early Tuesday?'

'At home with my partner. I do have a lecture scheduled, if that's all.'

Siv said goodbye and saw that she'd had an email from one of the constables who'd found the abandoned car.

The Vauxhall found by Mallow Cottage was previously owned by Ms Jill Winstanley. Aged 78, living in Walthamstow in London. She doesn't have a mobile or Wi-Fi, so I couldn't send her a photo of Warren, but from the description I gave her, she confirmed that she sold the car to him last February for cash, £450. She gave him all the documents because he said he'd see to the legal stuff and she wasn't sure what it entailed. She has no idea where he lived, but he answered an ad she'd put in the corner shop, the Short Stop. (Didn't think anyone still did that!) She commented that Warren was shabby and that he had an 'adorable little doggy' with him. She left nothing in the car and had no knowledge of Berminster Breaks, let alone why there would be a brochure for them in the car.

The Vauxhall shows up on ANPR on the motorway from London at 20.30 on Monday night and on the ring road approaching town at 22.30.

Siv glanced through her office window and saw that Ali wasn't at his desk. She forwarded the email to him with a message.

Warren saw an ad in a corner shop, which suggests that he must have some connection to that area of London. Can you contact the shop? See if anyone recognises him. I'm off to talk to Teagan Grenville about 'grave parties'. I'll explain later.

She phoned Teagan Grenville and discovered that it was her day off. She was at the Body and Soul Health Spa, having a pamper experience. Siv told her that she needed to talk and that she'd meet her in the reception area in twenty minutes. When Teagan began to protest, she hung up.

CHAPTER 12

The spa was nearby, on the far side of the harbour, so Siv walked there. The afternoon had turned bitterly cold, the light opaque. The water in the harbour was rough, slapping the sides of moored boats. Seagulls rode the rolling wash and grey plumed knots waded in the shallows by the slipway. She paused and watched the stocky birds, their feathers rippling in the wind. The story was that they were named after King Canute, because they moved back from the incoming tide, just as he had. The more prosaic explanation was that they were called knot because the onomatopoeic name referred to their call.

She headed on, skirting the block of flats where Mutsi had been living until now, keeping wary eyes open. One of the few compensations of her mother's move to Mortimer's house some miles away was that the centre of town would be safer.

Warm air hit her when she entered the spa and she unwound her scarf. A woman in a fluffy white robe, matching turban and mules was seated in the empty reception area by an array of potted plants, flicking through a glossy magazine. Her face was painted with a dark grey facemask.

'Ms Grenville? I'm DI Drummond.' Siv took a seat beside her.

'I resent this, Inspector. It's my precious day off work and I've paid a lot for my visit here. I had to hurry my balancing facial.' She spoke tightly through the constricting drying mask, barely able to move her lips.

'It might be easier if you washed the mask off,' Siv suggested.

'No thanks. It's bamboo charcoal, costs forty pounds. Has to stay on for half an hour to cleanse impurities.'

'I'll try to make this quick then. It's about Eugene Warren and Henry Kilgore.'

'That's what I expected.' Clearly, seeing her protest at being disturbed falling flat, Teagan had decided to treat the visit as a girly chat. 'Those two! They used to be a right pair. Funny how I didn't see Eugene for the flake he was. There was something about him that I found irresistible.'

Although it pained her greatly, Siv mimicked the bonhomie. 'We're all a bit mad when we're teenagers. I was, and my sister too. When you went out with Eugene, did you spend time in the grounds at the cemetery?'

Teagan sighed. 'Yep. Now and then. It was Eugene's daft idea.'

'I understand that he called your visits "grave parties". What did you do there?'

Teagan glanced around and tucked in the neck of her robe. 'Drank too much. Messed about.'

'Do you mean you had sex there?'

'For goodness' sake! Can't you lower your voice?'

'I have. There's no one listening. The woman on the desk is on the phone.' She pressed on, as if daring Teagan to tell her. 'So, did you?'

A hiss. 'Yes.'

Siv imagined her blushing under the mask. 'Was this at night? How did you get in?'

'When it was dark. Climbed over the gate at Barker's Way.'

'Where did you mess about exactly?'

'In the old bit of the cemetery. The mouldy graves. Eugene liked the spookiness. He chose neglected ones that had fallen in a bit. I just went along with him. It wasn't that often. It was bloody uncomfortable and there were insects.' She shivered. 'I hate anything crawling on my skin.'

'And drugs — they were involved?'

Teagan mouthed, 'Eugene always had some dope. We smoked a bit.'

'Did Henry Kilgore join you?'

She looked away, fidgeting with her sleeve. Her lips were bright pink against the dark mask. 'We went there in his car. He just drank and shared joints with us. There weren't any, like, *threesomes* or anything weird.'

Nothing weird at all about having sex in a graveyard, Siv thought sardonically.

Gosh, it was hot. She was overheating. She unbuttoned her coat and slipped it off. 'Might Henry have taken girlfriends there? He wanted Etta Parton to join you, but she refused, right?'

'Etta rated herself far too classy,' Teagan said spitefully. But Siv judged that she was wishing she'd been choosier herself.

'How about Bertie Greene, did he go there?'

'He might have.'

'Didn't it strike you as odd that Eugene's body was left at the crematorium, given your teenage exploits around there?'

Teagan stared at her blankly. 'No. I'd forgotten about all that until you just brought it up.' She touched her chin lightly with a finger, testing the mask. 'Eugene might have taken that other girl there.'

'What other girl?'

'The one he was two-timing me with, so I dumped him.'

Siv recalled Patrick's report. 'Your brother saw Eugene with her, right?'

'Yeah. On the beach.'

'I need to contact him. Can you give me his details?'

Teagan rolled her eyes. 'Gray's a fire safety consultant. He travels a lot, so email's probably best.' She gave Siv a phone number and email address. 'This mask needs to come off now. I want clean skin, not dehydrated.'

Teagan almost ran from the area. Siv called Gray Grenville, but his phone wouldn't take a message, so she sent him an email asking him if he recalled the name of the girl he'd seen with Eugene Warren on the beach.

The heat was draining her. She undid one button on her shirt, picked up a leaflet and read that for a hundred pounds, she could have a complimentary glass of Prosecco and a cream tea, partnered with either a body scrub and facial or a neck massage and manicure. *I'd rather use you as a fan.* She used the leaflet to waft air towards her. A small group of laughing women exited from the inner sanctum of the spa, bright-eyed and glowing. Siv wondered if a day here might work similar magic on her. It was doubtful.

* * *

Teagan lay with her eyes closed while the beautician removed her mask. Soothing panpipes played in the background, but Teagan wasn't calmed by either the music or the gentle ministrations to her skin. That inspector had thoroughly spoiled her day.

Teagan didn't care to dwell on difficult things and liked to put the past firmly behind her. She'd been uncomfortable when Henry had called by before Christmas. He'd seemed moody. Over coffee, he'd started talking about Eugene and things that had happened when they were at school, but Teagan didn't want to be reminded. The past should stay there. Buried.

Back then, she'd known of Eugene's bad reputation, but found him fascinating and got a kick out of being around him. Afterwards, she'd regretted ever getting mixed up with him and particularly sharing family details. He'd been amused when she'd described how she loved to snoop on people. He'd encouraged her habit, and it had seemed funny at the time. Evenings with him had been alive, colourful, never a dull moment, but the day Gray came home and told her he'd seen Eugene with another girl, she'd been humiliated, even though part of her had expected it would happen at some point.

She was still insatiably curious and a snooper. She went through her husband's emails and social media regularly. He watched porn, but that didn't bother her too much. Her mum had always told her you had to cut a man some slack. The way she saw it, if he was getting his extra kicks — because there was nothing wrong with their sex life, that's for sure — from a screen, he was less likely to screw some other girl in real life! If anyone left their phone unsecured and lying around at work, she peeked. Sue in Bedding had had an abortion, Tom in Luggage had regular dates via Grindr and Mr Vernay, the general manager, was a regular punter on betting sites. Even here, Teagan had squinted at the beautician's phone when she'd popped out of the room and read a text from someone called Baz, arranging to meet at a bar later. She'd examined her brother's diary, when they'd lived at home, and read all about his erotic dreams and masturbatory habits until he'd put a lock on his bedroom door to keep her out. Left alone in anyone's house, she'd rake quickly through drawers and shelves. Sometimes, she wondered if this compulsion to pry was a kind of illness, an addiction, maybe. Certainly, it brought her a rush of pleasure and excitement like no other.

However, now and again, the past did intrude, refusing to be put back in its box. She wished she'd never pulled that suitcase out from under her parents' bed and gone through her dad's things. She saw herself now as a teenager, kneeling on the carpet in her parents' bedroom, holding her breath and listening out for a tread on the stairs. At the time, she'd seen her action as clever. If only she'd put the letter back and not mentioned it, but she'd been high on the thrill, too full of the buzz, to stop herself.

She regretted that business with the suitcase because it had caused disruption in her family and made her own life uncomfortable. But right now, she was worried about what Henry had said when they'd met in November, and what might have happened to him. It had sounded as if Eugene was stirring things up, dredging up buried secrets. She didn't want any part of it. It had always been stimulating to explore other people's private business, but only for pleasure and the adrenalin rush. This was too much like discomfort.

Teagan could already feel her muscles tensing at the thoughts. She tried to breathe evenly and relax while fingers lightly moisturised her face. She wanted her forty quid's worth.

* * *

The head teacher at the primary school where Tara Warren taught had told her that she could take time off work if she needed, but she'd said she was OK and preferred to be at school. She tidied up the classroom after the children had gone home and neatened the bookshelves. Then she switched off the lights, took a battery lamp from her locked drawer and sat at her desk in its dim glow. It had been her Secret Santa present — a little brown china mouse held the bulb in outstretched paws.

Tara could tell that the head had given the kids her confidential chat about being caring and kind because someone has died. They were being unusually quiet and watchful. One of the children had said to her solemnly, 'I'm sorry about your brother, Miss. That's ever so sad for you.' She'd said thank you and accepted the sympathy card featuring stars in a night sky. If she was honest — as you were supposed to be with children, especially when death was involved — she'd have told her class that she wasn't particularly sad, her main emotion bitterness.

Tara's family life had been joyful and easy until her little brother turned fourteen and discovered drugs and alcohol. She'd liked being the big sister who he'd confided in and asked to string his conkers every autumn. She'd taught him how to tell the time, tie his laces and roller skate. Then, overnight, it was as if someone had thrown a switch. She'd been confused and stunned by his alteration from a cheery, cheeky but loveable kid into a sly, objectionable one. She'd heard all about his exploits from friends: the pilfering, the rows and foul language, his boasting that he'd spread chlamydia around town, the trail of girls he'd worked through. At least one girl had had an abortion without telling her parents. There'd probably been others. Tara's parents had aged before her eyes, worn down with worry, and yet Tara was just grateful that they'd never known the half of it. They never seemed to realise that she worried too, that she missed him and was embarrassed by his antics. They'd hardly noticed her after Eugene turned feral, and once he took off, she might as well have vanished with him for all the attention they'd paid her. She'd been relieved when he'd gone and hoped he'd never return. He'd ruined everything, and now she had to deal with the aftermath of his death, all on her own.

She stroked the little mouse's head. Eugene's death had brought back memories of the trouble he'd caused, the people he'd angered. Stuff she'd been glad to put behind her. Should she tell the police some of the things she'd recalled? Would it help them solve the case? Deep down, part of her wasn't sure she wanted to know what had happened to her brother, because it would bring everything back. It would make it real and *present* again. She wasn't sure if she could bear that.

* * *

The heating in the station had failed (again) and wouldn't be back on until the next morning. The temperature had dropped fast, and they all huddled in their coats for a quick early evening catch-up. Patrick wore a bomber hat with long faux-fur earflaps. He complained that his ears tingled in cold weather.

Just as they were about to start, Ali put down the water he was drinking and decided he needed the loo.

'Didn't your mum ever tell you to go before you went into class?' Siv asked. Her tone was light, but she was keen to get on and annoyed at the interruption.

'I've been thirsty. What goes in has to come out.' He pulled a face and rushed off.

When he reappeared, Patrick laughed, 'We'll have to get you a catheter at this rate, mate.'

'Yeah, yeah. Feel free to have fun at my expense,' Ali grumbled.

Siv went through the information she'd collected. 'Henry Kilgore appears to have been diverted from his visit to Bertie Greene by a phone call which he took at Larch Dell just before 11 p.m. Possibly a call from Eugene Warren or his killer. The abandoned Vauxhall at Mallow Cottage was Warren's. ANPR shows that he arrived in town around ten thirty on Monday night. Forensics have confirmed that his prints were on the steering wheel and all over the car. They've also reported that strands of fibre on the outside of Emmeline's Gate came from the jacket he was wearing when the body was found, as did some found in the wheelbarrow. Several of his hairs were in the barrow too, so that's how his body was moved to the steps. However, the only fingerprints on the wheelbarrow were Smeaton's and Robbins's.'

'Why bother putting the barrow back in the shed?' Ali asked. He yawned, rubbed his eyes.

'It was on the route back to the gate anyway,' Patrick said. 'A tidy- minded killer, maybe.'

'Or a killer with a tongue-in-cheek sense of humour who wanted to make life difficult for us,' Siv told them. 'Perhaps someone we've banged up in the past, or who has some other axe to grind. That would give us a wide selection.'

Siv checked her notes. 'What else have I got . . . Teagan Grenville owned up that she and Warren used to have sex in the cemetery, so it's likely that he took other girls there, and maybe Kilgore did too. I'm waiting to hear from Teagan's brother about the identity of the girl he saw with Warren on the beach back when they were teenagers, in case she's a lead. I also rang Bertie Greene. He denied ever attending "grave parties" in the cemetery. He emphasised that he didn't spend much time with Warren, but after his performance when we interviewed him, I'm not sure I believe him.'

Ali tightened his scarf. 'I spoke to Mr Kalnina, the owner of the Short Stop in Walthamstow. He was vague until I sent him a photo of Warren. Then he said he was an occasional customer, but he couldn't tell me anything else about him. Nobody's reported Warren as missing so far, so he might have lived alone. It also seems as if he lived off grid. I can't track him. But I'll keep on it.

'Techies also reported back on Kilgore's laptop, and I've searched through his emails and history. Nothing to flag. There was a work email, confirming his redundancy and asking him to contact HR. No emails featuring Warren or anyone else in Berminster in recent months.'

'Patrick, your turn,' Siv said.

'Guv. None of the crem staff have any form. Most have corroborated alibis for Monday night, except Robbins and Smeaton. Regarding other alibis, Bertie Greene claims that he went to bed, but he could have risked leaving his kids alone if he needed to commit murder. Tara Warren was at home alone preparing lessons. She didn't recognise the writing on the brochure, but then said she couldn't recall what her brother's was like. I've collected handwriting samples and none match the brochure. I contacted all florists in the area and none of them supplied the wreaths that were on our corpse. They all pointed out — a bit sniffily, I might add — that these days you can get wreaths online, including on Amazon.'

Siv rubbed the end of her nose to warm it. 'The three at Driftwood and Imelda Kilgore have accounted for where they were on Monday night, but it's possible that any of them could have been out and about after midnight. For now, though, I can't see that any of them had a motive for murder or making Kilgore vanish. Viv and Kilgore had a thing at uni, but that's been over for a long time. Warren hasn't featured in any of their lives, as far as I can make out.'

‘And where *is* Henry Kilgore?’ Ali asked.

‘It’s worrying,’ Siv sighed. ‘Let’s face it, the likelihood now is that he’s dead. Unless he’s out at sea, it’s strange that no one’s found his body. I saw the volunteers on TV, scouring the beach and the headland. I don’t think we’ve missed any tricks, but feel free if you can come up with any avenue we haven’t tried.’

They fell silent. The building was still. Most staff had gone home.

‘Right, no point in us getting frostbite.’ Siv pushed her chilled hands up her sleeves. She still hadn’t picked up her gloves from the cemetery. ‘Patrick, can you firm up all alibis? Etta Parton has one for Monday night that you need to check. The SOCOs have finished at the crem now. We should have results from Mallow Cottage tomorrow. Ali, please chase those first thing in the morning.’

Patrick hurried away. Ali was rummaging on his desk when Siv’s phone rang. She listened carefully and turned to him as she ended the call. ‘Are you due at home or do you fancy a drink on the way?’

He looked stunned. It was well established that Siv didn’t do random socialising. But he was about to be sorely disappointed. ‘I can spare half an hour,’ he said, perhaps too eagerly.

‘Good, because that was a bar worker at the Three Swans. She said that Henry Kilgore was in there one lunchtime with a woman about two weeks ago. We need to have a chat with her.’

* * *

The bar worker was called Rina and she was tiny, with a bubbly personality. She sipped a slimline tonic while Siv and Ali drank red wine. He’d bought pork scratchings and munched his way through the pack. The Three Swans had a thatched roof and etched windows but had been modernised inside and now styled itself as a gastropub. The three of them sat in an empty, narrow back room with an open fire. It had been done out as a library, with wing-back chairs and shelves of books. Siv's heart sank when she realised that most of the books were fake, with titles such as *The Insurmountable Problem* by Major Setback and *The Arctic Ocean* by IC Waters.

She showed Rina a photo of Kilgore and she confirmed that she recognised him.

'Yeah, I remember him,' she told them. 'He sat at the table just inside the door and the woman he was with sat opposite. They had mezze platters. I served them, and when I brought the order through, the woman pointed out that the falafel were missing. I had to apologise and fetch them. When I saw his photo on the news, I remembered him. He left a generous tip — despite the falafel mix-up.'

Siv loved a witness like Rina — sharp, straightforward, with good recall. 'What day was this?'

'It was my second day working here, a fortnight ago on a Wednesday. I checked the calendar before you arrived.'

'Did you recognise the woman? Can you describe her?'

'No. That's the only time I've seen her. She was thirties, brown hair, nice figure. She was confident, like someone used to getting what she wanted. Polite, though.'

'Did you hear what they were discussing?'

'Sorry, no. It was busy and I was still getting my head round the routines, so I was trying to focus.'

Siv tilted her glass at Ali. He was turned towards the fire and staring into it with his legs stretched out, as if he was at home, but she sensed that he was attentive. He straightened up and put his glass on the table.

'What impression did you get of them, Rina? Friends?' he said.

'Not sure. The woman was all business, in a sharp suit. Mr Kilgore was more casually dressed. Jeans, although smart ones, and a shirt and tie. They got along OK. She was laughing when I brought them coffee.'

'How long were they here?'

'I'd say about an hour.'

'Who paid?'

'She did. Cash. But I saw him put the tip on the table.'

'They left at the same time?'

'I can't be sure. Like I said, it was busy. She had big teeth, big and white, like all the celebs in Hollywood, you know?' She swirled her tonic water and said as an afterthought, 'I saw Mr Kilgore on Monday night as well, in the main lounge, with a man and a woman. Not the same woman as at lunch.'

Siv nodded. 'Henry was in here on Monday night, with friends.'

'Didn't look that friendly to me,' Rina sniffed.

This was news to them. 'What do you mean?' Siv probed.

'The woman must have gone to the loo or something, but he was arguing with the man. They didn't raise their voices, but I heard the other man telling Mr Kilgore that he could be a slimy bastard and to keep his hands to himself. He was rapping on the table.' She demonstrated with a pointed finger.

'I see. Did you hear anything else?'

'No, that was all.'

Rina went back to the bar when they'd finished. Ali emptied the last morsels of scratchings into his hand and popped them in his mouth. He took great care in dusting his coat off once he'd screwed up the packet.

Siv said, 'Removing any evidence in case Polly notices you've strayed from the dietary straight and narrow?'

He nodded guiltily. 'Although I don't know why — not much gets past her, no matter how hard I try. Rina's a goldmine, isn't she, guv? Interesting that no one's mentioned that Kilgore was here in town two weeks ago.'

'Presumably, no one knew. I'll check with his mother and Saffie. The way Rina described the meeting it doesn't sound like a romantic tryst, but Kilgore could've been having an affair. Maybe that's the case and he got found out.'

'A jealous husband went after him?' Ali didn't sound convinced.

'It's worth looking into. What was Kilgore up to? We need to find this woman with the Hollywood-style teeth.

Saul Robbins said that the woman in the cemetery who asked about the wheelbarrow was dark and in her thirties.'

'Plenty of women fit that description. You do. Maybe it was a meeting about a job. Kilgore could have been making enquiries.'

'Coming back to Berminster after his high-flying life in the big smoke? I doubt it. But I wonder what he and Kyalo were arguing about on Monday?'

Ali yawned and said reluctantly, 'D'you want to ask Kyalo tonight?'

She glanced at her weary sergeant. He looked done in. 'It'll keep until tomorrow. We'll get him into the station.'

'OK. I'd better head home. Are you coming?'

'I'll stay a bit.'

Siv savoured the last of her wine. She was tired. The deep, padded chair, the soothing Malbec, the glowing fire; she could happily fall asleep. Tomorrow, they needed to talk to Damian Kyalo, Viv Carpenter and Tara Warren again. She'd given a sketchy account of a wayward brother and she must know more about what he'd got up to. Even if siblings weren't close, they had a way of absorbing information about each other. A sort of osmosis.

She roused herself and rang Damian. His phone went to voicemail, as did Viv's. Siv left a curt message on his, asking them both to be at the station at nine in the morning. They could worry about the reason for the summons overnight. Then she called Imelda Kilgore. While she waited for the woman to answer, she found a stray crumb of pork scratching and threw it into the fire, where it flared. That said it all. How could Ali eat those things? Imelda said that she had no knowledge of her son visiting town earlier in the month. She added stoutly that the inspector must be mistaken, because he'd never have come to Berminster without telling her. There were traffic noises, the blare of a car horn.

'Just a minute, there's a bus going past,' she said.

'Sorry to have disturbed you when you're out.'

'I always hope it will be good news, but it never is. I'm walking the streets with Saffie, searching for Henry. The volunteers have finished for the night now. There's so much goodwill from people. If only that alone could bring Henry back. It's better to be active than sit at home moping, and we might find out something here in the town centre. Better than what you lot are doing anyway.'

Siv was surprised at the unlikely alliance. Desperation forged strange bonds. She ignored Imelda's jibe, knowing from her own experience how sharp grief can make you. 'Can I speak to Saffie, as she's with you?'

When Saffie came on the line she said, 'Did Henry mention that he was visiting Berminster two weeks ago, on a Wednesday?'

Saffie sounded lethargic. 'No. Why?'

'Someone says that they saw him in town. Could he have been here on business?'

'I suppose. He'd have mentioned it, surely?'

Yes, like he mentioned losing his job. 'Did he stay away from home any nights this month?'

'No. He was late some nights, but that was usual. I don't understand. Who says they saw him?'

'Someone in town. His mum wasn't aware of his visit either.'

'It can't have been Henry, then. He'd never come back here without calling on her. I keep expecting to see him in the street, but, of course, I don't.'

Siv left it there and finished her wine. She was sorry for Imelda and Saffie, traipsing around the chilly streets, uneasy in each other's company, trying to maintain hope. Henry Kilgore had been holding his cards close to his chest, compartmentalising information and keeping secrets. He'd deceived the two closest women in his life, but for what reason?

CHAPTER 13

Siv was waiting by the reception desk when Viv hurried into the station at 9.15 a.m., hand in hand with Damian. They were both out of breath. She didn't invite them to sit down.

The reception area was empty, so she asked immediately, 'Were either of you aware that Henry was in Berminster two weeks ago, Wednesday, lunching with a woman in the Three Swans?'

They looked clueless and said they knew nothing about that.

'Is that what you dragged us here for at this hour?' Damian asked.

'Partly.'

Siv told Viv to wait in reception.

'Why can't I come with Damian?'

'Because I want to check something with him, then I'll speak to you.'

'But—'

'Stay here, please. Shouldn't be long.'

Viv's posture slouched, and she went to sit on one of the hard, plastic seats.

Siv took Damian to an interview room. 'I said nine o'clock, Mr Kyalo.'

'We overslept, haven't even had breakfast.' He lifted his glasses and rubbed sleep from the corners of his eyes. 'Got any coffee? I'm not really awake yet.'

'No. Tell me again about Monday night in the Three Swans, when you were with Viv and Henry.'

'Tell you what? We were drinking and chatting.'

'Did you and Henry argue?'

'No.'

'A witness says that you did, when Viv may have been in the loo.'

Damian shook his head. 'Don't remember that. Mind you, we were pretty pissed, especially Henry.'

'The witness said that you appeared angry. They heard you call Henry a "slimy bastard", and you told him to "keep his hands to himself". Why would you have been saying that to him? Had he been hitting on Viv, wanting to revisit an old flame?'

'No way! You've got that all wrong.'

Siv studied him. His voice trembled, the lie not quite working. 'What was it about, then?'

Damian scratched his stubbly chin and relented. 'I wasn't angry, just a bit annoyed at him. He started going on about some hot woman at work, and I didn't want to hear it. He's got Saffie. He needs to behave. I told him that as well.'

'Did Henry mention this woman's name?'

'Nah. He changed the subject when I told him off. Then Viv came back, so we left it.' He grew truculent. 'Is this what you're asking Viv about as well? I don't want you upsetting her.'

'I'm sure she'll tell you what we've spoken about afterwards. Is there anything you want to change regarding your statement of what you did and where you went on Monday night?'

'It happened just like we told you. God, you do harp on.'

'Mind your attitude,' Siv bit back.

She led him back to reception and watched Viv leap up and kiss him as if he'd been released from years in incarceration.

'There's a machine over there with coffee,' Siv told him.

'That'll be crap,' he whined.

'Suit yourself.'

In the interview room, Viv sat in the chair he'd just vacated, took off her white furry hat, then tucked her hands into it, like a muff. She looked flushed and anxious. 'What's this about?'

Siv talked her through the argument between the men in the Three Swans. 'Were you aware that they'd had a disagreement?'

'No.'

'You didn't sense an atmosphere when you came back to the table?'

'They seemed fine. Who told you that they were arguing?'

Siv sat back and folded her arms, pausing for a moment. 'Were you and Henry having an affair?'

'No! Absolutely not!' She'd turned a deep shade of scarlet.

Siv gauged Viv and Damian wouldn't have had a chance to discuss their reactions. Viv was probably feeling guilty. Time to push.

She adopted a chatty tone. 'You're getting married, Henry was building up to proposing to Saffie — which he did on Sunday, and she accepted, by the way. Sometimes, people revisit old flames before a wedding — last-hurrah territory.'

It had happened to her before she'd met Ed. A man she'd gone out with briefly and hadn't seen for over a year had turned up at her flat one night with a bottle of wine, expecting a fling before his nuptials. He was sorely disappointed.

Viv had gone quiet. She was twisting her hands inside her hat. It was like a fluffy, snow-white kitten on her lap.

She said, 'I didn't know Henry and Saffie had got engaged.'

'They were keeping it under wraps so they didn't crowd your moment. Aren't you pleased for them?'

'Course, yes!'

Siv wasn't so sure. '*Was* there a last hurrah? Perhaps you're one of those people who quite like keeping a previous lover onside — having your cake and eating it too. It would add a certain frisson to life, no? From what I've heard about Henry, he's fun and charismatic, whereas Damian strikes me as a bit of a whinger. You spend most of your time mothering him.'

Viv flinched. 'That's really rude. You've no right to say that.'

'Oh, come on, Viv. I'm right, aren't I? I get it. You told me that you and Henry had been passionate at uni. More sex than chat. Maybe Saffie's more . . . *sedate*. Maybe Damian is too. Not my business. But solving crime is. I'm not judging you, as long as you haven't killed anyone. Have you or Damian killed anyone?'

'No.' Viv sighed and wriggled.

'If you tell me the truth, I can get on with my job. This is time-wasting for me. We've got teams of police colleagues and volunteers combing this area, but every passing day the clock ticks against Henry's chances of being found alive.'

Viv peeked up under her lashes. 'Will we get into trouble for not being truthful?'

'No. I can't be bothered.' Siv sat back in feigned weariness.

'*Please, please*, say you won't tell Imelda or Saffie!'

'Yes, fine.' She waved her hand vaguely.

Viv did a bit more hat wringing. 'OK. Henry came round to our place one night just after Christmas. Damian was out. We had a couple of drinks. He was worried about his job and I was so sorry for him. Anyway . . . we ended up kissing and things got a bit steamy. I stopped it, though. I do love Damian and I didn't want to hurt him. It was the only time that happened, honest!'

'When did you tell Damian?'

'A couple of days later. We talked it through. He was upset, but I promised him we didn't actually have sex and it had been a stupid one-off. I begged him not to say anything to Henry about it and, in the end, he agreed. I suppose it came up in the pub because we'd all had quite a lot to drink.'

'And you and Damian went back to Driftwood after you left Henry on Monday night?'

'Absolutely.'

Siv let her go and sat in the interview room a little longer. So Damian Kyalo did have a motive to remove his friend from the picture after all. But murder? And if he had killed Henry, surely Viv must know. Siv didn't quite buy it.

* * *

There was a log cabin decked out as a play hut in a corner of the school playground. The head told them that it was also used for support lessons when the weather allowed. It wasn't heated, but it was enclosed and dry and the school was pushed for space, so Siv and Ali had agreed to talk to Tara Warren in there. It had a fixed table, jolly cartoon cushions on the benches and the windows had curtains patterned with the planets.

The narrow bench creaked as Ali had trouble fitting his considerable behind on the slim seat, which was made for neater bottoms. He pushed a Minions cushion aside and perched, tilted forward. Siv couldn't help but marvel at his ample frame in the tiny space as he began to address Tara. 'We've found the car your brother travelled to Berminster in. We believe that he may have been living in East London.'

Tara had a grim expression. She was clearly put out that they'd turned up at the school. 'That doesn't mean anything to me. I'd no idea where he was.'

'You're sure he never gave any clue over the years?'

'I'm sure.'

Ali wriggled. 'We've been discovering a bit more about him. Apparently, as a teenager, he used to take girlfriends to the cemetery, which makes an interesting connection. Does that jog any memories for you?'

'Nothing that Eugene did would surprise me.'

'He must have said things to you. Boasted, maybe?'

'Like I said before, he became a mystery to me. We didn't have those kinds of chats.'

She sounded almost bored, yet Siv was sure she could see anger in Tara's eyes.

'Come on, Tara, don't mess us about,' she urged. 'You were what, just two years older than Eugene? This isn't a big town. Teenagers gossip. When I was at school here, it was hard to keep a secret. You might be able to hide stuff from your parents, but it would be more difficult with your siblings or mates. In the end, Eugene was still part of your family, even if he was semi-absent.'

Tara screwed up her lips. 'I hate all this. Raking over stuff.'

'It's tough but necessary,' Siv said briskly. She didn't have the time or the inclination to spare Tara's feelings.

She replied angrily, 'My parents should have done more to rein Eugene in, stop him destroying us. It was like they gave up. That meant they gave up on *me* as well.'

That's better — real emotion. 'You must have had some awful times, and I'm sorry for that, but we have to find your brother's murderer. I've been told that Eugene and Henry Kilgore took drugs. Correct?'

'Probably. I heard that, yes.'

'And you were aware that they went drinking and partying in the cemetery?'

Tara seemed to decide that she might as well get this over with. She took a breath and straightened up. 'I only heard about that because of what happened with the caretaker. His daughter was in my class and made a drama out of it.'

Siv glanced at Ali. 'Do you mean Andy Smeaton?'

'Yes. He found Eugene in there one night with Henry and some girl and threw them out. He was ranting on about it when he got home. His daughter thought it was highly amusing.'

Siv said more gently, 'You gave us Teagan Grenville's name. Do you remember any of the other girls that Eugene went out with?'

'I got the impression there was a stream of them.' Her distaste was apparent.

'Is there anything else you can tell us?'

Tara flashed straight back. 'What's there to say? Eugene made our lives shitty, then he vanished. My mum died of a broken heart. Then I lost my dad. That's it. An average tale of happy families.' She put her hands to her face. 'I'm sorry, that was rude. Are you anywhere near finding who killed Eugene? I just want this to be over.'

'So do we, Ms Warren. We're doing our best. I appreciate that this is a very difficult time for you, but it doesn't help when people keep information back or forget to tell us things that might be helpful.'

Tara nodded. 'Yeah, OK. I take your point. There's nothing else I can tell you.'

Siv had a spring in her step on the way back to the car. 'This could give Smeaton a motive.'

'Aye, especially as he's forgotten to mention that he'd met Warren and Kilgore,' Ali said.

'We'll talk to him straightaway.'

'I'll ring him now, shake him out of whatever corner he's in.'

* * *

Within fifteen minutes, they were sitting with Smeaton in the small room in Bere Lodge. He wore hi-vis orange waterproof trousers and jacket, a ribbed, hand-knitted hat and thick but slightly holey socks.

'Excuse the get-up, I was in the middle of sorting out the patio at the back, and what with all this wet weather, I didn't want to risk traipsing mud through the place. Phoebe would be on my case!' he said. 'What can I help you with? Is it more about that blasted wheelbarrow?'

Siv said, 'It's about Eugene Warren, the man whose body was left on the steps here. We're also searching for an old friend of his who's gone missing, Henry Kilgore. I'm sure you must have seen the publicity about him.'

'Right, I did see something,' Smeaton said.

'You've lived and worked in Berminster all your life.'

'Right again. I was born here.'

'Have you ever met Eugene Warren and Henry Kilgore?' Siv asked.

Smeaton's jacket crackled as he moved. 'Don't think so. But I meet lots of people, so can't swear to it.'

'We've been informed that you once found them in the cemetery and threw them out. This is going back some years, when they were teenagers. They liked to climb over Emmeline's Gate with booze and girls. Your daughter talked about the incident at school.'

Smeaton gave a rumbling cough. 'Did she? I suppose I must have, then.' He scratched under his hat. 'Hang on . . . yes, I do remember something. It was summer. A long time ago now, though.'

Siv wasn't convinced that he was struggling with recall. Judging by the look on his face, Ali didn't believe it either.

'I reckon you'd remember something like that, Mr Smeaton,' he said. 'I don't suppose it happens regularly. Try harder.'

Smeaton said indignantly, 'No need to take that tone with me, young man. Wait until you get a bit older. See if you're as sharp as you used to be.'

Ali said, 'You strike me as perfectly alert.'

'Oh, I see. I suppose that's a compliment. Let me think, then. Yes . . . It's coming back to me now. I did deal with some yobs. I was here later than usual. There'd been a leak, and I had to wait for the technicians to leave. There are taps up in the cemetery, so I'd gone to check them. I heard laughing and such. A girl giggling and glass breaking. There were three of them messing around. Disgusting behaviour. I marched them to the gate and gave them a piece of my mind. They were all plastered.'

'Did you take their names or report it?'

'Nah. Just kids messing. I didn't recognise them. The boys were Warren and this Kilgore, you say?'

'Yes,' Ali said. 'And Warren came to the cemetery a number of times, we believe. Are you sure you never saw him or Henry Kilgore here again?'

'No. I wouldn't have, would I, if they came here at night to mess about? I'm not usually around after eight.' He wagged a finger at Ali. 'I've always said that they should put spikes on top of Emmeline's Gate, but the suggestion's fallen on deaf ears.'

Siv asked, 'Can you remember where they were in the cemetery?'

'Now you're asking!' He took off his hat and spun it in his hands. 'Not exactly, but it was the older part, where the nineteenth-century graves are.'

'Have you been to that section recently?'

'No, we check it twice a year, in the spring and autumn, and remove bindweed and anything that's started to look dangerous. It's a deliberate policy; let nature have its way. A sort of wildlife haven. You'll notice the guide warns visitors to take care if they go there.'

They let him go and watched him through the window as he resumed his work outside.

Siv said, 'He has no alibi, but he'd hardly murder Warren for larking around years ago.'

'Aye, seems unlikely. Although he's kind of proprietorial about this place and he's strong enough to heave a body around.'

'Hmm. We need to go into his background again. Patrick can contact the local council about him.'

There was a tap on the door and Diane Lacey slipped in. Her brown coat had a deep, ribbed collar that buttoned up to her chin.

'I saw that you were here. Can I have a quick word?'

'Of course,' Siv said. 'Take a seat.'

Diane perched, fingering her collar. Her expression was grave. 'There's an issue I need to tell you about. I was hoping that Mr Foxwell would, but I'm sure he hasn't.'

'What is it you have to tell us?' Siv asked.

She wrinkled her brow. 'When you asked if there'd been any problems here, I said no, but that wasn't right. Someone stole . . . Oh, heavens, this is difficult. Toby will be mad at me for telling you. This is the only thing I've ever disagreed with him about, you see. It's just that Phoebe's come to me again, fretting about it, and I reassured her that I'd inform you.'

'Take it from the top,' Ali said easily.

'OK, right. We have a bereavement fund. It's for people who are hard up and struggling to pay for a funeral. The council contributes a grant to it every year, but we also have a collection box on the desk at Bere Lodge reception. Visitors are invited to contribute if they'd like to, and they're pretty generous, slot quite a few notes in. Staff often put spare change in there. Phoebe Palmer empties it each evening and gives the money to Toby. He puts it in the safe in his office.

'Last autumn, there were a number of times when the box was empty, or almost empty in the evenings, yet Phoebe had seen visitors put money in the very same day. She mentioned it to me, but she didn't want to approach Toby. He can be a bit impatient with her and they haven't always seen eye to eye. I told him about it. He said to leave it with him.' Diane looked out of the windows, craning her neck as if to check around.

'You're not doing anything wrong by talking to us,' Siv told her. The woman seemed weighed down with responsibilities. 'What did Mr Foxwell do?'

'That's just it, he didn't take any formal action. I assumed he'd report it to the police — that he'd have to. When I asked him about it around November, he said that he'd spoken to staff and no one knew anything. Then he said that there was no proof that anyone had stolen money and Phoebe could be a terrible fusspot. If anyone had been stealing, it had stopped. I could tell that he was annoyed that I'd raised it. Toby doesn't like anything that might affect the reputation of the crematorium. He's highly regarded by the council and he wouldn't have wanted his manager to hear that there was a problem. He won't like it that I've told you. I wouldn't have, but Phoebe came to see me about it yesterday and she's been bending my ear. She's annoyed that the culprit was never found. I said I'd speak to you.'

'Leave it to us,' Ali said.

Diane hugged her collar. 'I don't suppose it has anything to do with this murder, but I was uncomfortable not telling you, and Phoebe gets herself terribly worked up over such things. I'd better get back. I've left Saul in charge of the retort.'

'Are you and Saul an item?' Siv asked, not sure what had prompted the question.

Diane turned back from the door, blushing. 'Goodness, no! What makes you think that?'

'I wondered, that's all. You speak well of each other, and proximity at work has been known to spark attraction.'

'But I'm more than twenty years older than Saul.'

'I don't see why that would stop you being in a relationship,' Siv said.

'It's a professional friendship, Inspector. I've not had children. Perhaps Saul is the son I might have had if life had been different. I enjoy seeing him achieve his potential, spreading his wings.'

When she'd gone, they exchanged glances.

'Is the collection box something or nothing, do you think?' Ali unscrewed the top of a water bottle and took a gulp.

'Who can tell? I'll get Patrick to follow it up. It may be totally unrelated, but we'll see.'

Siv's mind had shifted to Henry Kilgore, to location and 'grave parties'. An idea sparked. What if Warren's killer had thought it would be neat to dispose of Kilgore somewhere in the cemetery too? She leaped up and threw her coat on. 'Let's walk over to the older part of the cemetery. I haven't been there yet.'

They met Toby Foxwell as they left Bere Lodge.

'I'm glad your colleagues have finished here, and we can get back to work,' he said. 'We've had to field lots of phone calls from concerned families. At least now we can tell them we're business as usual again.'

'We've appreciated your cooperation,' Siv told him.

'Have you found anything? The sooner the public are told the police have someone in custody, the safer everyone here will be.'

God, this man is irritating.

'Early days,' Ali said. 'But there's no suggestion there's a killer roaming the crematorium. Mustn't keep you.'

'I'm not sure you should have put that idea into his head,' Siv said as they walked away. 'No need to add to public anxiety.'

'Well . . . I get fed up with bureaucrats like him expecting us to work miracles.'

Siv frowned at him and phoned Steve Wooton for an update.

'Steve says his team didn't go in the old part of the cemetery,' she told Ali. 'It's a large area, and given the foul weather and the wheelbarrow evidence, they focused on the grounds between the chapels, the garden of remembrance and Bluebell Copse. They're going through Mallow Cottage now and he'll contact us later.'

Ali had lit up. His cigarette smoke lingered in the still, cold air. He stooped to retie one of his shoelaces, the cigarette hanging precariously from his lips. He muttered, 'Why exactly are we going to the cemetery?'

Siv shivered and stamped her feet. 'Both Warren and Kilgore are linked to this place. If what they got up to here is the reason for what's happened to them, it seems to me that Kilgore might have ended up in the same setting. It's worth visiting the area where Smeaton says he caught them.'

'Sounds a bit far-fetched to me.'

'We'll look anyway,' she said firmly.

They walked on, past new, clearly lettered headstones that stood sentinel to well-tended graves bearing flowers and garlands. Some were adorned with candles, angels, grave blankets and wind chimes. One was hung with a bird feeder. Others were edged with pebbles and shells. Signs of Christmas still lingered in holly wreaths, cards and tiny artificial trees with winking lights, shiny baubles and strands of tinsel. A sleigh pulled by reindeer and filled with tiny presents covered the grass on one.

The world was sombre grey; the sky, the stone and marble slabs all fused in shadow. Nature had joined the dead in sleep. The greens of grass and foliage were dull, lifeless. Siv veered onto a side path and stood in front of a grave. The simple oval headstone was in black marble with silver lettering.

GREGORY DRUMMOND
1946–2015
Truth is ever to be found in simplicity, and not in the multiplicity and confusion of things.
(Isaac Newton)

'My dad's grave,' she told Ali. 'Newton was his hero.' She'd considered adding, *Thanks for the cocoa*, when she'd had it made, and wished she had now. Watching her father make cocoa in a saucepan, taking his time while he told her about Newton's theories, had been a balm in her unsettled youth.

She turned on her heel and strode back to the main path. Ali respectfully made no comment. The path climbed slightly, and as they traced back through the years, the headstones became stained and marked, the lettering fading.

A notice stood at the entrance to the Victorian section.

PUBLIC WARNING. This part of the cemetery is fascinating but more than 150 years old. Some of the graves are deteriorating. Please take care when walking here. Do not touch the headstones or statuary. We appreciate your interest but please stay on the paths and look, don't touch.

Soon, all the graves became more elaborate and ornate. Headstones tilted and were covered with dark ivy, moss and lichen. Celtic crosses and angels abounded. The paths grew narrower and were lined with tall, ancient yews that blocked the light.

'The Victorians liked their symbols,' Ali said, admiring two clasped stone hands above the epitaph, *Never Parted, in Life or in Death.*

Siv was gazing up at an imposing, cracked urn set on top of a damaged granite obelisk. It tilted as if it might topple at any moment, and she moved away, not wanting an ignominious end. They paused to read a mildewed scroll on the grave of Norton Mobbs and were only just able to make out the faint script.

Remember Me as Thou Pass By
As Thou Art Now
So Once Was I.
As I Am Now
So Thou Wilt Be
Prepare Thy Way
To Follow Me

'OK, Norton, don't rub it in,' Ali said.

They wandered on, up and down the paths and along the graves, dwarfed by massive, cold statuary and the brooding trees. Acorns and pinecones were scattered among the leaves. An occasional clump of tiny purple violets provided the only colour. Siv kept hoping to spot a sign that someone had been here recently, but no one had come this way for a while.

'Hey!' she said. 'A mort safe!' She stepped from the path and bent to examine the broken and rusting iron cage that lay over a pair of graves covered in thistles.

'What's a mort safe?'

'They were put over graves to prevent disturbance. Some people were terrified of grave robbers stealing bodies for anatomy schools.'

Ali backed away and grumbled. 'This place does my head in. Talk about creepy! If we're expecting to find Kilgore's body, I can't see anything more recent than 1880 so far.'

'We'll keep going, anyway. Apparently, there are catacombs along the top boundary,' Siv told him. 'Come on, the exercise will do you good.'

'Not when I'm likely to end up with pneumonia. I've an awful headache today as it is.'

He had his hands stuffed in his pockets, his shoulders hunched. She guessed he was nervous. He'd told her last Halloween that he believed in ghosts and a spirit world, and in the dim winter light and chill wind, it was enough to give even the least sensitive of souls the heebie-jeebies. This dreary, dim burial ground would be firing his imagination.

As they moved back through the decades and came to the 1860s, several family vaults were set in a row. They were stern, grim structures, a little sunken. One had Doric columns engraved with lyres, another, two huge grimy angels with outstretched wings.

'These were the Victorian upper-middle classes,' Siv said, resting her hand on the foot of a wailing woman dressed in Roman robes, a hand to her distressed face. Ali grimaced. Siv grinned. 'Let's check them out.'

They walked around the vaults, their feet snagging on the uneven ground. Ali swore as he tripped on a broken branch, but there was no sign of recent tampering or disturbance. There was a dead pigeon, piles of leaf mould, ragwort, nettles and snares of dense brambles and ivy, but no unburied body. All was truly extinct, dank and still.

At the boundary, they saw the catacombs, guarded by tall, ornate doors. These were flanked by two Grecian-style columns, topped by coping stones and huge carved eagles. A hefty padlock secured them, and when Siv examined it, it was firm and undamaged.

'According to the brochure, there are five hundred coffins down there. It was a prestigious resting place and expensive, so only the very wealthy could afford the option.'

'I'd rather spend my money on living,' Ali said.

She peered through narrow vents in the door but could see only steps leading down and caught a whiff of chill, sour air. She was disappointed. She folded her arms and sighed.

Ali shrugged and lit another Gitane. 'It was a gamble, guv.'

'Yes. Just shows you can't always trust a gut feeling.'

'Aye, right enough. Tricky things, guts. I should know.' He tapped his protruding middle. 'Buy you a wee coffee? I just need the loo first. Would anyone mind if I nip behind a gravestone?'

'I won't, and I doubt you'll shock the dead. But be quick, we need to press on, trawl through all our info about Kilgore again. The bloody man must be around here somewhere.'

When Ali reappeared, they walked back at a fast pace to the car. Steve rang as Siv switched on the engine, his voice high and excited.

'Guv, you'd better get to Mallow Cottage. We've found a body. It's Henry Kilgore.'

CHAPTER 14

Steve was standing at the side gate to the garden of the small, detached cottage, waiting for them. He bristled as Siv walked towards him.

'I've got quite a few things to show you, DI Drummond,' he said with a little smirk. 'But first I wanted to clarify that uniforms searched this place when Kilgore was reported missing?'

'Yes, of course they did, on Tuesday night.' Siv was curious as to what he was getting at. There was always something with Steve.

'Well, if he was dead by then, heads should roll. First of all, there are tyre marks from Warren's Vauxhall Corsa outside here on the verge. So, it was parked against the hedge but moved into the turning to the field before Tuesday night. Now, come and see Kilgore with a knife wound in the neck,' he said leading them towards the cottage. 'This gate isn't kept locked, by the way.' He was pumped up, almost yelling in his excitement.

Siv and Ali looked at each other in dismay, before following the crime scene manager up the crazy paving towards the cottage. They paused at the door to don protective gear, then he led them across a decked area to a summerhouse at the bottom of the modest garden.

'There's a gap of about forty-six centimetres between this structure and the wall behind it.' Steve handed Siv a powerful torch. 'After you.'

She went first, shining the beam in. The space at the back of the summerhouse was littered with debris and soil. A thick, woody clematis obscured the wall behind it and trailed over the summerhouse roof, forming a dark cave. Some of the leaves had torn and scattered over Henry Kilgore. He was wedged sideways, his head lower than the rest of his body but Siv could see a gash, caked with dried blood, at the side of his neck. His blue trainers pointed towards them. His socks were patterned with polar bears. Siv stepped aside for Ali.

'I got a pair of socks like that for Christmas,' he commented.

'Very pertinent to the inquiry,' Steve remarked acidly, while herding them back towards the house.

'Now, just up here on the patio at the back of the cottage, there's a metal table and four chairs. Two of them have been set out at angles to the table, the other two are stacked. I checked with Ms Kilgore, and when she was here tidying up after the last guests, she stacked all four chairs together. Though we haven't fingerprinted them yet, it appears that our victim was having a nice little chat with someone. We're sifting through the cottage room by room and fingerprinting. There was no forced entry and the key is in the key safe. You can check if you want, but there's no evidence of a struggle in there.'

The cottage was a two-up, two-down with a shower room off the kitchen. It was neat and well maintained in the same basic style as Driftwood. It wouldn't have taken uniform long to search it. There was no sign of anyone else having been inside the cottage since Imelda Kilgore had last cleaned it. Siv and Ali left the team to it.

'The nearest houses to this are about half a mile away in both directions along this road,' Ali said. 'Doubtful that anyone will have seen anything.'

'Tell Patrick to get uniforms knocking, anyway. And not the idiots who might have missed a bloody dead body.'

Although the timing wasn't confirmed, Siv was fuming. She drove back through the drizzling rain to Imelda Kilgore's faster than she should, while Ali called Patrick.

'Uniform will be broke to the bone if they missed the body,' he said glumly.

'I'm guessing that means embarrassed. *Ashamed*, more like.' Ali shot Siv a sympathetic glance. 'Oh, come on,' she said impatiently, 'they must have missed it. I can't see our killer keeping Kilgore's body somewhere else. Given that Warren's car was initially parked outside Mallow Cottage, he and Kilgore must have gone there, and that's where they were murdered.

'This has caused us a huge delay, and Mortimer will be on the warpath. However, the way Kilgore's body was hidden away like that suggests he wasn't Warren's killer,' she concluded grimly. 'We're looking for another suspect.'

* * *

They could hear a vacuum cleaner when they rang Ms Kilgore's doorbell. She flung open the door, her cheeks flushed pink. She stared at them both while peeling off her rubber gloves. Her face dropped when they didn't say anything.

'It's not good news, is it?'

'I'm afraid not. We've found Henry's body. Let's sit down, Ms Kilgore,' Siv said.

They sat in a spacious living room decorated in various shades of blue, with many photos of Henry scattered about. Siv explained where he had been found. She informed his mother that it appeared he'd been stabbed, then steeled herself for the inevitable questions.

'I don't understand,' Imelda said slowly. 'The police searched all my properties. You organised it. They got keys from me.'

'That's true. We don't know yet when Henry's body was hidden there. The side gate wasn't left locked, so it might have happened after the search. If he was there before

Tuesday night, then something went badly wrong and I can only apologise.'

Imelda blushed bright scarlet. 'Apologise! An apology hardly covers it! I've spent days worrying and wondering where my son was and I could have been spared the anguish! All those people tramping along the coast and looking around rocks and scrub could have been saved the effort. All pointless. My poor Henry, lying there in the cold and dark—'

Ali asked if he could use the bathroom. Siv frowned. This was hardly the moment. Imelda gestured impatiently at the hallway and he vanished.

Siv said, as reassuringly as she could, 'We will enquire into what happened when Mallow Cottage was searched, I guarantee that.'

Imelda's breath came fast, her heavy frame trembling. 'Oh yes, you bloody will! I've been traipsing around the streets with that lacklustre Saffie, looking in pubs and down alleyways, searching around the harbour and Larch Dell, that rubbish-strewn area that calls itself a park. I can guarantee *you*, you haven't heard the last of this from me.'

Siv had seen grief affect people this way before, erupting in anger, lashing at the world. She took a deep breath. 'Of course, I understand. In the meantime, did Henry have a key to the cottage?'

'No, but he might have had the number for the key safe. I keep a list in the kitchen drawer. My God, was he murdered in the cottage?'

'We can't say yet where he died. Did Henry use Mallow Cottage or any of your other properties when he was at school?'

'Of course not. They're businesses, kept for rental guests or the occasional use of family and friends, such as Driftwood at the moment.'

'Ms Kilgore, did you ever have the impression that Henry still carried a flame for Viv Carpenter?'

Imelda tutted. 'Of course he didn't. That relationship was over years ago. What are you trying to suggest now?'

'Just a line of enquiry. Also, we've been told that Eugene and Henry took drugs when they were school friends. Were you aware of that?'

The woman blanched. 'No! I mean, I could believe it of Eugene, but not of Henry. I never witnessed any sign of drug use. He was always a fit and healthy young man. He was on the fencing team, for goodness' sake. No, no, you must have been misinformed.'

There was no point in tormenting her with stories of parties in the cemetery.

Siv asked, 'Do you want me to call anyone to be with you? I could wait until Saffie or Viv get here.'

'I'd rather be alone.'

It was time to go. Siv got up as Ali come back into the room. 'Again, we are so sorry for your loss. A family liaison officer will call you later. We'll be in touch as soon as we have any updates, Ms Kilgore.'

'When can I see my son?'

'We'll be in touch to arrange that with you.'

As they got in the car, Siv looked askance at Ali. 'What was with your bathroom timing? Not helpful. Thanks for leaving me with the fallout.'

'Aye, sorry about that. Just couldn't wait.'

'Hmm.' She raised a sceptical eyebrow at him. He looked away.

'We'll assume that the same person killed Warren and Kilgore,' she said. 'As yet, we have no motive, but murders are often close to home. I can't see Saffie heaving two bodies around. Imelda could, or Viv and Damian, working as a team. But I can't imagine Imelda killing her own darling son, and even if Henry had been coming on to Viv, it's hardly a strong enough motive for murder.'

'Surely this must reach back, given that message on the holiday brochure. It has to be connected with Kilgore's and Warren's adolescent shenanigans.'

'I agree.'

When they arrived at Driftwood, Viv and Damian were lounging on the sofa, this time watching *Once Upon a Time in Hollywood*. Viv paused it on Margot Robbie's face. Saffie had gone for a walk on the beach, she said. Siv told Ali to find her and break the news. When he'd gone, Siv informed the couple about their friend.

Damian exhaled loudly, closed his eyes. Viv's brimmed with unshed tears.

'Oh, God! His mum must be gutted. Have you told her?' Viv said.

'Just now. Maybe you could go to her, see if she needs anything.'

'I'll do that.' Viv sniffed.

'How was he killed?' Damian asked.

'Probably a knife wound, but the post-mortem will confirm that,' Siv said. 'Do either of you recall Henry mentioning Mallow Cottage?'

'He'd told us his mum owned a few places in town,' Viv murmured. 'Henry called it her seaside empire. He didn't say anything about that cottage in particular, though.'

Damian shrugged. 'First time I've heard of it.' He gave Siv a shrewd look. 'Hang on, when did Henry die?'

Siv knew what was coming. 'We haven't established that yet. We have to wait for the pathologist's report.'

'Right. Didn't the police search all of Imelda's properties on Tuesday?'

'We did, yes.'

He pursed his full lips. 'So, if Henry was dead by then, you managed not to find his body during that sweep?'

'That's correct.' Siv didn't like the satisfaction in his tiny smile.

He glanced at Viv, arching his eyebrows. 'Oops, bit of an own goal there, if that's the case. I wouldn't like to be in your shoes when Imelda comes gunning for you. And she will, if you cocked up. I wouldn't cross her where Henry's concerned.'

'I've apologised to Ms Kilgore, but as I've said, we've yet to determine when Henry died.'

Damian persisted, 'Imelda won't rest at an apology, I bet—'

'I'm sure the inspector wants to get on now, Damo.' Viv took his hand. 'Let's leave it.'

Siv nodded. 'Thanks.'

She couldn't see any point in keeping these people here much longer.

The chalet was in a terrible mess with stuff strewn randomly. It smelled cheesy. She resisted the urge to throw open a window. Cleaning the place would provide Imelda with therapy.

'We need DNA samples from you all, then you can go home when you like. Are you back at work on Monday?'

They nodded. Viv started to cry, quietly. Damian put his arm around her and kissed the top of her head.

Siv walked outside onto the porch. She watched Ali and Saffie walking up slowly from the beach. He was puffing away on a cigarette. The woman said something to him and he patted her shoulder. Her hair blew around her face. She took a band from her pocket and tied the long strands back. As they came closer to the porch, Siv saw that Saffie was dry-eyed.

'I knew he was never coming back. I just knew,' she said. She gestured at the sea. 'I hate this place. I wish we'd never come here.'

'I'm sorry,' Siv said, walking towards her. 'We'll need to search Henry's flat in London before you go back there. Once we've taken a DNA sample, you can head for your parents' home. Can you give me your keys to the Farringdon flat?'

Saffie dug in her pocket and handed them over. 'Is that it?'

'Yes. DS Carlin will do the DNA swab, then that's it.'

'Good. I'm so tired of questions. I've one of my own, though. This woman that Henry was seen having lunch with. Was he having an affair with her?'

Siv knew she should be delicate but this line of questioning could provide a vital lead. 'What do you think?'

Saffie moved into the sheltering wall, away from the snapping breeze. 'If you'd asked me last week, I'd have said impossible, but after hearing about Henry losing his job . . . I can't tell. It's as if . . . as if I never really knew him.'

She began to sob. Darting into the chalet, she slammed the door.

Ali pulled a face. 'She told me that Imelda turned on her last night and said that she'd been a drag on Henry, sapped his energy. I said that people come out with things they don't mean when they're worried.'

'Or they say what they're truly thinking, because the usual filter's not working.'

'You're a sceptic.'

'Undoubtedly. Either way, she'll be better off out of here. Kyalo latched straight onto the possibility that our search missed Kilgore's body.'

Ali grimaced. 'He would. Saffie was too distraught to consider that, thank goodness.'

* * *

Patrick had been busy checking out alibis. Now he was worn out and ravenous. He'd spent the night with Kitty and hadn't got much sleep. Her energy and stamina amazed him. He supposed it must come from working outside, in all weathers. She was hardier and tougher than him. And he was out of practice. Years of being there for Noah had rather blighted his love life. Maybe he'd buy some vitamins, the ones that muscly male models advertised. He'd seen the guv's message that they'd found Henry Kilgore, so he'd better stay alert. She could get impatient and sarcastic if he dragged his feet, and he was aware that he'd been distracted at times when the going had been tough with Noah.

He was sitting at his desk, devouring a tray of lasagne from Gusto and reflecting on Kitty's wondrous thighs, when a call was put through to him.

'It's a Gray Grenville. He tried DI Drummond, but she didn't pick up so he rang here.'

Patrick swallowed a mouthful of pasta and took the call. 'Hello, this is DC Patrick Hill. I work with DI Drummond. She emailed you about Eugene Warren.'

'That's right. I've just got back from a work trip. Has something happened?'

Patrick explained that they were now investigating two deaths.

'Good heavens. What can I say? How awful for their families.' Grenville's manner was light, easy.

'Did you know them both?'

'A little. I was a year ahead of them at school. DI Drummond was asking me about the girl I saw on the beach with Eugene.'

'That's right. Do you remember who she was?'

'I think it was Leah Steele, because she had long, distinctive hair. Strawberry blonde, I believe it's called. I can't be sure though, especially after so many years, and I was some distance away at the time. Teagan dodged a bullet there with Eugene Warren.'

'You didn't rate him?'

Grenville laughed. 'He was dynamite, on a collision course with life. Not the kind of boy you want your sister to hang around with. I'm glad she broke up with him after I told her what I'd seen. She was furious with me to start with, when I spilled the beans on him, but then when she challenged him, he mocked her, told her to like it or lump it.'

'Thanks for that. We also know that Eugene and Henry did drugs and hung out in the cemetery. Did you know about that or were you aware of them falling out with anyone?'

'Sorry, long time ago and I didn't mix with them socially. The cemetery? Not a comfortable place to have fun. I suppose they thought it was naughty.'

'Do you live in Berminster, Mr Grenville?'

'No, I'm in Brighton. I prefer the city.'

Patrick thanked him, put the phone down and finished his cooling meal while running some searches on Leah Steele. He found a local phone number and rang it. A woman answered and confirmed that she was Ms Steele. Patrick could hear a car engine. He explained why he was calling. Her tone changed.

'Eugene Warren! I saw that he'd been murdered. I'm not surprised, I'm sorry to say.'

'Why's that?'

'He was a right little shit when we were at school.'

'Did you ever go out with him when you were teenagers?'

She snorted. 'Hang on, I'm going to pull in. Your call's been put through to my mobile — on Bluetooth. Don't worry, officer! I'm in Northumberland at the moment. One sec.' There was a pause and the sound of an engine slowing and then she resumed. 'No, I didn't go out with him. I'd rather have had teeth pulled without anaesthetic. He didn't wash much, apart from anything else. Who told you that?'

'It came up. Have you got strawberry-blonde hair? Or did you have as a teenager?' As he asked, he was searching Facebook and saw that her photo confirmed it.

'I have. Assisted these days. Why?'

'Someone said that they saw you on the beach with Eugene. They told me they recognised your hair.'

'Sorry, but their memory's playing tricks. I was on the beach loads, but never with Eugene. I wouldn't have touched him if someone paid me.'

Patrick chased the last drips of tomato sauce with his fork. 'Can you recall any other girls who had hair like yours, who could have been mistaken for you?'

'Not offhand. Eugene could have invented the term *promiscuous*. There must have been lots of girls who didn't mind his sweaty smell. Some people find it an aphrodisiac, I believe. Either that, or he had hidden talents that made up for his lack of hygiene.'

At that thought Patrick gave up on his meal and pushed for one last try. 'Do you recall any girls he took to the cemetery in the evenings?'

'Nope, but sounds like the kind of thing that would've been right up his street.'

* * *

'There'll have to be an internal review, if Henry Kilgore was dead when we searched,' DCI Mortimer growled. 'That would look very bad, DI Drummond, the police failing to find a body. It's pretty basic stuff, after all. We'll be a laughing stock. The press will have a field day, and as for Kilgore's mother . . .'

Mortimer's head was too small for his bony frame, but his new style of wearing his hair longer compensated for it a little. His faded roots had vanished and toffee highlights gleamed in his thinning locks. Mutsi must have bought him a different dye. His skin was clearer and less inflamed than when Siv had first met him. She hated to acknowledge it, but maybe Mutsi was having a positive effect on him.

'It was dark, sir, and the overgrown gap between the summerhouse and the wall wouldn't have been obvious at night,' she offered.

'That's hardly a reason we can put forward legitimately. It sounds . . . lame. It *is* lame.'

'Yes, sir.'

'A double murder now. Any suspects?'

'No. Working on it, sir. We're waiting for the post-mortem results on Kilgore.'

'I see. Well . . . I believe you're with us for lunch tomorrow.'

'That's right.'

'Good, good. Your mother and I had a lovely weekend on the boat recently. Took her across to near Boulogne and back, had a delicious meal in a little bistro on the coast. Your mum's learning the craft of seafaring quickly. I'm impressed!'

Oh yes, she's a fast learner when it suits.

'Sounds great. Mum will have enjoyed the food. She hates cooking, but then I expect you've discovered that. Hopefully, you're nifty in the kitchen, sir!'

He gave an awkward laugh. 'You'll have to come out for a trip on *Quicksilver* sometime.'

'That's a lovely offer, sir. Better get on.'

'Thank you, DI Drummond.'

'Thank you, sir.'

She stopped on the stairs. In the hectic activity of the week, she'd forgotten about her email reply to Mutsi, grudgingly agreeing to lunch. Might as well brace herself and get it out of the way. Now she quailed at the prospect, her thoughts racing. She needed back-up.

S.O.S. Mutsi has moved in with Mortimer, she texted Bartel. *I've agreed to have lunch with them tomorrow. Will you please come with me?*

Ali was signalling to her as she headed for her office. He rubbed his temples with his thumbs.

'Just took a call from an Orlando Golding. He contacted Waltham Forest Police this morning to say that he'd seen news of Warren's death. Sounds as if Warren was his part-time lodger. Golding lives in Walthamstow.'

It was gone five and dark outside. 'We'd best get ourselves to London. We need to visit Kilgore's flat anyway, so we can go to Farringdon after we've seen Golding. Are you OK?' Ali was still massaging his temples.

'Crappy headache, is all. Had it all day. Can't shift it.'

Siv nodded. 'Take some aspirin. Then ring Golding back and say we'll be with him in a couple of hours.'

Optimistic, in Friday night traffic but needs must.

CHAPTER 15

They reached Golding's flat at half eight. They'd had to stop at a service station for a loo break for Ali, and by the time they reached the city, the traffic was heavy and grinding. Siv drove fast, checking road reports. Ali fell asleep, his head propped against the window, arms folded. She didn't mind; it saved having to make conversation and she could concentrate on the route. She'd read Bartel's reply to her text while she'd waited in the services for Ali.

OK for lunch. Should be fun. I'll referee if the gloves come off.

Golding's flat was on the ground floor of a terraced house near Walthamstow Central station. It was chilly inside, but the living room was furnished comfortably. Golding was a large man, dressed in layers, with long dreadlocks tied back with elastic.

'Sorry about the cold,' he said. 'I haven't been in long and I forgot to set the central heating. It should warm up soon. Coffee?'

They accepted, sitting on a small sofa. The kitchen was in an alcove off the living room and Golding talked to them as the kettle boiled.

'I was getting a bit worried about Eugene as he's not usually gone this long, and then I saw the newspaper when I was on the bus. Poor guy. It's really weird what's happened. What was he doing in Sussex?'

'He grew up in Berminster,' Siv told him.

'Oh, I see. He never mentioned that.' Golding spooned coffee into earthenware mugs and brought them over to the sofa with a tin of chocolate biscuits. 'Here, you've had a long drive.'

Ali's eyes lit up, and he dived in. 'When did you last see Eugene?'

Golding pulled a chair forward and sat, legs akimbo. 'Saturday before last. He'd stayed for a couple of days. He came and went with his dog, you understand.'

'So, was he a lodger?'

'Kind of. He paid me fifteen pounds for every night he slept here.'

'Cheap accommodation,' Ali observed.

'Yeah, but the deal was that he cleaned the flat while he was here and did odd jobs. He was reliable, thorough. He stayed roughly half a week, did laundry, showered, cooked some meals. He was a nifty cook and he'd leave stuff in the freezer for me. Then he'd take off for three or four nights, maybe more. It varied. That's why I wasn't thrown when he hadn't shown up, although I was starting to wonder where he was.'

Siv asked, 'Where did he go when he wasn't here?'

'Dunno. Slept in his car a fair bit, from what he said. In warmer weather, he pitched a tent in various places. He was a nomad, really. There might have been other people he stayed with, but he never mentioned them.' Golding ate half a biscuit in one bite. 'I knew him, but not well.'

'Explain,' Siv said.

'I met him about six years ago. I work in a city farm and he came in. Seemed a bit lost and worse for wear. We got chatting. He needed somewhere to live part-time and I have a tiny spare room. He was polite in a distant sort of way. Our arrangement suited me because I like my space, and I didn't want anyone else here twenty-four-seven. The extra money was handy, though. He always paid up promptly and his meals were tasty. He made these biscuits.'

Ali saw that as an invitation to help himself to a fourth. Siv finished hers. It was good, the chocolate dark.

'Did Eugene work?'

'He never mentioned a steady job or anything, but then again he didn't have much conversation. When he was here, he stayed in his room mostly, reading. I'd forget he was around until he walked the dog. The ideal sharer, if you like.'

Ali mumbled through his biscuit, 'What did he do during the days?'

'I'm not sure. He walked a lot. Sometimes he mentioned the local marshes and the wetlands. They're a site of special scientific interest, internationally renowned. Invertebrates fascinated him. He had quite a few books about them in his room.'

Siv finished her coffee. 'He never referred to his past, or his life in Berminster?'

'No. He was pleasant but never talkative. We were ships that passed in the night.'

Ali dusted his fingers. 'Did you have a sexual relationship with him?'

Golding smiled. 'No. I wondered if you might ask that. I'm straight. I never asked what Eugene's inclinations were. We didn't discuss the subject, and as far as I'm aware, he never had anyone staying here. Although . . . it might not be relevant, but someone visited him here a couple of weeks back. That was unusual. I was on my way home and this guy had just left. I saw him turn out of the path and walk up the road, towards the Tube. He might have come from the flat upstairs, but when I got in, Eugene was washing mugs and he seemed a bit . . . excitable. Restless. I asked him if he'd had a visitor and he said, yeah, someone he used to know. Then he vanished to his room. He left the next day.'

'What did this visitor look like?'

Golding hesitated. 'It was getting dark and I only saw his back. Medium height, dark coat, dark hair. That's about it.'

Siv showed him a photo of Henry Kilgore on her phone. 'Could it have been this man?'

Golding took his time. 'Maybe. Hard to say, because of the back view. Similar build, I suppose.'

'We need to inspect Eugene's room,' Siv said. 'Have you been in there or moved anything?'

'No. I assumed he'd be back until I saw the paper.'

The room was narrow, just space for a single bed, a chest of drawers piled high with books and a patterned curtain attached to a curved rail that acted as a wardrobe. The floorboards were painted cream with a cheap coir mat by the neatly made bed. The walls were bare. Ali opened the wardrobe while Siv went through the drawers.

'Just two pairs of jeans, a couple of sweatshirts and a denim jacket. All well-worn and clean. All pockets empty except for this,' Ali reported.

He held out a business card, dark brown with white lettering.

Pie Mad
Come and taste our delicious, handmade pies and pasties.
Or let us bring them to you. We deliver throughout North London.

'Bag it, and we'll contact them,' Siv said.

'I could do with a pie right now — my stomach thinks my throat's been cut,' Ali replied. He squatted down with a grunt and peered under the bed, pulling out a long object. 'Here's Warren's tent, all packed away for the winter.'

Siv had found a sparse collection of underwear, T-shirts and socks. No personal documents. The bottom two drawers of the chest were empty. As Golding had said, the books on top were almost all about invertebrates: field guides, their biology, habitats, tracks and signs, intelligence, neurobiology, embryology and reproduction. She flicked through them all. The top one was a spiral notebook with various lists and notes. She scanned the first page.

Walthamstow Wetlands:
Speckled wood butterflies
Thick-kneed beetles
Fen raft spider
Clubtail dragonfly
Downy emerald dragonfly
Water spider
Froghopper

Ali had sat on the bed and was yawning. She joined him with the notebook. Someone trod heavily on the floor upstairs. She leaned back against the wall and gazed at the uneven ceiling.

'The handwriting in this isn't the same as on the brochure found in Warren's car. He was a troublesome, drug-taking, promiscuous teenager. He left Berminster aged eighteen and vanished. We've no information what he was doing for about four years after that, but he met Golding and has been living this come-and-go life here for six years, spending part of the week on the road, sleeping in his car or camping. No obvious means of income, but he could have been doing bits of work off the radar for cash. You might predict that such a dissolute teenager would become an equally degenerate adult, maybe a complete down-and-out. Warren turned into a quiet, polite man with an interest in nature and wildlife and lived an alternative but self-supporting lifestyle. If you're still awake, what do you make of it?' Siv finished.

Ali stretched his hands above his head and cracked his knuckles. 'He dropped out, simple as that, and got over his bad boy stage, calmed down. It happens. I knew tykes and tearaways back at school who're bank managers and solicitors now.'

'Were you ever a tyke or a tearaway?'

'God, no! My daddy would have killed me. He always seemed to know everywhere I'd been and everything I was doing.' He glanced sideways. 'How about you?'

'I had my moments. My sister took the main bad-girl role.' Siv tapped the notebook against her leg. 'I'm getting fed up with these mysterious people we're accumulating. The woman who lunched with Kilgore in the pub, the man who visited Warren here and the girl snogging him on the beach, the woman in the cemetery and the person who wrote on the brochure. Wakey-wakey, Ali. We need to get off this bed and search it, then we're done.'

They tipped the bedding and mattress off the bed, looking all around the base. Siv removed the duvet cover and shook it out. Nothing. Ali ran his hands all over the mattress before he replaced it.

'Chuck me a pillow,' Siv said.

They took one each, pulling off the pillowcases. Feathers floated from a tear in the cushion Siv was shaking and she sneezed loudly.

'Bless you!' Ali smiled. 'Yes, result!'

He pulled a crumpled Berminster Breaks brochure from his pillowcase and held it out. They looked at the handwriting across the top, heads bent. It was the same as on the one found in Warren's car, but the message was different.

Funny how fun suddenly isn't funny.

'Now, how did this get here?' Siv said. 'It was posted or delivered by hand, so someone knew where Warren stayed. Maybe the person who Golding saw visiting him here brought it.'

'It's threatening, unlike the first message. Upping the ante.' Ali rubbed his eyes.

Siv slipped it into an evidence bag and put the notebook in another. 'Before we head to Farringdon, there's just one more thing.'

On the way out, she asked Golding, who was standing in the kitchen eating a Pot Noodle, if Warren had owned a mobile phone or a tablet.

'Never saw him with a tablet. He had one of those pay-as-you-go mobiles, but he never offered me the number, and I never asked for it.'

'I see. You need to leave his room as it is for now and not enter it.'

'OK, I understand. I was wondering — what's happened to Eugene's dog?'

'I'm not sure.'

'I wouldn't mind having him, if he's not been rehomed.'

'Call the RSPCA in Berminster,' Siv told him. 'They should be able to advise you.'

'Ta. I might do that.' He shovelled another forkful of noodles into his mouth. 'Eugene was an inoffensive guy. Why would anyone kill him?'

Because he wasn't always so inoffensive.

'We'll be in touch, Mr Golding.'

* * *

On the way to Farringdon, they stopped to pick up a couple of burgers and coffee at a McDonald's. Ali devoured his ravenously and Siv didn't lag behind. The car was silent while they ate companionably.

'That's better,' Ali said, tidying rubbish into a brown paper bag. 'I was running on empty.'

'Me too.' Siv was gazing at the handful of people inside the restaurant, sitting alone at window tables. 'These places always remind me of Edward Hopper paintings on such bleak, cold nights. Solitary people needing light and warmth.' She'd been one of them now and again after Ed died. Late at night, sleepless and distraught, she'd walk to a café and sit with an unwanted coffee, just needing to be amid the wash of humanity. She handed Ali her paper bag to add to his. 'I'll carry on driving, and you can do the journey back.'

Kilgore's flat was small but lavishly furnished. The walls were covered with framed photos of him and friends engaging in sporting activities. A wide sofa in gold velvet stood against one wall of the living room. Above it hung a portrait of Saffie with a self-conscious expression. She wore a low- cut black evening dress and was seated on a floor, on a white rug, her legs curled to one side. Definitely a trophy photo. There were half a dozen tall candles under glass domes on the unit framing the TV.

Ali took the bathroom and bedroom, Siv searched the living room and kitchen.

'He's got a lot more clothes than she has,' Ali called. 'Why does a man need more than twenty shirts?'

Siv finished the kitchen, which was so clean it was hard to believe that anyone lived there. When she flicked the bin open, it was empty. The fridge contained bottles of wine, cartons of kale and cucumber juice and expensive ready meals, mainly Thai. She moved into the living room and examined the industrial-style wheeled bookcase. Lots of glossy magazines about car racing, skiing and snowboarding and a stack of *Vogue* and *Elle*.

On the bottom shelf were three tall, grey cardboard boxes. Siv carried them to the coffee table and sat on the sofa to go through them. They contained Kilgore's important documents, pertaining to his car, the flat, mortgage, insurance, his birth certificate, education, fencing diplomas, medical card. All the usual details of a life. Unlike the orderly kitchen, they were in a jumble. She smoothed them out as she replaced them. She heard Ali flushing the loo and then running the bathroom tap as she opened the third box. There were folders with essays from university and old school exercise books with the Fulbrook Upper crest on the front, including Kilgore's record of achievement. She flicked through, noting that he'd scored high marks in biology and maths. On the front of a history book he'd written, *History is bunk*. Below this, another hand had corrected in red, *History is more or less bunk. If you're going to quote, get it right!*

She contemplated the correction and the by-now-familiar handwriting from the brochures. The same hand. So, whoever had written the messages on the brochures had known Kilgore when he was at school. That was a step forward. She placed the book to one side on the table. Another couple of books in, she found Kilgore's physics textbook and saw that he'd studied Newton's laws of motion. She couldn't help but smile at the thought of her dad.

Towards the back of the textbook, in a chapter about experiments with electric circuits, there was a folded piece of paper, torn from a notepad. She opened it and read the message in blue biro.

Kilgore, tell your prick of a friend to leave my sister alone. He thinks he can ignore me and take the piss, but he'll be sorry if he doesn't stop fucking about with my family. GG

She placed the note beside the history book and sat back for a moment. It was almost midnight. The grease from the burger still coated her throat and she regretted eating it. She longed for an apple or a tart pear to cleanse her mouth. Tiredness pricked at her eyes, her skin itched and her muscles ached. This day seemed endless.

She called out to Ali. 'I've found something.'

He came through, grumbling. 'What have you got? I've seen nothing except more clothes and smellies than I'd use in a lifetime.'

'This could be a treasure trove,' she told him. 'See the comment in red on the front of the history book.'

He sat beside her. 'That's the same writing as on the brochures.'

'Yep. Are we looking for a teacher here? The red pen indicates that, and the correction.'

'Could well be. And this wee threatening note, different handwriting from the brochures and on the history book, but signed "GG".' He turned to her. 'Gray Grenville, Teagan's brother.'

'Must be. I'm not sure it's significant, though. It must refer to Warren, and he did leave Grenville's sister alone — well, she dumped him after her brother dobbed him in.'

Ali rubbed his face. 'We've clocked up some miles and made headway.'

Siv placed the book and the note in evidence bags. 'Let's hope so. You've got water on your forehead.'

'I splashed my face. Trying to keep awake.'

'Sure you're OK to drive?'

'Aye, no problem.'

Siv tuned the car radio to Classic FM and, lulled by the Pastoral Symphony, fell asleep for a while on the way back to Berminster. She was dreaming hazily of Ed, a peaceful, joyous reverie where they were in parkland, when she jolted awake, aware that the car had stopped. Her mouth was dry, her thoughts full of her dead husband. She looked around, dazed. Ali was out on the verge, bent double and holding onto his knees.

She scrambled out of the car. 'What is it? Are you ill?'

'I needed to pee and then I came over funny. I'm so tired and my head's killing me. Guv, I need to get to hospital. Blood sugar's not right.' He staggered and she caught him. He was as heavy as a ton of bricks.

'Come on, lean on me. I'll get you to hospital. You'll be OK.'

Would he, though? He looked awful close up, bleached and exhausted. She braced against him and managed to stumble to the car and get him into the passenger seat. The night was black and she couldn't see any signs.

'How far are we from Berminster?'

'About twenty miles.' His eyes were drooping.

'Ali!'

'Sorry, just so sleepy.'

Siv stuck the blue light on, pulled out into the traffic and put her foot down. She rang Polly and explained what was happening, heard herself gabbling and slowed her speech, trying to stay coherent. Now and again, she glanced at Ali. His head lolled.

'Come on, Ali. Stay with me. We're almost there.'

Her breaths were short, her hands clammy on the wheel. She'd been sleeping while Ali was becoming seriously ill. Why didn't he wake her? He could have passed out and crashed. *Take it steady*, Ed murmured. *Keep your cool, just drive.*

Half an hour later, Siv slewed the car in front of the entrance to Berminster A & E and ran in, leaving Ali slumped in the passenger seat. Polly was already there, grim-faced. She collared a nurse and Siv announced an emergency with a police officer. They hurried Ali through in a wheelchair, while Polly gave them details.

Siv walked up and down by the windows in the crowded reception, cursing herself. Ed had been diabetic. He'd kept it well controlled, but he'd once had a hyperglycaemic attack. She should have recognised the symptoms, but she'd been so wrapped up in these murders, she'd failed to note the warning signs: peeing frequently, headache, fatigue. Instead, she'd ribbed Ali about his loo visits and his tiredness. He might die. God, what sort of partner was she? People could and did die in these circumstances. Fear made her pace faster. She tried to slow her breathing and pressed her hands to her scalp, massaging it. It wouldn't do for her to have a panic attack while Ali was fighting for his life.

When Polly appeared, scanning the room for her, Siv dreaded what she was going to say. She waved, her heart racing.

Polly said with relief, 'It's all right. They're rehydrating him and giving him insulin therapy. He'll be OK.'

'Are you sure? He looked so awful. It's been a long day and Ali's been working flat out on these murders. He won't have eaten properly. It takes its toll.'

'Yes,' Polly said tightly. 'He pushes himself when he should be more careful. He loves the job and, of course, he thinks very highly of you. Wants to keep up with the pace you set.'

Siv's stomach knotted with guilt. The job was everything to her, but she wasn't sure that was such a good example to be setting.

'I don't know what to say, Polly. Murder enquiries are always pressured.'

‘Hmm. You might have noticed that he wasn’t well.’ She was a kindly woman usually, but her tone was now scathing.

The accuracy of the accusation hit home. ‘I am sorry.’

‘Well. Here we are. They’ve reassured me, anyway.’

‘Would you like me to stay? Is there anything I can get you?’

‘You go on home,’ Polly said. ‘No point in both of us losing a night’s sleep.’

‘You’re right, though. I should have realised.’

Polly sighed, relenting. ‘Yes, but he doesn’t take the best care of himself, whatever’s happening. I’ll bet he’s been eating rubbish.’

‘Biscuits and burgers,’ Siv confessed.

‘Well . . . no surprises there.’ Polly gave a small smile. ‘I’ll update you later on. I’d best get back to him now.’

Siv reached home at gone four in the morning. As she got out of the car, she saw eyes gleaming from the hedge and watched a dark shape scurry away. *Goodnight, Mr Fox — or rather good morning!* She was exhausted but wide-awake.

The wagon was cold and dark, and her feet were numb after hours of sitting and driving. She switched on lamps, put kindling and logs in the stove and threw in a match. She kicked off her boots and donned Ed’s sweatshirt and a pair of thick walking socks. Then she poured a glass of akvavit and took some poppy seed crackers from the cupboard. She sipped the akvavit, eyes closed, welcoming the spirit’s fire. When she’d finished the glass, she poured another and nibbled a cracker, then needing something more substantial, fetched a wedge of Gruyère cheese and sliced a gleaming red apple to go with it.

The logs crackled, filling the stove with blazing flames. This was comfort. Not that she deserved it, with poor Ali flat on his back in a hospital bed. If he was conscious, he was probably cursing her for a slave driver.

She checked her phone and saw that she’d had an email from Rik.

I can only feel sorry for Mortimer. But sorrier for you. I've got a not very comfortable sofa bed if things get too bad. Hope you survive lunch. x

Siv smiled, enjoying the tangy apple. Feet on top of the stove, she went over the week, reflecting on the two dead men and the gaps in what she'd learned about them. Their pasts linked them, so that must be where the key to unlocking the case lay. Bertie Greene had hung out with them. And despite his insistence at the interview, he must know more. She grasped at an idea concerning him as she warmed through and her limbs grew heavy. He was definitely hiding something.

CHAPTER 16

The crematorium was open on Saturday mornings. Patrick arrived early, driving through a low mist, and walked into the reception in Bere Lodge. Phoebe Palmer was on the phone. Patrick lifted the white plastic collection box on the counter and shook it gently. Empty. The bottom section had a simple clasp that would open easily. It was shaped like a chalice with a purple label.

Berminster Crematorium Bereavement Fund.
For those in need at a distressing time.
Please give generously.

He slipped in a pound coin as Ms Palmer put the phone down. It rattled noisily.

When he introduced himself, Phoebe Palmer said, 'Mr Foxwell's not in this morning, I'm afraid.'

'That's OK. I want to talk to you.'

'Me?'

'Yes. I see that this collection box is empty. Is the money removed each evening?'

'That's right. Thank you for the contribution.'

'My pleasure. Do you make much for the fund?'

The woman seemed uncomfortable. 'A fair bit . . . It depends, of course . . . Sometimes there might be twenty pounds in there at the end of a day.'

'Not bad. I hear you were concerned about money going missing from the box last year and you reported it to Diane Lacey.'

Phoebe shifted a folder on the counter. 'Did Diane tell you?'

'She did.'

'You should speak to Mr Foxwell.'

'Of course, but right now, I want to talk to you. You seem uneasy.'

'I don't want to exceed my authority . . .'

Patrick was happy to nudge Phoebe forward. He said gravely, 'I have the authority where there's a question of theft. I'm not asking now, I'm instructing you to tell me and I'll inform Mr Foxwell of that.'

Phoebe gazed at him gratefully. 'I see. It was last October. I always check the box at lunchtime, DC Hill, just to keep a tally. Sometimes, people put quite a lot in, not just loose change, and it's not right to leave too much in there. I remove the money each evening as well. A couple of weeks running, I noticed that the box was empty on some days, which is highly unusual. I'd seen a woman put a twenty pound note in one morning, but it wasn't there at lunch. I told Diane and she informed Mr Foxwell.'

'What did he do?'

'He spoke to me and seemed cross. He asked how I could be sure that money was missing. Obviously, I couldn't swear to it, but I knew. We've run that collection for more than fifteen years, and it's a rare day when the box is empty. Mr Foxwell suggested that a member of the public might have taken money, but that didn't seem possible. Maybe once, but not over weeks. He didn't like that. I believe he spoke to all the staff then. I heard nothing more, but there was no more tampering with the box, so I suppose that suggests it was one of the team here who was being light-fingered. It was horrible. We'd never had anything like that here before, and we avoided discussing it.'

'Is this reception area ever left unattended?'

'Not for any length of time, but there would be occasions when I've popped to the loo or to get something.'

'And any member of staff could legitimately be in here?'

'Of course. We hold meetings in here and all the general admin happens in this building.'

Patrick leaned against the counter. 'So, Ms Palmer, you've been here a long time. Did you suspect someone?'

She coloured and fiddled with her wedding ring. 'Oh dear, no. I couldn't imagine who would do such a thing. You don't want to believe ill of the people you work with day in, day out. I wouldn't point a finger.'

Patrick sensed that she'd have liked to but didn't dare. 'If you have an idea, you really should tell me.'

'No . . . Honestly, I couldn't say.'

He sensed her growing discomfort. There was no point in leaning on her. 'I'll leave you in peace now. I'm glad the theft stopped.'

'Yes, thank goodness! And you will tell Mr Foxwell that I had to speak to you?'

'Of course.'

Patrick wondered if he was wasting his time with this tale of petty pilfering. But as the guv said, with a murder enquiry, you left no stone unturned.

The guv rang as he left Bere Lodge. She sounded a bit flat as she explained that Ali was in hospital, but he was doing OK and she'd call in to see him during the morning.

'All the signs were there. His tiredness, the loo breaks . . . I should have realised what it signified.'

Patrick felt mortified. 'Oh, that's tough. I feel bad now because I laughed at his nipping to the loo.'

'Me too. I should have twigged what was happening.'

'How's Polly? She must have had a terrible fright.'

'I've spoken to her just now. She's relieved that he's stable.'

'I bet. I'll go and see him later today.'

The guv went on to tell him about their visit to Kilgore's London flat and the two schoolbooks they'd found, with different handwriting.

'I'll send you photos of both. The writing on the history book matches the brochures. Try to track down Kilgore's old history teacher. The note is signed "GG". It looks as if it's from Gray Grenville, aimed at Eugene Warren and warning him to stay away from Teagan, but we should check that out. I need you to phone Grenville and confirm whether he wrote it. Get some details. Find out where he was on the night of the twentieth as well.'

'Is Grenville a suspect now, guv?'

'Seems unlikely, but belt and braces at this point.'

Patrick decided to give the hospital a ring before he got on with his tasks. He needed to salve his guilty conscience. Poor old Ali. He waged a constant battle with his health and this job did encourage sugary snacks. In future, Patrick promised himself he'd be more alert to signs of illness in his colleague. It wasn't just the guv's responsibility to keep tabs on this.

* * *

Mutsi insisted on giving Siv and Bartel a guided tour of Mortimer's house, which rejoiced in the unimaginative name of Clifftop. It was detached, with large front and rear gardens, and blandly decorated in browns and greys.

'It's architect-designed, you see, and in a prestigious position,' Mutsi said, sounding like an estate agent. 'This is the master bedroom, with splendid views across the channel. We're going to redecorate and get a new bed for in here, aren't we, Will? This is the previous marital bed, so we'd like to ring the changes.' She hooked her arm through his. She oozed allure in a black leather skirt and cerise-striped silk shirt, clasped at the waist with a wide buckled belt.

Mortimer smiled, both entranced and bewildered. As well he might be. The top of the chest of drawers beside him was covered in paint testers and fabric swatches. Siv avoided looking at the bed and gazed out at the sea view. She was ragged from too much akvavit and not enough sleep. She'd tossed and turned, waking to fret about Ali. Her only comfort was that she had a free pass to bail out of this lunch by three o'clock for Henry Kilgore's post-mortem. It spoke volumes about her relationship with her mother that she'd rather listen to grim details about a corpse than eat with her. That would amuse Rik — she'd have to email her.

Bartel sounded hearty. 'This is a fine view. Lovely to wake up to. I have just a little terraced home, but it's my own. Mind, my home is bigger than *madame's* here.'

Siv saw that Mutsi wasn't sure what to make of him or their relationship. He towered over her and Mortimer, stroking his long, pointed beard. He wore a three-quarter length, red-and-black embroidered jacket over a black shirt with a green bow tie and jeans tucked into grey biker boots. It certainly was an eye-catching look, but it suited him.

'Why do you call Siv *madame*?' Mutsi asked.

'I'm not sure. She strikes me that way,' Bartel said. He turned to Mortimer. 'As well as your interior improvements, you need to get the guttering at the left-hand corner of the house fixed. I noticed it's cracked on the way in.'

'Thanks, I hadn't spotted that.'

'I'm a roofer. My eyes always travel upwards when I approach a house.'

He sniffed. 'Something smells good. I'm as hungry as a mountain wolf.'

Mortimer tittered. He was sporting crisp blue denim jeans and shirt. The youthful outfit aged him and emphasised his stringy neck. 'I'm sure we can do something about that. Let's go down and have some nibbles.'

The living room had black leather armchairs, cement-coloured Anaglypta wallpaper, grey velour curtains and photos of sailing boats. Mortimer offered them wine and little bowls of olives and pretzels. The snacks were like toys in Bartel's huge hands.

'How is Sergeant Carlin?' Mortimer asked.

'He's doing OK, s—' Siv almost said *sir*, stopped herself and swigged wine. Hair of the dog. 'I called Polly this morning. He should be home tomorrow, but he'll need to rest for a day or two.'

'He should take more care of himself,' Mortimer said.

'Self-control, that's what it's all about,' Mutsi remarked. She pushed the pretzels away. 'He should read my blog, Siv, take note of the dietary advice I put on there. If he followed that, he wouldn't have these problems.'

'I'm not sure it's as easy as that. It's a complex illness.'

'Oh no, that's just an excuse,' Mutsi said airily. 'If you treat your body well, it will treat you well. I hope I don't sound boastful if I say that I'm an example of that. I eat carefully, do my dance exercises and Pilates every day. People often tell me that I have the figure of a woman in her twenties.' She caressed her arms with polished fingertips.

Siv speared an olive with a little more force than needed. 'I can't imagine you ever sounding boastful.'

'You write a blog, Crista?' Bartel asked.

'Yes, a highly successful one called 60Chic. I had eighty thousand followers at the last count. I give style, nutritional and makeover tips and general life advice for the mature woman.'

'Fascinating,' Bartel said.

'Crista's going to give this room a makeover,' Mortimer said gallantly.

'Definitely — as soon as the bedroom's finished! That wallpaper's *so* nineties. We need colour and warmth in here, fabrics and textures. I'm contemplating apricot and gold, which will light up with the evening sun. Sivvi, your landlord makes throws and rugs, doesn't he?'

'Hmm.'

'I could come and chat to Corran, call in on you while I'm there. I still can't understand why you want to live at the bottom of a soggy field, like a gypsy. It's hardly the kind of address a professional woman should have. You're of the same mind, aren't you, Will?'

'Erm . . . well . . .' Mortimer busied himself with topping up glasses.

Siv stretched her legs out. 'It's a meadow. I like it. I can listen to the river.'

'But so odd and remote!' Mutsi exclaimed. 'Anyway, I'd better see to the lunch. Don't want it to be overcooked.'

Siv couldn't help herself. 'Surely the instructions were on the packet?'

Mutsi stood and smoothed her skirt. Siv saw Mortimer's eyes swivel to her long legs in sheer black tights.

'Always so witty, Sivvi,' her mother said, gliding from the room.

Bartel and Mortimer started chatting about fishing. Siv tuned out. She flicked through a book on the coffee table, *Sailing for Beginners*. You had to hand it to Mutsi, she always did her homework diligently. She scanned a few lines about how wind moves a boat, but she was trying to recall the idea she'd had about Bertie Greene in the small, akvavit-fuelled hours. It eluded her now. Her phone pinged and she saw a text from Ali.

They're saying I need to rest, but that's baloney. Much better already. Sorry for giving you a fright.

Hugely relieved, she texted back.

You'll do as the doctors tell you. Polly had a bigger fright than me. Behave and follow orders.

Mortimer was waxing onto Bartel about sea fishing and a wonderful turbot he'd caught. He was more human and relaxed away from work, his face softer. Siv could only feel sorry for him and anxious about the trickiness of the situation. If Mutsi stayed true to form, she'd grow bored as soon as she'd spent enough of Mortimer's money on redecorating his house. If her mother then legged it, working with him would be awful. She might have to find another job. Her wine tasted sour, but it was her mood, not the expensive Chablis. Just as she'd found her feet and a measure of stability, Mutsi had to turn up and spoil everything.

Come on, Sivster, buck up! Ed murmured. *Mortimer might be relieved to see the back of her in a year's time.* She smiled and drifted into picturing what today would have been like if Ed was still alive. He'd have accompanied Mutsi to the kitchen and absorbed her attention.

Bartel broke into her daydream, nudging her. 'Lunch, come on!'

They made their way through a melon starter, *lihapullat*, the Finnish meatballs, served with rice and salad, followed by chocolate torte. Bartel had second helpings of the meatballs, informing Mutsi that in Poland, there was a similar dish called *klopsiki*.

'You'll have to give me the recipe,' he said, nudging Siv's foot under the table.

'Of course. I made them with the leanest ground beef and just a tiny bit of whipping cream.'

Siv was sure that they tasted exactly like IKEA's meatballs, and the melon and torte were undoubtedly from Waitrose, but the ordeal was almost over and she should make up for her earlier crankiness.

'Delicious,' she said. She glanced at her watch as she finished her dessert. 'I'm afraid I'll have to go to the mortuary soon.'

'On a Saturday! Surely not!' Mutsi cried.

'Dr Anand often does a Saturday when he's busy,' Siv replied.

'Well, it's a conversation stopper!' Mutsi collected plates. 'Just help me make some coffee, Sivvi.'

In the pine kitchen, Mutsi switched the coffee machine on and gestured at the wall tiles, featuring clusters of cherries. 'It's so dated in here as well! Really, the whole house needs to be modernised.'

She sidled close. Her subtle scent was woody and sensual. Siv moved back a little.

'Your hair's better, Sivvi. That's a flattering style, although a little longer around the ears would be good. You have quite big ears. I remember remarking on that when you were born.'

'Thanks.'

'Is Bartel your boyfriend?'

'He's a good friend.'

Mutsi tutted impatiently. 'Yes, but are you sleeping with him in your eccentric little wagon?'

'Why do you ask?'

Mutsi raised a perfectly plucked eyebrow. 'I understand you miss Ed, and any port in a storm and all that jazz, but he's hardly *suitable*. Personable, yes, but rather uncouth. His hands are like shovels! Those ragged nails!'

'He rips off roof tiles, what do you expect? I like him. He tells me fascinating stories.'

'Oh, Sivvi! I just don't understand you.'

'That's true.'

'You need to get out and meet more people instead of playing with your paper shapes.'

Siv ignored her. 'Shall I get some cups?'

'They're on the tray, but I need a jug. Have you heard from Rik at all? She never replies to me. I've no idea what she's up to. I don't know what I'm supposed to have done to her. I'm sure I always tried my best with both you girls. Rik's so edgy and *trying*. You always had a gentler nature.'

'I hear from her now and again. She seems OK.'

'Does she ask after me?'

'No. Can we change the subject?'

'For goodness' sake! I am her mother and—' Mutsi paused as the doorbell rang. 'Ah, good. We have a guest who's joining us for coffee.' She smiled slyly. 'Now, this is someone who would be *perfect* for you. I'm sure Will thinks so too, although he's discreet about these matters. Of course, we asked him along before you said you were bringing your roofer friend and dashing off. I'd planned for the four of us to go for a walk, and then tea on the yacht. Pour the milk in that jug and you'll see what I mean!'

When they returned to the dining room, Siv's heart sank. Tommy Castles was sitting at the table, swiftly demolishing the last slice of chocolate torte. He wore a chunky blue polo neck jumper over his athletic build, and he'd had his hair cropped short. Not for the first time, Siv wondered if he was ex-military. An SAS type, sinewy and gung-ho.

'Hi, Siv! This is amazing pud, Crista. It'll set me up for an afternoon hike.'

Siv swallowed fortifying black coffee. 'Good to see you, Tommy. You met Bartel at the Halloween party last year.'

'That's right, just in passing. You had to rush off. You always seem to be rushing off when I see you, Siv. So, Crista, are you all moved in now?'

'All done.' She took Mortimer's hand. 'We're over the moon.'

Mortimer wrinkled his nose at her. 'We are, and we're glad that family and friends could come and celebrate today.'

Tommy winked at Siv. 'What's Siv going to call you outside of the station, then? She can hardly say *sir*.'

Mortimer fiddled with his coffee. 'Will, of course. Same as everyone else.'

'That's settled, then. Hey, Siv, I hear Ali's in hospital. Too many doughnuts, as per. Hope he never has to chase a suspect. He'd probably have a heart attack.'

Siv controlled her response. 'He's much better today. I expect he'll be given stern advice.'

Tommy laughed. 'Not that he'll follow it. He's led by his stomach, that one.'

Bartel popped two lumps of sugar in his coffee. 'You admire Ali, don't you, Siv? He's reliable and skilful.'

'That's right, and a team player. I trust him. You need that in a colleague. Apologies, everyone, but I have to talk to a pathologist.'

'Going so soon?' Tommy winked at her.

'Afraid so. I have to leave the field to you. Want me to drop you on the way, Bartel?'

He nodded, thanking Mutsi and Mortimer for their hospitality.

* * *

Siv almost skipped to the car. Sweet relief! That was done and dusted and she'd ensure that she was unavailable for social visits for as long as possible.

'You did well,' Bartel commented as Siv accelerated from Clifftop.

'Thanks. And thank you so much for coming. Lifesaver.'

'I was entertained. The wine was terrific. Is your mother trying to matchmake between you and Tommy Castles?'

'That's her idea.'

'You can't trust a man with narrow eyes. I enjoyed the food, but those meatballs *were* from IKEA.'

'Definitely.'

'Your mother fibs without blinking.'

'Always. It's one of her skills.' But Siv had had enough of Mutsi as a topic. 'Are you fishing at the moment, or is it too cold?'

'It's never too cold to fish as long as you wear layers. Good pike and perch to be caught in January.'

Siv wasn't the slightest bit interested in fish, unless on a plate with chips, but she liked watching Bartel by the river. His stillness and concentration were soothing. 'Let me know when you're going. I'll take a walk and bring you coffee.'

'Yes. Um, I have a little thing to tell you,' Bartel said, pulling at his beard.

'Oh yes?'

'I have a new friend. A lady. She's from Estonia.'

'What's her name?'

'Astrella. I met her in *Polska*. Early days. We'll see.'

Was he trying to hint that their fishing rendezvous were a thing of the past? He was usually direct but perhaps he felt awkward. And now, so did she. She made her voice upbeat. 'I'm pleased for you.'

'You are?'

'Of course.'

Bartel hummed. 'Your boss man needs to get that guttering fixed.'

'Uh-huh. I'm sure Mutsi will remind him.'

'I must read 60Chic, get some lifestyle tips.'

'You can learn how to contour your cheekbones.'

'Essential for when you're up a ladder.'

She smiled. She was genuinely pleased that he'd met this Astrella but hoped she was a woman who had no interest in fishing or riverbanks.

CHAPTER 17

'So, your victim, Henry Kilgore, was stabbed in the neck with a thin, fairly blunt blade, such as a small kitchen knife — it didn't hit an artery but it cut his windpipe, so he bled out internally. Basically, he drowned in his own blood. Nasty way to go. Treacle toffee?' Rey Anand, the pathologist, proffered the bag of sweets towards Siv.

'I'll pass this time.'

'We found no phone on him,' Rey added, 'just a set of keys and his wallet.'

Rey went on to explain that the angle indicated the killer had stood slightly to his right side and behind him, so Kilgore might not have seen his assailant until it was too late. However, skin cells recovered from beneath the middle fingers of Kilgore's right hand revealed trace DNA that didn't match his or Eugene Warren's, suggesting that he might have managed to grab at his attacker. Estimated time of death was in the early hours of Tuesday morning. Post-mortem bruising on his head and body indicated that he'd been shoved behind the summerhouse soon after the attack.

'Kilgore died around the same time as Eugene Warren then,' Siv said.

'That's correct. Those two men must have made someone very angry.'

As Siv was saying goodbye to Dr Anand, Steve Wooton called.

'We've finished at Mallow Cottage. Reports back from Forensics confirm that tiny traces of Kilgore's blood were on the back of one of the chairs on the patio and also on the decking that led to the summerhouse. We found fibres from Eugene Warren's fleece on the back of the other chair. No prints or other DNA in the house except Ms Kilgore's. She's a thorough cleaner. No sign of the strap or belt used to kill Warren, or the knife used on Kilgore. The killer tidied up.'

The bad news, Siv decided as she returned to her car, was that Uniform were in trouble about Tuesday night. It had been shoddy work and Ali had been right in saying that the team — and the Force — could be embarrassed. It seemed likely there'd be an inquiry and possible disciplinary measures. Imelda Kilgore would understandably be on the warpath. Siv decided to send an email to Mortimer, avoiding any more direct contact with him over the weekend.

That done, she drove to Berminster General and stopped at the shop on the ground floor. Ali would be missing his Gitanes, but they were contraband on the ward. Instead, she bought newspapers, sugar-free chewing gum and a black fidget cube with bright red buttons and levers. The box assured her that it was ideal for people who needed distraction.

She found Ali sitting beside his bed, attached to an IV drip, and chatting away to the two men in the beds nearest him. He'd be loving the company, the bustle of the ward and the camaraderie of his peers.

He beamed when he saw her. 'Guv! This is cracking! Pull up a chair. You can swish the curtain round for a wee bit of privacy.'

She drew the bright blue curtain, as he requested. 'How are you doing?'

'Much better. They've pumped me full of the good stuff. I should be back home tomorrow.' He pulled a face. 'My own stupid fault. I wasn't checking my blood sugar levels regularly. Everyone's told me off. Will I never learn?'

'Up to you. You should have said something though, you know. I've been kicking myself for not noticing you were going downhill.'

'Ah, don't beat yourself up.'

He looked embarrassed, so Siv just said, 'I'm glad you're OK, anyway.' She scanned his face. He looked definitely worse for wear, but his eyes were bright enough.

'Aye, I'm flying it.' He examined the fidget cube. 'This should keep me occupied for a while. What's the story on our dead men?'

Siv knew she should protest that he was meant to be resting, but she also knew Ali, and that wouldn't work, so she updated him.

'Running with the forensics, this is how I see it playing. Warren and Kilgore agreed to meet someone at Mallow Cottage. Warren drove there from London and Kilgore got the call as he was on his way to Bertie Greene's. Whatever the reason for the meeting, it was persuasive enough to make Kilgore change his plans. It would have been around a twenty-minute walk from Larch Dell to the cottage, during which Kilgore left Saffie a message. He and Warren sat on chairs on the patio. Who knows whether our killer was part of this catch-up or just ambushed them. We don't know which one died first. The killer shoved Kilgore behind the summerhouse and then took Warren's body to the crem, either in his car or their own.'

'So, the cottage and the crem were significant places for the killer.'

'Seems so. Maybe that significance led to the different ways in which the bodies were dealt with. Warren's placement below wreaths suggests to me that his death was the more meaningful to the killer. Patrick's looking into it, but I'm not sure what to make of this alleged thieving at the crem.'

'Except that small crimes are often linked to bigger ones.'

'Yeah, or it might be a blind alley. I need to crack on. Can I get you anything else?'

'No, that's OK, this is more than enough. Polly will be in soon.' He had a smug expression. 'But don't rush off. I've got something for *you*. I rang Pie Mad earlier on. Spoke to the owner-cum-manager. The shop's at the back of Euston Station. The manager confirmed that Warren worked for her most weeks, Thursdays and Fridays. Casual basis, cash in hand. He'd been doing it for about two years. Just wandered in one day and asked if she'd got any jobs going. He seems to have lived on an ad hoc basis, taking his chances where he found them. The manager was annoyed when he didn't turn up last week, and couldn't raise him on his phone. She hadn't seen the news about his death.'

'What did he do? Make pies?'

'Better than that. He delivered them to businesses in the area, using one of those tricycles with a box attached. There's one brings ice creams around here in the summer. Pie Mad has regular customers as well as occasional ones. I asked the manager to email me a list of clients that he'd been to over the time he worked for her. There are around ninety.' He picked up his phone, pinched the screen, zooming in on something, then held it out to Siv.

Footprint, King's Cross, she read, as Ali exclaimed, 'Bingo! Warren hadn't seen Kilgore for years, but one day he pedalled his trike to Footprint to hand over his tasty lunches. He could well have bumped into Kilgore. We have blanks to fill in from there, but I reckon that has to be how they came back into contact.'

'Thank you for this. Although, of course, you shouldn't have been working while you're ill.'

Ali grinned. 'Of course. Total bed rest, but if you see Polly on the way out, don't mention it.'

'Patrick's at the station today, chasing stuff up. We're not idle without you, you know,' Siv said. 'But it's very strange that Kilgore hardly mentioned Warren or Greene to his friends. Warren featured prominently in his life at one time, and if they did meet at Footprint in recent months, it would surely have rated a comment. Which makes me think they had something to hide.' And Siv reckoned she might know just where to find it.

A nurse approached, saying that she needed a couple of minutes with Ali, so Siv said her goodbyes.

'I'll be back at work soon, promise,' Ali told her.

'We'll see. I'll keep my fingers crossed, but I'd say you're being overly optimistic.'

In the car, she rang HMP Berminster and asked to speak to the governor. Within fifteen minutes, she was on her way there.

* * *

Siv stopped at Corran's and Paul's on the way home and handed over a bottle of wine and posh chocolates, which she sometimes dropped off in return for the logs and occasional meals they gave her.

Corran kissed her on both cheeks. 'Paul's out, but come in for a cuppa — or a glass of this, even.'

'I won't tonight, thanks. I've a complex case on and need to work.'

'Those murders, is it?' Corran asked sagely.

'That's right.'

'Tell you what, then, take a portion of macaroni cheese back with you. I made loads. Just the thing for a cold night. Cold enough for snow. Weather report said we might get a dusting.'

It was almost half eight and a long time since lunch, so she accepted. She sat at the farmhouse table in the wide kitchen of the converted barn, while Corran dished a portion of the meal into a container with small, deft hands. He was short and light on his feet. He and Paul had made a lovely home and were almost fully self-sufficient. They seemed an ideal pair, but she'd occasionally overheard them arguing fiercely when she'd walked by. She smiled while Corran told her that the vet had been round to trim the goats' hooves and Judy had been uncooperative, but she was keen to get on home and go over the investigation.

As she was leaving, Siv said, 'Just to give you a heads-up, my mother might swoop on you for advice about interior décor. She's settled in town now. And it would give her an excuse to come this way.'

Mutsi had phoned Corran when she'd been snooping around last year and had made derogatory comments even then about her daughter's choice of accommodation. Corran was diplomatic and appreciated Siv's desire for privacy.

'OK. I'll keep the discussion to business.'

'Thanks.' Siv paused. 'She's got a partner with plenty of money now, so make sure she buys your most expensive products.'

Corran grinned. 'Understood.'

When she opened the wagon door, she recalled that the log basket was almost empty. She brought it out to the wood store at the side of the patio and chucked logs in, releasing the oaky scent of apples. She looked up at the full moon. A wolf moon with Venus glittering nearby. Something rustled in the trees. One of the goats bleated, an owl hooted mournfully.

In the wagon, Siv longed to head straight for the akvavit but made herself wait. She lit the stove, chucked the meal in the microwave, changed into jeans and Ed's sweatshirt, then opened the fridge and poured a glass. She held it up to the light — water of life, liquid fire or liver destroyer, depending on your viewpoint.

'*Kippis!*' She drank, savouring the caraway notes, and then put a large dollop of ketchup on her mac 'n' cheese, stuck it on a tray and sat by the stove.

When she checked her messages, she saw that a Ms Jane Ferris had contacted the station to confirm that she'd met Henry Kilgore for lunch two weeks ago in the Three Swans. Siv had also asked Patrick earlier in the day to provide her with an update and was pleased to see that he'd sent one.

Guv,

Kilgore was already scouting jobs. I checked with Footprint and he'd taken that Wednesday when he came to town as leave. I spoke to Jane Ferris. Very sparky lady. She owns and runs an events company, based in town, but with a lot of work around London. She said that Kilgore had phoned her because he'd heard she might be recruiting. It was a preliminary meeting and the job won't be available until May. She was impressed with him and was about to ask him to send in a CV.

I spoke to Gray Grenville about that note you found at Kilgore's flat. Grenville had a bit of trouble remembering it. Then he said he'd given it to Kilgore to pass to Warren, warning him to leave Teagan alone. He was at home on his own on the twentieth. He'd also previously given me the name Leah Steele as the girl he saw with Warren on the beach.

I contacted Leah Steele. She denied ever hanging out with Warren and made it clear she hadn't liked him.

Tried to get hold of the council about Andy Smeaton, but no one available until Monday. The head at Fulbrook Upper went into the school to check records. Kilgore's history teacher was a Liam Jamieson, now retired. I've got his address in town. Want me to see him?

All alibis now checked.

Jane Ferris. That was one unidentified woman off the list. Saffie would be relieved to hear that her fiancé hadn't been having an affair. There were still two mysterious women out there, though — the one who'd stopped Saul Robbins in the cemetery, and the one who'd been with Eugene Warren on the beach.

Siv finished her food and set the tray aside. It had been a productive day, the lunch at Clifftop aside, and that could have been worse. Sometimes it was well worth scratching an itch, and her trip to HMP Berminster had struck gold. In the records, she'd seen that Bertie Greene had few visits during his time there: three from his ex-wife, a couple from old colleagues and one, last October, from Eugene Warren.

She'd photographed the entry and emailed it to Patrick and Ali, with a message.

> *Warren visited Greene at Berminster jail.*
>
> *Patrick, I need you with me tomorrow to visit Greene and then Liam Jamieson. We won't tell Greene we're coming. I'll pick you up at 9.30.*
>
> *Ali, rest up. Keep you posted.*

She found Eugene Warren's notebook, put her feet up on the stove and flicked through it. On closer inspection, it was a series of descriptions and musings with some amateurish pencil sketches of birds. Most seemed to be about days he spent at the Walthamstow Wetlands.

> *All day today at Lockwood Reservoir. Hot and sunny. Air was amazingly clean for London. Only saw two other people. The reservoir is the highest in the wetlands, so amazing views across the water to the city skyline, and I could glimpse the Orbit sculpture in Olympic Park.*
>
> *Saw several dunlin, a Siberian dusky warbler, tern and common sandpipers.*
>
> *When Lockwood was being excavated in 1903, they found a log boat, possibly prehistoric. Also swords — some Viking — spearheads, a Palaeolithic flint, and Roman pottery and tiles.*
>
> *Lockwood is deep, at least eight metres, and tranquil. Undisturbed. So peaceful, I wanted to cry. Sat for ages by the water, wondering what other treasures and oddities might be in the deep. It would be the best reservoir here for slipping away quietly, joining the ancient bones, settling into the silt. No fuss, no trouble. Night, night.*

This was a very different man to the stroppy teenager she'd heard about. Introspective, sensitive, melancholic. Also, from his final comments, a man who was possibly contemplating suicide.

She put the book away, refilled her glass and took out her folding. She was working now on the steam yacht, using navy and black paper, and shaping the two funnels. They were tricky, demanding concentration. For a few minutes, she listened to the silence. It would make Ali jittery, but Siv relaxed into it.

At one in the morning, she glanced out of the window and saw that the meadow was covered in a fine dusting of snow.

CHAPTER 18

'Guv, you know that Noah has a friend called Eden now?' Patrick was sharply dressed and groomed, his shirt as white as the snow outside.

'He mentioned her at Christmas.'

'Well, she told Noah that she'd met Eugene Warren back in the day when he lived here.'

'Oh, well, that's convenient.'

'I know, right? Anyway, I asked her if she'd talk to us. She'll be at the house around lunchtime.'

'OK, that might be useful.'

The snow on the roads was thawing, making the drive a little easier, but the streets were still pretty, the sun glinting on the white pavements. The harbour was inviting as they drove past, with boats rocking gently on the water. Siv could just glimpse Mortimer's blue-and-white boat at the far end. She wondered if he was on board with Mutsi, preparing to sail away for lunch. He was only in his early fifties, but senior officers sometimes retired fairly young, courtesy of robust pension pots. Maybe he'd decide to take his hefty pension soon and set sail with Mutsi on a long, around-the-world voyage. What a lovely idea.

Patrick drummed on the window, shattering her reverie as they pulled up in front of Bertie Greene's home. Siv wondered whether she should have bought him a fidget cube too.

He asked, 'What made you check the visitor records at the prison?'

'Not sure,' she said. 'I'd got the impression that Greene was concealing something. It struck me the other night that it might be to do with his time in jail, so it was worth a try.'

Greene answered the door wearing a tatty cotton dressing gown and holding a mug of coffee. He looked and smelled stale.

'We need to speak to you urgently, Mr Greene. This is DC Patrick Hill.'

He shrugged and waved them in. The living room was cramped and chilly. Two men on the television were cooking and exchanging banter. One of them was handling a lump of pork, the other juggled onions. Greene rolled up a large duvet that was bunched on the sofa and indicated that they could sit there. The two cushions were stained and one was leaking stuffing. There was just one other chair, the tall-backed, padded kind that you found in care homes. Greene sat in that. The ceiling above his head bulged, the plaster radiating cracks. Moisture dimpled the walls and there was mould around the window frames. The ceiling light flickered through a torn lampshade, casting shadows. The carpet badly needed vacuuming. The only dash of brightness were the children's drawings attached to the back of the door. This was a man only just holding back the tide of chaos.

'I won't bother asking how I can help you,' Greene said wearily.

Siv nudged empty cider cans with her foot. 'It's straightforward,' she told him. 'You lied about having no contact with Eugene Warren. He visited you in prison. I've seen the record. You need to tell us about it.'

Greene shivered. 'I hoped I might get away with that, but I should have known better. I never get away with anything.'

Amazing, how liars so often try for the sympathy vote.

'Poor you,' Siv said.

'I didn't kill him, or Henry.'

'Let's say that we accept that for now, unless we find evidence to the contrary. Just tell us about Warren.'

Greene crossed and recrossed his legs, pulling the dressing gown over his hairy knees. 'Eugene wrote to me in prison. He'd read local news online and saw that I'd been sent there. He asked if he could visit me. I was gobsmacked. It was the first time I'd heard from him in years. I didn't particularly want to see him, but I wasn't overwhelmed with visitors, so I said yes. He came just the once last autumn, a couple of weeks before I got out. Brought me some books. He was different to the old Eugene. Quieter, nicer. Not taking the piss. That was it, really.'

Siv asked, 'How long was he with you for?'

'About forty-five minutes.'

'What did you talk about? What prompted him to travel from London to see you after so long?'

Greene said, 'I wondered about that. We chatted a bit about the old days. He asked if I ever saw Henry, so I told him now and again. I got the impression he was a bit lonely. He didn't say anything about where he was living or what he did. Just seemed to want a trip down memory lane.' He sniffed and pinched his nose. 'He asked about what had happened to me, how I ended up behind bars instead of guarding them.'

'Did Eugene tell you that he'd seen Henry in London?'

Greene looked surprised. 'No, nothing like that. Had he?'

Siv frowned. 'Mr Greene, why did you want to get away with not mentioning this visit?'

He tucked his chin in. 'I've had enough of the police in my life. I deserved jail, I did my sentence, but now I want to make things right with my kids. This place is no palace, but my kids can stay here. I've got a job. I can just about pay the bills and maintenance for them. I didn't have anything to do with what happened to Henry and Eugene. I was trying to keep trouble from my door, but it backfired.'

Patrick said solemnly, 'It might be a good idea to keep an eye out for trouble. It appears that your friends died because of their previous connection here. You were part of their circle.'

Greene gaped. 'You reckon I might be in danger? Who from?'

Siv pressed the point. 'It's a possibility, and if I could tell you that, I'd have made an arrest by now. Of course, if you're the killer, you've nothing to worry about.' She left the comment heavy in the air, but Siv didn't suspect him. He struck her as a man who'd been frightened and battered by life. He was too timid to have organised a complex double killing. 'Anything else you want to get off your chest while we're here?'

He shook his head.

'Really?' Siv raised an eyebrow. 'But you haven't mentioned your link to someone who works at the crematorium.'

'What?' He shifted, his chair creaking. 'Oh, you mean Saul. I don't have much to do with him. He's so distant he's barely family, that's why he didn't cross my mind.'

Siv stood. 'Bear in mind that I could be charging you with wasting police time. Think it over and ring me if you suddenly remember something I should know.'

Back in the car she said, 'I'm convinced he's still not telling us everything. But if what he did say is true, then Warren was keeping an eye on what went on in Berminster. His notebook indicates a man who was solitary and sad, possibly depressed.'

'Maybe he was homesick and it was a way of touching base. Reaching back into his old life?' Patrick said.

'If it was just homesickness, he could have contacted his sister. No, it's more complicated than that. Now for Mr Jamieson.'

* * *

Liam Jamieson had a flat in Waterside, the art deco building by the harbour that Mutsi had just vacated. He was on the second floor and waiting for them at the door.

'Do come in. I've never had a visit from the police, so this is quite the novelty. I see you have your noses to the grindstone, even on a Sunday!'

'The wicked never rest, so neither can we,' Siv told him.

'Well, quite! Do sit down. Can I get you coffee?'

Siv quelled Patrick with a glance. 'No, thank you. We need to speak to you about a former pupil of yours, Henry Kilgore. You taught him history.'

Jamieson was tall and elegant, with a domed head, thinning hair and a bony Adam's apple. He hitched his flannel trousers up at the knees and crossed his legs. 'I saw that Eugene Warren and Henry Kilgore had been found murdered. I have to say, if it doesn't sound harsh, that I wasn't too surprised about Warren. I always thought that he was the kind of boy who might come to a bad end. Kilgore was a surprise. He was well brought up, even if he tried to pretend otherwise.'

'Did you teach both the boys?'

'I taught Warren for a year and then he dropped history. Kilgore kept on with it — a pointless choice, really, as he had no interest in it. I believe he saw it as an easy option, just a load of old stories that you could read and regurgitate. He liked not to have to extend himself too much. One of those sporty males who do the academic work grudgingly. The bane of every teacher's life — unless you're a PE teacher. It was a shame, because Kilgore had a good brain when he put his mind to it. Of course, as an educator one sees a lot of that.'

He settled back in his chair and steepled his fingers beneath his chin. 'I have to say, I was glad to retire. I'd started to despair about my time in the classroom. Now I give talks to groups of other retired people who are appreciative and insightful listeners. In fact, I've just signed up to present some sessions to the BSS, Berminster Senior Students—'

Siv interrupted. 'If we could get back to Henry Kilgore, that would be helpful.'

'Why, yes, of course.' If Jamieson was offended at the interruption, he didn't show it.

Siv took out the evidence bag. 'We found this history exercise book in Kilgore's possessions. There's a comment in red on the front. Did you write it?'

Jamieson took a pair of reading glasses from his shirt pocket and examined the front of the book. 'No, that's not my handwriting. The amendment is correct, however. Typical of Kilgore's sloppy attitude to misquote, although Henry Ford's words often are.' He removed his glasses and twirled them by one arm. 'You're both downcast. Is this writing important in some way?'

'It could be,' Patrick said. 'Can you show us an example of your handwriting?'

'Ah, of course. You need comparative verification. I've always been of the opinion that the police are, in fact, very like historians. Like us, you have to check many sources, seek material evidence, follow a discipline, cross-check and test rigorously. In this case, we have the test of identification — is the source's origin clearly authenticated? I've often considered writing a paper on the similarities between historical research and detective work. My mature students would find it fascinating. Perhaps you'd be willing to share some of your experiences with me if I were to do so?'

'Just an example of your handwriting for now please, sir,' Siv replied. Although Jamieson's passion for his subject reminded her of her father, right now, her patience was wearing thin.

'Sorry, yes, of course! I'm afraid I get carried away!' He rose and crossed to a table strewn with paperwork. He selected a piece of paper and brought it across to Siv. 'Here are my preparatory notes for a talk on Hannibal — the man and the legend.'

Siv and Patrick stared at the page. An entirely different hand. Siv handed it back.

'Thank you. Is that writing in red pen familiar to you? Could another teacher have written it? Maybe a supply teacher if you'd been ill?'

Jamieson resumed his chair and pleated his trousers again. 'Inspector, I never had a day off sick during my career. I don't recognise the hand. Colleagues wouldn't usually encroach on each other's pupils, and I taught Kilgore for five years. Perhaps another pupil wrote it — one who was better educated than Kilgore.'

Siv was disappointed. They'd had to sit through Jamieson's pontificating with no result. Her thoughts went to Etta Parton, but she had a confirmed alibi for the time of the murders. Still, it would be worth getting a sample of her handwriting. 'Is there anything else you can tell us about Warren and Kilgore? Warren left school and town suddenly, before taking his exams.'

'I can't help you, I'm afraid. I stopped teaching Warren when he was fifteen, and it was a relief. He didn't cause outright trouble in class, but he was a devious, unpleasant boy. One of those with a bland, insolent stare. I confiscated a pornographic magazine from him during a lesson, and of course, he made the most of saying that I wanted it for my own perusal. As for Kilgore — he did the minimum to get the grades he needed, but he wasn't a troublemaker, as it were. Have you any idea why they were killed?'

'I'm sure we'll find the perpetrator,' Siv said as she got up.

'Thank you, sir,' Patrick added. 'I'm interested in what you said about the similarities between detectives and historians. Do contact me if you'd like to discuss it. It's the kind of thing I like to post on Twitter.'

Jamieson's initial expression of delight at Patrick's interest dropped and he raised an eyebrow. 'Twitter . . . I see. I don't indulge in tweets myself, but I must keep an open mind about all opportunities.'

'Sucking up to teacher?' Siv joked as they left the building.

'I liked him; he was old school, literally. I've always been keen on history — I did it for GCSE.'

'You don't think Jamieson might have droned on in class, liking the sound of his own voice?'

'Maybe, but I bet he's a master of his subject. Hannibal fascinates me. Taking his army across the Alps was an amazing feat. Historians are still arguing about the route he planned. I'd like to hear that talk.'

This was a new angle to Patrick. 'Maybe the BSS would let you attend as an honorary senior.' Siv chuckled. 'In the meantime, can you contact Etta Parton for a sample of her handwriting? She was a swot at school. Maybe she wrote on Kilgore's book.'

'But her alibi . . .'

'Even so. She might have written on the brochures for some reason that has nothing to do with the deaths.'

'We're not much further forward,' Patrick said glumly.

'Yeah. That interview got us exactly nowhere. We're following lots of leads and just going around in circles.'

* * *

Noah sat contentedly next to Eden. The house was the tidiest that Siv had ever seen it. The bright light showed clean surfaces instead of the smears and clutter that used to greet her last year. It smelled much better too. Patrick brought through coffee and biscuits.

'Eden saw the news about Eugene Warren,' Noah said. 'She wasn't sure about talking formally to the police, but I told her you don't bite.'

'Rarely, anyway,' Siv said, smiling. Eden struck her as a woman who wouldn't be scared of much.

Eden laughed and nibbled a biscuit. She was pretty, with brunette hair and delicate wrists and ankles. 'If Patrick's anything to go by, the police have got more user-friendly.'

Patrick inclined his head. 'This is just a chat over a cuppa.'

Noah patted Eden's arm. 'Go ahead. Tell them what you told me.'

'OK.' Eden put her mug down and said matter-of-factly, 'I met Eugene because he was a client. I started sex working when I was seventeen. My dad had thrown me out and I needed to make a living. I'd say Eugene was about that age when he first came my way. I didn't see him that often, maybe half a dozen times. He was a bit full of himself, bragged about all the girls he slept with. Made me wonder why he needed to pay me if he had that much sex for free, but I wasn't going to turn down a client. He seemed all mixed up. Troubled. I could tell he was on drugs. Sometimes when I saw him, he was really high.' She reached for her coffee and glanced at Noah.

'Did he tell you things?' Siv asked. Some men used sex workers as a confessor or a therapist.

'He talked about someone he bought drugs from. He called him "The Wheel". Seemed a bit in awe of him and . . . well . . . dependent on him. He'd get anxious about meeting him. I got the impression that this "Wheel" kept him dangling, but he was a reliable supplier, so Eugene was hooked.'

'Did Eugene ever mention a proper name?'

'No, just that nickname. I felt sorry for him, because he was young and in a bit of a state. One night, he was ever so upset. Really shaken and sort of sweaty. He said something terrible had happened, and he was going to get out of Berminster and never come back. I asked him about it, but he clammed up. I never saw him again.'

Siv asked, 'When was this?'

'I can't remember exactly. I reckon it was 2010, around April time.'

'Eugene left school and town that May,' Patrick said. 'I've never heard of a dealer called "The Wheel". How about you, Noah?'

'Doesn't ring any bells with me. Hope you're not implying I was ever into the drug scene. I am now, of course, with my blood thinners.' He winked at Siv. 'I wonder if they've any street value?'

'I wouldn't be surprised,' she said and then thanked Eden. 'That's really helpful.'

At the front door, she said to Patrick, 'We'll meet first thing in the morning to catch up. There's lots of information here that we need to pull together.'

'Will Ali be back?'

'Not sure. If he isn't, we'll just have to forge on. Enjoy the rest of your day.'

In the car, she sat for a moment, going over all the things the team hadn't yet pinned down. There were two sets of handwriting they still needed to identify, unknown people hovering on the edges of the enquiry and now a drug dealer called 'The Wheel'. This afternoon, she'd go into the station and list it all on the incident board.

She considered going to the café at Bere Marsh Nature Reserve, which did amazing soups, but decided to defer gratification and found Toby Foxwell's home details. An unannounced call on a Sunday would annoy him, but he could suffer for not divulging information about the thefts the previous year.

His address was a three-storey house not far from the hospital. Four cars were parked on the drive outside, indicating visitors. When she rang the bell, a portly man wearing a striped cardigan and holding a large gin and tonic opened the door. He asked cheerfully if she was Maddie's friend, Lucinda.

'I'm afraid not, sir. DI Drummond to see Mr Foxwell.' She held up her ID.

He stepped back to let her in, and she was greeted by music, the buzz of chatting and laughter and the mouth-watering smell of Sunday roast. The portly man winked roguishly at her and popped his head through a door off the hallway.

'Toby! It's the police for you. What have you been up to, you naughty boy?'

The voices stopped, leaving Michael Bublé singing that he couldn't help falling in love. Foxwell appeared, followed by a perplexed woman holding a wine bottle.

'What are you doing here? Is there something wrong at the crematorium?' Foxwell asked. He was in smart chinos and an open-necked shirt. Siv could smell his aromatic aftershave.

'I'm sorry to disturb your Sunday, Mr Foxwell, but I need to ask you about something.'

'Can't it wait until tomorrow? We've got lunch guests.'

'Afraid not.'

He turned to the woman. 'Do apologise to our guests, Maddie. I'll be as quick as I can.'

She looked daggers at Siv. 'OK, but I don't want lunch to spoil.'

Foxwell hurried Siv into a cramped study on the other side of the house.

'This is very inconvenient, Inspector.' He didn't invite her to sit down.

'I'm sure. However, Mr Foxwell, I find it inconvenient when people keep information from me in a serious investigation.'

'What do you mean?'

'I mean the problem about the bereavement fund collection box.'

'Oh, that!' He seemed relieved. 'It was hardly worth mentioning to you.'

'Really? You strike me as a thorough kind of manager, one who's keen on the rules. I'm surprised that when I asked if there'd been any problems at the crematorium, you didn't see fit to tell me about an allegation of theft.'

He'd lost ground. 'That was last year,' he said weakly.

'Only last autumn. Quite recent. What did you do when the matter was brought to your attention?'

'Has this come from that fusspot Phoebe Palmer?'

A boy was trampolining in next door's back garden. He rose and fell, arms held wide, snow flying. Siv could hear him chuckling, carefree.

'Just answer the question.'

He sighed heavily, a put-upon man. 'I asked all the staff members if they knew anything about it. They said they didn't. As there was no real evidence that any money had gone, just Phoebe's word for it, I left it there. After that, there was no further problem with the collection box. Inspector,

Phoebe Palmer is a conscientious person, but prone to getting agitated. A fussbudget. She sees her work as an extension of herself, rather than a job to do. She makes mountains out of molehills.' He attempted humour. 'I expect she counts the teabags in the staff kitchen.'

Siv asked, 'When you spoke to your staff, did anyone come up with the name of a possible thief?'

'No. They were all surprised and baffled.'

'Did you report the matter to your manager?'

'No. It didn't warrant it.'

Siv thought as much. 'I suppose you worried that it might reflect badly on you, and you wouldn't want that.'

'Not at all,' he clearly lied. 'As far as I'm concerned, I dealt with it appropriately. I really don't see what this has to do with a murder enquiry.'

Neither do I right now. 'You're sure there's nothing else that you haven't thought worth mentioning?'

'Nothing. I'd like to get back to my guests now.'

'By the way, Phoebe Palmer was right to speak to us, albeit reluctantly. Enjoy your lunch.'

She hurried through the raw air to the car. Soup. She needed soup and a mound of garlic bread.

CHAPTER 19

Monday morning, and Siv could see her breath in the office as she updated the incident board. Ali had been discharged from hospital and was on the phone.

'To be honest,' he was saying, 'I'm still a wee bit watery, but doc says if I rest up today, I can come back tomorrow. Polly's at work and I'm bored witless.'

She could hear the cheery voices of morning news presenters in the background. 'Take your time,' she replied, not meaning it. 'They still haven't fixed the heating here, despite promises, so best to stay warm.'

'What's the problem with it?'

'Sludge in the pipes or something. I'm sure there's a more technical term. We've been "assured" that it will be back on later today, but I'm not taking my coat off. I'm having a catch-up with Patrick. D'you want to listen in?'

'Does a one-legged duck swim in circles?'

Patrick had sneaked in a fan heater from home. They'd set it on maximum and were sitting beside it. It gave off a faint smell of burning. Siv hoped they wouldn't cause an electrical fire. They'd been told they weren't allowed to bring their own heating in because it would contravene health and safety rules, but as Siv had said to Patrick, 'What are they going to do, arrest us?' They'd pulled their chairs over to the incident board and were both drinking hot chocolate.

Siv switched her phone to speaker, naming and crossing out all the people on the board who had confirmed alibis for Monday night.

'That leaves us with Saul Robbins, Andy Smeaton and Tara Warren. Also, possibly Bertie Greene and any of the three at Driftwood.'

'So still an open field,' Patrick said.

'Too open,' Siv agreed. She sat down. 'To recap. Warren was a difficult, wayward teenager, into sex, drugs and alcohol. Kilgore seems to have matched him on the addictions, but he was Teflon-coated and stayed in the mainstream socially. Eden Jarvis told us that Warren was upset about something and determined to leave Berminster. He'd been drifting since he left town, with casual jobs and an ad hoc home life. He was part renting, part camping out or sleeping in his car. He'd mellowed since his school days, turned to nature. Kilgore went to university and got a well-paid job. He was good at concealing things and compartmentalising his life.

'Someone got Kilgore and Warren to head to Mallow Cottage late on Monday night. Kilgore was stabbed in the neck, Warren was strangled. He and Kilgore had a connection to the crematorium with their "grave parties" and Kilgore's mother owns the cottage. We've heard that Warren was deeply upset about something that had happened the April of his final year at school. It made him determined to leave home just weeks later, abandoning his exams. Those brochures we found indicate that Warren and Kilgore died because of something that took place when they were having fun, possibly at the crem or at Mallow Cottage. Warren could have come across Kilgore at Footprint when he was making deliveries for Pie Mad. He was also keeping up with Berminster news online, visited Bertie Greene in prison and talked about old times. Greene said he'd changed and was quieter. Lonely too. Warren used to use a drug dealer here called "The Wheel". I rang Bertie Greene, but he claimed never to have heard the name. Ali, does it ring any bells?'

'Nope. Going back a bit, though. Some of those guys move on or get out of the game when they've made enough from it.'

Siv bent and held her hands out to the wheezing fan heater. 'Then we have our two sets of handwriting. There's the history exercise book with handwriting in red pen that matches the brochures. That means that whoever wrote the messages on the brochures knew Warren and probably Kilgore too, when they were at school. That person wanted to get at Warren, make him feel uncomfortable. We also have the note we found at the back of one of Kilgore's textbooks signed "GG". Gray Granville has confirmed that he wrote it to Warren, warning him to leave Teagan alone. That sounds pretty straightforward and fits what he told us previously. Patrick, fill in the other details.'

Patrick moved closer to the phone. 'We've now got someone's DNA from Kilgore's nails, which could be the killer's. We need samples from Saul Robbins, Andy Smeaton and Tara Warren. It doesn't match Warren, and Greene is on record. We still don't know the identity of the woman on the beach with Warren or the guy who visited him in Walthamstow. Then there's Andy Smeaton — I haven't as yet been able to check out the fracas he had with Warren and Kilgore when he chucked them out of the cemetery. Etta Parton sent me a sample of her handwriting. Doesn't match, so we're no further forward there.'

Ali asked, 'Do we really believe that Damian Kyalo had forgiven his friend for getting overfamiliar with his fiancée?'

'Hard to break their alibi,' Siv said. 'Let's see what DNA comparison with Kilgore's nails tells us.'

'Guv,' Ali said, 'I've had an idea. Tommy Castles worked here ten years ago, and he was involved in drug investigations at one point. He might have heard of "The Wheel". Worth asking him.'

'And you could do that from the comfort of home,' Siv replied quickly. She was not going to be left with the task of speaking to Castles if she could avoid it. Being the boss had some benefits. 'I'll leave that to you, Ali. Patrick, you get those other DNA samples and chase Forensics for matches. I'm going to check out Jane Ferris, the woman who interviewed Kilgore for a new job, in person, in case she can shed any more light on his mindset, and I'll contact the council about Smeaton.' She underlined the name 'The Wheel' on the board. 'And I'll look at drug-related offences for 2010.'

She wrote across the top of the board.

Remember fun at Mallow Cottage.

Funny how fun suddenly isn't funny.

She stood back and read them aloud. 'But what I'm thinking is, how does it all lead back to this?'

* * *

Generate, Jane Ferris's company, was based in a modern office block at the rear of the library. Siv helped herself to a complimentary coffee while she waited on a high-back sofa, designed to look like stacks of speckled brown eggs in grey boxes. It made her smile, but she'd sat down gingerly, half expecting a cracking noise. Perhaps Jane Ferris liked to discombobulate her visitors. The small foyer was just the right temperature, and she wondered how the place was heated, as she couldn't see any radiators. The wide video screen beside the curved reception desk showed images of packed events with the words *Achieve*, *Enthuse*, *Fulfil* running across below. Siv flicked through a booklet.

> *Our spirited team takes pride in managing and delivering live, virtual and hybrid events with skill, passion and efficiency.*

Generate facilitated conferences, virtual events, corporate parties, team-building and company fun days — Siv tried and failed to imagine one of those with Mortimer. *Fun* was the last word to come to mind. There were dozens of glossy photos of smiling, enthused people. Inside the back cover was a brief biography of Jane Ferris.

Jane Ferris graduated with a BSc Hons in business and marketing from the University of Brighton. She worked for Brighton & Hove City Council before setting up Generate. Ms Ferris is deputy president of the Berminster Chamber of Commerce, an active member of Berminster Business Forum and a patron of the town's theatre.

A woman breezed through the outer door, her long black coat draped cape-like around her shoulders. Her shiny hair was short and feathered around her oval face. She had a briefcase under one arm and she advanced with hand outstretched.

'Inspector Drummond? Jane Ferris. I hope I haven't kept you waiting. Some idiot blocked my parking space. Do come through.'

It was a light, minimalist, hi-tech environment. They passed white kidney-shaped desks clustered in circular pods and screened meeting booths. The staff were all young and informally dressed in bright colours. Siv caught flashes of lime, turquoise and vermilion. She followed Ms Ferris into an airy, wood-panelled office. They sat in apple-green chairs made of fabric and mesh, the kind that ensured you sat with your spine aligned, your lower back supported. The walls were lined with blown-up photos of conferences. A huge olive tree stood in a ceramic planter. The desk was of the sit/stand variety and was raised, with the computer screen at eye level. Generate must make serious money.

Siv recalled what Rina the waitress had said about Ms Ferris's teeth. They were indeed large and white. She'd thrown her coat across a spare chair and kicked off her stilettos. Her suit was burgundy plaid, teamed with a pink-and-lavender striped shirt. The effect was dazzling.

'Would you like more coffee, Inspector?'

'No, thank you.'

She crackled with energy, her cinnamon-coloured eyes dancing. 'Before I forget, I must tell you that I absolutely love your work!'

'Pardon?'

'Your art, your origami. I saw the beautiful miniature stage you made for the theatre. So unusual and intricate! It must have taken you hours.'

'Thank you. It absorbed me.'

Jane Ferris had pale, clear skin, which made her lively eyes all the more arresting. 'I have to say — no offence intended — it seems an unusual interest for a detective.'

'What interests should a detective have?' Siv asked.

'Well . . . let's see. The TV ones seem to drink, run, play chess, knit or do crosswords. Some of them garden. Sherlock Holmes played the violin, which was artistic. I suppose that shows there can be hidden depths. But then again, he did a lot of drugs too.' She clapped her hands together. 'Presumably, you accept commissions? I was considering asking if you'd make something for our reception area. It needs a conversation piece.'

Siv wasn't sure if Jane Ferris was genuine or amusing herself at her visitor's expense. 'I could consider it, but not now. I'm investigating a double murder and I want to ask you about Henry Kilgore.'

Ms Ferris looked solemn. 'Of course. I'm distracting you and I see from your expression that you disapprove. I can be a bit of a wild card, but it works in the world I've built here . . . Mr Kilgore, yes. That poor man. How terrible and tragic! I only met him the once, but he was so personable and enthusiastic. Do pass my condolences to his family.'

'I will.'

'Do you know why he was killed?'

'I can't discuss that. Tell me about your meeting with him.'

Jane Ferris touched a lever that tilted her chair back slightly, crossed her shapely legs and put her hands behind her head. 'There's not a lot to tell. I explained when I contacted your DC Hill. Henry heard on the business grapevine that I'm planning to expand the company. He phoned me and I agreed to have lunch. We met in the Three Swans. He told me about himself and his career to date. I thought he'd fit well into our team. We agreed to stay in touch.'

'Did he tell you that he worried he might be made redundant?'

Ms Ferris stretched a foot. 'Oh, yes. I'd done my homework on his employer. I always like to form my own opinion about why someone wants to jump ship. I could see Footprint weren't doing so well. Henry didn't seem too worried. He had a confidence in his abilities that I liked. I could tell that we'd get on. I was particularly interested in his experience in London-based events. I could have used that to develop our business in the capital. Sadly, that particular opportunity has vanished.' She looked down, tilted her foot sideways. 'Bugger, I've got a hole in my tights.'

Siv followed her gaze and saw a flash of pink skin by her little toe. 'Did Henry seem troubled in any way, other than about his job?'

'He didn't appear so. Of course, not knowing him, I can't really say, Inspector. And he was showing me his self-assured persona, given the nature of the meeting. It's what I'd have expected, as a prospective employer with a thriving business that candidates are keen to join.'

The woman's own self-assurance was grating on Siv. She couldn't think why. Usually, she was drawn to assertive women. Maybe it was the hint of teasing running through her conversation, or the sense of arrogance.

'Are you from Berminster?'

'I was brought up in Eastbourne. I moved here after uni. It's a lovely little town. Are you a native?'

'Partly. I read that you're well woven into the town's business community.'

'Of course. It pays dividends to network and influence.'

'How long have you been running Generate?'

'Twelve years or so. I started in two rooms above the sweet shop on the parade and moved to these premises seven years ago. Excuse me a moment.' She picked up her phone on her desk. 'Tessa, sweetie, could you pop out and get a couple of pairs of black tights for me? Sheer, Wolford brand. They have them in Ormonde. Yes, that's right, on my account. Thank you.' She smiled at Siv. 'I have a meeting soon and I can't negotiate if I know I have flawed clothing. Is that daft?'

Siv thought of Ali, who often had holes in his socks but still managed to do an excellent job. 'Whatever makes you comfortable. Have you ever met a man called Eugene Warren?'

'Warren? Don't think so. In what context?'

'At the moment, in the context of murder. He grew up here.'

'Oh yes, he's the other man who died. I saw it on the news. No, I can't help you there. I hope coming here hasn't wasted your time.'

'Thank you for contacting us.' Siv stood.

'My pleasure. Do give me a buzz when you're free to talk about creating a piece for me. I have some ideas we could discuss, but, of course, I'll be led by your artistic talent. I must get these tights off — they're annoying the hell out of me!'

* * *

Patrick had brought Andy Smeaton to the station on Siv's instruction. The heating had just kicked back in — thank goodness — but the interview room was still chilly. Smeaton pulled his scarf up around his neck, touched the radiator with calloused hands.

'Are the police economising? I know you've had cuts, but even so . . .'

Siv wasn't disposed to offer a hot drink. 'Maybe the cold will wake up your memory.'

'What's that supposed to mean?' he said testily. 'Sounds like it's you lot who need waking up. I saw Henry Kilgore's mother on the local news, saying you'd missed her son's body when you searched her properties. She was livid. I'd say you're in for an uncomfortable time.'

'Let's stick to why you're here, Mr Smeaton.' Siv would rather not think about the paperwork that Uniform's cock-up was going to leave her with.

'Fine. So, why have you dragged me away from work?'

'As DC Hill will have told you, you're helping us with our enquiries. Do you have a problem with that?'

Smeaton folded his arms. 'Go on, then.'

'I contacted the council earlier. They have a record of a complaint made against you in 2009 by Eugene Warren. It was regarding the incident in the cemetery, when you found him and his friends. You didn't mention it when we asked you about that.'

His brow furrowed. 'A complaint? Cheeky bugger. Can't say it came back to me when we were talking. I suppose nothing came of it.'

'I wouldn't say that. You were reprimanded.'

'Was I?' He jerked his head back. 'If I was, it must have been a slap on the wrist. I honestly don't have any memory of it.'

'Just as you didn't recall the incident with the three young people when we first asked you about it. Let me read what I was told.' She tapped her iPad.

'"Mr Eugene Warren phoned us to say that he and two friends had been visiting the cemetery, because they were interested in Victorian grave monuments. They hadn't noticed the time passing. Mr Smeaton appeared, very angry and shouting at them, accusing them of trespassing. He made them walk to the main gate, and when Mr Warren protested at the treatment, he alleged that Mr Smeaton twisted his arm, leaving a bruise.

We interviewed Mr Smeaton, who informed us that he'd found Mr Warren and another male and female in the cemetery after 8 p.m. They were drinking and carousing. He'd escorted them to the gate and warned them not to come back. He denied any physical contact. Mr Smeaton said that one of the men had been verbally abusive and all three were drunk and laughing. He stated that they seemed to find the whole thing hilarious. Mr Smeaton was reprimanded for not reporting the trespass at the time, or taking the details of the trespassers, in keeping with council regulations. He acknowledged that he should have done this, but stated that he'd had a long and busy day because of water problems at the crematorium.

When we phoned Mr Warren to attempt to conclude the complaint, he didn't respond to our calls or subsequent letter, so the matter ended there."'

Smeaton said, 'There you are, then. Warren was just being mouthy and trying to make trouble for me because I'd thrown him out. I expect he thought it was funny to complain and get his own back.'

'You do recall it then?'

'Not really. Vaguely. I can't have paid it much attention. It talks about a reprimand, but that probably means my boss told me to take it easy and make sure I ticked the boxes in future.' He wagged a finger at Siv. 'You understand how it works in organisations. Half the time, complaints are from troublemakers and whingers. You must get plenty of that—' he looked at her pointedly — 'and you have to waste your time jumping through hoops and doing the paperwork. All that "transparency" crap. You're wasting your time again now, going over this. If Warren was still alive, he'd be wetting himself.'

He didn't appear concerned, but Siv continued. 'Mr Smeaton, you must understand that you failed to mention both the incident in the cemetery and then Mr Warren's complaint. Withholding such information in the course of a murder inquiry is frowned upon, to say the least, and can result in criminal charges. You could have held a grudge against him and Henry Kilgore.' It sounded thin and unlikely to her own ears.

He pulled a face. 'Oh, give me a break, Inspector! I didn't even know who they were, did I? I hardly waited around all this time planning murders because some hooligans were getting pissed and "having a laugh"! They were just stupid oiks.' He shoved his chair back. 'I've had enough of this now and I'm bloody freezing. If you want to ask me any more ridiculous questions, I want a solicitor.'

'OK, Mr Smeaton. First, DC Hill would like to take a DNA sample, with your permission.'

'You can take blood, hair and bone marrow if it means I can get out of here and not have to listen to any more of this crap. I might make a complaint of my own, about being kept in icy conditions!'

Siv left him to Patrick and went back to her office.

Although the room was cold, the radiator was clanking by her desk, and when she put a hand on it, it was amazingly hot. Her feet were numb. She pulled her chair over, slipped her boots off and put her feet against the warmth. *I know the where and the how, I have the shape of an idea about the why, but I've no clue as to who's the perpetrator.* Andy Smeaton had no alibi, but his annoyance had seemed genuine enough. He might lash out verbally, but she couldn't see him planning two murders, using his prized wheelbarrow and buying wreaths.

She started as she heard Mortimer behind her.

'Getting warmed up, DI Drummond?'

She swivelled around. 'That's right, sir.'

'Thank goodness we have our heating again. Have you heard from DS Carlin?'

'He's doing some work from home today and he hopes to be back tomorrow.'

'Good, good. Any progress on these two murders? A week's gone by now. I hope you're on top of things, cracking the whip.'

She hoped he wasn't going to make a habit of popping by her office now that they had a family connection. 'I was about to send you an email update, sir, as soon as I've checked one or two outstanding matters. We're making progress, some promising new information to follow up.' That might get rid of him.

'I look forward to it. Lovely lunch on Saturday. Your mother pulled out all the stops.'

'Indeed.'

He hesitated, seeming to find the standard-issue calendar on her wall fascinating. 'Good. I have a meeting now regarding this Uniform balls-up at Mallow Cottage. It would be good to hear that you've caught Kilgore's killer sooner rather than later. Might take the steam out of it and stop Ms Kilgore talking to the press. She's already given one interview. Scathing, to say the least. I'll have to meet with her, and it would be good to have a positive spin for the conversation. I'm looking for a constructive outcome.'

'Doing my best. Giving it one hundred per cent, sir.'

'Right. Make sure everyone is.' He nodded and left.

When he'd gone, she put her boots back on, sat at her desk and searched crime records for 2010. She found a number of drug offences. Most arrests had resulted in warnings and cautions. Three deaths were logged. A fifty-three-year-old man had died from heroin in February, a twenty-three-year-old man from cocaine in September and a seventeen-year-old woman from MDMA on 2 April. That could be interesting. She was about the same age as their victims would have been at the time. Siv clicked on the file.

Freya Blewitt, aged seventeen, was found outside the door of the speech therapy clinic attached to Berminster General Hospital on the night of 2 April 2010. She was unconscious and died two hours later. Cause of death was a severe reaction to the drug MDMA, commonly known as Ecstasy.

Emergency services received an anonymous call at 22.46 p.m. from a phone box on the corner of Bere Hill, alerting them to Ms Blewitt's whereabouts. An ambulance was despatched immediately.

Ms Blewitt's parents believed that she was at the cinema with a girlfriend, Leah Steele, that evening. When questioned,

Ms Steele denied any such arrangement and, in fact, she had spent the evening at home, watching TV with her mother.

No trace of Ms Blewitt's movements that evening was established, or the identity of the person who made the phone call. Neither Ms Blewitt's parents, nor any of her close friends were aware that she took drugs. Scrutiny of Ms Blewitt's social media failed to find any recent contacts other than her main circle of friends, none of whom knew where she'd been the night she died.

Siv called Patrick in and showed him the report.

'You spoke to Leah Steele, didn't you?'

'That's right. She said that she'd been at Fulbrook Upper with Warren. So presumably, Freya Blewitt might have been there too.'

'Get hold of her again. This has to be an important connection. It seems likely that Freya Blewitt was with Warren and Kilgore when she took the Ecstasy, and that was the terrible event that made Warren run. The timing certainly fits.'

Patrick was excited. 'What if they took the drug at Mallow Cottage?'

'Whoa. Step by step. Phone Leah Steele. I need to contact the Blewitts.'

* * *

Ali called her as she drew up outside the Blewitt's house and parked in the grey slush.

'Guv, I got hold of Tommy Castles. He was in Uniform back then. "The Wheel" was a name cops heard, but the dealer was never identified. Tommy said that it could have been someone operating anywhere along the south coast.'

'OK. Thanks for trying.' She updated him quickly on the day's events.

'Tommy said he'd seen you at Mortimer's for lunch on Saturday.' Ali sounded amused. 'Are Mortimer and your mum living together now?'

Oh, for the anonymity of London life! 'Yes, they're tucked up cosily. I have work to do. You seem better.'

'Aye, back tomorrow. Anything else I can be doing?'

'Yes please. Contact Footprint. Send a photo of Warren and ask if anyone who worked with Kilgore remembers seeing him with the pie deliveryman. It would be useful to have corroboration.'

Julie Blewitt lived alone now, in a semi-detached house on a dilapidated seventies estate. It was clean and neat but faded, and the living-room carpet had bald patches. Ms Blewitt's salt-and-pepper hair was cut in a fringe that hung almost into her eyes. She insisted on giving Siv a cup of mint tea and made herself hot water with a slice of lemon, while explaining that she was now divorced.

'I'm sorry to have to talk to you about your daughter, Ms Blewitt. It's in connection with another enquiry.'

She had a lopsided smile. 'Don't be. I don't mind. It's good to hear her name, actually.'

'Thank you. Which school did Freya attend?'

'Minster Academy.'

'So how did she know Leah Steele?'

'They met at Brownies when they were about nine and remained firm friends.'

'Was Freya friendly with Eugene Warren or Henry Kilgore?'

'They're the men who were murdered, aren't they? I don't think she was, no. Is that why you're asking, because of them? Shocking, two young men being killed like that.'

'These are general queries for now. I've gone through police records concerning Freya. I read that you believed she was at the cinema with Leah Steele the night she died.'

Ms Blewitt pushed her fringe back. It fell down again into her eyes. 'She told me she was going to see *Clash of the Titans* with Leah. But Leah was at home, said they hadn't planned anything.'

Siv asked quietly, 'Why did Freya lie?'

Ms Blewitt was inhaling the steam from her tea. 'I suppose because she was going somewhere, seeing people I'd disapprove of.' She prodded the slice of lemon with the tip of a finger. 'I wasn't getting on with Jack, my husband at the time. Things were very tense here. The marriage was on its last legs. We weren't paying Freya enough attention. I was glad that she went out that evening, because I was tired from rowing with Jack and I needed space and quiet. I'll have to live with that sadness until the day I die. I sit here at night on my own and I'd give anything to hear her playing her music.'

'I'm sorry. That night might have been the first time that Freya took drugs, or she might have been using them for a while. Did you or her father notice anything about her behaviour, or did she mention any new people she'd met?'

She shook her head. 'Inspector, Freya could have been in all sorts of trouble and me and Jack wouldn't have spotted it, because we were taken up with our own problems. I'd have denied that at the time, but I see it plainly now. It hurts me to say it, and God knows what you think of me for admitting that to you, but that's how it was. I racked my brain after she died. At the time, I told the police that I wasn't aware if she had any boyfriends, or their names. Leah said Freya wasn't going out with anyone, but I wasn't so sure about that. I can't say why. Freya had seemed a bit secretive, and she came and went from the house more often . . . but I was preoccupied. I can only say that I didn't notice anything very unusual about her apart from that. Nothing that worried me.'

'Are those photos of Freya?'

Ms Blewitt reached for a trio of photos in beaded metal frames that were sitting on the bookshelf and handed them to Siv. 'She's sixteen in these.'

Freya had been short and plain, with a snub nose, a tiny mouth and a bashful smile. In the first photo, she had dull-brown, shoulder-length hair, in the second, short, fluffy, caramel-coloured waves and in the third, rippling coppery-blonde tresses.

'Freya liked her hair styles and dyes,' Siv commented.

Julie Blewitt smiled. 'The brown was her natural colour. She went through a phase of wearing wigs. Don't ask me why. She wore one in a school play and liked the easy change of image. One of those teenage fancies, messing about with her appearance. I took those photos on the same afternoon, with her trying out the wigs.'

Siv studied the third photo. Gray Grenville had mentioned a strawberry-blonde on the beach with Eugene Warren, the girl he'd named as Leah Steele. She tapped it and asked, 'Was Freya maybe trying to copy her friend Leah's hair?'

'Probably. She thought her own was boring. She envied Leah's colour. It was indeed lovely, so bright and eye-catching.' Ms Blewitt put her untouched drink down. 'It would be good to understand why Freya took that drug and who she was with — who dumped her like an unwanted parcel on the pavement. I'd like them to pay for what they did. I'm not saying Freya was forced to take anything, but just to leave her like that . . .' She placed a hand over her heart. 'I'm paying every day for what happened to Freya. I wasn't a good enough mother. I should have spotted something. She should have been able to confide in me. I'm sorry. I suppose you hear this kind of thing all the time.'

'I hear it quite often,' Siv replied.

'Thank you. Thank you for not saying I have to forgive myself, or that it will get easier.' There was a sudden gleam of hope in her eyes. 'Did Warren and Kilgore have something to do with Freya's death? Is that why you're here?'

'I can't say at the moment, or if we'll get answers for you. But it's possible, that's all.'

CHAPTER 20

Patrick knocked on Siv's door and reported that Leah Steele had confirmed that she'd been at home the evening Freya died, and there had never been a plan to see a film. They'd been good friends, although at different schools, and according to Leah, Freya had never had a steady boyfriend.

'Leah said that they found all the boys their age "juvenile and immature".' He grimaced. 'I suppose that's what girls said about me when I was at school.'

'I expect you've improved over time,' Siv told him. 'I'm not sure that Leah was up to speed about her friend.' She explained about the photo and the strawberry-blonde wig. 'I borrowed these photos from Ms Blewitt. If that was Freya on the beach with Warren, she might not have wanted Leah to find out about the relationship, because her friend had such a low opinion of him. Girls can like their secrets and that feeling of power. Freya looked girl-next-door, but maybe she was after a bit of spice — Warren certainly offered that.'

Patrick checked out the photos. 'Freya was the same kind of build as Leah. In this one with the strawberry wig, she could be mistaken for her, for sure, especially from a distance.'

'That would explain Gray Grenville's mistake. Find Smeaton and show him these photos. Ask him if Freya's the girl who was in the cemetery.'

'I predict he'll say he can't remember.'

'Do your best. Promise him we'll get his wheelbarrow back for him.'

Siv made coffee and saw that an email had arrived from Forensics. The DNA under Kilgore's fingernails matched Saffie Armand's. But the information came with advice that the skin cells could have come from ordinary close contact with his partner. Siv mulled this over. She didn't see Saffie Armand as a killer and wasn't keen on another slog to London. She called her number. Saffie answered after two rings.

Siv asked, 'Are you OK to talk?'

'Yes. I'm in Acton. Work gave me a couple of days' compassionate leave. Have you got news for me?'

'Of a sort. Can you explain why Henry might have had your skin cells beneath fingernails on his right hand?'

There was a silence. 'I'm not sure what you mean.'

'Forensics have told us that they identified your DNA from his fingernails.'

Saffie made a strange noise. Siv wasn't sure if it was a laugh or a cry.

'Saffie? Are you there?'

'I'm trying to think. It must be from . . . This is so awful, having to disclose personal things.'

'I understand.'

'I . . . that is . . . sorry, give me a minute.'

Siv crossed to the window and waited. Freezing rain had fallen and clear ice framed the branches of the trees. She took in the stark beauty of the scene as she listened to Saffie sob quietly and then blow her nose. Listening to grief was perhaps worse than observing it. It felt intrusive.

Saffie said hoarsely, 'It would have been before we went out to eat on Monday evening. Henry and the others got back from kayaking and he had a shower. Then we had a . . .

a cuddle in our bedroom. Henry liked to scratch my back and then I'd scratch his. That would explain why my DNA was under his nails, wouldn't it?'

'It would, yes.'

'It's like everything is ruined now, even our last time together. Strangers know all about us. Gosh, I hate it.'

'It's hard for you. I'll leave it there for now. Thank you. Take care.'

Siv pressed her forehead to the window. Yet another setback with this DNA match. Her assurances to Mortimer were sounding thin. She pictured him chatting to Tommy Castles. They'd be agreeing that she just wasn't up to the job. Wrong appointment. She kicked the roasting pipe that ran along the skirting. Now that the heating was back with a vengeance, her office was baking. One extreme to another. She inched a window open and watched the ice-filmed trees swaying in the breeze. Their branches sounded like bones knocking.

* * *

By the afternoon, Siv was stuck and out of ideas. Andy Smeaton had told Patrick that Freya Blewitt might have been the girl in the cemetery, but he couldn't be sure. Ali had emailed her to confirm that two people in Kilgore's team at work recalled Warren delivering food and seeing Kilgore chat to him. Useful, but it didn't get her any further forward. These were just confirming facts that she'd suspected already. They really needed a break in the case — not only to get Mortimer off her back, but to get justice for the families. Finding out who 'The Wheel' was would be something. Ali had told her that St Michael the Archangel was the patron saint of police. *Come on, St Michael, give me a steer here!*

Mid-afternoon, she grabbed a tuna sandwich and a coffee from Gusto. The sun had made an appearance, so she decided to make the most of it and sat on a bench at the side of the museum. She was missing Ali and his solid, reliable presence. When she'd finished eating, she'd ring him and see how he was doing.

She'd eaten the sandwich and was taking the first sip of coffee when a stooped man walked slowly past the bench, paused and then doubled back. He was slight and very pale, with a heavily lined face enlivened by bright blue eyes.

He asked hesitantly, 'Would you be that police lady?'

'I'm a detective, yes.'

His accent was soft and Scottish. 'You might be the person I need to speak to. I was just heading to the station. It's about those men, Eugene Warren and Henry Kilgore.'

She indicated the bench beside her. 'Take a seat. I'm DI Drummond, and you are?'

'My name's Jock Keyes. Are you sure this is OK — me interrupting your lunch like this?'

'I'm used to it.'

He sat, placing his jute shopping bag beside him. Tins of baked beans, mackerel and soup were wedged in beside a loaf of white sliced bread. A solitary man's meals. His matching hat and scarf were blue and white with circular logos, Queen of the South.

'It's good to see a bit of sun. You have to make the most of it, although your bones would freeze if you sat here for too long.' He squinted up at the sky.

Keyes gave the impression of a reticent man, but there was a warmth to him. 'That's why I chose here when I had time for a sandwich. My coffee is keeping me thawed. So, Mr Keyes, what can you tell me?'

'I read that Mr Kilgore's body was found at Mallow Cottage. Maybe that sparked my memory about Mr Warren.' He tapped his forehead. 'I knew I had something about him in here. I used to deliver the post around that way, you see. I was watching *Midsomer Murders* last night, and during the ad break, it suddenly came back to me, where I'd seen him. Funny how your mind does that, isn't it? I suppose it might have been the country lanes and cottages that stimulated the old grey cells and made me remember.'

'You mean you'd seen Eugene Warren?'

'I did, a long time ago, though. It's probably not important, but I'd nothing else to do this afternoon, so I decided I'd pop by.'

'Tell me about what you've remembered.'

'I'm going back some years now. This Warren was a teenager. He looked the way he did in that photo in the news. That skullcap was unusual. It was one morning when I was on my rounds. He was coming out of Mallow Cottage with a young girl, and I recognised her because her dad had an allotment at the site I'm on, and she was there with him sometimes. I knew the house was a holiday place. You get to learn those kinds of things on a postal round, you understand. I only ever delivered rubbish like flyers and charity appeals through the letterbox.'

'I can imagine.'

Keyes had a scrape of stubble on his chin and he rubbed it. His hands were veined and cold. He needed the gloves to match his hat and scarf.

'Warren was putting the key in the key safe at the side of the house. It struck me as a bit odd, because they were so young and she was a local lass, so she'd hardly be renting somewhere. I've always been a postie, and you get to be alert to anything unusual, particularly places where old folk live. I've had a couple of instances where I've noticed curtains not drawn or lights left on, and it's turned out someone's been taken ill. So, I asked them if they were staying there, if they had the owner's permission.' He rubbed his hands together.

'How did Warren respond when you questioned him?'

'He was very rude, I recall. Told me to mind my own business and get on with my job or he might contact the Queen and tell her the Royal Mail was being abused. The girl said nothing. I suppose she was embarrassed. I said something like, he should mind his manners, and he laughed and told me to eff off. Then they walked away. My son was in the van. He heard Warren using foul language and he wanted to have it out with him, but I told him not to get involved.'

'What was the girl's name?'

'She was called Freya. I don't recall her surname. Sadly, she died that year. Drugs, I believe.'

Freya? Siv's day lifted. Was she the missing link after all? There it was, a significant connection between the murdered men, the dead girl and Mallow Cottage. 'Thank you so much, Mr Keyes. Can I take your details, in case we need to come back to you?'

He gave her his address and number. 'Have I helped at all?'

'Oh yes, definitely.'

'Better than being a hindrance, anyway. I'm sure you get plenty of time- wasters.'

She smiled at him. 'You're certainly not one of those. What's the logo on your hat and scarf?'

'Queen of the South, my football team back in Dumfries. Usually called the Doonhamers. They play in the Scottish Championship. Whenever I can, I go up there to cheer them on.'

'You'd better get on now, before you get chilled. Your hands are frozen.'

'You've heard the saying — cold hands, warm heart.' He smiled. 'I'll head home now and have a drop of soup. Have a good day, Inspector.'

Back at the station, Siv updated the incident board and then sat studying it. Freya Blewitt had been at Mallow Cottage with Warren, and probably in the cemetery with him and Kilgore. Kilgore must have given Warren the code to the key safe at the cottage. Surely, Kilgore and Warren had been with Freya that night she took the Ecstasy. They'd panicked when she became ill and left her near the hospital. That's what the second message on the brochure had been about: *Funny how fun suddenly isn't funny*. The two men had been summoned or drawn back to Mallow Cottage a week ago because of Freya's death. The central question was, who else had known about that terrible event and why wait more than ten years before exacting punishment?

She kept returning to the belief that Bertie Greene must be keeping back information. The way he was acting, something wasn't adding up. His weasel tactics, the way he tried to say as little as possible. She went back to his file, reading through each page slowly. Then she clicked her fingers, as she came upon a name. Ian Keyes. He was the prisoner who'd been Greene's downfall. Keyes, that was the surname of the surprise witness who'd interrupted her al fresco lunch. Could they be related?

She rang the prison and confirmed that yes, Ian Keyes was the only son of Mr Jock Keyes, who was named as his next of kin. That meant it had been Ian Keyes in the van with his dad that day. It also meant he'd witnessed the incident when Warren and Freya Blewitt were leaving Mallow Cottage. Maybe he'd written on the brochures. She urgently requested an emailed sample of Keyes' handwriting.

Time to lean on Greene again. The threads were all starting to come together, she could feel it. She found Patrick, brought him up to speed and told him to bring Greene in.

* * *

Greene brought a pungent whiff of curry to the interview room.

'I was in the middle of making a chicken madras,' he complained.

Siv said, 'Nice to have time for cooking, isn't it, DC Hill?' She'd instructed Patrick that she needed a pacey, pressurised interview, the kind that Ali easily raised his game for. She hoped Patrick was up to it too.

'Very nice,' Patrick agreed, unsmiling. 'Wish we did, but we're too busy trying to solve two murders.'

Greene looked from Patrick to her uncertainly. 'Why do you need to see me again? This is the third time.'

Siv said, 'Tedious, isn't it? Of course, if you'd told us the truth the first, or even the second time, we wouldn't need to keep questioning you.'

'Who says I'm not telling the truth?'

'I do,' she snapped. 'If you keep pushing your luck, I'll arrest you. You're on borrowed time after your previous lies, so don't tempt me.'

He asked quickly, 'Arrest me? What for?'

'Wasting police time, for starters. I'm tired of your evasions. You need to get real, Mr Greene. There's a lot riding on this interview for you.'

'You've no idea how much,' Patrick added. 'That's why we double-checked if you wanted a solicitor.'

At that, Greene rubbed his hands on his knees and blinked rapidly. 'What do you want from me?'

'You knew Freya Blewitt,' Siv stated.

Greene licked his lips. 'Yes. B–back when we were teenagers.'

'And you were aware she went out with Eugene Warren.'

'Eugene told me one time.'

'She died. What can you tell me about that?'

'Nothing, honestly.'

Siv shook her head. 'Not good enough. Let's try, what did you *suspect* when you heard about her death? Clock's ticking.'

'I . . . I wondered back then if maybe Eugene or Henry had something to do with it.'

'Yet you didn't say anything.'

'I wasn't sure. I didn't want to point a finger.'

'You told me that they only smoked dope. Freya took Ecstasy.'

'That's all I took when I was with them, just dope, honestly.'

'*Honestly*,' she mocked. 'Just because you keep saying the word like a mantra doesn't mean you are honest. You said, "back then". Did Eugene Warren talk about Freya when he visited you in prison, having his little trip down memory lane?'

Greene hesitated. 'Yeah. He told me that he and Henry were with her at Mallow Cottage that night. They had some

Ecstasy tabs. Freya was fine one minute, then she collapsed. They put her in Henry's car and left her by the hospital. He and Henry were amazed they'd got away with it. But Eugene said it had played on his mind ever since, and the memory got worse instead of better. Tormented him. He was guilt-ridden. It was like he wanted to make up for it in some way, but he couldn't work out how.'

Siv wanted to applaud. Finally, concrete, nailed-down information. Maybe that was why Warren had been drawn to Lockwood Reservoir, a place to quietly end his life. End all the torment over an innocent girl's needless death.

'And you still didn't say anything,' Siv probed. 'Her parents still don't understand what happened to their daughter that evening.'

'I had enough on my plate,' Greene muttered.

'Was there anyone else with them that night at Mallow Cottage?'

'Just the three of them.'

Siv laughed. 'Why should I believe that you weren't there? Those three are dead, so that's an easy fib for a practised liar like you.'

Greene was sweating. 'I wasn't. Like I told you before, I didn't actually mix that much with Henry and Eugene.'

Patrick leaned forward. 'You'd have liked to though, wouldn't you? We've been told you were a bit of a hanger-on. They didn't have much time for you, was the truth of it.'

Greene reddened and cast his eyes down.

Nicely done.

'Ian Keyes. Tell us about him,' Siv said briskly.

It was the briefest of tells, but the slight widening of his eyes and the faltering gaze told Siv everything she needed to know. It was this name he'd been dreading, not Freya Blewitt's.

'He . . . he's in prison.'

'Yes. He's one of the reasons why *you* ended up in prison, correct?'

'Yeah. You can read all the details.'

Patrick said, 'We have. He had you over a barrel and threatened you with exposure about failing to report finding a mobile phone. Truth is, that was only half the story, right? I bet he's still got you where he wants you.'

Greene squirmed in his seat.

Siv leaned in. 'We don't have all the info, but we'll dig and we'll find out. If we need to, we'll visit Ian Keyes. He won't like the prospect of any additions to his sentence. Ian Keyes saw Warren and Freya leaving Mallow Cottage one morning, and having that kind of mind, he probably put two and two together when he heard that Freya had died. I'm sure he's the kind of shrewd man that stores such information away for future use, plays the long game. He found a use for it when you turned up working at HMP Berminster. Keyes knew that you used to knock around with Warren and Kilgore, and no doubt, he was aware of their playing with drugs. Just like him, you'd had your suspicions about how Freya died, yet you'd withheld information about a serious crime. It was just another bit of leverage that Keyes had on you. If you tell us the truth now, we'll see if we can make things easier for you.'

Greene said nothing. He wiped his damp forehead. Siv gave a little nod to Patrick.

'Let's try going through other names and connections we have from back then, Mr Greene, see if anything jogs your memory,' Patrick said encouragingly. 'Leah Steele was Freya's friend, but she's told us she wasn't aware of Freya's relationship with Eugene. Then we have Gray Grenville, Teagan Grenville's brother, who seems to have been pissed off with Eugene for the way he treated his sister.'

Greene gulped like a drowning man seeking air. 'Gray, yeah, Gray Grenville. He's Freya's sort of brother!'

Siv and Patrick exchanged stunned glances.

'Explain "sort of"', Siv demanded.

'Half-brother or whatever.' He gripped the table. 'They had the same dad.'

'How do you know that?'

He mumbled, 'Eugene told me at school. Thought it was hilarious.'

At last, something to get our teeth into. Siv hurried on. 'Back to Ian Keyes. I'm sure you can tell us more about him, now you seem to have found your tongue. You'll feel better once it's all out there.'

Greene laid his arms on the table and rested his face on them. Patrick raised crossed fingers. After a long minute, Greene spoke. He sounded defeated and relieved. 'OK, but I want three things first.'

'That's a lot considering how you've messed us around, Mr Greene, but try me. I'm in a good mood,' Siv said.

'A coffee and a solicitor. Also, I said I'd phone my girls tonight. I'd like to make that call.'

'Fine. In the meantime, DC Hill is going to arrest you on suspicion of withholding information.'

* * *

Siv reached home after eleven, poured a glass of akvavit and texted Ali.

Are you awake?

The answer was immediate.

Yes, binge watching The Crown.

She rang him while a bowl of casserole spun in the microwave. 'We finally nailed Bertie Greene. We have his statement that Warren, Kilgore and Freya Blewitt took Ecstasy at Mallow Cottage and they dumped her by the hospital.'

'Yes!' Ali whooped.

'Greene spilled the lot, at last.'

She explained her encounter with Jock Keyes and the hold that his son had over Greene concerning what he'd seen at Mallow Cottage. 'Ian Keyes also threatened Greene's kids. Since he was released from jail, Greene has been sending in drugs and phones to Keyes via a maintenance contractor. I hoped that Ian Keyes might turn out to be the writer on the brochures, but his handwriting's nothing like.'

'Shame. That'd have been a break.'

'Yep. Greene really irritates me, but he's a sad man. He'd have been in less trouble if he'd contacted us with his suspicions about Freya Blewitt in the first place, but he's a limited sort of person and Ian Keyes had him backed into a corner. We've charged him and he's in custody at present. But, even better, Greene gave us a gem of information when Patrick mentioned some of the names we've pulled together from back then. Hold on, I just need to stick some toast on.'

'Don't leave me with a cliffhanger,' Ali pleaded.

She put two slices of bread in the toaster. 'Greene told us that Gray Grenville was Freya Blewitt's half-brother. I checked with Ms Blewitt and she confirmed it. Freya was the result of a brief fling that she had with Grenville's father. He didn't want to have anything to do with the child, so when Julie Blewitt married, Freya took her stepfather's surname.'

'So, hold your horses,' Ali said. 'That note we found at Kilgore's flat might have been about Freya, not Teagan?'

'Exactly.' She picked up her phone, scrolled to her photo of the note and repeated the message they'd found. '"Tell your prick of a friend to leave my sister alone. He thinks he can ignore me and take the piss, but he'll be sorry if he doesn't stop fucking about with my family." If Grenville realised that Warren had moved on from Teagan to Freya, he might have been furious and he might well have suspected who'd been with her when she collapsed.'

'That would mean Grenville lied about who he saw Warren with on the beach.'

'If he's our killer, he would lie about that.'

'But if he did find out about Freya and Warren,' Ali said, 'why wait years to make a move?'

'That's a good question. But they do say that revenge is a dish best served cold. Maybe we'll get the answer in the morning. Are you fit to come to Brighton with me tomorrow?'

‘Try and stop me. What are you eating?’

‘Tuscan bean casserole from Gusto. Toast with lots of butter.’

Ali groaned. ‘I had fish stew earlier. I’m craving chocolate eclairs now but all I’m allowed is a handful of almonds.’

‘And that’s being generous.’ Siv heard Polly call faintly from the background.

‘Never mind, eh? You’ll feel virtuous.’

It was chilly in the wagon, but Siv couldn’t be bothered to light a fire tonight. She downed her food, poured another drink and went to bed with it and her iPad. She plumped the pillows, pulled up the duvet and searched for Gray Grenville. He worked for a fire safety company called Ignis. The only social media hit was Facebook, but his page had scant information and no updates since 2017.

Warmed through by the akvavit, she lay back and listened to the ripple of the river and the sound of foxes barking. Snug in the warmth of the duvet, she reached a hand out to the cold sheet beside her and realised that she hadn’t thought about Ed for a couple of days. Too busy, no headspace. He’d get it. He’d always understood when she’d been absorbed and distracted by work.

Night. Sleep tight, she said to him. He didn’t reply.

CHAPTER 21

Gray Grenville had said that he'd be at home, writing reports. He lived on a long, terraced street that sloped down towards the flat, steely sea. The houses were painted in blues, pinks, greens, oranges and greys. A couple were a more mundane magnolia. All had tall chimney pots. Grenville's was a rosy peach colour with window boxes packed with yellow violas and trailing ivy.

'Very Mediterranean with these colours,' Ali said to Siv as they parked. 'Great view.'

He was cheerful, although he still looked watery around the eyes. On the journey, he'd been full of good intentions about food and lifestyle, stating that he had to stick to the rules of DEP: diet, eating and physical exercise. Siv had smiled in agreement, although she wasn't convinced, especially as he'd been finishing a Gitane on his front path when she picked him up.

Grenville was in navy jeans, a ribbed red sweater and despite the cold, brown flip-flops. He was boyish, with a smooth, fresh complexion and a side parting in his dark brown hair. The living room was on the first floor and they followed him up the hessian-covered stairs. His work desk was stationed by the back window. He seemed businesslike and at ease but offered no refreshments despite their journey.

'I told your colleague, DC Hill, what I could on the phone,' he said.

Grenville's voice was low pitched with a mellow timbre, and the moment he opened his mouth, Siv was struck by the uncanny similarity to Ed's. It was like he was in the room with her. She struggled with the surprise. *Keep it together, Drummond.* She cleared her throat and concentrated on the pattern of his sweater.

'We need to clarify a few matters. You told DC Hill that you saw Eugene Warren on the beach in Berminster with a girl. You said it was Leah Steele, because she had strawberry-blonde hair.'

'That's correct. I knew that Teagan was going out with Warren, so I told her that he was a two-timing sleazeball.'

'Remind me again — how well did you know Warren?'

'Mainly by reputation. He was a troublemaker. I didn't mix in his company.'

'Were you aware that he took drugs?'

He said without hesitation, 'No. But looking back, it wouldn't surprise me.'

'The thing is, Mr Grenville—' Siv looked up at him — 'Leah Steele has told us that she never associated with Eugene Warren. But rather, we have information that suggests the girl he was with was someone else you knew.'

Grenville maintained steady eye contact. Not even a flicker. His hands lay relaxed on his knees. 'All I can say is that I thought it was Leah Steele. I wasn't that near them and it was in the evening, but I was sure I recognised her hair.'

Ali said, 'Tell us about Freya Blewitt.'

Grenville stiffened a little. 'She was my half-sister. She died.'

'Yes, from an adverse drug reaction. Were you aware that she took drugs?'

'No. We didn't live in the same household or have a relationship. Why are you asking me about Freya?'

Ali rocked forward in his chair. 'We believe that Freya was mixing with Eugene Warren and also with Henry Kilgore. They might have had a connection to her death.'

'I've never heard that. Do you mean they gave her drugs?'

Siv didn't respond but showed Grenville a copy of the note they'd found at the back of the textbook in Kilgore's flat. 'Do you recognise this? It's to Henry Kilgore, issuing a warning to his friend. It has the initials "GG". DC Patrick Hill rang you about it.'

He half smiled. 'Gosh, yes. I explained to DC Hill that I gave it to Henry Kilgore. That seems such a long time ago. Where on earth did you find it?'

'In his possessions. I'd like you to explain again what it's about.'

Grenville traced a fingertip across the note. 'It's about Teagan. I'd seen her terribly upset a couple of times when Warren had behaved badly or stood her up. She was worth ten of him anyway, and I'd told her he'd mess her about. But she was taken with him, so, of course, she ignored me. I'd warned Warren to treat her right and he'd laughed in my face. Then I saw him on the beach with that other girl. Teagan dropped him, thank goodness, but it took her a week of agonising to tell him. I was furious with Warren. I wrote the note just before Teagan ended it, to warn him off.'

'Why give it to Kilgore and not to Warren?'

'There was no point in talking to Warren. He was such a weasel. Kilgore was basically a decent bloke. I'd sailed with him once or twice in the town regatta. He hung out with Warren, and I reckoned he might have some influence on him.'

It sounded reasonable, but Siv wasn't convinced. 'The way it's written, it could be referring to Teagan or Freya, or maybe both of them.'

Grenville's expression darkened. 'I don't understand you. I told you, I had no idea that Freya was mixed up with Warren. Why do you keep asking me about her?'

'She's relevant to our investigation and you were related,' Ali said sternly.

Grenville squared his shoulders. 'Let me make something clear here. I didn't even know that Freya existed until I was in my teens, and she wasn't aware of Teagan and me. Teagan was a nosey parker with a dramatic streak, always poking about in other people's stuff. I learned to keep anything personal locked away. She was going through our dad's things one day and found a letter that Julie Blewitt had sent to him. It talked about Freya. Teagan produced the letter over dinner with one of her theatrical flourishes, and my dad admitted reluctantly that we had a half-sister. That was quite a meal. He told us that he'd had a brief affair with her mother. Our mum knew about Freya, but there was no contact. When my dad confessed, it was one of the conditions my mum laid down.'

Ali asked, 'What ages were Teagan and Freya at that point?'

'Teagan was thirteen, Freya was twelve. My dad was clearly a busy man when they were conceived.'

'What happened then? Did you meet Freya?'

'Just once. We sat in a café with our fathers — our dad and Freya's step-dad. It was horribly awkward. Freya was a dull, shy sort of girl. She seemed bewildered and a bit nondescript. We didn't have anything in common and I couldn't think what to say. Teagan chatted on. She's never short on conversation, but Freya hardly said a word. That was it. We were told that there wouldn't be any more meetings, and that Freya had been upset and didn't want to see us again. I've no idea if that was true — it was probably more that our mothers didn't want the families linked. Don't ask me why. I suppose there were wounded feelings. I was relieved. I didn't want to repeat the experience in the café. I had a sister and didn't need another. When we heard that Freya had died, it didn't really affect us. I hope that doesn't sound insensitive.'

'It sounds very strange,' Ali told him. 'You and Teagan never saw Freya again?'

'I didn't and I doubt that Teagan did. Our paths didn't cross, and the Blewitts lived on the other side of town. All Teagan said after that meeting in the café was that Freya was a drip.'

If he wasn't telling the truth, he was an accomplished liar. Siv showed him the photo of Freya in the strawberry-blonde wig.

'Your half-sister went through a phase of wearing wigs. Could she have been the girl you saw on the beach with Warren?'

'I suppose . . . Where did you get this photo?'

'From Freya's mum. Given that Leah Steele wasn't with Warren, he might have found it amusing to swap between one sister and another. Are you sure you didn't realise that it was Freya that evening?'

He said angrily, 'Of course I didn't! I wouldn't have kept quiet about that. If it's true, Warren was even more of a shit than I thought.' He stared again at the photo and then handed it back.

Siv asked, 'Can I confirm that you were on your own on the night of the twentieth of January? That's what you told DC Hill.'

'Let me check.' He picked up his phone. 'I had a work appointment in Bognor Regis. I got back here about half seven, had a meal and dealt with emails. I didn't go out again.'

'Can anyone verify that?'

'I live alone.' His phone vibrated and he checked it. 'Sorry, I'll have to answer this email. I've a busy day, I really must get on. I can't tell you anything about these two murders, or Freya's death. I wish you well with your investigation.'

'He's not the sentimental type,' Ali said in the car. He took a packet of pecan nuts from his pocket. 'Want some?'

'Please.'

He tipped some nuts into Siv's open hand. 'Should we have asked for a DNA sample?'

'What's the point? The only DNA we have for a match is from Saffie. Her back-scratching story rings true.' She wiped condensation from the windscreen with her glove. 'I couldn't find any obvious holes in what Grenville told us. We've got a number of people without confirmed alibis, but I just can't see that any of them have a strong enough motive for murdering these two men.'

'Let's head back to the station and go through everything again,' Ali suggested.

'That's the only plan I can come up with. Give me some more nuts.'

Her phone rang as she was chewing. It was Julie Blewitt.

'Inspector, it occurred to me that I should get in touch, because you and your colleagues seem interested in Freya. I told DC Hill about her biological father.'

'That's right. We've just spoken to Gray Grenville and he gave us more background. He said that he and his sister only met Freya once, in a café.'

'Well . . . that's it, you see. Freya told me that Teagan Grenville met up with her a couple of times after that. She warned Freya not to tell anyone, because it would cause trouble. Then Teagan seemed to have got bored and she told Freya there was no point in meeting. Freya was upset by that and confided in me. As an only child, she liked the idea of having siblings. She was rather taken with Teagan, who was a year older and obviously more mature and into clothes and make-up. The secret meetings had been fun.'

'What did you do when Freya told you?'

'Nothing. I was annoyed with Teagan Grenville and I didn't like seeing my daughter upset, but to be honest, I was glad. We were getting on fine without the Grenvilles in our lives, and I preferred it to stay that way.'

Siv thanked her for the information and relayed it to Ali. 'Teagan Grenville's a piece of work. I wonder what else she's not telling us? Call Patrick and get him to invite her to the station straightaway. No delays or excuses.'

* * *

They kept Teagan waiting for half an hour while they had coffee. Siv said that she could kick her heels. Ali offered to lead on questioning and Siv agreed. When they entered the interview room, Teagan was stabbing a message on her phone with long, glistening red nails. She'd slipped her coat off and wore a grey pleated shirt tucked into a short black skirt, with a leather belt. Her customer service badge hung around her neck.

She asked, 'What's with the delay? I'm supposed to be at work, I've left them short-handed.'

'Never mind that and put the phone away,' Ali told her, yanking out a chair. 'Now, we've been talking to your brother and to Julie Blewitt. Fascinating stuff about your half-sister, Freya. You seem to have been a bit of a troublemaker where she was concerned.'

Teagan's false eyelashes swept up and down, and she tossed her hair back. 'Oh, her. What are you getting at?'

'Tell us how you found out that Freya existed.'

She rolled her eyes. 'I found a letter from her mum to my dad. That's how it all came out. Then we met her, just once. We didn't start playing happy families. That's it. Anyway, what's she got to do with anything? Is that why you've dragged me away from work?'

'I've not started yet,' Ali said. 'And before you tell any more lies about Freya or anything else, think carefully. It's a crime to lie to the police.'

Teagan bit her highly glossed bottom lip. 'I don't understand. What are you on about?'

Ali smacked the table with the palm of his hand. 'Ah, come on, Teagan. Don't mess with my head. I'm just out of the hospital and I'm tired. Tell us about your secret meetings with Freya.'

Teagan's lashes went into overdrive and she picked at a nail. 'Who told you about that?'

Ali laughed. 'Well, not Freya, obviously. Come on, come on, time's a- wasting here.'

Siv said quietly, 'Just tell us, Teagan. It's for the best.'

Backed into a corner, Teagan took a combative stance. 'What a lot of fuss about nothing! OK, OK, so I saw Freya a couple of times. We met in that café at the harbour after school. I didn't see why we shouldn't, just because our parents couldn't be civilised. I fancied having a sister, but it turned out we didn't have anything in common. She was a bit boring and hard work. Kept going on about how her mum wouldn't like us meeting. In the end, I couldn't be bothered with her.'

You had to hand it to her for brutal honesty. 'When did you last see Freya?' Ali asked.

'Must have been a couple of months after we first met. So like, years ago.'

'Did your brother know that you'd seen her again?'

'No way! He wouldn't have been interested anyway. It's ever so hot in here. Can't you turn the heating down?'

'It has a mind of its own,' Ali told her.

'Very funny — *not*,' she said.

'I'll tell you what you won't find funny. It turns out that you and Freya had more in common than you realised. He was called Eugene Warren.'

'Oh, here we go. Not him again! How'd you work that out?'

Ali said, 'We believe that Freya was the girl your brother saw with Eugene on the beach. He was cheating on you with your own sibling. He may have had something to do with her death.'

'You're having me on!'

'Afraid not.'

Teagan rubbed under her right eye, leaving a tiny smudge of mascara. 'But that can't be right. Gray would have recognised Freya.'

'Aye, you'd think so,' Ali replied, 'but he hadn't seen her for a few years. She was older and wearing a wig.'

Red weals flashed on Teagan's neck. 'That complete and utter bastard!'

Siv got up and opened a window, but only a notch. It seemed the heat was working to their advantage. 'Now, Teagan, this is important. Did you tell Eugene that Freya was your half-sister?'

'Yeah. I told him all about it, how I found out and everything, but as I said, she turned out to be ever so dull. It gave him a good laugh.'

'More than you knew,' Siv said.

Her eyes filled. 'Now I remember . . . he said that poor, dreary Freya deserved a bit of excitement in her life. I never thought he meant anything by it. Oh God, what a mess.' She clenched her hands and put them to her chin. 'Did Eugene give her the drugs?'

'Probably,' Ali told her. 'What's it they say, guv? Careless talk costs lives.'

Teagan wailed. 'You can't blame it on me! I never meant any harm!' She tapped her nails together fast, making a sound like a clicking insect. 'Listen, when I spoke to Henry in November, he said he'd seen Eugene, and Eugene said there were things he regretted that he needed to put right. Henry was a bit funny, said Eugene was like a hand grenade waiting to go off.'

'Did Henry say when or where they'd met?'

'No, no details. I should have told you that before, but I didn't like the sound of any of it. I didn't want to hear about Eugene.'

Finally, they were getting somewhere. 'Eugene sourced his drugs from someone called "The Wheel". Can you help us with a name?' Siv asked.

'No, I never had anything to do with all of that. Like I told you, I just smoked a bit of dope with him now and again. I didn't even like it much. Can I please, please go now?'

'Yes, go on. DS Carlin will show you out,' Siv told her.

When Ali came back, Siv put her feet up on a chair. 'I think the worst Teagan's guilty of is carelessness and callousness,' she said.

'Aye. It amused Warren to go after Freya. What a nasty wee shite he was.'

Siv ran a finger across the fiery radiator. Her brain was cluttered and sluggish. 'Kilgore's and Warren's paths crossed again after so many years, and Kilgore understood that Warren was feeling guilty about Freya's death. I just have no idea who decided that their fun had to be paid for. I'm going to take a quick lunch break, then let's meet with Patrick in my office and review. Can I get you anything? I can stop by Gusto.'

Ali said in a tone of utter misery, 'I'd love a huge slice of pepperoni pizza with garlic bread and a vanilla *bombolone*, but I've an avocado, walnut and apple salad to relish upstairs.'

'That sounds like brain food, which is very much what we need right now.'

CHAPTER 22

Siv needed to speak to Janis, the museum curator, about her origami exhibition. Heading to the museum, she discovered that Janis was out and not due back for an hour or so. She decided to eat in the museum café and made her way through a plate of fish in a parmesan and herb crust with chunky chips. Poor Ali, with his virtuous salad. If she ate that in this winter season, she'd be hungry again in an hour. While she enjoyed her food, she thumbed idly through the well-stocked information rack on the wall beside her and saw flyers about guided cemetery walks, similar to the one Diane Lacey had given her. She took one down and read it.

Conducted Tours of Berminster Victorian Cemetery

By Diane Lacey, BA MA

Diane is the senior retort technician at Berminster Crematorium. She has a master's degree in death, religion and culture.

Tours are on the fourth Tuesday of each month, 14.15–15.30

Meet at the main cemetery entrance.

The tour will trace the fascinating history of the oldest part of the cemetery. You will hear about burial customs and some graves of interest, including those of survivors of the Charge of the Light Brigade and the Crimean war, a Victoria Cross hero, burials from both world wars and the influenza epidemic in 1918, as well as many others. Your visit will end at the catacombs.

Please take care on steps and keep to the paths.
Please wrap up warm in cold weather.
Admission: £4

Except admission was no longer £4. Siv set down her fork with a clatter, the last chip still speared on it. The £4 had a single line through it and someone had written in black ink *£5, or £3.50 for senior citizens*. The handwriting was familiar. She searched in her bag for the forgotten flyer that Diane had given her. It was scrunched in the side pocket and was printed with the updated pricing, so from a more recent batch.

She abandoned her plate and hurried to the reception desk with the altered flyer. The languid, rake-thin man in his twenties who was on duty grinned at her.

'Hi, I've heard of you. I'm Albie Bailey. We're really looking forward to your contribution to the exhibition.'

'Thank you. I'd like to ask you about this flyer. Someone's corrected the admission price by hand.'

He cultivated an absent-minded professor look, round tortoiseshell glasses, flannel shirt, tweedy jacket with elbow patches and a wispy beard. He said cheerfully, 'Oh yes, that was me. Diane phoned and asked if we'd do it. She'd just had a load printed when the council told her she needed to hike the price and include a concession for older people. She didn't want to waste lots of paper, so I agreed to alter them. She does free talks for us here, so I was happy to return the favour. I did it over a couple of days. Boring, but we have to respect the environment, right?'

'Of course.' Siv returned his artless smile. He was around the right age to have been part of Warren and Kilgore's world. 'I need to speak to you as a police officer. Can we go somewhere private? This is urgent.'

He stepped back. 'Oh, crumbs. Hold on, I'll need to get someone to cover the desk.'

He dithered around for a couple of minutes and at last found a colleague. They met in a windowless back office. Bailey switched the strip light on. It buzzed and flickered. He had a dreamy air and seemed puzzled. He pulled the one chair out for Siv and perched against metal shelves stacked with labelled boxes.

'This is a bit weird,' he said. 'What's the urgency?'

'Mr Bailey, I'm investigating the murders of two men, Eugene Warren and Henry Kilgore. Did you know them?'

'I knew Henry. We were in the same cricket team for a while. I've seen the news about both of them being murdered.'

'Did you attend Fulbrook Upper School?'

'No, I went to Halse Grange.'

'OK. This is your handwriting on this flyer. You altered a batch of them for Diane Lacey.'

'That's right.'

Siv found the photos of the Berminster Breaks brochures on her phone. 'Is this your writing?'

'Yep, course.'

'Can you tell me why you wrote on those brochures?'

'Sure. Someone asked me to.'

'Who?

'A friend of Diane's.'

'Name?'

He made a vague gesture. 'Sorry, I don't know. I mean, I only know him by sight.'

Siv took a deep breath. 'Tell me exactly how it happened.'

'Like I said, Diane gives talks in here sometimes about the history of the cemetery. This guy who asked me the favour was at one of her talks. He popped in one day and said Diane was family. He was playing a practical joke on a friend. They had this thing going where they sent each other odd stuff as a surprise.' He laughed. 'Anyway, he wanted to tease this friend of his with baffling messages in handwriting he wouldn't recognise, so he asked me to write them.'

'Didn't that strike you as a strange request?'

He pushed his glasses up his nose with his thumb. 'Umm . . . not really. My dad's always playing practical jokes. He sets up really complicated ones, spends days on them and ropes people in, so this guy's was comparatively straightforward. I suppose I'm used to it.'

Siv stared at him. He was so laid-back, it was amazing he didn't fall over. She pointed to one of the brochures. '*Funny how fun suddenly isn't funny*. You didn't find that remark a bit odd and hostile?'

He spoke the words silently, his lips moving, and shifted against the shelves. 'I suppose maybe it is . . . At the time, that didn't occur to me. I mean, he knew Diane and he seemed very friendly. It just took a minute to write the stuff and then this guy was gone.'

'Have you seen him since?'

'No.' Slight concern crossed his face. 'Has it caused trouble?'

'Did this man say what the messages referred to?'

'No. Just that it was a joke. I haven't done anything wrong, have I?'

'I can't tell yet. What does this man look like?'

'Ordinary, really. In his twenties. Medium height.'

'Hair colour?'

'I can't say. Fairish, maybe. He was wearing a baseball cap both times I saw him.'

'Local?'

'Probably. No particular accent.'

'When did you write the messages?'

'Sometime last year — maybe November. I can't remember exactly. I'd completely forgotten about it until just now.'

Siv showed him a photo of Kilgore's history book. 'This is also your handwriting.'

'Gosh, yes, it is. That's a blast from the past.' He scratched his head. 'This feels weird, as if you've been tracking me.'

'How did you come to write that comment?'

He didn't need to mull it over. 'We were in the cricket pavilion. There was a rain shower, so we were stuck inside for a while. Henry was catching up with homework. I picked up his history book and told him he'd got the Ford quote wrong. I wrote that as a joke — as if I was his teacher. He said he preferred his version, because as far as he was concerned, history was complete bunk.' He cracked his fingers together. 'This is freaking me out now. What's my handwriting got to do with your murder investigation?'

He'd volunteered information easily and frankly. She stood and regarded him for a moment. He seemed genuinely mystified.

'Thanks for clarifying these things. Where were you on the night of Monday, the twentieth of January?'

Now Albie looked really worried. 'At home. I always stay in with my partner on Mondays.'

'Someone will be in touch again to check that with your partner. I appreciate your help.' His shoulders dropped with relief.

He called after her as she hurried away. 'Aren't you waiting for Janis? She'll be back any minute.'

Siv waved a hand and dashed through the automatic doors. At least she knew where Diane Lacey would be on this fourth Tuesday of the month.

* * *

Ali drove to the cemetery through light, steady snow. A traffic accident held them up and they sat waiting to be waved on. Ali tapped the wheel impatiently.

'I believed Bailey,' Siv said. 'He struck me as the day-dreaming type. He's well suited to a museum. I'm sure that our baseball cap wearer used him to try to stay anonymous.'

'And he said this fella was someone from Diane's family?'

'Apparently. But did she know about it, and if so, will she tell us? There is a young man who might regard Diane as his family.'

'I was just thinking that.'

They didn't speak further. The windscreen wipers gave a tiny squeak that made Siv grit her teeth. Messages on a couple of brochures didn't amount to evidence of murder, but it would be interesting to hear what Diane Lacey could contribute.

'It's just gone a quarter to three,' she said as they left the car. 'We'll be there for the end of the tour. They should be in the catacombs.'

They hurried along the slippery paths. Snowflakes stung Siv's eyes and she pulled her hood up, hunching into her coat. The realm of the dead looked so pretty, draped in white. Her thoughts circled around Diane Lacey's mentoring of Saul Robbins, and then students, higher education and the cost of obtaining a degree nowadays. People had to fund themselves in all kinds of ways, especially if they didn't have a bank of mum and dad behind them. Some might be tempted to turn to crime and easy pickings.

She stopped suddenly, one foot sliding, and put a hand on Ali's arm to steady herself. Not for the first time, she was glad of his comforting sturdiness.

'When did student grants stop and the loan system start?'

He was bare-headed and white crystals glinted in his cornrows. 'Umm, late 1990s, I think. It's a bit freezing for questions about higher education.'

That confirmed her own memory. 'I was thinking about coming from humble beginnings and wanting to achieve and get qualifications. Let's push on.'

The tall gates to the catacombs stood open. Siv could hear Diane's voice as she led the way down the ten steps. There were just five older people inside the brick-lined vaults, all holding folded, dripping umbrellas, their faces obscured by scarves and hoods. One had brought a folding stool and was perched at the front of the group. They were intent, listening carefully. They might well be members of Berminster Senior Students and participants in Liam Jamieson's lectures.

Rows of coffins in various stages of deterioration were stacked along the walls, standing on deep stone shelves. Diane Lacey was gesturing to an ornate coffin, which was decorated with the same snakes and torches as the gates.

'These elaborate coffins were clearly for wealthy Victorians who could afford a stylish burial. Don't worry about any decaying wood. Coffins not buried in the ground have to be lead-lined, so the core is untouched by decay. These were the most expensive interments, private and secure. If you were very rich, you could buy a whole section of shelves. You could visit your departed without the prying eyes of the hoi polloi.' She smiled at an appreciative titter from her audience. 'The torches on the coffin represent death, while the snakes that twine around them symbolise life. The circular serpent swallowing its own tail indicates eternal life and . . .' She paused as she spotted Siv and Ali enter. 'Oh dear, you're very late, we've almost finished the tour.'

Siv's voice rang in the cavernous space. 'Do carry on, it sounds fascinating.'

Diane continued to talk about burial symbols, but she kept glancing at Siv and Ali, standing at the back of the group, and now and again, she stumbled over her words. It was much colder below ground, and the flagstone floor added to the chill.

Ali hissed. 'Should we not just put a stop to her gallop and get her in for questioning?'

'Let her finish. She's uncomfortable, wondering why we're here.'

'She's not the only one who's uncomfortable. This place is horrible,' he muttered.

Diane was speeding up, rattling off a story about a murdered corn merchant who was supposed to haunt the catacombs. 'We'll call a halt there,' she said. 'It is very cold and the light will fade soon. I want you all to get back through the cemetery safely. Thank you for braving the weather today. I do hope you've enjoyed the tour and managed not to get frostbite.'

There was a thin round of applause, muffled by gloves, and the audience started to file up the steps. One man hung back and asked Diane a question about the size of the catacombs. Siv waited impatiently while he fiddled with a hearing aid and asked Diane to repeat her answer. Finally, he was satisfied and slowly made his way out.

Diane was wearing a red baker-boy hat. She tugged down the brim. 'Can I help you?'

'We need a word with you at the station,' Siv said. 'If you'd like to lock up, we'll walk back to the car with you.'

'But what's it about?' Diane asked.

Siv wasn't going to question her among the dead, breathing in this bitter air, and Ali might be tiring. 'We'll talk in the warm, Ms Lacey.'

They watched while Diane secured the padlock on the doors. The snow had stopped. They walked back, crunching single file through the silent, dank afternoon, with Diane in the middle.

* * *

Diane Lacey removed her hat and stroked her flattened hair. She smiled and asked again how she could help them, trying to look at ease. The perspiration at her hairline told a different story, and it wasn't just that the heating was at full strength in the interview room.

Siv said, 'You informed us that you didn't know Eugene Warren or Henry Kilgore. Is that correct?'

'Yes.'

'You don't want to reconsider that answer?'

'No, why would I?'

Ali took printed photos of the two Berminster Breaks brochures from a folder. 'Do you recognise these? We're aware that you know the person who wrote the messages.'

Diane looked at them closely and paled. 'I know the handwriting. It's Albie Bailey's. What's this about?'

'We believe these messages set out to threaten Eugene Warren.'

'Oh. But Albie's a poppet. He wouldn't threaten anyone!'

Siv said, 'Albie Bailey has told us that a man in his twenties asked him to write these messages as a practical joke. He informed Mr Bailey that he's a member of your family. He was at one of your talks at the museum.'

Diane wiped her forehead with the back of a hand. 'I can't think . . . my *family*?'

'Yes. He wore a baseball cap when Mr Bailey saw him. Do you have a relative who matches that description?'

'I don't . . . I don't know.'

Liar. Siv coughed.

'Have you such a massive family that you lose track of them?' Ali asked sarcastically. 'You gave us the impression there's just you and your grandad.'

'This is so difficult. I'm terribly confused.'

Siv said, 'You don't come across as someone who confuses easily, Ms Lacey. You're a rather clear-headed type. Two degrees to your name, dedicated to your job and the heritage of the cemetery. You're highly respected at work. I don't believe you.'

Diane was silent, taking stock of the situation. 'I need time. This is all very sudden.'

'We don't have time,' Ali said. 'It looks as if you did know Eugene Warren, because someone who claimed to be in your family sent him these brochures. One was in his car, the other in his accommodation.'

'Eugene Warren was an unhappy man,' Siv added. 'He was remorseful about his rackety youth and something that had happened at Mallow Cottage. Was he making waves with his guilty conscience? Did it impact on this young man who's related to you?'

'I know nothing about Mallow Cottage. I didn't know Eugene Warren. I don't have a relative who . . .' Diane winced, picked at a button on her sleeve and stopped. She regarded Siv. 'This is very complicated. Sometimes, events spin out of control and you're left bewildered, wondering how things got this way so quickly.'

It was as if she was referring to Ed's sudden, awful death and Siv's own situation. One moment, she'd kissed him goodbye before he cycled to work, the next she was being told that he was dead by the side of the road. Siv took a breath. 'Carry on.'

Diane sighed. 'Maybe that's why I like working with dead people. There are no more surprises.'

'True,' Siv said, 'except surprises can be pleasant. I suppose you're speaking of nasty ones.'

Diane replied, 'Inspector, haven't you ever done anything in your life that you've regretted?'

The room smelled of damp wool and something rotten, as if the foetid air of the catacombs had travelled with them, clinging to their clothing. Siv banished images of mouldering shrouds, dust and decay.

'Of course. I could probably make a list. But this interview isn't about me. Is there something you need to say?'

Diane gave a strained, fleeting smile. 'You make it sound enticing and comforting, like a priest in the confessional.'

'We are like clergy at times,' Siv said. 'People can experience a huge sense of relief when they've confessed to us. Of course, their penance can be a prison sentence rather than a few prayers.'

'You're a wise woman, Inspector.'

'Thanks for the compliment, but let's stick to the subject. Eugene Warren was regretful about past actions that had led to someone's death. Henry Kilgore didn't seem to be burdened by misgivings, but then he was less prone to self-doubt.'

Diane said flatly, 'I can only repeat that I never met Henry Kilgore or Warren.'

Ali said, 'But you know who this young man is, don't you? The one who conned Albie Bailey into writing messages with talk of a practical joke.'

Diane seemed about to reply, then stopped and looked up at the ceiling.

Siv and Ali stayed silent. Siv was pondering the pieces as they started to fall into place. Theft from a bereavement fund, people wishing to better themselves, the current cost of higher education. She contemplated this highly qualified, yet diffident woman and sized her up in a different light. Diane was in control, as you'd expect, but she was also unsure and struggling.

Siv switched tack and aimed directly for her Achilles' heel. 'You're fond of Saul Robbins, aren't you?'

Diane twitched, a little ripple running from head to toe. 'Yes, I am.'

'You've gone out of your way to help him.'

'I've wanted to encourage him.'

'His experience mirrors yours. Like you, he started off with few advantages. He's trying to better himself, and he has to finance his academic studies. Degrees don't come cheap. Saul isn't a big earner. He must have struggled to pay his way.'

'That's true.' Diane licked her lips.

'I think that Saul Robbins stole from the bereavement collection to fund his studies and either you suspected him or you knew.'

Diane swallowed. 'That's nonsense. I alerted you to the thefts.'

'True, but you were fairly sure that there was nothing we could do,' Siv told her. 'You're caught up in something, Diane. Maybe you wandered into it unwittingly. Are you shielding Saul Robbins?'

Diane flinched. 'You know when the sea looks inviting and you wade in and then suddenly, the bottom shelves away and you start sinking . . .' She sounded overwhelmed.

'Where is Robbins today?' Ali asked.

'Off on a study day,' she murmured.

'Diane, indications are that you might be linked to two murders,' Siv told her. 'Those brochures were used to intimidate. Maybe you killed two men or assisted someone in the killing. If you weren't involved in murder, then anything you tell us that will help to find the person who was might go in your favour.'

Diane took a shuddering breath and started talking about how she'd met Saul and grown fond of him. They listened as she stumbled over her words in a raw, pained voice.

'He came to me in my office, told me about problems he was having. Confessed things to me. He'd done something foolish that was troubling him. It wasn't such a terrible thing, but it was worrying him. He was afraid it might jeopardise his future if it ever got out. I could see why. It was hard to credit that he'd acted so rashly—' Her voice tailed off and she cleared her throat.

Siv could guess what that was. 'Can you tell us more about what Saul had done?'

Diane took a moment to respond. 'It was all such a mess. Saul talked about his past. He'd been in love with a girl called Freya. Besotted with her from the way he talked, but he'd lost her and he'd never got over it.'

At that, Ali twitched in his chair, but Siv touched his arm. *Let her carry on.* It was as if Diane was talking to herself, attempting to rationalise events.

She gazed at a wilted plant in the window of the interview room. 'I was so worried about Saul. He seemed very on edge. I'd wake at night, going over what he'd told me. I'd never had to deal with anyone else's personal difficulties before and I wasn't sure I was making the right responses. It felt like a tremendous responsibility, but I wanted to help him stay on the right path.' Suddenly, Diane broke off and stared at Siv, a muscle twitching in her cheek. 'Why *did* you talk to Albie Bailey this afternoon? I can't understand why these brochures are so important.'

The question threw Siv for a moment. She said carefully, 'How do you know when I spoke to him?'

'He rang me, said you'd been at the museum asking about my relative and some brochures he'd written on as a favour. I'd no idea what he was talking about. But after he rang off, I realised he must have been referring to Saul.' She ran her tongue over her lips. 'Is Saul in trouble?'

Siv's heart sank. 'Diane, did you contact Saul?'

'I tried to. I left a message for him, asking him about Albie and what he'd been up to.'

Ali gave a heavy sigh, muttered under his breath.

'What's happened with Saul?' Diane was sounding insistent. She lifted her head and stared at Siv. 'I'm really worried.'

Siv rallied, shoving her chair back. 'You should be. Saul Robbins is a suspect in two murders. We have to find him now. You need a solicitor.'

Diane gulped water down and named a solicitor. Siv said they'd see to it. They left her with custody colleagues and hurried to Saul Robbins' home. There was no time to waste.

* * *

They arrived just after 10 p.m. It was a top-floor flat in a block of twelve. They heard blues music thundering as they approached the door. After Ali had rung the bell and then hammered on it several times, a young man opened it with a bottle of beer in hand.

Ali flashed his ID. 'Is Saul Robbins in?'

'Afraid not. He was here earlier on, studying and stuff, but he went out a couple of hours ago.'

'Are you his flatmate?'

'That's right. Tony Prudence.'

'Can we come in?' Siv asked impatiently.

Jimi Hendrix was singing 'Hear My Train a Comin'' as they stepped into the living room. It was so loud Siv's ears hurt. She mimed to Prudence to turn it down.

'I bet your neighbours love you,' she said.

Prudence shrugged and hitched up his tracksuit bottoms.

She asked, 'Do you know where Saul is?'

'Nah. He came home about six, after he'd been for a run. He'd been sitting for hours writing an essay, so he needed exercise. I'd just given him a beer when someone phoned him, and when he finished the call, he said something about the shit hitting the fan. He was a bit weird, actually, pacing around and listening to phone messages. I asked him if he was OK and he gave me this funny stare. He said something about going back to where it started, and then he rang someone. He took off again after that.'

'Do you know who he called?' Siv asked.

'No. He went to his room.'

'Do you expect him back?'

'I presume so. He didn't say he wouldn't be home tonight. He's been a bit odd recently. Agitated. I've heard him get up during the night.'

Ali asked, 'Does he have a partner?'

'Not for a while. Never mentions anyone, anyway.'

'Try ringing him,' Siv said to Ali.

'No point,' Prudence told her. 'He left his phone in the kitchen, and that's weird too.'

Siv slipped gloves on, found the phone and rang the last number on incoming calls. When she'd finished speaking, she turned to Ali. 'That was Andy Smeaton. He said he'd phoned Saul this evening to find out if he had any news of Diane. Smeaton saw her coming with us this afternoon. Later on, he spotted that her car was still parked at the rear of the retort. I'm just going to try the last number Robbins called.' She rang and listened to an automated message saying that the number wasn't in service.

'What's going down?' Prudence tipped his head back and finished his beer.

'We're not sure. How does Saul get around?'

'He cycles.'

Siv handed him a card. 'If Mr Robbins comes back, please ring me immediately. I need to take his phone with me. We have to search this premises — don't go into his room. Officers will arrive with a warrant soon.'

Outside the flats, Ali reached for his cigarettes, checked himself and took gum from his pocket instead. 'Bloody

Smeaton, sticking his nose in. Now Robbins has had warnings from him and Diane. He'll know we're onto him.'

'Damn. I could kick myself. I should have warned Bailey not to speak to anyone. I was in too much of a hurry to get to Diane.'

'Never mind. Where the hell's Robbins gone? "Going back to where it started." To the crem, maybe?' Ali yawned and shook himself.

Siv leaned against a streetlight. Snow was falling again, casting a strange silence on the world. Perhaps this road was taking them back to where it began. 'That's a possibility. Come on. We'll try the chapel steps.'

'We'd better ring Smeaton, get him to open the gates.'

'No. It'll take too long. We'll climb over Emmeline's Gate, like our killer did.'

In the car, they were both tense. The heater hummed and the windscreen wipers swished the snow away. The streets were quiet, with people huddled indoors.

'Sounds like Robbins was wired about something,' Ali said.

'Yeah. Panicking, I'd say. I wish we knew the last person he called.' Siv had a horrible, sinking sensation that they might be about to find another body. Mortimer would make a caustic comment regarding the head count.

'D'you think Diane Lacey was aware of what Robbins was up to with Bailey?' Ali asked.

'She's protective of Robbins. When I mentioned him, her eyes filled up. She seems an unlikely murderer, and she has an alibi. But she indicated that she'd got out of her depth.'

'Well, I have a feeling she's going to find the lifebelt's missing,' Ali said.

They parked in the deserted road, beside Emmeline's Gate. Siv climbed over first, with Ali puffing behind her. Holding their torches, they ran through Bluebell Copse and down the path towards the chapels. The snow scattered under their feet. The chapels loomed through the dark — tall and eerily beautiful, watching over the ranks of the dead.

One external light shone over the central door. Siv slowed and caught her breath. She half turned to Ali. 'Quiet now. Turn your torch off.'

They approached silently. Wind whispered in the trees behind them. Siv feared seeing a body on the steps. She stopped, inching forward, heart thudding. They were snow dusted, empty. She exhaled with relief. They walked around the chapels, but all was hushed and still. Ali was panting hard. Siv let him take just a moment. She was sure where to try next.

'Mallow Cottage and fast,' she told Ali. She took off, running back to the car. Her torch played on the frosted bushes, conjuring strange shapes from them. She was filled with dread now.

Siv drove at full speed, tearing around corners.

Ali gripped the dashboard. 'If he's not at the cottage, where next?'

'I reckon we won't have to cross that bridge,' Siv said grimly.

When they drew up outside the cottage, no lights showed.

Ali tried the door. 'No sign of a break-in.'

'Round the back,' Siv whispered, switching on her torch.

She led the way and halted as she turned the corner. A bike leaned against the side of the cottage. She carried on slowly, each step silent in the soft snow.

The back garden was in complete darkness. She stopped. No sounds. She lifted her torch beam from the floor and gasped as it danced on a dark shape. That of Saul Robbins. He'd used one of the garden chairs to stand on. Now, it lay on its side and he dangled from the rope he'd attached to a downpipe.

They hurried forward. Ali grasped his legs, lifting his windpipe away from the knot.

Siv felt for a pulse. 'Nothing,' she said. 'No sign of life and he's cold to the touch. Call it in. Ring Patrick as well and tell him to come here. I want you to go home as soon as he arrives.'

'I'm fine,' Ali protested, 'there's no need—'

She held up a hand. 'That's an order, non-negotiable.'

'Fine, fine.'

When he'd made the calls, Ali looked up at the body.

'D'you think he and Diane were lovers?'

'No, I believe it was platonic. They gravitated towards each other because they each recognised a fellow traveller in life. Fighting the odds, overcoming adversity.'

They waited with the body in the cold. Siv watched Ali move down the garden, by the summerhouse, and give in to the craving for a cigarette. She stood by the fence. Looking up at the dark shape in the gloom, Siv's thoughts raced. Robbins had loved Freya Blewitt. He had to be their killer, but it didn't make sense. There were still too many holes. They had nothing to link him directly to Warren and Kilgore. Every question answered just posed another.

Snow glittered in Robbins' mousy curls and clung to his padded jacket. It hung open, exposing just a thin T-shirt, and Siv had an irrational urge to zip it up. Nothing would warm him now.

CHAPTER 23

It was two in the morning by the time Siv got in. On the way home, she'd received a call from the station. Diane Lacey had just seen an email that she'd received from Saul Robbins the previous evening, when they'd been interviewing her. They'd forwarded it to Siv. She also had a USB stick that uniformed officers had taken from Robbins's PC.

She kicked off her boots and woke up the stove, feeding in kindling. Then she poured a large glass of akvavit, took marinated artichokes, feta cheese and olives from the fridge and ate them with her fingers, standing by the kitchen window. Outside, the snow had stopped, but a rising breeze scattered flakes from the spindly trees. She saw the reflection of the stove's red and orange flames as it blazed into life. The sight was a comfort after the grim scene at Mallow Cottage.

She sat by the fire with her drink and opened her laptop. When she inserted the USB stick, she saw various folders named *Course/Syllabus*, *Essays*, *CV Notes*, *Textbooks*, *Submission Dates* and *Dissertation*. *Essays* contained more than thirty documents with titles like, 'Adding value in a marketing team', 'Describe the most important features of competitive strategy' and 'Explain your understanding of organisational culture as a leadership tool'. Siv saw from the *Course* folder that Robbins was doing his MBA via the Rother Business School.

She switched to her email. Robbins had sent Diane the message at six thirty the previous night. The subject line said, *Give this to the police*. Above the attachment was one word. *Sorry*. Siv clicked the attachment and read, reaching for her glass now and again. The tone and content contrasted sharply with Eugene Warren's elegiac musings on nature. Robbins was prickly, resentful, angry. He'd certainly hated his menial work at the crematorium and relied heavily on Diane's support.

> *I murdered Eugene Warren and Henry Kilgore. My friend, Yaz, helped me, but I planned it and I did it.*
>
> *This is in case I get the bad breaks and the police are smart. I've no intention of being questioned for hours and going to jail. I've had enough of being bossed around and treated like dirt. I've left this because I want Diane to understand. She deserves that. She and Yaz are the only people who've ever helped me. Diane's the only one who treats me with any respect at work. Yaz has been amazing regarding my MBA. She's given me lots of encouragement and advice.*
>
> *I hate my fucking job. It's OK when I get to help Diane in the retort now and then, but the rest of the time is just shit-shovelling. Toby barely notices me. Andy acts as if I'm his sidekick, and that old bat, Phoebe, treats me as if I've got dog muck on my shoes. No idea why she reckons she's so special — she's never done anything with her life except stand behind a desk. The way she goes on about how much her collection makes, you'd think she was running an international charity. I decided that as I'm a case in need, I'd help myself and benefit from her fund. I started by taking a twenty.*
>
> *It all kicked off last November. I helped Bertie Greene move some second-hand furniture into his place. He's such a loser, but he needed a hand. It's a grotty flat, but when you've done time, you can't expect much. We got some beers*

in afterwards and a takeaway. Bertie got pissed, saying that life picked on him. Other people's crap had spread over him and it wasn't his fault. He started to drone on about Eugene Warren visiting him in prison. I wasn't really listening until he mentioned Freya. He told me that Eugene had screwed Freya and they'd hung out at the cemetery, drinking and taking drugs. Eugene got them from someone called 'The Wheel'. Henry Kilgore joined in sometimes. He went to Mallow Cottage with them and they took Ecstasy. Freya collapsed and they dumped her by the hospital. Lots of stuff about how much Eugene regretted what had happened.

I loved Freya. I know I'm still young, but I'd say she was the love of my life. I fancied her for ages before I asked her out. I had no confidence in myself and I was over the moon when she said she'd come out with me. She was so calm, sweet and understanding. She never took drugs. A sheltered kind of girl, but she was preoccupied with her parents' rows. She didn't like them much, because they were at each other's throats all the time. I realised she was upset because of all the crap going on at home and I liked protecting her. We didn't go out for long, but I really felt we got each other and we'd be long term. I could never understand why she suddenly said she didn't want to see me anymore. I was heartbroken. I couldn't concentrate at school and my marks started to slide. Then when I heard she'd died, I hit rock bottom, couldn't be bothered with anything. It's why I left school with mediocre grades and ended up in that crap job at the crem.

Then I understood that Eugene stole her from me. I'd heard he made a habit of hitting on other guys' girls, but I never thought that was why Freya dumped me. Never occurred to me that she'd be interested in him. So, he took her away and then he filled her full of drugs and killed her.

I was beside myself. After what Bertie had said, I went to Diane's office and told her about Freya and me and that Freya had died. I didn't mention Eugene or give her Bertie's details. I couldn't burden her with that. I just said that I might have an idea about who'd been involved in Freya's drug overdose. But then, everything got on top of me. I broke down and confessed I'd stolen from the bereavement fund. Diane was shocked, but she told me as long as I promised not to do it again, she'd say nothing. She urged me to go to the police about my suspicions regarding Freya. I said it was all too unclear. I wanted more time.

I wanted to do something about Warren and Kilgore but I needed to find out who 'The Wheel' was before I decided. Bertie mentioned that Eugene worked at a place called Pie Mad in London, so I went there and hung around. He was hawking food about on a stupid trike. What a loser, and yet even though he'd ruined Freya's life, stolen it from her, he got to live! I followed him home to a grotty terraced street. On the way back from London, I kept remembering Freya. She was so small and dainty. She fitted under my arm. I loved her but Eugene couldn't have given a toss about her. I should have done more to keep her safe. If I'd persisted with her, kept in touch and insisted on finding out why she'd stopped seeing me, I might have found out about Eugene, and I could have stepped in. But I was too knocked back.

I decided to torment Eugene a bit. I'd seen the Berminster Breaks brochures around town, so I picked a couple up. A pretty photo of Mallow Cottage, where Freya spent her last evening. I got Albie Bailey to write messages on them. Then I sent the brochures to Eugene. He could sweat. A week later, I sent Eugene a note with my phone number. Just said my name was Saul. I told him I knew what he and Henry had done to Freya and he'd better call me.

Siv rubbed her eyes. She was so tired the words were blurring. She started to read the next entry, but fell asleep, the screen glowing on her lap.

* * *

When Siv reached her office the next morning, she spent the first hour or so finishing Saul Robbins' account and highlighting pages. Ali and Patrick were continuing to interview Diane Lacey with her solicitor present. Mid-morning, her stomach was rumbling, so she popped to Gusto and bought a team brunch of coffee and a selection of croissants, with a fruit-topped porridge for Ali. Mortimer appeared in her office with a jaunty air just as she arrived back.

'I'm joining you for your debrief,' he announced.

Ali raised an eyebrow. Patrick looked pleased. Siv tried for bland.

'Of course, sir. I'd have brought you a coffee from Gusto if I'd realised. But you can have a croissant.'

'Very kind. Are you well on the road to recovery, Carlin?'

'Aye, sir, thanks. Steaming onwards.'

'Headlines first,' Siv said when they were all seated. 'We have confirmation that Robbins died from suicide by hanging. I've been reading his account of the murders. He's our killer, by his own admission, but he had a helper. Bertie Greene told him about Warren, Kilgore and Freya Blewitt. The confession he wrote clarifies quite a few things and tells us how he murdered Warren and Kilgore. But it leaves one big question dangling, and that's the identity of the person he describes as his helper. All he writes is that it was a woman called Yaz. I believe Robbins's last phone call before he killed himself was to that person because he rang a pay-as-you-go mobile and that number's now dead. Ali, you take us through Diane Lacey's interviews.'

Ali tore his eyes away from her croissant. 'Diane got friendly with Saul Robbins at the crem. Took him under her wing and helped him with his studies for an MBA. He came from a similar background to her, hadn't had many advantages, and she saw that he was fragile and easily crushed. So, she identified with him and wanted to urge him to aim higher. Seems to have been a big sister or mother figure to him.

'Then, last autumn, a couple of things happened. Phoebe Palmer reported the theft from the bereavement collection. Robbins went to Diane, upset and agitated. He told her he'd been in love with Freya and explained how she'd died from a reaction to Ecstasy. Diane described a difficult, emotional scene. She claimed that Robbins made no mention of Warren and Kilgore's part in it. He did indicate that he had suspicions about who'd been with Freya when she became ill. He confessed that he'd been stealing from the collection box. The way she described it, she slapped his wrists and told him not to do it again. She pitied him.' Ali ate a blueberry from his pot of porridge before he continued.

'Diane's a highly competent professional where her job's concerned, but when it came to Robbins, her judgement deserted her. After Warren was found, she started to wonder about Robbins's notions concerning Freya's death. He was jittery and lacked concentration at work. She had no reason to believe he was connected to the murder, but she was uneasy. She claims she asked him if he knew anything about it, and he got terribly upset and accused her of doubting him, so she left it there.'

Patrick said, 'She told us about the theft from the bereavement fund because she had no other option.'

'That's right,' Ali confirmed, 'but also because when Phoebe Palmer first broached it to Diane, she said she suspected Robbins. Diane thought that Phoebe was just indulging her dislike of him and cautioned her not to make allegations. She gave us the info about the theft because if she hadn't, Phoebe Palmer might well have. That way, Diane controlled the story before we saw Foxwell. She maintained that she had no idea about the messages on the brochures and that she knew nothing about the murders.'

Siv swallowed the last of her croissant and picked up the thread. 'Saul Robbins's account confirms what Diane has told us and fills in other parts of the story. As we know, last year, Warren visited Greene at the jail. He told Greene about what had happened with Freya and Kilgore at Mallow Cottage. What Greene omitted to tell us was that Warren also mentioned his job at Pie Mad. That man has lied through every interview with us. I'm glad we finally pinned him down.

'When Greene was released in November, Robbins helped him with a few things in his new flat,' she continued. 'They spent an evening drinking. Greene told Robbins all about Warren's visit to him in jail. Greene was unaware that Robbins had been keen on Freya when they were teenagers — held quite a torch for her, in fact. They went out for a while, but then Freya lost interest in him because, unknown to Robbins, she'd fallen into Warren's orbit. Robbins was devastated. Seems to have seen himself as her champion, and being with her had boosted his self-esteem. Then Freya died. Robbins attributed his failure at school and being in a dead-end job to the impact of losing her—'

'Fertile soil for grievance to take root in,' Mortimer interrupted, 'albeit many years later.'

'Indeed,' Siv agreed. 'After listening to Greene's ramblings, Robbins knew who'd been responsible for Freya's death, and he'd also learned that someone called "The Wheel" had supplied the drug that killed her. It tormented him. He brooded about it and he started to nurture the idea of identifying "The Wheel" and making Warren and Kilgore pay for what they'd done. He went to London and followed Warren home from Pie Mad. He got Albie Bailey to write on the brochures and sent them to Warren, and a while later, he also sent a note with his phone number, saying that they needed to talk about Freya Blewitt. Warren did call him, according to his account.'

A shower of rain rattled noisily against the windows, making Patrick jump. The slats on one of the blinds clicked together in the draught.

Siv turned to her laptop and read aloud. '"Eugene rang me. He was very agitated about the brochures and my note and asked what I wanted. I wouldn't tell him anything about myself, just that I lived in Berminster and I'd heard the whole story from someone. It was good hearing him squirm. He was very keen on owning up, but concerned that he'd get Henry and 'The Wheel' into trouble as well. He said he'd met Henry in London. Henry had come to his place and pleaded with him not to stir up the past. Henry was happy now. He had a partner, and it would ruin everything for him. I told Eugene I wanted to know the identity of 'The Wheel'. He hedged about that. Finally, he told me who 'The Wheel' was. I was stunned when he said it was Yaz. I couldn't sleep, thinking about it. Couldn't believe it.

'"I contacted Yaz, said I knew about the drug dealing. We talked for ages. She told me that she'd stopped dealing years ago. She knew she'd done wrong, but she explained she hadn't intended to hurt anyone and she'd mainly stuck to selling weed. When she was young, she took a wrong turn, got caught up in that world. She didn't know Freya, had no idea that she'd died, or why. She got really upset and tearful. I could tell she was genuine. I wanted Eugene and Henry to pay for what they did, but I didn't want to mess up Yaz's life. She's been kind to me and generous with her time and expertise. She and Diane have been my two angels, guiding me on. Eugene was completely different. He didn't care who he damaged back then. If it came to it, I'd stop him destroying Yaz. I already had the germ of a plan."'

Siv stopped, looking around the room at her team. She drank coffee, pausing to allow for questions, but they were all just gazing at her, as if mesmerised by Robbins's story.

She carried on. 'So, we don't know who Yaz is. And we've been mistaken in referring to "The Wheel" as male. Robbins describes more phone conversations in December, with Warren agonising about what to do. He said Kilgore wasn't returning his calls. I imagine that Kilgore was avoiding him, hoping it would all go away, and he'd plenty to think about already with his job under threat. Robbins was still trying to steer Warren away from naming Yaz. Then in January, Warren made the call that clinched his and Kilgore's fates.'

Mortimer's phone rang. He got up and stepped away to take the call. Patrick clicked his fingers together, impatient to hear the rest. Ali finished his porridge and smiled at Siv as if to say, *There, haven't I been good?*

Mortimer ended the call and sat down again. 'Sorry about that. Do go on, DI Drummond.'

She looked down, continued reading.

'"Eugene rang me again. He said he'd decided that he was going to go to the police. He'd managed to get hold of Henry, who was furious and said that if Eugene went ahead, he'd deny everything. Henry told him that there'd be no evidence to back him up after all this time, but if he wanted to be a martyr, so be it. Henry said he had a lot going on in his life. He'd be in Berminster for a week in January and asked Eugene to leave his confession until after then.

'"I talked to Yaz. She was really worried and she said if Eugene went to the police, it would destroy her. I told her I wouldn't let that happen. She said I was her knight in shining armour.

'"I didn't want to take lives. It's not who I am, but I couldn't see any other way. Eugene and Henry would bring Yaz down with them. They deserved to die, both of them, for what they did to Freya. Even if there was enough evidence to put them on trial, what sentence would they get? Something nonsensical.'

'He had a point,' Ali said. 'I see where he was coming from.'

'An eye for an eye,' Patrick added.

Mortimer gave them both a pained look. Siv hurried on.

'"I put my plan to Yaz. She agreed to help me and we split the tasks. She'd contact Eugene from now on and I'd talk to Henry. She called Eugene, told him that I'd spoken to her and if he was going to go to the police, she'd like to meet him and Henry first to discuss it. She piled on how sorry she was about what had happened, and pitched the idea that she wanted to help him persuade Henry that it would be best to own up. The three of them should go to the police together and make a clean breast of things. Eugene bought into it. He sounded relieved and agreed to a meet in Berminster. He gave her Henry's number.

'"I rang Henry, said I was a friend of Yaz. I told him that Yaz wanted to meet him and Eugene so that they could try and persuade Eugene not to go to the police, or at least to leave them out of his confession. He hesitated, but finally said yes to a meet.

'"I bought myself one of those all-in-one suits. Ran through it all again with Yaz. She thanked me for looking out for her and promised she'd keep making amends for past mistakes. She'd already made a big contribution to a charity that helps young drug addicts. The plan felt right. It brought justice for Freya. Henry and Eugene would die at Mallow Cottage, where they'd drugged her. Henry would stay there, because he provided the location for their crime. I'd lay Eugene out at the crem. See if he'd think it was such a great place for party after all. Yaz suggested I buy wreaths online as a nice touch. She'd pay me for them. I loved imagining the shock the old staff die-hards would get, how much it would put Toby's sharp nose out of joint and how angry Andy would be when he found out about his prized wheelbarrow.'

'What a piece of work this young man was,' Mortimer said, wiping a flake of croissant from his chin. 'I'm only sorry that he escaped justice by killing himself. Carry on, carry on.'

'Almost finished now,' Siv told him, picking up from where he'd butted in. 'On the Monday, Yaz rang Eugene and told him to come to the garden of Mallow Cottage at half ten that night. She said that she and Henry would be there. I wasn't a bit afraid. I was full of energy. When Eugene arrived at Mallow Cottage, I told him I was Saul and that Yaz and Henry would be along any minute. He sat in the chair like a little lamb. I strangled him from behind with a belt. He struggled but it was remarkably quick, and I took the belt off and left him sitting there. Then I rang Henry and told him where to come. It was so dark when he arrived, he didn't realise that Eugene was dead. He sat down and I stabbed him in the neck and shoved him behind the summerhouse. I drove Eugene to Emmeline's Gate in his car and used Andy's wheelbarrow to take him and the wreaths to the chapel steps."'

Siv said, 'For Robbins, these crimes amounted to the perfect box ticking. He dispensed justice to Warren and

Kilgore, protected his friend "Yaz", and he got his own back on the staff he despised at the crematorium. There are just a couple of paragraphs after that, some of it self-justification. Robbins notes my interview with him and says he invented the woman in the cemetery who asked him about the wheelbarrow, just to confuse matters. It amused him to give me a description of myself. I'll read you the last lines.

'"Maybe you won't get to Yaz. She's clever. If you do, tell her I'm sorry. I tried hard to protect her, but it didn't work out. In the end, I want Diane to have the truth."'

'Seems like Kilgore was probably heading to Bertie Greene's on the Monday night to offload about the situation with Warren,' Patrick said.

'He must have been sick with worry. He did well to conceal it,' Siv agreed.

'What a messy, shabby, sordid tale,' Mortimer said. 'At least Freya Blewitt's mother will have some closure.' He rubbed his hands. 'Also . . . when Ms Kilgore hears what her son was party to, she might well reconsider her complaint about us. Yes, I'd say that's almost a certainty. She'll hardly want to draw adverse attention to herself. Where's Diane Lacey now?'

'We sent her home after this morning's interview,' Siv said. 'She was in pieces over Robbins's suicide. She failed to report that Robbins had confessed to being the crem thief, but I'll wait and see if her employer wants to make anything of it. She might lose her job when Toby Foxwell finds out. I dread to think what she'll do if that happens. That cemetery is her life.'

Mortimer stood. 'She drew a short straw when she took Robbins under her wing, didn't she? I'll leave you to get on and establish Yaz's identity. Make sure that's quick, so there are no loose ends. Good work, everyone.'

'Every cloud has a silver lining for Mortimer,' Ali said when he'd gone. 'Imelda Kilgore will be devastated.'

Siv stood up, stretched, leaned forward and picked up the last croissant. She noted Ali watching as she tucked it back in its bag, but she didn't want him to be tempted. 'We urgently need to track down this Yaz. There are no clues, other than that she was "The Wheel" in her younger life and she offered Robbins support with his studies.'

'Do we think she's local?' Ali asked.

'Hard to say,' Siv replied, putting the bag down beside her. 'The confession indicates phone calls, so possibly not. She must have been reasonably local when she operated as "The Wheel". Between you, can you ring Foxwell and Tony Prudence? Ask if they have any idea about Yaz and tell Foxwell that his deputy manager won't be at work. Check Robbins's call and email history. Then contact Diane Lacey and ask her about Yaz. I'll visit Ms Kilgore and Ms Blewitt, and then I'll enjoy myself trawling through the folders on Robbins's memory stick.'

She sat at her desk after her team had gone, marshalling her resolve to see two grieving women. She'd add to one's agonies and perhaps relieve the years of anguish for the other. And then there was Saffie. She'd feared that her fiancé had been having an affair. Siv couldn't even begin to imagine how she was going to cope with the news that Henry had once left a girl to die.

CHAPTER 24

Siv woke at six in the morning, one of those abrupt starts from sleep. A wrenching into the world. There was a rustling and scratching in her brain, like a mouse behind a skirting board. She reached out to switch a lamp on and stared into the darkness. They'd had no luck establishing Yaz's identity the previous day. Diane Lacey had declared she'd never heard of her. No one with a similar name was in Robbins's phone or email contacts. The last number he'd called was listed just as *Y* and it looked as if the SIM card on that phone had been destroyed. Trying to get any trace on it would take time.

Yet she knew she had a hint of something. She lay very still, clearing her mind and then visualising the incident board.

She sat up. She had it, surely? Was it all in a surname? Was it really that simple? She threw on a dressing gown, perched on the side of the bed and reached for her laptop. She'd copied Robbins's folders and she looked through several of his essays again, knowing that she'd spotted something. Fifteen tedious minutes later, she saw it, in an essay titled, 'The challenges of entrepreneurship'. She seized a pillow, threw it in the air and punched it when it landed.

She donned jeans and her purple sweater, made coffee, then pulled her boots on. There had been a hard frost overnight, and when she stepped outside with a torch, the ground was cold and dry. She paced in the dark by the river. It was covered with a thin glaze of ice. The snowdrops looked bedraggled. The sky was scattered with fragments of fast-moving clouds, the moon scudding between them. The coffee was strong and bracing. She'd need to be fortified for what lay ahead.

She was impatient, but there was nothing she could do just yet. Back in her wagon, she poured more coffee, sat at the little table and worked on folding a dark green coracle. She shaped the central seat across the middle. The chest strap and the oars would be in black. The work calmed her, allowed her to control her urge to act.

At eight o'clock, she was dressed and ready to leave the wagon. She made a phone call, breathing deeply as she heard her questions answered, and instructed the person on the other end not to mention the conversation to anyone. Then she rang Ali.

* * *

The Generate offices were full and busy at eight thirty. Two young women pushed their fold-up bikes through the foyer. They still wore their helmets, emblazoned with the Generate logo of an upward-pointing arrow. The screen at reception showed an audience standing and clapping with the flashing message, *We Make Magic Happen*. The man behind the desk told them that Ms Ferris wasn't in yet.

'Nor will she be able to see you when she gets here,' he said. 'She's already late for her 8.15 breakfast meeting, so she'll have to go straight into that.'

'Have you tried contacting her?' Siv asked.

'No. I've told Tessa, her PA.'

'Get Tessa for me, please.'

He blinked. 'Sure. Take a seat.'

Ali regarded the egg-themed sofa suspiciously. 'Think I'll stand.'

'I spoke to Tessa when I rang at eight,' Siv told Ali. 'One of your shirt buttons is undone. You don't want to frighten the PA.'

He fumbled to do it up with his thick fingers. 'Tessa's the one who confirmed the name?'

'Yes. Jane Yasmine Ferris, known generally as Yaz. I don't like the fact that she's late, doesn't bode well. Tessa also confirmed that Saul Robbins once spent a couple of days here, observing the business for his MBA. I found a reference to Generate in one of his essays.'

Siv tapped her foot, willing the PA to appear. The man at reception was on the phone, arranging a meeting, his fingers flying across his keyboard. He wore the kind of narrow-cut suit that Patrick liked. The audience on the screen beside him were applauding and whooping at a woman wearing a mike. Behind her was a presentation titled, *Make Your Dreams Reality*.

A young woman with a moon face, plump knees and a too-tight skirt hurried up to them. She smiled cheerily. 'Hi, I'm Tessa, Yaz's PA. Can I help?'

Siv showed her ID. 'I spoke to you half an hour ago. We need to see Ms Ferris urgently. Is she due in?'

Tessa's smile dimmed. 'She's late, actually, which is really unusual. I was just trying to get her on her phone, but it must be switched off. There are a couple of people waiting for her.'

'When did you last see her?'

'Yesterday evening. We left the building together. Is there something wrong? Why do you want to see her?'

Siv asked, 'How was Ms Ferris yesterday?'

Tessa tugged at her skirt. 'She was fine, fine.'

Siv asked Ali to phone Yaz Ferris and to get Patrick to join them immediately. She turned back to Tessa, who was looking anxious. 'We need Ms Ferris's home address.'

'Oh, right. She lives in Saltmarsh Court on Rosemount Avenue. Number five. But I'm sure she'll be here any minute—'

'And her car details. Do you have those?'

'It's a red Audi hatchback. I can get you the registration. We have to record them for parking.'

'Great, thanks. Text it to me immediately. Our colleague DC Patrick Hill will be here shortly. If Ms Ferris calls you, you're not to tell her that we're here, and you must inform him immediately. Got that?'

Tessa nodded. 'But what's this about?'

'Thank you. You can get back to work.'

Ali had finished his calls. 'Patrick's a few mins away. I couldn't raise Yaz Ferris.'

They hurried from the building to the car. The air was so cold, Siv caught her breath.

'Looks like Yaz Ferris must have run after Robbins's phone call last night,' Ali said.

'In her shoes, so would I. I feel in my bones that she's already flown the nest.'

'What led you to Jane Ferris being Yaz?' Ali asked when they were headed for Rosemount Avenue.

'Her name. Think about it.'

Ali stared at her, fingering his scrubby beard. 'Nope. Don't get it.'

'Her name was there on the board in front of us. Ferris. Ferris wheel. So obvious, we couldn't see it. When you say "The Wheel" in the context of drugs, it sounds a tad sinister, but it referred to that least ominous of things, an amusement ride.'

Ali threw his hands up. 'Stall the ball! Tell me I'm dreaming! It's hard to credit that a successful woman like her would have got involved with Robbins. It was high risk.'

'Yaz Ferris is used to risk,' Siv replied. 'She built up her own business. That takes guts and the ability to step into the unknown. And the stakes were high. If she'd done nothing, she faced the prospect of her life unravelling.'

'Yeah. It would have been a fall from grace, all right.'

Siv didn't respond. She was thinking of the combative light in Yaz Ferris's eyes when she'd interviewed her. She was a woman used to giving orders and thinking strategically.

Robbins had been a murderer, but maybe he'd also been something of a pawn in her skilful, controlling hands.

* * *

Rosemount Avenue was a wide street lined with liquidambar trees. Some of their spikey, globed fruits had survived the winter. Saltmarsh Court had once been a convent and was now six high-end flats. Siv took in its elegant symmetry. The building was coated with white stucco and had marble steps to the entrance, arched windows, crenellated parapets, a porch and octagonal corner buttresses. Well-tended shrubs and flowerbeds completed the attractive picture. The parking bay for flat five was empty.

Ali pressed the bell labelled 'Ferris'. There was no response. He tried the other bells, and finally a deep male voice came through the intercom.

'Yes?'

'Police here. We're concerned about Ms Ferris in flat five. Have you seen her?'

'Yaz? Not in the last couple of days.'

'Who are you?'

'Fabian Draper. I live below Yaz, flat two.'

'Let us in, please.'

The buzzer sounded. When Ali pushed the door open, a barefoot man, dressed in a sweat-stained T-shirt and black waterproof trousers, appeared in the hall. He was holding a whole peeled orange and had a towel draped around his shoulders.

'Excuse my appearance, I'm just back from a run,' he apologised. 'Yaz will be at work.'

'We've tried there, and Ms Ferris isn't answering her phone,' Siv explained. 'Does anyone have a key to her flat?'

'I do, for when she goes away.' He cradled the orange in his cupped palms, as if it was a small offering.

'Fetch it, please. We'll try knocking on her front door first.'

'But what's the problem?'

'Just get the key, please,' Siv told him.

They ran up the stairs and found flat five at the end of the corridor. There was a subtle smell of polish and candles. Siv wondered if the building was still permeated with convent scents. The door was sturdy oak and flanked by two planters holding ferns and trailing ivy. Ali banged on it, but there was no reply.

They donned gloves and waited for Fabian Draper. He soon appeared, minus his orange and holding a key. Siv asked him to stay outside while Ali opened the door. A quick sweep of the flat showed that it was empty. Siv returned to Draper, who was wiping his face on his towel.

'Ms Ferris isn't here. Do you know if she has any family in town?'

'I don't think so. She's mentioned a sister in Eastbourne. But we don't really do much family talk. She's a private woman.'

'Thanks. We'll be here for a while and we need to hang onto the key. Is Ms Ferris friendly with anyone else in the block?'

Draper shrugged. He had a direct gaze and a sheen of sweat on his arms. 'I doubt it. People live here for the privacy.'

'What about other friends in town?'

'I can't tell you about those. What do you think has happened to Yaz?'

Siv could feel the warmth from his body and stepped back. 'We hope to find her safe and well. Thanks for your help.'

He seemed to be about to speak but held his hands up instead and turned away. Siv joined Ali in the flat, which overlooked the rear gardens. The living room was large and high ceilinged with thick green-and-red-striped rugs on oak floorboards, deep bookshelves, a tiny TV and two Chesterfield sofas in a mustard fabric.

Siv picked up the iPhone from the coffee table and placed it in an evidence bag. 'This explains why no one can get hold of her. No sign of a laptop.'

There was one good-sized bedroom and a white-and-chrome kitchen with an adjoining utility room. No dirty pans in the kitchen, just one wine glass rinsed and standing upside down on the draining board. Siv opened the dishwasher. It was full and the crockery was clean.

'Everything's neat and ordered,' Siv said. 'The wardrobe hasn't been ransacked, although it's so full, it'd be hard to say if clothes have been taken. There are two suitcases stored on a shelf. Nothing to suggest that she left in a hurry. But then, she wouldn't. I got the impression of a highly organised, efficient woman. It's worrying that I can't find a passport anywhere.'

'I'll put out an alert on her car,' Ali said.

'When you've done that, ring Tessa and ask if she knows of any family to contact. And get uniform to relieve Patrick. We need to keep a presence in that office, in case Yaz does return.'

While Ali was busy on the phone, Siv walked around the flat again. There were few photos and none that looked as if they were of family. Apart from two landscapes, they were of work colleagues, taken in various settings and usually with Yaz standing in the centre of the group. On the bedroom window ledge was one of Yaz, a selfie of her sitting in a canvas chair. Behind her, above her left shoulder, was a glimpse of a blue gable with *86* in white numbers on it. Siv put it in her bag and then returned to the living room and looked down at the mature garden. Fabian Draper was out there, dressed in jeans and jacket. He was smashing the ice on birdbaths and filling them with clean water. She watched his deft, rhythmical movements. He turned and she stepped back quickly, not wanting him to see her.

'All done,' Ali said, speaking just behind her and making her jump. 'I spoke to Patrick. There's been no word from her at work. Tessa's wearing holes in the floor. OK there, guv?'

'Fine, thanks.'

'You look a wee bit pink.'

'It's warm in here.'

Draper appeared again when they were in the foyer.

'Any news?'

'Ms Ferris isn't at home,' Siv told him. She handed him a card. 'If you see her, can you ask her to contact me urgently?'

'Siv Drummond,' he said and smiled slowly. 'Just to mention, Yaz goes away fairly regularly for weekends, sometimes a bit longer. Not that much in winter. She doesn't say where, but she pings me an email, just asking me to keep an eye on the place. She does the same for me when I'm not here.'

'Thanks,' Ali said, opening the door. 'Grand job on the birdbaths, by the way. Isn't that right, guv?'

* * *

Hailey Laurie, Yaz Ferris's sister, had three children, two dogs and a husband who was in bed, recovering from an emergency appendectomy. She looked flustered, harassed, weary and none too pleased to have two detectives in her house while she was trying to prepare dinner. They refused tea and sat at the table in the messy, steamy kitchen, waiting for her to dry her hands.

'Dad could have *died*,' the oldest child, a solemn-faced girl of about twelve, told Siv and Ali. 'His appendix nearly *ruptured*, and if it had, he could have got peritonitis.'

'Lucky it was caught in time,' Siv said impatiently. They'd driven like the wind to get here and she didn't want to hear about Mr Laurie's medical problems.

'I can draw you a diagram of an appendix,' the girl offered. 'I've been reading up about it.'

'Scram, Chrissy,' her mother said, to Siv's relief. 'Check on your brothers and finish your homework.' She closed the kitchen door after her daughter and ordered the dogs into the conservatory with loud commands of 'Stay! Stay!' Then she stood and stared at them, gathering her thoughts. 'I don't understand what you mean about Yaz. Is she missing?'

Siv tapped her heel on the floor. She was aware of the need to close down this investigation, but that wasn't going to happen with a major suspect at large. And a clever suspect at that. She'd had enough of dogs, children and domestic chaos. 'Yaz isn't at home, not at work and she's not answering her phone,' she explained. 'Have you heard from her?'

Hailey was unlike her sister, apart from the same colour hair. She was short, squarely built and gruff. She came and stood by the table, leaning against a chair. 'Not for six months or so. We're not in touch regularly.'

'You didn't hear from her at Christmas?'

'Just a card. She'll have been away somewhere luxurious. Last year it was Hawaii. I'm baffled. Where is she?'

Ali had been checking his phone. 'We need to find her, in relation to an ongoing enquiry. We've just been informed that her car has been found parked at Berminster Station. Do you know of any other family or friends she might be staying with, or any idea where she might be heading by train?'

'We're her only family and she doesn't bother much with us,' Hailey said, with an edge to her voice. 'I could have done with a sisterly hand recently, but I know better than to ask her. She doesn't like children. I don't know her friends. She never mentions them. Yaz lives her own life.'

'One of her neighbours told us she goes away quite often for the weekend. Any idea where that would be?'

Hailey shook her head, darted across the room and switched on the microwave. 'Yaz has her own business, plenty of money and only herself to please, so the world's her oyster. That's all I can tell you.'

Siv took the photo from Yaz's bedroom out of her bag. 'Would you have any idea where this is?'

Hailey came over and looked. 'Sorry, no. Could be anywhere. Could be abroad. Yaz has always travelled a lot. She can afford expensive holidays. When she was eighteen and off to uni, she decided that Jane was too ordinary a name and she became Yaz. She's been up herself ever since then.' She pushed her ratty hair back. 'Should I be worried?'

'It's hard to say at present,' Siv told her.

Someone started hollering upstairs and the dogs were barking, their noses pressed to the conservatory door. Gusts of steam rose from two saucepans and the microwave beeped. Siv gave Hailey her details and said they'd be off.

Ali laughed once they were outside. 'She asked if she should worry as an afterthought. No love lost there.'

'No, but at least we know that it's unlikely Yaz Ferris will turn up here.'

Ali pointed up at the clear sky. 'More snow forecast tonight. Hope your wee wagon will be warm enough.'

'It will be. It's cosy.' Siv looked back at the Laurie's brightly lit house. They'd issued an alert at all ports and airports, but there was no report of Yaz Ferris. Her sister and her work colleagues said that she kept her life private. Her laptop was missing, presumably with her. Patrick was looking into her bank and credit card transactions, but Siv guessed that there wouldn't be any. Yaz Ferris would have had a plan.

CHAPTER 25

They were fifteen miles out of Eastbourne, on the way back to Berminster in tumbling snow, when Hailey Laurie called Siv.

'I'm really worried now. I've been trying to think if Yaz ever mentioned anything that might help you. I don't know if it's significant, but Chrissy just reminded me that Yaz gave us a bowl a year or so ago. It's pottery, made in Whitstable.'

'Is there a name?'

'No. Just *Made in Whitstable* on the bottom. I've got it on the table now.

'You will let me know as soon as you hear from her?'

'Of course. Thanks for ringing.'

'Anything useful?' Ali asked.

Siv told him. 'Probably nothing, a gift, a pottery bowl,' she said. Yaz could have bought it anywhere. There was a gallery in Berminster that sold such items from a variety of sources. It was probably mass produced. She watched the snow splatter the windscreen and thought of the photograph with the deck chair. Deck chair. Seaside. It was worth a try. 'Pull over.' She took out the photo, switched on the light and traced a finger along the glimpse of blue gable numbered 86. 'Does that look like a beach hut to you, behind Yaz?'

Ali held the photo up to the light. 'It's hard to say, there's so little of it.'

'Fabian Draper said that Yaz went away regularly for weekends, but not so much in winter. If she rents or owns a beach hut, she wouldn't stay there in inhospitable winter months. Whitstable has a train station, so she could get there easily by rail. I'd say we need to find a beach hut around there with that number.'

Ali's eyes widened. He reached for his phone, searched and groaned. 'There are hundreds of beach huts along that coast, in Whitstable and Tankerton.'

'But we have a number. We'll take a look, and if we can't find it, we'll contact Kent colleagues to widen the search.'

'It's not much to go on, a pottery bowl and a photo.'

Siv rapped the dashboard. She had a good feeling. 'It's all we have. Come on, turn the car and we'll head for Whitstable.' She glanced at the time. 7 p.m. Neither of them had eaten and this would take a while. She had no intention of driving Ali to hospital again and facing Polly's wrath. 'Have you got any food with you?'

'Aye, in the glove compartment. Nuts and bananas.'

She took out a banana and handed it to him. 'Here, you eat and I'll drive.'

They left the car to swap seats. The snow was dense and fast. Siv moved the seat forward and turned the heater to full. The roads were slow and slippery. She couldn't put her foot down in the treacherous conditions. Peering into the whirling white flakes, she willed the dark miles away, anxious to reach her target.

* * *

Whitstable was cloaked in snow, the streets empty when they arrived.

'I came here with Polly last summer, to the oyster festival,' Ali said. 'I'm not too bothered about eating them, but the craic was great. Dancing, music and such. Hot sun then. Looks like a ghost town now.'

Siv parked in the town centre, near the seafront, and told Ali to stay put. She'd get them both a coffee from a mobile van that advertised takeaways and deliveries.

'I can go. I'm not an invalid,' he protested.

'Quiet, and eat your nuts.'

The young woman in the van smiled cheerily. 'You're lucky, I'm just about to close. Snow's keeping people inside. What brings you out on a night like this? Not sunbathing, anyway!'

Siv showed her ID. 'Two coffees, one black, one white. Oh, and a flapjack, thanks. Do you know this area?'

'I grew up here.'

'I'm looking for a beach hut, number eighty-six.'

The woman turned back from the hissing coffee machine. 'Bit of a needle in a haystack in this area. There're huts along the front here and at West Beach and further along at Tankerton Bay. All I can say is that I sometimes deliver breakfast to number twenty-three, and that's to the right, past the fish restaurant.'

Back at the car, Siv gave Ali his coffee and opened the flapjack.

'Are you allowed any of this?'

'One wee piece,' he said. 'I deserve it on a night you wouldn't put a dog out in.'

'Are you implying I'm treating you cruelly?'

'Aye. You're a torment to me.'

She passed him a morsel of flapjack. 'Don't say I never give you anything. We'll take a steer from the coffee woman and turn right along the seafront.'

'The seaside looks so forlorn on a winter's night,' Ali said. 'Kind of mournful.'

'If Yaz Ferris is here, it won't be doing her mood any good.'

They finished their coffee, donned hats and gloves and set off with their torches. An east wind coming straight off the sea was whipping the snow up and flinging it through the air, blinding them. The tide was in and the waves lashed angrily. The beach huts were dark beneath their uniform white covering, many with padlocked doors and drawn blinds. Some had verandas and steps up. All looked empty, abandoned until the sun and warmth returned. Ali shone his torch so that they could see the numbers increasing. They plodded on. Siv wiped snow from her eyes, hoping that this grim exercise was going to bear fruit. She saw number eighty-one and put a hand on Ali's arm.

'Nearly there. Go slowly. Drop your torch beam.'

Eighty-six had four steps up to a door set within a porch. When Siv played her torch on the ground, there were no fresh footprints in the snow. There was no padlock on the door but thick black blinds were down. They walked around the hut, looking up at the small back window, which was curtained. A dim light showed.

'Someone's in,' Ali whispered.

They returned to the front. Not a soul around, just the driving snow and the pounding sea. Ali shook himself and knocked powdery snow from his sleeves. His eyes gleamed down at Siv and she knew he was eager for action.

'I'll do the traditional thing and knock,' Siv said. 'There's no other exit.'

She took her glove off and rapped on the door. A faint sound within, then silence. She rapped again.

Ali stepped forward and banged with his fist. 'Coastguard here. This is an emergency!'

A long pause and then the door was opened slowly. Ali shoved a foot in the frame.

'Hello, Ms Ferris. Yaz. You've met my DI.'

She froze. Jane Ferris looked past them into the snowy night, as if momentarily considering flight and then made a defeated gesture and turned away. They entered and Ali closed the door. She sat in a blue wooden armchair, hitched a tartan rug around her shoulders and picked up a glass of whisky. They stood dripping on the white painted floorboards. The hut was warm from the heat thrown out by a portable gas fire that resembled a traditional stove and made the room homely.

'You look like snow people. You'd better sit down. Clever old detectives, finding me here, and so soon! How did you manage it?'

'Jane Ferris, I'm arresting you on suspicion of being an accessory to murder,' Siv said, completing the caution.

Yaz waved a hand. 'Yes, yes. I absolutely deny it. I had nothing to do with it, but I'll come quietly and all that. I haven't exactly got an escape route, have I? Take a pew for a minute. Want a hot drink or a whisky? Or even a hot whisky?'

Siv would have loved a hot whisky but shook her head.

They sat down on wooden chairs. The hut was beautiful, painted lemon and cream, with a tiny built-in kitchen, a table with benches and a radio. Paintings of seascapes decorated the walls.

Yaz sipped her drink. 'Well, this is cosy, we three in here on a snowy night. Safe against the storm.'

Siv asked flatly, 'If you deny being an accessory to murder, why have you run away? Why are you holed up here?'

'Who says I've run away? I own this place. I needed time to think. I'm aware that Saul Robbins will have been telling terrible lies about me. I just wanted peace and quiet.'

Ali grunted. 'That's a likely story.'

Yaz had picked up her game. She smiled at him. 'It's the truth, I'm afraid. I've been in a terrible state, worrying over Saul's false accusations. I've been calming my nerves with rest and whisky.'

So that's how you've decided to play it. Crafty.

Siv asked, 'What would those lies and accusations be?'

'The rubbish Saul was spewing when he turned up at my home out of the blue the other night.'

Siv interrupted. 'Robbins came to your home? He didn't ring you?'

Yaz widened her eyes. 'No, he was at my door, sweaty and wild-eyed. He was panicking, all over the place, saying that he'd murdered those two men and he was going to say I'd helped him. He ranted on about how Eugene and Henry had killed someone called Freya at a cottage and how he'd planned their deaths and ordered wreaths. I couldn't believe what I was hearing. It was as if he'd gone completely mad. Saul said he was going to use the fact that I'd dealt some drugs way back to blame me. I was utterly shocked, as you can imagine. I tried to reason with him, but it was hopeless. I was actually worried that he was going to attack me. I was on the point of trying to dial 999, but I managed to calm him a bit and persuade him to go. I was worried that he might come back and harm me. I had to clear my mind, so I headed for my refuge.'

That's astute, casting yourself as a victim.

'Right,' Siv said. 'Most people would head for their local police station in that situation.'

'I'm not "most people", Inspector. Never have been. I do things my way, in my own time. And I just wasn't thinking straight. I was frightened. Mud can cling when it's flung at you. I did tell Saul he should speak to you, but I wasn't going to be pressured by him or the police. I know I'm innocent. The only things I'm guilty of are some bad choices in my youth and letting Saul latch onto me. I admit to drug dealing and I deeply regret it.'

Siv made no response. Hubris didn't come near it. She had to hand it to Yaz for getting a story prepared. *Keep chatting.*

Yaz said warmly, 'After all, I came to you about that meeting with Henry. I had nothing to hide, you see. Funnily enough, it was about a job, despite whatever Saul has said. When Henry contacted me, I knew who he was, but he didn't recognise my name.'

'He'd never met you and he'd only known of you as "The Wheel",' Ali commented.

'Correct — that stupid name that Eugene gave me. I didn't enlighten Henry. In fact, he would have been an asset to my business had things worked out differently.' Yaz drew the rug closer to her. 'I love this little hut. I bought it five years ago. No one else has been in here before you turned up, spectres from the snowstorm. People think that I always take expensive, exotic breaks. I do indulge in those, but I also adore this simplicity. It's an antidote to the job, the noise and the pace. I realise I'll have to accompany you and help you with your enquiries. I won't be able to visit here for a while, I suppose. I'll miss sitting and looking out at the sea and sky with a glass of Macallan.' She was ashen but composed. Her amber earrings glinted warmly in the glow of the brass lamp beside her chair.

Siv could imagine. It felt like a retreat. Yaz reminded her of herself, sitting by the fire wearing thick socks and a fleecy sweater, a drink to hand. It was an uncomfortable reflection. They sat in silence. The fire hissed.

'I suppose they're going nuts at work,' Yaz said.

'Pretty much,' Siv confirmed. 'What to do when the boss vanishes?'

Yaz stuck her hands in her sweater pockets. 'Hopefully, I've trained them well enough to cope for now. I've been an idiot, though. I should never have helped Saul Robbins with his degree. He's a curious combination of intense and biddable, and there's always a downside to those extreme characteristics. I suppose he's been telling you lie upon lie. I don't know why I ever wasted my time with him. He was too needy, but he was so appreciative and I derived gratification from his devotion. If I'd had any idea of the trouble he was going to cause me . . .'

'He's dead,' Ali interrupted. 'Hanged himself.'

'Oh.' She took a sip of whisky. Her eyes flashed with satisfaction. 'Can't say I'm saddened. Oh, don't look at me like that. It just didn't seem fair, you see, when he blurted out his story about how those two morons, Eugene and Henry, had raked everything up and he'd decided to deal with them because he was lovelorn. Bloody Eugene indulging in his guilty conscience. I'll admit I got into bad ways at uni and was too keen on easy money, but you should be able to leave your youthful indiscretions in the past. I've done far more good in my adult life than a lot of other people — certainly considerably more than Eugene, who seems to have hung around bemoaning his fate. I've worked hard at becoming successful and shared that with charitable causes.'

'Other people's misery helped you to finance your road to success. A girl died,' Siv said.

Yaz Ferris threw back the rest of her whisky. 'Spare me the sermon. I honestly don't feel responsible and I'd no idea at the time. That happened because Eugene Warren was a fool. I couldn't stand him when he was a customer. Jumped-up loudmouth. He nagged me to get that E for him, and in the end I did, just to shut him up. I wasn't one of your evil pushers. Just enough harmless weed to supplement my student income. So, how did you get to hear Saul's lies about me if he killed himself?'

'He left a confession,' Siv told her.

Yaz rolled her eyes. 'How awfully old-fashioned.'

'He wanted Diane Lacey to know the truth. He thought of her as family.'

'Oh, yes, Saint Diane. He certainly had her on a pedestal.'

Siv couldn't conceal her dislike of this arrogant woman. It was all about her. No mention of grieving families and friends, or of broken lives.

'Diane is in bits. She was genuinely fond of Saul and interested in his life, his career. She thought of him as the son she might have had.'

Yaz had a hard expression. 'How touching, but she was fooling herself. She could have found a more promising protégé. Saul wasn't very bright, you know. He had ideas about himself. Seemed to think I'd give him a job when he got his MBA. That wasn't going to happen.' She raised her empty glass to the light. 'Better not have another, I suppose. Clear head and all that. . .'

Siv eased her scarf from her neck. 'What was your next move going to be then, after this?'

She replied innocently, 'Once I'd recovered from the shock and felt safer, I was going to call you, of course, explain everything.'

'Sorry to have interrupted your convalescence,' Siv told her.

She fixed her gaze on Siv. 'I could tell you were sharp. Takes one to know one. I really do like your origami, by the way, I'd love to learn to do it. I wasn't bullshitting about that. I would have offered you a commission in time.'

'I'd say that's irrelevant now,' Siv told her. *Hopefully, the bullshit you've just come out with won't wash and you can teach yourself the art of folding in prison. It will help pass the long hours.*

'Yep. How *did* you find me? Come on, don't keep me in suspense.'

Siv stood. 'We need to go. You'd better put the fire out and lock up. This hut will be empty for a long time.'

* * *

They finished dealing with Yaz Ferris and her canny solicitor late the following afternoon. She was in custody, pending a decision by the Crown Prosecution Service. Siv went to Mortimer's office when he buzzed her.

'It's with the CPS now,' Mortimer said. 'It's difficult to know how they'll call it. The only hard evidence is Saul Robbins's confession. They'll have to weigh up if it's admissible. With Warren, Kilgore and Robbins dead, it's a tough one.'

'Yes, sir. Ms Ferris's solicitor has already queried Robbins's state of mind when he wrote it. Her team will certainly argue that it's unreliable and a false confession where she's concerned. Then there's the problem that she never called Robbins from her phone. She probably used burner phones, and his calls to her could be explained as being related to her mentoring. She's lying when she claims that Robbins went to her home and intimidated her. I'm sure he made that last call to her, to a burner. She stated that Robbins knew where she lived because he called by not long ago to discuss an essay. Of course, that will handily give us some of his DNA in her flat, backing up her story that he visited her to issue threats before he hanged himself. Other than that, she said that they only ever met at the Generate offices. She's covered a lot of angles, and Robbins's suicide has actually helped her.'

Mortimer steepled his fingers. 'She was clever, responding to the police appeal about Kilgore's meeting in the Three Swans. Puts her in a good light, possibly. Astute too, admitting to past drug dealing, so looking as if she's shouldering some responsibility, while subsequently doing her best to make amends. She may be clever enough to dodge this bullet, despite the fact that she ran.'

'She and her solicitor made great play of her utter shock at Robbins's appalling lies.' Siv frowned, contemplating the odds. 'The very least I'm hoping for is a successful prosecution for drug dealing.'

'Indeed. Well, we've done what we can for now.'

Siv liked that *we*. She waited. 'I'll tell the team you're pleased then, Sir.'

'Yes, yes, of course. Please do. Clearly, there were cock-ups along the way, but overall, a decent enough result.'

Back in her office, Siv stood at the window. She'd spoken to Tara, Imelda and Saffie, listened to their tears. Nothing she said could console them. The prospect of some measure of justice was cold comfort at such a time. It had been a long day. She rubbed condensation from the glass. Sleet was falling from a stone-coloured, forbidding sky. This dour, harsh month was almost over and she was sick of it, couldn't wait for it to be gone. On the way home, she'd shop for spicy and vivid foods: pimentos, aubergines, beetroot, red onions and cabbage, blueberries, raspberries, crimson apples. She'd no idea what she'd make with them. She just wanted her wagon to be filled with colour. A plant too. Something big, blowsy and joyous. She recalled one she'd seen at Nutmeg. It had long green stems with beak-shaped flowers in orange, yellow and blue — Bird of Paradise, that was it. She must have one. Something shifted inside her, like ice melting. Maybe a hint that she could finally enjoy life again.

She picked up her phone and considered. She'd never yet invited anyone to her tiny home. Time for a step forward. She wrote an email to Hope Merrick.

Don't die of shock at this invitation. You might be busy, but if not, would you like to come round tonight for a bite to eat?

Her finger hovered. She pressed *Send.*

THE END

ALSO BY GRETTA MULROONEY

DETECTIVE INSPECTOR SIV DRUMMOND SERIES

Book 1: THESE LITTLE LIES
Book 2: NEVER CAME HOME
Book 3: MURDER IN MALLOW COTTAGE

THE TYRONE SWIFT DETECTIVE SERIES

Book 1: THE LADY VANISHED
Book 2: BLOOD SECRETS
Book 3: TWO LOVERS, SIX DEATHS
Book 4: WATCHING YOU
Book 5: LOW LAKE
Book 6: YOUR LAST LIE
Book 7: HER LOST SISTER

Thank you for reading this book.

If you enjoyed it please leave feedback on Amazon or Goodreads, and if there is anything we missed or you have a question about, then please get in touch. We appreciate you choosing our book.

Founded in 2014 in Shoreditch, London, we at Joffe Books pride ourselves on our history of innovative publishing. We were thrilled to be shortlisted for Independent Publisher of the Year at the British Book Awards.

www.joffebooks.com

We're very grateful to eagle-eyed readers who take the time to contact us. Please send any errors you find to corrections@joffebooks.com. We'll get them fixed ASAP.

Printed in Great Britain
by Amazon

66374147R00192